SOLDIERS OF BABYLON

A PETER O'KEEFE NOVEL

DAN FLANIGAN

Publisher:
Arjuna Books
5301 Pawnee Lane
Fairway, Kansas 66205

ISBN Paperback — 979-8-9912325-3-1
ISBN eBook — 979-8-9912325-4-8
ISBN Audiobook — 979-8-9912325-5-5

Book cover & interior design by – Deena Rae; E-BookBuilders, adaptation for ebook

File version: 202512048.025

Dan Flanigan's Books

Peter o'Keefe Series

Mink Eyes

The Big Tilt

On Lonesome Roads

An American Tragedy

Soldiers of Babylon

Other Books

Tenebrae: A Memoir of Life and Death

Dewdrops

SOLDIERS OF BABYLON

Think not that I am come to send peace on earth: I came not to send peace but a sword.

Matthew 10:34

CHAPTER 1

IT WOULD HAVE been better if someone had been killed. Or at least maimed.

The explosion had nicely ripped the face off of the one-story clinic and gutted the inside. Likely they couldn't afford to rebuild it. At first they might believe it was a gas-line leak, but not for long. If it wasn't instantly obvious that it was his work, his letter to the local media would make that undeniably clear. One less extermination camp. A real one, not the fantasy ones the Jews had fooled all the gullibles into believing.

Yet it could have been so much more.

At the last hour he had faltered, deluding himself that it would be enough this time to detonate it in the middle of the night instead of during the working day, when the blast itself and the flying shrapnel and the collapsing roof and walls would have torn apart or crushed most, if not all, of the murderers. It had been an unwelcome surge of moral cowardice, an insufficient commitment to the necessary work and acceptance of the necessary consequences. He hadn't even managed to kill the security guard, who a few minutes before the blast had unfortunately decided to leave the building and retrieve something from his car parked a half-block down the street.

So ... he had failed. They needed to understand that they must pay a price for mass murder. Eye for eye. Life for life. Once he made that clear to them, maybe some of Herod's soldiers—the doctors and nurses and administrators, even the expectant mothers themselves—might think twice before ever again dipping their hands in the blood of the Holy Innocents.

Next time he would redeem himself.

It would be difficult for them to discover that it was he who had done this thing. The bomb materials were simple, acquired carefully over a long period of time from many different sources, thus hard, if not impossible, to trace. He hadn't visited this city beforehand, and during the two nights he spent there he'd slept in his car. He often did that on his scouting expeditions, choosing locations where a strange car parked overnight was unlikely to draw attention.

In this city he'd spent only the time required to carry out the necessary surveillance: driving by the clinic several times and confirming its fairly isolated location, as if the city were trying to tuck this slaughterhouse out of sight where it could almost forget that it was harboring such an abomination; walking past the front of the building to make sure there were no security cameras and that the shrubbery would effectively conceal what he intended to place there.

He repeated the process several times and at various times of the day, parking his car two blocks away and approaching the clinic, dressed as a businessman—suit and tie, briefcase at his side— determining the least busy time of day for vehicle or pedestrian traffic and comings and goings to and from the clinic. On each pass he mentally rehearsed how he might quickly stash and conceal the briefcase in the shrubbery, then stroll casually away.

When he heard the explosion, he quickly but carefully moved on, resisting the temptation to hang around to enjoy the carnage, and climbed the nearest ramp to the interstate. Having checked the car daily for a missing taillight or other defect that might attract a highway patrolman seeking to fill his monthly quota, he now held the speedometer at five miles per hour under the speed limit.

He headed due west, to a place he knew would offer refuge— until the next time...

CHAPTER 2

THEY HAD TWO tasks that day. First, continue the surveillance on Richard Maxwell. Second, on the way back, take another look at Country Bank, the small suburban bank they'd successfully robbed a few months earlier. Well, more or less successfully. They hadn't come away with much money, but it looked like there was no chance they were suspected of it, and they'd learned some valuable things, so they thought they might try again. Maybe they'd score big next time. If not, it would be a useful rehearsal for more ambitious efforts.

As for Richard Maxwell, he needed to be restrained. Through intimidation, or if that didn't work, obliteration. It wasn't enough that Maxwell had made both fortune and fame in the computer business. Deciding he was some kind of "goo-roo," he had embarked on a campaign to take advantage of his celebrity and massive earnings to buy two radio stations and had recently announced his intention to buy a third and fourth, hinting in the press release that a television station purchase would be coming soon. He had also recently acquired a sort-of-newspaper, a weekly rag with a countercultural bent and minimal readership, but he had big plans for its future.

On all fronts the man was quickly revealing himself to be a minion of the Antichrist, attacking every sacred thing in existence, not content with spreading filth and lies but directly attacking their beliefs, practices, values, and leaders, unleashing his snarling writer and radio talk-show host attack dogs in a virtual reign of Jewsmedia terror. Another situation like Alan Berg out in Denver—one that needed to be handled similarly.

They had learned through careful, stealthy observation that Maxwell was a man of fixed, almost ritualistic habits. He rose at 5 a.m. every day, watched and listened to certain news programs on television and radio, and read both the local paper and the major nationals, which were specially delivered to his surprisingly modest two-story brick, Tudor-style house, located not in some suburban gated fortress community but in an older neighborhood long favored by the city's old-money class. He left his house at 8:30 a.m. every weekday and on many weekend days as well. In good weather he drove a black Mercedes SL convertible, usually with the top down (so simple and easy to just pull up beside him at a stoplight and casually pull the pin and toss in a grenade). On snowy or icy days he traveled in a black Jeep Grand Wagoneer. Destination: his company headquarters in the newest, shiniest high-rise office building in the city, the company's name (*MAXWELL*, of course) in giant, egotistical letters at the top of the building.

During the day he would occasionally visit one of his media properties, sometimes driving himself, sometimes being driven, but in the main the media managers and other personnel came to him. The only irregularity in his typical day was the time he left the office, which varied from 6 p.m. to very late.

They had concluded it would be simplest to strike on one of the nights he traveled home after dark. They could station shooters in cars at two or three different places along his homeward route and blast the unsuspecting arrogant nerd with fusillades of automatic rounds. If a first opportunity had to be passed on due to the presence of witnesses or other issues, they could signal the second car, then the third.

But after heated debate, the Prophet decided to send him a warning first. That was too much for Sinclair. "It's both stupid and cowardly," he spat, right to the Prophet's face.

As usual, the Prophet remained calm. "Or maybe," he said, "it would be a foolish and suicidal act to hit him now. Are we really ready to bring the war on … over *him* … and right now?"

"We keep putting it off," Sinclair said. "I didn't come here to play kiddie games."

"It will come soon enough. Just a few more things to put in place."

"How 'bout we at least blow up his radio tower?"

"Like we tried to blow up that synagogue, and failed, taking all that risk for nothing?"

"Eventually, we need to *do* something," Sinclair said churlishly.

"And we will, Matthew. God will say when. And when we do, it'll be a far more powerful statement than killing one stinking kike."

"He's a Jew?" someone asked.

"If not," the Prophet said, "he might as well be. He's doing their work. Trash what you easily can and send an unmistakable message. That's enough for now."

CHAPTER 3

Some years earlier Peter O'Keefe had reluctantly concluded that his new profession required him to at least skim through the morning newspaper each day, a mostly distasteful task that he nevertheless dutifully performed and was presently engaged in.

Efforts were underway to measure and understand the extent and effect of the massive spill of 11,000,000 gallons of oil into Prince William Sound after the Exxon Valdez tanker had collided with a reef on March 24. An accompanying photo showed sea otters and sea birds coated head to foot with oil.

Briefs had been filed in the U.S. Supreme Court by a number of scientists, informing the Court that developments in medicine and technology had not reduced the period of viability of a fetus to less than six months—and were not likely to in the future.

"I was only following orders" was the headline's characterization of Oliver North's defense during his trial for aiding and abetting the obstruction of a congressional investigation. His skillful lawyer was painting a picture of a good soldier trying to do his duty to the administration of President Ronald Reagan, an administration utterly contemptuous of Congress and the law it had passed forbidding sales to the right-wing Contra militia fighting to overthrow the left-wing Nicaraguan government. North had become one of the major executors of the "solution" engineered by the administration to divert to the Contras profits from the sale of arms to the pariah government of Iran, which was officially designated by the United States government as a state sponsor of terrorism.

Real-estate tycoon Donald Trump was trying to buy the Eastern Airlines New York-D.C. Shuttle operation out of bankruptcy.

In a still mostly rural township on the edge of the encroaching city, avowed Ku Kux Klan members running for office in a local election had lost. O'Keefe was trying to decide how much of a good thing that was—or whether any good in it was cancelled out entirely by the fact that here, in 1989, they'd come as close to winning as they had.

The S&L Crisis—financial institutions choking on bad real-estate loans and crashing into insolvency all over the country—was only getting worse. That bad news would bring good news: even more legal work for his best friend and major client, lawyer Michael Harrigan, and then from Harrigan to the Peter O'Keefe & Associates private detective agency. Was that *irony?* A complex concept that he was never sure he understood sufficiently to apply it correctly in particular instances.

He let the paper down on the desk, looked out the window to a perfect spring day, and vowed to enjoy this and *every* good day this spring in case they were forced to endure another brutally hot summer like last year's.

The intercom line buzzed.

"It's Paschal," his receptionist said, still laughing at something Paschal had said. "Can I put him through?"

O'Keefe hadn't talked to Paschal McKenna in a while. He took the risk of asking his journalist friend how he was doing.

"I'm doing very well, thank you."

Which hopefully meant he was still sober.

"You ever heard of Richard Maxwell?" McKenna said.

"Somewhere. Can't think where."

"Made a fortune selling computers. Also owns radio stations and in the process of acquiring a television station. And he's my new boss. Bought our little journal here."

"A fool and his money?" O'Keefe said.

"But a *holy* fool. He intends to develop an alternative, maybe even a checkmate, to Russ Limbaugh among other things."

"Could that mate be Paschal McKenna?"

"Oh, no. It's only the written word for me. I can't fulminate well enough."

O'Keefe waited for Paschal to tell him what he was really calling about.

"You'll probably get a call from Richard soon. You'll want to take his call."

"About what?" O'Keefe said.

"He'll tell you. I've spoken highly of you. Do your best. We need it."

Maxwell called within the hour. "I'm told you have a security operation. Executive protection."

"Yes," O'Keefe said, low and slow, a cautionary reflex since the basic security operation had taken off well, but the highfalutin executive-protection aspect was more hope than reality at this point.

"Can you meet with me right away?"

"I think so. I'd want to bring my partner who runs that operation."

"That's George Novak?" Maxwell said.

"You know him?"

"No. But Paschal McKenna and the local newspaper archives have told me a lot about you and your operation."

"I'll talk to George and get right back to you."

"ASAP, please. And full disclosure, I'm talking to other companies."

"It would help us to know what your basic problem is."

"Apparently," Maxwell said calmly, "someone intends to kill me."

O'Keefe found George in the office of Sara Slade, their other partner.

"Ever heard of Richard Maxwell?"

Neither had, so O'Keefe briefed them on the two calls, ending with, "What do you think?"

George stood up. "Could be a big deal. Let's go."

CHAPTER 4

An eager-looking Maxwell was standing next to his receptionist's desk when they arrived. He lurched forward and offered them each a brief handshake, muttered "Welcome" without looking any of them in the eye, and led them down a short hallway to a conference room. Nothing opulent. The office was comfortable but simple and unadorned, even bland. Maxwell himself seemed much like his unpretentious office decor: white button-down shirt, khaki belt and pants, brown loafers, sandy hair and pencil-thin, barely detectible blondish mustache that clashed with the black frames of his glasses. He evinced the aura of the type of nerd who'd carried a briefcase in high school, but also exuded quiet intelligence, focus, intensity.

Their threesome lined up on one side of the table and Maxwell sat at the head.

"Two nights ago my wife and I woke up in the middle of the night to a loud crashing sound. Thankfully, the kids slept through it. I came downstairs and checked the front door. It's double entry—a decorative glass door and then a heavy wooden one. The glass door was shattered, and this was the condition of the wooden one."

He slid a Polaroid snapshot over to them. "I took some better photos, but they're not developed yet. The police took some of their own, but this will tell you all you need to know."

At the top of the door, painted in surprisingly fine detail, was a swastika. At the bottom, a Star of David. In the middle, big block letters declared *STOP!*

"Nazis?" George said.

"Kristallnacht," Sara said."

O'Keefe understood her reference. George looked confused.

"It means," she said, 'Night of the Broken Glass. A night in the 1930s when the Nazis broke the glass windows of Jewish shops all over Germany."

"Are you Jewish?" George asked Maxwell.

"No, but I might as well be. We're all Illuminati, in league with the Jews to take over the world. They call us not the news media but the 'Jewsmedia.'"

"Real Nazis?" George said. "Here? Now?"

"Not quite," Maxwell said, "Not full bore. But close enough. Apparently, they do think they're the master race, love Hitler, and hate Jews and their supposed co-conspirators like me. They did a similar thing at my little newspaper's offices and at our local radio station."

"Doesn't that radio station run all night?"

"Yes, but it's automated. No human after 1 a.m. Only pre-recorded music and ads."

"No security guard?"

"Yeah. But apparently asleep at the switch. It wasn't even discovered until the first employee arrived that morning. Obviously, that security company's not on my current interview list."

"What did the police say?" George said.

"They didn't seem to take it seriously."

George nodded. "Yeah. That kind of thing happened a few times when I was on the force. They paint a swastika on something, but nothing happens after that and it's forgotten about."

"The police don't like me anyway," Maxwell said. "Not after we did that series on police incompetence and brutality. And"— hesitating, reluctant—"there's something I didn't feel I could disclose, not right then anyway."

Like puppets, strings pulled, all three raised their chins expectantly.

"I was warned something like this might be coming. Someone came to me and told me that a survivalist group living in some kind of camp down in the lake country was planning to do me harm. At first I didn't quite believe him. I thought he might be a nutcase. I get some threats and don't want the police treating me like the boy who cried wolf. Plus, my maybe-not-so-nutty informant insists that I *not* go to the police. He claims, not just vehemently but violently, that he'll never talk to the police and will deny everything if I call them in."

"'Insists'?" George said. "Have you told him about this recent thing?"

"I have. He wasn't surprised, but he hasn't changed his mind about who he'll talk to. I still don't think the cops'll take him seriously, and I don't want to scare him off."

"You think he'd talk to us?" George said.

"Don't know. I'd have to be careful how I approach that. I definitely don't want to run him off now that he's proved not to be a complete lunatic."

"So how can we help?" O'Keefe said.

"*You* tell me. I don't want to overdo it, but I have to protect my family and my employees. The receptionist at the radio station already quit. Paschal's told me about you more than once, and of course I've read about you in the papers from time to time. But I know you're also pretty new to this security and bodyguarding business. Why should I hire you instead of a large, well-established operation?"

"Like the one that was asleep at the switch the other night?" George said.

O'Keefe worried that the rebuff might have come across as too sarcastic, but Maxwell smiled.

"I understand. I was a startup not all that long ago myself. But then, most startups fail."

George charged on, surprising O'Keefe again that his laid-back old friend could summon up such a supercharged sales persona. "We've already got a small but highly qualified staff of security people, plus a list of others anxious to come work for us as soon as we can bring them on, including some with a lot of executive-protection experience—ex-police, ex-FBI, ATF too. Plus, you don't have to force-fit into our cookie cutter. We'll make the cutter for your cookie."

And he's become a master of whimsical wordsmithery too.

Maxwell said, "How about a detailed proposal and budget?"

"Right away," George said. "And if you want, we'll put some people on the job while we're negotiating. You need it right now, and it'll show you what we can do."

George was overextending himself big time, but O'Keefe let it go. It was George's game here after all, and too late to stop him anyway.

"Good," Maxwell said. "Let me know PDQ on that. The existing security group is falling all over itself trying to make up for their dereliction, but I can't bring myself to trust them anymore. How 'bout if I can persuade my informant to meet with us? And after that, you make me a detailed proposal?"

"Done," George said.

Maxwell looked at Sara. "So what's your role in all this, ma'am?"

"I work mostly on fraud cases, but I get on the street whenever I can. I've had extensive weapons training, and I'm a blue belt in Brazilian jiu-jitsu and close to a purple."

"Interesting," Maxwell said. "But I'm wondering what my informant might think about a woman being involved. These people aren't exactly feminists. They claim the Bible commands the complete subjugation of women."

Not trying to change the subject, genuinely innocently confused, George said, "I've never understood that Old Testament fixation by these radical Christians. It's all about the Jews, who they *hate,* as God's Chosen People."

"They've got that all figured out," Maxwell said. "They've come up with a doctrine called 'Christian Identity.' According to them, the lost tribes of Israel weren't Jews at all, but *Aryans* who migrated up from the Middle East until they reached northern Europe. *They* were and are the *real* Chosen People."

"What about the real Jews, the ones in Israel?"

"Maybe they were the real Jews, but *not* the real Chosen People. George, my man, you apparently aren't aware that Eve had *two* lovers in the Garden. Not only Adam, but the serpent, Satan himself. It wasn't just an apple involved. Two seeds were implanted in her. One was Adam's, The result: Abel, the good twin. The other, from the Devil's seed: Cain, the evil twin. Abel's seed became those lost tribes that eventually migrated to northern Europe. Cain's seed, children of Satan, became the Jews that stayed in the Middle East and interbred with all kinds of trash there. They are, literally, Satan's children."

"Makes all the sense in the world," George said. "How could I have missed that?"

"Their compound down in the lakes is actually a tiny little sort-of-town of eighty people or so. A lot of them are children because they believe in doing their part to make sure the white race prospers. They call it the New Ark or Ark II. They believe in the so-called End Times. They call the period we're in now the "Tribulation," prelude to the Apocalypse and the Final Armageddon Battle, which are imminent—if not tomorrow then the day after tomorrow. Not flood this time, but fire. Civil war. Race war. But the people of the Lord, the few real and true Christians, will survive and welcome the return of Jesus to the once sinful but now purified earth. That's what they're preparing for.

"It's the Christian version of the Islamic Revolution. Iran, 1979. America, 1989. And there are wannabe ayatollahs all over this country, including this guy down there they call the Prophet. And, according to my informant, they're damn well prepared. They have a virtual armory, all kinds of weaponry. They even run a survivalist training program, a boot-camp-like thing where anti-black, anti-Jew, antigovernment neo-Nazi warriors from all over country come for a month-long training regimen. They say it's survivalist training, but it could also be described as terrorist training. They charge for it, and it's the financial mainstay of the place right now."

Maxwell said he would contact his informant and set up a meeting, then added, "I found him a good job, and he's appreciative, but he's reluctant to talk much. We need to be really careful about spooking him."

On the ride back, George said, "This could be the best thing that could possibly have happened for us right now."

"And the worst if we screw it up," O'Keefe said.

"Duh," George said. "That's always true."

O'Keefe asked Sara what she thought of Maxwell's reservations about presenting her to his informer.

She shrugged. "I understand completely."

"Ready for anything and everything?" O'Keefe said.

"Of course," she said.
"As always," O'Keefe said.
George laughed.
Sara frowned.

CHAPTER 5

THE RECEPTIONIST ESCORTED them into the conference room where Maxwell sat with a small blob of a man placed intimately next to him as if under Maxwell's special protection. A straw Stetson rested on the table in front of the guest. Seeing Sara, the guest stood and made a small bow. His black hair was well greased and combed up and back into a short pompadour. He wore a wrinkled cowboy shirt purchased long ago for a more slender man. The snaps down the front barely contained the bulging flesh, threatening to burst open at any moment. His belly spilled over his beltline.

Maxwell held out both hands, palms open, gesturing to each side of the table. O'Keefe took one side, and George the other, directly in front of Maxwell's guest. They hadn't planned it that way, but O'Keefe thought it was perfect. George could buddy up with almost anyone. O'Keefe was more reserved by nature, reluctant to engage.

Sara took a seat at O'Keefe's side, leaving an empty chair between them, as if in acknowledgment of at least a slightly inferior position. He guessed that interval was deliberate. Although she usually wore minimal makeup, at least that O'Keefe could detect, she looked even plainer today. Her blouse and skirt were on the dowdy side. She looked modest but still attractive in a simple way, and he guessed that was deliberate as well.

Maxwell introduced them to his guest—Norbert Cahill—then addressed the group. "I discussed this a little bit with Norbert before you guys arrived. I don't want to cause any unnecessary trouble for the Ark people. Live and let live. That's my motto. But they don't seem to feel the same way about me."

Norbert smiled at that.

"So, Norbert, it seems essential to learn as much as possible about them with the help of these people at the table."

It wasn't just about him, he continued. Not at all. It was his family, his innocent employees. If he failed to protect them given what Norbert had told him, all of his previous doubts now scoured away by the recent attacks, it would be downright idiotic, even criminal on his part, to sit idly by and just let them come to him.

"I know you're uncomfortable about all this, and I've scrupulously honored your unwillingness to go to the police, even after what those people did the other night."

Norbert was squirming. "Course you can't be sure it was them," he said.

"True," Maxwell said, "but there aren't any other obvious suspects, and it all fits with what you've told me. So I hope you understand that I desperately want … *need* … to get these people involved and give them as much information as possible so they can do their job and protect me, my family, my employees. They are *not* the police."

Norbert closed his eyes and nodded in what looked like a gesture of acceptance.

"All of these people know your feelings on this and won't do anything to out you with the people down there or with law enforcement unless it's absolutely necessary to protect the innocent from harm."

"Yeah," Norbert said. "Please. I still got friends down there. Don't want to burn every bridge. We were there from the start, me and the wife."

Under Maxwell's gentle questioning, Norbert explained how he and his wife, Linda, had slipped into meth addiction in their younger days. After they'd lost essentially everything, they'd heard about a small church in a neighboring country town where the preacher, a man named Dodd, welcomed people like them: nowhere-left-to-go people. He took them in, even let a few set up camp and live on church property.

The reverend was known as "the Prophet" by his small flock. Norbert asked the Prophet what he and Linda could do to escape the hell they'd created for themselves. The Prophet repeated what Jesus had said to the rich young man who asked him how he could achieve eternal life: "Give up everything you have. Give it to the poor, and follow me."

"That's easy for you two," the Prophet said, "since you've got nothing left but your meth-obliterated, stripped-naked souls and bleeding selves. You're the lucky ones. You've got absolutely nothing, not one thing, to lose except the addiction that's killing you."

And Norbert and Linda did exactly that. As the Prophet had promised, they were saved, joining several others, most of them former drug addicts or alcoholics who, under the Prophet's teachings and spiritual care, had managed to shed their crippling dependencies and live clean.

Eventually, the local authorities grew alarmed by the spreading campground, which apparently was intended to become permanent. The whole thing seemed more and more like a cult, and they certainly didn't want to end up with a Jonestown on their hands. They warned the Prophet that he needed to disperse the residents and act like a regular church instead of a commune.

Not long after, the Prophet enjoyed one of his periodic visions, where the Lord spoke directly to him and told him clearly what the Prophet had been suspecting for a while. "The Jew-controlled governments," Norbert said, squirming again and looking simultaneously defiant and guilty as if someone might scold him for the outburst, "the whole country, the whole world's choking to death on its own wickedness."

After proffering that little gem, Norbert expatiated further, delivering what sounded to O'Keefe like something the Prophet must have preached to his flock ad nauseam until every one of them could recite it by heart. God's people desperately needed a refuge from the brutal chaos that would soon descend, a new Ark, where they could find shelter while the rest of the New Babylon wallowed in its orgy of self-immolation.

And following on that vision came a miracle—God's fulfillment of His promise. New land for the making of a new covenant. Someone told the Prophet about a large property that some city family had inherited and been trying to sell for years.

More than 200 acres, it had never been farmed or occupied by any human as far as anyone knew. Its timber had been cleared a century or more earlier, but the land was now bulging with cedar and other large trees. A portion of the property abutted a remote cove of a huge man-made lake that sprawled over many miles, and neither real-estate developers nor resort operators had yet been attracted to that part of the lake.

There was a small town a few miles up the road. The nearest neighbors, isolated farms, were separated from this property by natural barriers including thick brush infested with thorn and bramble bushes, copperheads, water moccasins, and even, it was said, timber rattlesnakes, as well as the occasional wild boar.

The Prophet persuaded the owners to sell cheap and accept a minuscule down payment and a mortgage with payments stretched out over twenty years. The desperate and grateful sellers failed to impose any restrictions on the use of the land or its exploitation. The Prophet called it the New Ark and sometimes Ark II. The people had spent the first years clearing parts of the land for habitation and sustaining their community by felling and selling timber from their abundance of trees. They fished in the lake and raised chickens, goats, sheep, and rabbits for protein. They didn't farm on a large scale but did cultivate ample gardens for vegetables and fruit trees and bushes. They managed to grow enough in the summer to put up large stores of those fruits and vegetables for the winter months.

They began with tents and lean-tos and a few miserable-looking house trailers but before long began milling their lumber and constructing simple but substantial houses. Soon the tents disappeared and only a few trailers remained among the new stick-built residences.

For the Prophet, his wife Naomi, and their four children they built a special house with an imposing foundation of fieldstones and strong timber above. Over the years they kept building additions until it was a sprawling complex that served also as an administrative and communications headquarters.

Norbert spoke about these things with obvious longing. "We were a godly group, in a rough but beautiful paradise our own Eden. We didn't have much, but we had all we needed. We didn't have to worry about temptation for ourselves and especially not for the children. I never saw such happy kids."

George, sympathetic, no trace of the tough policeman he'd once been, said, "How did you feed all those people?"

"We had our gardens and fruit trees, and the domestic stock, but mainly we relied on food stamps. Actually, we always ate pretty darn good."

George, leaning in, gently chiding, "Guess you weren't *entirely* anti-government, eh?"

Norbert laughed. "We figured if all the deadbeats could sponge off the government, the good people might as well do a little of the same.

George chuckled sympathetically. "Where'd you get money?"

"Most of us would go out to work, doing odd jobs or handyman-type work at some local place and turn the wages over to the Prophet for common use. And we had all that timber. We started cutting it—"

"By hand?"

"At first, yeah."

"That had to be hard," George said, all brotherhood and solidarity.

Norbert held out his hands, revealing heavily callused palms, and said, "You bet it was. Even with gloves, these were solid blisters for a while. But then we scraped together enough to get hold of some chainsaws and really went to town, so to speak. Sold to lumber yards and sawmills around that part of the state. Like I mentioned, over time we figured out how to mill some of it ourselves. With that, and trades we made with the lumber yards, our raw timber for finished boards, we did really well on that alone ... at least as long as the big trees lasted. But pretty soon they were gone, just the more recent growths left. Still a lot of trees, but they weren't large enough to fell and mill and sell. So it was sort of ... what next?"

CHAPTER 6

OTHER THINGS CHANGED.

"The Prophet started having visions … of … you know … the coming End Times … how they'd play out. There'd be total chaos. No food and hardly any police to protect people from marauders. And the people in the Ark would have no protection. So we needed to put ourselves in a position where we could defend ourselves from horrors we didn't create but that could still come bangin' on our doors, so to speak."

They began to compile a protective arsenal of weaponry. "We started with a few hunting rifles … you know, nothin' special … but then we started buyin' 'em."

Once they had the weaponry, they needed to learn how to use it effectively. One of the men, Leon Lomax, had served as a drill instructor in the military and was assigned the task of developing a training program, which, as time went on, became more and more elaborate and intense, eventually including everything from target shooting to hand-to-hand combat, martial arts, constructing booby traps, and more. Lomax was more than gung-ho, and what he didn't already know, he tried to learn, making many trips to the dinky public libraries in the region, eventually obtaining cards at some of the larger regional town, city, and college libraries. Norbert described how Lomax had used their interlibrary-loan services to read everything he could on the subject. He'd also badgered the Prophet to let him buy certain "mission-critical" items, as he called them. Many of those were devoted to subjects like urban and guerrilla warfare, featuring the IRA, the Viet Cong, Castro, and

Che Guevara. He even studied the exploits of Joseph Stalin—the pre-revolution version, when he was known as "Koba" and robbed banks to support the cause.

George said, "So much for 'turn the other cheek,' eh?"

Norbert reacted sharply, vehemently, so much so that George flinched a little. "Enough of that. That got us exactly nowhere, and all the time things were getting worse. The noose was drawin' tighter and tighter all the time. Look where we ended up—out in the wilderness, and even then they wouldn't leave us alone with their unconstitutional gun laws and all. There's plenty of Scripture, Old Testament and New, and sayings of Jesus too, in favor of violence and war against the heathens bent on our final destruction. The Prophet and our chaplain Caleb assembled all that in a booklet. The General—that's what we took to callin' Leon—really did it up right on the training program. Put all the men through it. Even some of the women got involved. My wife, Linda, was one of 'em."

O'Keefe, adopting the friendly tone that George had used, leaned forward. "How'd that square with women being subservient and all that?"

"When the Tribulation and the End Times come," Norbert said, "everyone'll need to grab a gun. Just like that song, 'Keep Your Rifle By Your Side,' says. There's scriptural justification for that too. And it don't mean she don't know her assigned place in Creation … Anyway, like I said, we developed a real serious training regimen, and somebody had the idea to open it up to outsiders and charge for it—"

Maxwell, interrupted, "We haven't talked about that much. How's that work?"

"Darn well, actually. Came at a good time, when we were gettin' short on dough … We dedicated a separate area and put up some nice tents and organized a food-service operation along with it. We called it Christian Soldiers Survival School. Then the General convinced us to put up some building facades to make a decent imitation of a city block so we could simulate hand-to-hand fighting in a city. Our customers loved that. The kids too. They love to play in that thing when the training isn't happenin'. I guess everyone thinks that's where the main battles of the next war's gonna be … mostly in the cities. Anyway, we've been makin' a pretty penny on that, I'm sure."

"How long is the training?" Maxwell said.

"Four tough weeks."

"How many do they do a year?"

"Varies. I think we're up to six or seven. But so far we don't do 'em in the dead of winter." He embraced himself and shivered. "Too cold."

Maxwell seemed excited to hear all this. "When's the next one?"

"Not sure. Easy enough to find out. We got a special phone number set up with people assigned to answer and take questions and orders and all that. We even do some sales stuff to get the word out."

"Like what?"

"A table or booth at gun shows and little ads in a couple magazines."

"Any requirement to get admitted?"

"Cold cash," Norbert said, chuckling. "I can't recall hearing about anyone gettin' turned down. But it's not like the queers and hippies and ACLU and"—he hesitated, searching for the word—"nigras and such are bangin' on the doors to get in."

"How about women?"

"We've had a few. Like I said, they'll likely have to do some fightin' when the time comes. And the word got around to the more serious Christian survival groups all around the country. People started comin' from all over. It's making us some serious money."

"What groups, Norbert?" Maxwell said.

"Various," Norbert said.

"Like the group up in Idaho?"

"That was one."

Norbert was becoming increasingly uncomfortable, but Maxwell kept prodding. "They're called Aryan Nations, right? Neo-Nazis."

Norbert reeled back defensively and straightened up. "Yes, sir."

Maxwell kept on. "That's where those guys, 'The Order,' came out of, right? Killed Alan Berg, the disk jockey in Denver. Robbed banks, spread the money around to different groups."

Norbert, more prickly now, started to shut down. "I guess."

"You know if the Prophet got any of that money?"

"I wouldn't know," he said, looking and sounding like a surly, evasive child.

"And there were also some Ku Klux Klan groups?"

"Some."

"Skinheads? Bikers?"

"Those too ... Mostly good people..."

"But..." Maxwell said, and waited.

"Well, over time it's attracted some people to our place that weren't really interested in the original mission, just the war part. And the Prophet's gotten to be a pretty big dog all around the country, speakin' all around about preparin' for the Tribulation and the End Times, and all kinds of big shots comin' to our place to visit. He started wearing military garb like the General, so the rest of us followed."

"Did you follow ... all of it?"

"I did. I believed. Still do. But I was a bit uncomfortable, I'll admit. It seemed like we wasn't just self-defending anymore but about to go the other way and carry the war outside. We kept building up an arsenal, and the General figured out how to do things like turn semi-automatic rifles and pistols into machine guns and make homemade silencers. We started selling 'em. Illegal. All of it. And all of a sudden we were hearin' about the Feds checkin' us out, including that they might be sneakin' informers in. And there was rumors about certain things that certain people went out to do. Only the inside group—the Elders, they're called—were actually involved in it, but in a tiny town like that, secrets are hard to keep. And we heard there were other things in the planning stages. Like maybe doin' somethin' to Mr. Maxwell here ... and other things..."

"Like...?" George said.

"I ain't talkin' about any of that. I'm not here for anything but to warn Mr. Maxwell because that's somethin' I knew about, and I don't want his or anybody else's blood on my conscience. But that's it. I don't know nothin' else. None of you are recording this, are ya?" He looked at Maxwell. "You promised."

Maxwell said, "No recordings. Promise kept. If you want, I'll frisk all three of them, strip them down right here in front of you."

Norbert shook his head. "Nah. I believe ya."

George leaned forward, soothing. "Is all that why you left?"

"No. Like I said, I believed. Still do."

"Then why?"

"He took my wife."

George looked confused. "Meaning?"

"He had another vision. He showed us where the Bible approved the taking of multiple wives. He'd always had an eye for a handsome female, and, misfortunately, my wife is a looker, and shapely too. He had her in his mind for his number two."

"But another man's wife?"

"Well, not quite. We called each other husband and wife, but never got actually married. And she was more than willing. Ambitious. Always wants to be the queen bee. And we was childless. Couldn't make it happen somehow."

"You didn't object?"

"She and I weren't all that fond of each other anymore anyway. And like I said, I believed in him, and still do, even though I think he might've been stretchin' that particular divine vision a bit through wishful thinkin'. But nobody else, not one person, said a contrary word about it. And right away she got pregnant. Seemed like a sign there for sure. And I tried to stick it out, but it was just too uncomfortable. And I could tell I wasn't welcome anymore. Not by him. Not by the others either. It wasn't quite a shunning, but close."

"Would you like to return?" George asked.

"Sure. I miss it a lot. But I've accepted that was part of God's plan for me."

CHAPTER 7

After Norbert left, Maxwell said, "I reviewed your security plan. I like it."

George turned his head away from Maxwell and toward O'Keefe and actually winked! O'Keefe was shocked that Maxwell had so quickly accepted the proposal. They hadn't low-balled it. Just the opposite. They'd put a big price tag on it with plenty of cushion to make sure it would be profitable.

"But," Maxwell said, "it's not enough. I want to go a step further. I want someone to go down there … sign up for that training … even try to join the community."

"One of *us,* you mean?" O'Keefe said, his voice rising embarrassingly high and cracking a bit.

"Yes."

"We've got a business to run. There's only the three of us in management. We can't just drop out of the world for weeks or months."

"You could if I paid you more. A lot more. Way more than you could earn here even if you succeeded beyond your wildest expectations. And you'd have all my business—not just the radio station, the newspaper, and the television station I'm gonna buy soon. The computer companies too. And I'd be pushing everyone else I know or do business with, now and in the future, to hire you."

O'Keefe was about to continue to object, but George cut in. "Pete, let's at least think about it … talk about it."

O'Keefe nodded, curtly, but kept a sullen silence.

"And there's one other thing," Maxwell said. "I think it needs to be you, Pete."

Now O'Keefe was angry. And he must have looked it because Maxwell hurried to explain.

"You were a Marine, weren't you? That amateur military stuff ought to come easy."

"It didn't come easy then, and it sure as hell wouldn't now. George is the ex-cop, and he's head of our security operation."

"Exactly. That's why it needs to be you. George needs to be here to implement and manage what's a very ambitious plan that I'm not so sure you've got the bandwidth to pull off, at least right now. And forgive me for saying that I think your chances of pulling it off without George spending most, if not all, of his time on it aren't all that good."

George flashed O'Keefe an "I'll kick your ass if you keep this up" look, which O'Keefe recognized from all the way back in grade school, and said, "Okay, like I said, we'll think about it. But if we agree to do this, it's gonna cost you."

"Call me Don Corleone. I'll make you an offer you can't refuse."

Maxwell didn't disappoint. $40,000 per month plus expenses, plus a discretionary bonus of up to double the monthly fee if results were good. And, thanks to lawyer Michael Harrigan's advice, they also negotiated a provision for arbitration if the parties disagreed on either the quality of the information or the amount of the bonus.

George was chomping at the bit, but O'Keefe was still resisting. There was probably some danger involved, which he'd recently been trying to avoid, but that wasn't the real problem. His disclosed objection: the assignment was entirely outside their business plan and certainly outside the role he was supposed to play in that plan. His undisclosed reason: he hadn't been a volunteer Marine but an unlucky draftee, and he'd disliked everything about the Marine Corps, especially boot camp. Having to endure anything close to that again would break a never-again vow he'd made to himself long ago. The pain of that would be geometrically increased if he was also forced to play the role of a violent, antisemitic, racist neo-Nazi for an indefinite period of time.

George wasn't buying the disclosed reason. "Executive protection," he said, "is damn sure part of the plan. And I might add, Boss"—George had always called him that, and always with a sardonic edge—"it's been the most successfully implemented part of the plan so far."

O'Keefe frowned but couldn't disagree and gave an involuntary slight nod in affirmation.

George leaned over and locked in on him. "The problem is, if we don't agree to the whole deal, we might not get the job at all, any part of it, even the exec protection. That's a big opportunity to just piss away. And I believe the guy when he says he'll beat the drum for us everywhere."

"Maybe we'd still get the protection job. He didn't exactly tie them together."

"Well, that's what I heard," George said. He looked at Sara. "How about you?"

She looked sympathetically at O'Keefe but said, "'Fraid so. That's what I heard too."

As a last resort, despite being afraid of the answer, O'Keefe asked her what she thought.

"I have to vote with George."

He didn't play chess or billiards but recognized what had just happened.

O'Keefe had given in but kept it to himself for now and said he was close to a decision but wanted one more meeting with Maxwell and Norbert.

"Well, let's get after it," George said. "They may kill the guy while you're fucking around here, Boss."

Which startled O'Keefe. He hadn't thought about that.

George continued, "Like I promised, I've already got a guy on him … gratis … to show him our initiative and good faith."

"You've become quite the businessman," O'Keefe said.

"Your fault, Boss. You've made me a slave to this shit."

It was déjà vu when the detective trio entered Maxwell's conference room—Maxwell at the head of the table, Norbert standing at his side and bowing to Sara.

After O'Keefe asked a number of questions about how New Ark was governed and operated, Maxwell turned to Norbert and said,

"Big question for you. With this latest thing, where they essentially invaded my home and threatened my family and employees, I'm not comfortable just sitting around twiddling my thumbs and waiting for something to happen. I don't want to go to the police any more than you do because my experience is they won't do anything until someone gets badly hurt or killed. And even if they actually do something, who knows what can of crazy worms they'll open ... or create themselves. So I'd like to know a lot more about what's going on down there. If I send someone down there, maybe George here, or Pete, and he tells them he wants to join, you think they'll take him in?"

"For the training, sure, but I don't know about the other."

O'Keefe was reeling. Maxwell's disclosure of the plan to Norbert was entirely unexpected, and he wasn't sure it was a good idea. Then again, maybe Maxwell had just opened the door for a way out of this thing. He said, "I'll tell you one thing, guys. I already did boot camp once and didn't like it. I sure don't want to put myself through that kind of thing again, especially if it turns out I still don't get accepted into the community."

"Can't be sure," Norbert said. "That would be a big deal. But the Prophet wants to grow the community as much as possible. But then, like I said, they've been gettin' sensitive about possible infiltrators."

"Norbert," O'Keefe said, "you think I'll get a chance to meet the Prophet and any of the Elders during the training?"

"Probably. Not sure though."

There was a silence that no one seemed eager to disrupt as Norbert, head down, eyes on the tabletop, seemed to be giving the situation further consideration. Then he looked up with a sly smile and said, "I'll tell you this,"—he nodded toward Sara—"if you take *her* with you, you'll get in for sure. I don't doubt in the slightest that the Prophet would regard her as the finest possible breed mare..." He caught himself, embarrassed. "Uh, sorry, ma'am, but that's the way the Prophet thinks about such things."

Sara blushed. The men chuckled nervously, and now catching themselves, quickly stifled their amusement.

"Are you serious?" George said.

"Our Prophet is quite fond of handsome women. A weakness, I guess."

CHAPTER 8

Watching Norbert leave, O'Keefe noticed him glance back over his shoulder, with a troubled look. Suspicion? Regret?

"Richard, I'm not so sure you should've told him the plan. What if he changes his mind and decides to get back in good graces by blowing my cover?"

"That won't happen," Maxwell said. "I'm taking the very best care of him."

"What if he gets one of those divine visions? You think you can compete with that?"

"Won't happen either. He was acting coy about it with you guys, but he's told me enough about some things down there that could put him in the pen."

O'Keefe wasn't so sure. He thought a direct command from God Almighty Himself would undoubtedly override all purely worldly concerns, but he decided not to argue the point. "If I go down there and go through that training, and they don't take me in, I want a special bonus."

"Easy enough to get past that," Maxwell said. "Take Sara."

O'Keefe shook his head. "If I do that, I might as well shut down."

"Well, thanks, Boss," George said.

"You know what I mean."

Maxwell smiled slyly. "I'll double your payment."

O'Keefe shook his head again, more vigorously this time.

"At least think about it," Maxwell said. "Why should I pay you a special bonus if you're unwilling to reduce the risk they won't accept you?"

"Request withdrawn," O'Keefe said, "No bonus."

George intervened. "Richard, can we have a minute to discuss this?"

"Yes, please," Sara said. Rather sternly, O'Keefe thought. Not a good sign.

"Sure," Maxwell said, and quickly rose from his chair. "Take all the time you want. Just poke your head out the door and tell Denise when you're ready for me."

At the doorway, he stopped and turned back to face them. "I hate to appeal to your humanitarian impulses, guys, our country being the citadel of capitalism and all, but this is about a lot more than money. My little life isn't the only thing at stake here. It's also my employees, my wife, my kids ... and who knows who else is on their hit list."

It was playing out just as if George and Sara had planned it all in advance.

"Are you crazy?" George said. "That's more than we could make in our wildest dreams. And remember, that's on top of what we'll charge him for my part. And how about the reputation bump the whole thing'll give us? This ain't hard, Boss."

"And *you* need to remember that there'll be an opportunity cost to it. We won't be able to hustle for the things we're really supposed to be doing. And Sara's working on projects for Harrigan. He's our friend, but he can't let us risk his own client relationships by us abandoning him."

"The way I see it," George said, "this assignment has a about ten tons more opportunity upside than *anything* else we could do."

"You don't have a problem with dangling our partner here in front of that Prophet character? I'd feel like a pimp."

Sara cleared her throat. "Gentlemen, you think maybe you ought to ask the bottom girl what *she* thinks?"

George laughed while O'Keefe's forehead folded in confusion. *Bottom girl?*

Noticing that, Sara explained, "That's what the pimp's main girl is called."

How does she know that? O'Keefe wondered.

"We ought to do it," Sara said.

"You know this isn't just playacting," O'Keefe said. "We could get killed down there."

She shrugged. "Could get that just walking down the street."

O'Keefe emitted a small, sharp snort of disgust. "Great analogy. I know you're a badass, but you could get hurt … badly … killed even. No amount of money is worth that."

"Thank you, Daddy, but I'm of age now and can make decisions for myself."

"I didn't know money was so important to you."

"This is about a lot more than money," she said. "This isn't our usual chasing deadbeats and guarding buildings. These are killers. Or they harbor killers. They're gonna creep out of there someday and who knows what havoc they'll wreak. They have to be stopped."

"Boss, I would say the bottom girl has spoken," George said, his smile triumphant, irritatingly so.

O'Keefe smiled, a little sourly. "Alright, but it's on your greedy heads. And I'll do the talking when Maxwell comes back."

Maxwell returned, looking anxious.

"The vote was two to one," O'Keefe said.

Further consternation on Maxwell's face.

"In your favor. You can probably guess who voted for what."

Broad smile from Maxwell. "Thank you, Sara."

"I have to be honest," she said, "I was really voting *against* those bastards down there at that Ark place."

"But," O'Keefe said, "we have a couple of conditions. It has to be an additional 50,000, not 40,000. So 90,000 per month."

Without hesitation, Maxwell agreed, dashing O'Keefe's last remaining hope. *I should have asked for more.*

"We'll start right away and move as fast as we can, but it'll be a lot of work, and the clock on the monthly payments should start ticking right now."

Maxwell thought on that for a moment and said, "How long will it take you to get down there?"

"If you help us with some things, like fake IDs and solid backstories, a month, six weeks at most."

"Okay, but the payments shouldn't be so high until you actually go down there."

"And you would propose what?"

"Half until you go down. 45,000."

O'Keefe looked at each of his partners, giving them a chance to send Maxwell back out again and confer. But both nodded.

"Okay," O'Keefe said and remembered something Harrigan had told him to insist on: "He might find some excuse not to pay you," Harrigan had said. "Might say you breached the agreement somehow … or who knows, he could go broke. Get your money up front."

"You need," O'Keefe said, "to deposit the first month in advance and always be one month ahead. If they don't accept us, or we bail out at any point without your direction or consent, we'll return that month's advance deposit."

"Fair enough," Maxwell said. "Should I have a contract drawn up?"

"And our expenses for the prep period are on top of the fees."

Everyone in the room except O'Keefe visibly squirmed. Later, both George and Sara would ask if he'd been trying to kill the deal.

If he had, it hadn't worked. "Alright," Maxwell said, for the first time unenthusiastically.

"And," O'Keefe said, "that will include our lawyer fees for reviewing the contract."

"*Alright. Goddamn, alright* … if you'll promise to get the fuck out of here without gouging anything else out of me."

Maxwell seemed to be mostly joking, but O'Keefe couldn't let that comment go unanswered.

"I swear I'm not doing that. You're a businessman. You have to know what a big opportunity, but also a big risk, this is for us. It could blow up in our faces, figuratively and literally."

They rose and shook hands with Maxwell, Sara last. Maxwell kept her hand after the shake and said to O'Keefe, "You know what this pricing means, don't you, Pete?"

"I'm afraid to think about what it means."

"It means that Sara's worth more than you are. 50 versus 40 per month."

George smiled big. Sara seemed to be trying not to.

"Clearly so," O'Keefe said. "But I knew that anyway."

CHAPTER 9

The Prophet had warned Sinclair that "you're pushing your luck, Matthew" by undertaking this mission on a Saturday, the Sabbath according to their beliefs. Yet the Prophet had also been badgering him to get this done. The Prophet had a way of talking out of both sides of his mouth on things, especially important things—intentionally, Sinclair suspected, so the Prophet could claim prophetic accuracy no matter how things turned out. That was alright. He respected the Prophet for his shrewdness, one of the things that made him a great leader, worth following to the Promised Land or anywhere else. When he told the Prophet that the buyer insisted this was the only day he would be traveling to their area for a long time—that if they wanted to sell him weapons, it was now or never—the Prophet said nothing. *Yes, shrewd.*

At least the buyer prick had agreed to meet early in the morning, time enough to make the sale and get back to the Ark in time for Sabbath services. So he had risen long before daylight, replaced the existing license plate with another, loaded the trunk with an array of the weapons their expert armorers had converted from semi to fully automatic rifles and handguns, plus plenty of ammunition. As usual, he strapped on a shoulder holster holding a pistol and placed a machine pistol on the front seat next to him.

They had agreed to meet at a remote forest clearing, far from even the nearest farmhouse, where the buyer could try out the weapons. Sinclair arrived a little early, but the buyer was already there, leaning against the trunk of a black Mercedes, wearing a cocky smile, black leather jacket, crisply creased blue jeans, and fancy black cowboy boots. The unzipped jacket revealed a white shirt, top buttons unbuttoned, and a thin gold chain resting on a fluffy nest of chest hair.

Sinclair deliberately waited until the last minute to hit the brakes, swerving into a skid, sending the rear end of the car sliding toward the man arrogantly leaning against the car trunk. The man lurched into a crouch like a football linebacker, ready to dive either way.

"Sorry about that," Sinclair said as he exited the vehicle. "Lousy brakes. I keep forgetting how bad they are."

After a suspicious look from the buyer, they got right down to their business, neither wanting the other to know his name and not trusting that the other would offer his real name anyway.

The buyer picked one of the converted AR-15s and fired multiple rounds, single shot and fully automatic, at targets they rigged up on trees at various distances. After that, he tried out one of the silencer-equipped pistols.

Sinclair had given the price of each item over the phone and expected no haggling. The buyer said he'd take four fully automatic AR-15s, two silencer-equipped single-shot pistols, and a similarly equipped machine pistol, and said, "How about throwin' in the ammunition for goodwill's sake?"

"Sorry, friend," Sinclair said. "Really I am. But we're poor, and it's hard work to make these things. High risk, too, because it's illegal. We can't afford to be a discount operation. Just the demo ammo you shot here today was costly to us."

"Okay. I can understand that. But is there anything special about this ammunition?"

"No."

The buyer's face was a question mark, as if he'd sensed that Sinclair had left something open for negotiation. He pulled a wad of cash out of his jacket pocket. "I think you're overpriced on the ammo since there's nothin' special about it."

"Might be. Might not. But I've got no authority to discount."

"How about if I buy the whole bunch, the whole shootin' match? No pun intended."

It was tempting. Clean out the trunk. Good total price even with a discount. No illegal weapons on the return ride home to get him in trouble if the police stopped him for something. But the Prophet might publicly scold him for taking less.

"Like I said, no authority."

A slight sneer from the buyer. "Seems kind of dumb."

He fought an impulse to draw the pistol and at least scare this prick. Or more. He could wipe that smug smile off the hotshot's face … or why not his whole face … with a bullet … grab the wad, and drive calmly away. *Wonder what the Prophet would say about that. Maybe: "Just another heathen. Who cares … as long as no witnesses. You gave him what he deserves. Let Yahweh sort him out."*

"Take it or leave it," Sinclair said.

The buyer shrugged. "Your loss."

Which made him want at least to coldcock the sonuvabitch. He really was tempted, but he refrained since it was a good sale … and it *was* the Sabbath after all.

The buyer selected a few rounds for each of the purchased weapons, passing up the rest of the ammunition.

"You don't take checks, I suppose."

Now the prick was trying to cheat him. He couldn't have been clearer that it was to be a cash sale. "Fraid not."

"I was hoping to reserve as much cash as possible for the gun show."

"No can do. I made that clear on the phone."

The buyer fingered through his wad, plucked out a few bills, and handed him more than enough for the cost of the items. "I don't have the exact amount. Got change?"

"Think so," Sinclair said, reaching into his pocket and pulling out his own smaller clump of bills. But he couldn't make the exact change.

"So what do we do now?" the buyer said with a smart-ass grin.

Sinclair didn't know what to say.

The silence continued, the buyer's grin too.

You're giving me no choice, asshole … I'll wipe that grin…

But, just in time, the prick said, "Well, since you're so poor and all, I'll let you keep the change. But maybe you'll look more favorable on me next time. Maybe remember me and give me a credit, maybe even a discount. Or maybe we'll see each other at another gun show down the road and you can make it up to me then."

For some reason he couldn't understand, the situation made him ashamed. He wasn't sure what to say so he responded only with a slight nod. They stood, silent again, waiting. If he left first, the buyer would see his license plate. Not happening.

Again, it was the buyer who broke the silence. "Nice doin' business with you."

Sarcastic prick. You'll never know how lucky you were to live out this day.

As the buyer drove away, Sinclair made sure to stand at the rear of his car, his body covering the license plate.

It had been a successful transaction despite the Prophet's warning about the Sabbath, but his mood remained foul, his bubbling anger distracting him into pressing a little too hard on the gas pedal and exceeding the speed limit—not by much, but enough to attract a patrol car looming up in his rear view mirror, no siren but roof light flashing.

The weapons in the trunk and the one beside him on the front seat were supposedly unlawful, but those laws violated higher law, natural law, God's law, to say nothing of the Constitution of the United States. But the police goons would enforce those laws anyway. This goon would certainly check the license plate and find it matched a different vehicle. Darned if the Prophet hadn't turned out to be right about the Sabbath after all. But maybe the goon would be lazy, not bother to check on the plate, just ask for his driver's license, check that out, which would yield nothing, then maybe just give him a verbal warning and let him go. One good ol' boy to another.

But when he looked in his rearview mirror as the trooper emerged from his car … Not a good ol' boy at all. A son of Ham. An outrage. The ultimate insult that this Godless government could inflict on a white Christian man. Someone had once asked the Prophet how God would judge a white Christian man for killing one of these. The answer: "About the same as He'd judge you for killin' a dog."

He pushed the seat as far back as it would go, grabbed the machine pistol in his right hand and the door handle with his left, exited the car with his back to the approaching trooper, whipped around and unleased two bursts of automatic fire.

Several bullets hit home—the head and the heart. The trooper pitched backward and lay sprawled on the ground, face to the sky. His left arm and leg twitched in unison one time, then no movement at all.

He jogged over to the body.

Still breathing.

He looked down at it with revulsion and fired another burst, blowing the trooper's face off.

As he drove away, he was surprised by how calm he felt, how easy it had been. He couldn't recall anyone driving by from the time the trooper had started after him until he'd finished the goon off and left the scene.

He would tell no one. Except maybe the Prophet. Well, yes, he would have to tell the Prophet, though not about the speeding. The Prophet wouldn't likely scold him, except to remind him of the warning about undertaking the trip on the Sabbath, and that next time he shouldn't be prideful, arrogant, rebellious. Maybe they would even joke about it, recalling the old saying about "the only good one."

And he had surely made this one into a good one.

CHAPTER 10

Gᴇᴏʀɢᴇ ᴀɴᴅ Sᴀʀᴀ set about working with a couple of Maxwell's people to produce fake IDs and fictional personal histories for Sara and O'Keefe that would withstand at least a limited amount of scrutiny.

O'Keefe's first task: Figure out how to replace Sara and himself during what could be months at the Ark with little to no contact with the world outside.

He had the rueful thought that she would be harder to replace than O'Keefe himself would be. He had lately morphed into a combination of promoter/salesman and business manager. But in terms of their primary work, he'd drifted into a hit-and-miss existence of working on whatever task he bumped into, or, as was more often the case, bumped into him, a "utility" player who filled in wherever he was needed in the moment. So be it. *Chop wood, carry water.*

She'd come a long way from the day when, in response to his ad in the classified section of the newspaper, she'd appeared in his office from what seemed like, and, indeed, maybe had been— nowhere. He had just started out and desperately needed some support. He'd received no answers to his ad until she showed up on a particularly bad morning—bad in a good way because he suddenly had not one but two new cases that needed immediate attention—but bad in a bad way because he was days behind in returning some important calls and weeks behind in paying his bills and keeping his simple books. The phones had been ringing, often without being answered, as he struggled to juggle a variety of tasks. His voice recorder had suddenly and mysteriously stopped working, and it, along with everything else mechanical, stretched far beyond his ken. The computer was there on his desk, but, at best, he could do word processing with it, nothing beyond. He was a good typist but had some difficulty with the prevailing software programs, DOS and WordPerfect (which he'd adopted because Harrigan and his other lawyer clients used it). A Lotus spreadsheet might as well have been Egyptian hieroglyphics.

Not knowing that it was a desperate man on the other side of the desk (and it probably wouldn't have changed anything about her manner and approach even if she had known), Sara had, paradoxically, acted both diffident *and* serious. She'd presented no résumé or even a willingness to discuss her past, including any job qualifications. But she was well spoken and generally exhibited an assured self-possession. She could type, had some other computer skills, and had made it clear that she was exceedingly anxious to learn, describing herself as a "Jill of all trades," willing to do pretty much anything. She sealed the deal by leaning forward, capturing him in an intense, dark-eyed gaze, and saying, most *un*-diffidently, "I think this work would be extremely interesting."

Although he was already having to scratch and scrounge every two weeks just to pay his current lone employee, ex-MP, ex-police officer, and O'Keefe's childhood buddy, George Novak, it made both of them laugh when he nodded toward the phone trilling unanswered for the second time during their brief interview and said, "Can you start right now?"

She said she could, and she did. To this day O'Keefe hoped he'd made that offer on the basis of her intensity and his desperation, not the sex appeal she so effortlessly radiated. He immediately installed her at the desk in the small reception area and brought George from his office to introduce them.

Later, he apologized to George for not consulting him before offering her the job. "I didn't want to take any chance she might escape."

"No problem," George said. "I understand. Quite a babe. I'd've been mad at you if you'd let her get away."

"You horny bastard," O'Keefe had said. "That had nothing to do with it."

"Go tell lies to someone else, Boss. Is she married?"

"I didn't ask."

"No ring."

"I didn't notice."

"I did. Did you ask her if she has a boyfriend?"

"Oh, yeah. That would've been a real appropriate question, butthead."

"Boss! What kind of detective are you?"

"One who learned the hard way—no pun intended—how to keep it in his pants."

"How dull you are. But anyway, good choice. What's her background?"

O'Keefe had no idea. He was just grateful that she'd appeared seemingly miraculously from seemingly nowhere and taken the job.

It had soon become clear that a second coming of Radar O'Reilly had manifested in their midst. In addition to the usual receptionist and secretarial duties, she took on the bookkeeping and bill payments and brought them out of the messaging Stone Age by securing a good finance deal for proper computers connected to a new phone system that furnished voicemail to replace the often-malfunctioning message-recording machines.

She had only two downsides. One required him to be led not into temptation, or at least not act thereupon. The other was the terror that one of his lawyer clients would spirit her away with a promise of more money, a long list of benefits, and the near certainty of career advancement when O'Keefe couldn't in good faith even offer the certainty of a future job. In what he knew to be a feeble preemptive strike, he bestowed on her, entirely voluntarily, without a hint of a request or expectation on her part, a salary increase that he couldn't afford.

But it had turned out that Sara wasn't in it for any of that. Her motive, initially undisclosed, for taking the job was that she wanted to become a detective and looked for every opportunity to "get out on the street" as she put it.

She was not only fearless but, O'Keefe suspected, a danger freak, and she tended to get in over her head. O'Keefe had tried but been unable to infuse into her some traditional notions of what she needed to be protected from. He wouldn't admit that this was sexism on his part. Just reality. This could be a damn dangerous job. O'Keefe's short detective career had seen him suffer near fatal gunshot wounds, a car bombing, and more. And for that reason—right or wrong, paternalistic, patriarchal, or for whatever other politically incorrect impulse—he wouldn't be able to forgive himself if he allowed, or let her allow, something terrible to befall her.

He didn't mind her ambition, was even willing to support it, but he rebelled against putting her in, or allowing her to put herself in, dangerous situations in which she might be physically overwhelmed. He'd once illustrated this to her by grabbing her and roughly pinning her to the floor. She'd been able to muster only the feeblest resistance.

Her response: martial arts training. Now he'd be reluctant to try that move again and had taken up martial arts himself to keep up with her.

Yet he still resisted assigning her to anything dangerous or allowing her to intrude into perilous situations, though the latter was hard to control. He'd tried to make her into a fraud investigator—numbers and legal documents—which she'd accepted because that was her entry ticket to the profession, but she clearly had no intention of accepting that role forever. Which resulted in a fairly constant tension between them. Now he had to worry not only that some law firm or competing detective agency would hire her, but, her ambition frustrated, she might even go out on her own.

So the chains he'd clamped onto her had gotten looser and looser. This Maxwell thing was a further loosening. In Maxwell's office that day, he'd tried to resist but found himself in the tightest corner and he'd agreed to the mission under duress, unable to fully focus on and assess how that choice might affect one very formidable person: the guy who was still their primary source of work, lawyer Michael Harrigan, who was not just the agency's primary meal ticket but O'Keefe's childhood best friend and blood brother. They'd fancied their younger selves to be modern knights of the Grail, which meant to them the ultimate sacred meaning of life—or, at least, a soulful long-haired girl.

The work for Harrigan had started amid the chaos arising from the financial institution failures in the S&L Crisis that had erupted in the mid-1980s. That work was still coming in and looked as if it would continue to come in for at least a few more years. Sometimes it involved rescuing failing businesses whose lending sources had dried up. More often it was about dealing with the struggling, barely surviving financial institutions' recovery efforts, or representing the entrepreneurs who acquired the loans left behind by the failed banks. In both cases, it required a sophisticated form of "chasing deadbeats," as Sara had characterized it in Maxwell's office that day. Occasionally, where they could navigate the conflicts of interest, Harrigan and they might even defend a "deadbeat" or two.

O'Keefe had informed Harrigan about the Maxwell situation and obtained his advice on structuring a possible agreement, which Harrigan had dispensed in his usual bemused, skeptical manner, though this time, as on a few previous occasions, with what seemed like a touch of envy for the more dangerous but adventurous life his old friend had stumbled into. That life was thanks largely to Harrigan himself, who, on one very bad morning some years ago, had bailed O'Keefe out of jail, essentially lifted him by the scruff of his neck as he would a puppy who'd soiled the carpet, and dragooned O'Keefe into what amounted to involuntary servitude as Harrigan's own private PI. With Harrigan's support, O'Keefe was consistently adding new clients. But now it had developed that Harrigan might be deprived of not only O'Keefe but the currently far more useful Sara for an indefinite period.

"When do we tell Harrigan?" Sara had said.

"As soon as I get a sign from above ... you know, like the Prophet gets. But it won't be on the wings of a dove, I don't think."

O'Keefe needed that sign soon. He owed Harrigan that. But it refused to quickly manifest. At one point he even consulted Karma, his noble German Shepherd and former police dog. But Karma, if he knew, refused to share.

Finally, more in desperation than enlightenment, two words came to him, more a last straw than a biblical bolt from the blue.

CHAPTER 11

T HOSE TWO WORDS were Dagmar Sibelius.

The person to whom they referred perched only a few yards away from him, in the reception area of the office. Sentinel, secretary, and many other things.

Sara had been in charge of recruiting her replacement and showed up at his door with a tall, thin, vivacious creature with rapidly blinking eyelids and a scrambled profusion of the springy curls favored in the 1980s, hers an eye-popping fiery red. She was the opposite of Sara in almost every physical and emotional characteristic. She held out her hand and said, "Dagmar Sibelius. That's *Si,* like Sister, *Bay* like San Francisco, *Lee* like Robert E., and *Us,* like you and me. Si-be-li-us." She said her dad had told her they enjoyed a distant family connection of some kind to the Finnish composer. O'Keefe was a bit proud of himself for being able to say "Frederick Sibelius?". She rolled her eyes and said, "Yes. I don't know if it's true, but Dad sure thinks so."

She'd recently dropped out of junior college. "Not because it was boring," she said, "which it was, but because I couldn't afford it. I need to work and make my way in the world."

He refrained from telling her that dropping out of college wasn't a good start for making such a way, as his own experience had painfully punctuated.

Like Sara, she said she was attracted to the job because it seemed so interesting. "It seems different, maybe even exciting. I read about you in the paper last year."

"I'm hoping it won't be that exciting ever again."

"I get it," she said, but he sensed a bit of disappointment in her tone.

He saw no reason to disappoint Sara and thought that the brightness this person would bring might be quite a good thing for an office where the boss was given to brooding and melancholia, George was out most of the time, and Sara was quiet, dark, and deep.

When he offered her the job, she leaned over his desk toward him, not in a come-on sort of way but in utmost earnestness, and said, "I'll tell you one thing, sir. I won't disappoint you. I don't disappoint."

Indeed, she did not disappoint. She turned out to be an unexpected boon, like Sara before her. But what he was about to ask of her might be too much. She was a college dropout. But so was he. So was George. And who knew whether Sara was or not? But that aside, Harrigan's work would relegate this exceedingly social creature, who seemed to relish human connection and interaction, to mostly lonely hours poring over pesky numbers and laborious documentation. She might hate it or just be bad at it, disappointing Harrigan while crushing her morale in the process. Or she might perform exceedingly well, and he would lose another office assistant to what Dagmar might consider a higher calling.

The first miracle, Sara, had been improbable. The second, Dagmar, seemed almost supernatural. Finding a third was unimaginable.

He asked Sara for her opinion on whether it would work.

"Maybe," she said. "She dropped out of junior college, but that was because it bored her, not because she hasn't got the smarts. I doubt she knows much about financial stuff, but neither did I. She seems like a riser to occasions … She's so social though. I wonder if she could really force herself to spend mostly solitary hours analyzing documents, including a bunch of legal documents and financial statements, doing spreadsheets, all that stuff."

They agreed that, for it to have any chance of succeeding, Sara would have to work triple time to train her as best she could in a short amount of time.

Now the only question remaining: Which one should he talk to first, Harrigan or Dagmar? If he talked to Dagmar first, and Harrigan nixed it, she might be sorely disappointed, unhappy, her morale compromised. If he went to Harrigan first, and Harrigan agreed but Dagmar refused, that could profoundly disappoint Harrigan, twisting a knife in the wound of losing Sara. Best friend or not, Harrigan could only put up with so much.

So, Dagmar first.

She listened carefully, without visible enthusiasm, and asked for a little time to think about it.

She took not one but two days. When she knocked on his door and came stiffly in and sat down across from him, he thought for sure it would be a no. But instead, she said, "I'll admit I'm scared, but I want to do this … for the cause."

"I appreciate that," he said, "but if it's not for your own cause, don't do it."

"Oh, it's that too," she rushed to say. "If I want to advance myself, I have to take chances. I'm just not sure I'm good enough for this."

Spreading his hands to take in the desk and the room, he said, "*I* don't know if *I'm* good enough for *this … any* of this. I have to answer that question every day, again and again, and the answer isn't always the one I'd like it to be."

"Have you talked to Mr. Harrigan about me helping?"

He explained that he didn't want to go to Harrigan with the bad news about Sara without having a replacement to suggest, but he felt he should talk to Dagmar first. He didn't want to lift Harrigan's hopes, then dash them. "It won't be an everyday thing, but I won't kid you, at times it'll be hard, doing what George needs you for here and helping Harrigan too."

"He seems like a very serious man," she said. "I hope he doesn't think I'm an airhead."

O'Keefe laughed. "Actually, he might have that suspicion, but he'll figure it out soon enough, and I guarantee that a dose or two of you a day will improve his mental health wonderfully."

"Thank you, sir. I hope it'll work out."

"If it doesn't, I hope you won't be heartbroken."

"Oh, no. My heart's stronger than that."

That handled, O'Keefe went to Harrigan.

"First, *you* leave me. Then I take a risk on Sara, which I admit was well rewarded. But no sooner do I become dependent on her than you take *her* away on what occurs to me is a pretty crazy expedition."

"I can't argue with that, but Sara wants it, George wants it, and you can't say it isn't for a good cause … and likely a lucrative one. Just what Maxwell said it would be, an offer I can't refuse—"

"If you survive it," Harrigan interrupted. "Sorry to say it that way, but those are some damn dangerous characters down there. You sure Sara really wants to do that?"

"Rarin' to go and won't countenance a contrary word."

"And Dagmar, I like her, but she doesn't have a clue about this stuff."

"Sara will train her. No charge for that, and no charge for Dagmar either while Sara and I are away."

Harrigan scowled, then pressed back in his chair. "I guess that's an offer *I'd* be an idiot to refuse."

"Thank you, " O'Keefe said.

With a weary shrug of resignation, Harrigan said, "Like it or not, all things must evolve. But now you owe me double." He reached to his left, picked up and handed O'Keefe a thick document. "The appeal brief. We filed it today."

"Nice," O'Keefe said. "But like I keep having to tell you, on this one I think *you* owe *me.* It might be your ticket *out* of Hell and might even earn you a little less time in Purgatory … Do we still believe in Purgatory … or did they make that disappear somehow?"

"How would I know?"

"Maybe it went with Saint Christopher. Dante would be disappointed."

"Well, you can bet we still have Hell."

It was the case of "Miss Ginny"—Virginia Montrose, former preschool teacher of O'Keefe's daughter, Kelly. Last year, Miss Ginny had been convicted of sexually abusing several children in her care. Reluctantly, in response to Kelly's tearful plea, O'Keefe had worked pro bono as an investigator in the case. He and many others considered the conviction a gross miscarriage of justice, even a "legal lynching." It had so devastated Ginny's lawyer Scott Hartley that he'd walked away from active legal practice and taken a teaching position at a local law school. O'Keefe had pulled out all the guilt stops with Harrigan and persuaded him to convince his law firm to partner with Hartley on the appeal and actually take over and lead the effort, as Hartley had scant access to the human resources a law firm could muster in such a cause.

"What's next on this?" O'Keefe said, nodding at the document. "How soon do we get a hearing?"

"Hard to tell. But not soon. The prosecutor gets the time to file a response, then we respond to that, then the court finds a place for us at the end of a crowded docket. Months for a hearing, maybe a year or more for a ruling."

"The Goddamn wheels of justice," O'Keefe said, "grind so slow they might as well be walking … and with a limp. Meanwhile, Ginny's life is bleeding away in that prison cell."

"Not to be cynical," Harrigan said, "but write your congressman."

"I've got enough futility in my life already. What about the governor?"

"We're pressing her hard. Our friends in the civil liberties community are doing the same. But I don't think the governor'll preempt the courts, at least not until the appellate court has a chance to reverse the trial court. There's still Satanic and moral panics swirling around out there, and lots of people are certain Ginny's guilty. Maybe if the gov loses the election, she'll do a good deed on her way out."

"How about Marvin?"

"A lot harder since he took a plea. That really hurt him. It hurt Ginny too. And it will keep hurting her, and him still more. It helps that it was an Alford plea, which didn't require him to affirmatively admit guilt, just acknowledge they had enough evidence to convict … But I think his only chance is with the governor, and probably not until, and unless, Ginny gets relief."

"Are you guys in for the long run?"

"Oh, yes. My partners might wish we hadn't agreed to get involved because those Save Our Children people are vicious and relentless. They've even applied some direct heat on our individual partners, even their families, even their kids at school. But I won't let our guys weasel out. If they do that, it'll be the old 'my way or the highway' … though I'm not sure they wouldn't wave me goodbye."

"I'm feeling bad now."

"Don't. I don't regret it. It's redemptive. I should be begging for any chance for any remission of sins I can get."

It was the sacrament of confession Harrigan was referring to, and it amused O'Keefe that even though neither of them believed anymore, had not set foot in a church in years except for a funeral, wedding, or concert, they still instinctively reached back to their childhood and the old sacramental-catechistical mythic structures and rituals to interpret and give meaning to many of the deep, defining moments of their lives

As O'Keefe rose to leave, Harrigan said, "You're becoming a worthy knight, my brother…And I *am* an idiot. I *will* pass up your offer. I'll pay Dagmar."

CHAPTER 12

O'KEEFE STEEPED HIMSELF in all things fundamentalist (Apocalyptic Christian version), survivalist, antigovernment militarist, and racist white separatist. He forced himself to read the main texts of the Christian Identity ideology, so false and foolish and ponderous it was hard to slog through it. But by the end he knew the details well enough that he would be able to discuss the ins and outs with a believer (*another* believer, he corrected himself, for a believer was a role he would soon need to fully inhabit).

Somewhat more interesting were the survivalist tracts of John Todd and others. Far more interesting, and sobering, was what seemed to be the foundational document, both inspiration and blueprint for what the Prophet and the people of the Ark might be in the process of becoming: *The Turner Diaries*—a novel, fiction, but fiction they yearned to make terrible fact, dreaming of, even if not always actually intending and planning, actions necessary or desirable to make it so. The blood and gore in the book included obliterating an FBI building with a truck bomb.

He immersed himself in gun culture. His prospective new companions at the Ark seemed to love their weapons as much as they loved their children and, certainly, their wives (though many wives were also gun lovers). As part of his self-education, he read all he could including back issues of the major gun mags, *Guns & Ammo* and *Soldier of Fortune*. In one of these he found a small ad in the "Personals" section for the Christian Soldiers Survival School: *Are you prepared for the End Times, the Final Armageddon Battle? WE ARE.*

Then there were the gun shows. He was startled to find that a large, immensely popular gun-show circuit had developed around the country. Hundreds every year. Not just in the big cities. Many medium-sized towns hosted them too. Two were scheduled for that very month, less than a half day's drive away.

He drove up to a large structure at one end of a suburban industrial park. Forget parking in the lot, it was full, the cars spilling over onto the adjacent roadside and the grass median strip. The building's foyer was packed: lone men leaning up against the wall, thumbs hooked in the belt loops of their jeans; groups of two and three, some speaking in low tones suggesting secrets shared and conspiracies afoot, others gesturing, laughing, boisterous, loud. Noise and cigarette smoke, probably cigar smoke too (cheroots no doubt), poured out of an opening in a wall marked with a "Café" sign.

O'Keefe lined up for a ticket, paid in cash, and entered the main "Hall," actually an auditorium. The size of the crowd inside surprised him even more than the multitude of cars outside. And not just men. There were many couples, even families. Personal weaponry was allowed if unloaded, the ammunition supposedly checked at the door, thus a significant number of customers strolled around with pistols or revolvers in shoulder or hip holsters or with rifles slung over shoulders. The inspection and security procedures seemed halfhearted if not downright sloppy. And there was ammunition for sale within easy arm's reach throughout the place. All that made him nervous. A mad-dog shooter wouldn't last long in here with all these trigger-happy would-be warriors, many of whom might actually *be* tough, but the shooter could inflict tremendous carnage before they overwhelmed him.

Rows of tables, stretching the full length of the auditorium, maybe thirty or forty yards long, displayed every conceivable type of legal firearm—and as he later discovered—outside, in the parking lot, out of car trunks and the backs of campers and vans, *illegal* ones could be easily obtained. Many of the guns were of the same type but manufactured under different brand names. Alongside them was an array of hunting and military clothing and paraphernalia.

He found himself almost lost in the blur induced by the display but was determined to see it all.

Jammed into niches, corners, and smaller adjacent rooms were more tables laden with militant expressions of militant ideas likely favored by most of the attendees and the organizations purveying to them. Signage, flags, banners, bumper and other stickers, and stamps with messages of protest against and demonization of restrictions on ownership and use of firearms, the government (pronounced gov'ment, especially the federal gov'ment), the United Nations, Communists, Jews, blacks, liberals, homosexuals, and, oddly, ghosts long passed away but still haunting certain minds—hippies.

After tramping up and down row upon row, he noticed along a far wall, barely visible in the jumble of tables and booths an unexpected treasure: a small table with a large sign behind it, towering well above the man sitting in attendance:

WAR GAMES

MILITARY SURVIVAL TRAINING

BROUGHT TO YOU BY THE NEW ARK

He remembered Norbert saying that they were trying out "some sales stuff."

As O'Keefe got closer, he got a better look at the man sitting at the table. His face was familiar.

The man jumped up and spread out his arms. "O'Keefe, you shitbird!"

"Spud," O'Keefe mumbled, trying to recover from the surprise.

Spud scooted around the table, rushed toward him, and stuck out his hand, not to shake but to grab O'Keefe's arm and squeeze hard and pull O'Keefe toward him. "What the hell is Pete O'Keefe doin' in such a place as this?"

O'Keefe groped for a story. "Well, I've been getting more and more curious about this kind of thing, and I was down here on some other business, had a couple of hours to spare, thought I'd drop by."

"Well, I'll be a Goddamn (pronounced "God *dahm*") hornswoggled tadpole. We been livin' in the same town for all these years and never laid eyes on each other ... but here we are."

Gesturing toward the table and the sign, O'Keefe said, "What's this?"

"I'm helping these guys out. It's a helluva thing they got goin'. A military thing. A survivalist deal. Important shit. Gettin' people ready for the comin' End Times. The Apocalypse. Just like the Bible lays it out … slicker'n owl shit."

The table Spud presided over was meagerly supplied with a few promotional materials describing the program and the beliefs of the Ark II people. O'Keefe took two copies of each. There were also two stacks of *The Turner Diaries*.

"Help yourself to a book there," Spud said. "I usually sell 'em, but I've got the authority to *give* 'em to the right kind of people."

"Don't need it. I own it already."

"Good for you. Ain't read it myself. Never been much of a reader. But I've heard all about it so many times I think I know it by heart."

He thoroughly surveyed O'Keefe. "No shit. Pete O'Keefe. If I thought I'd see you anywhere, it'd be the opposite of here. It'd be some antiwar rally or somethin'."

O'Keefe managed a laugh. "Not anymore."

"Really?"

"World's slidin' down into the shithole, Spud."

"Sure thing. And you come to the right place with that kind of thinkin'. But I'll be a mouse-fucked turtle if I ever thought I'd see Pete O'Keefe in a place like this."

"Was I that bad?"

"You sure as shit were. Damn near offended me. But I knew you were a good guy beneath that. Let's go have a coffee."

"How about your table?"

"I'll get my neighbor next door there to watch it. But nobody'd bother it anyway. No scumbag thieves here. Law abidin' people here. I could lay down a hundred-dollar bill on that table, if I had such a thing, and leave it there. Nobody'd touch it. This is a brotherhood. Yeah, man, you've come to the right place."

CHAPTER 13

O'KEEFE HADN'T MET Spud until he was back on U.S. soil, having miraculously survived Vietnam and only a few weeks away from being discharged. Never a social sort, even less so then, O'Keefe had been close to downright hostile in those days, fed up with everything Marine Corps and on the verge of a self-defeating outburst of insubordination likely to land him in the brig for a stint that would have extended his tour of duty, perhaps for a long time, and might even have led to a less-than-honorable discharge, which would have punished him in unpredictable ways for the rest of his life.

Spud, also a short timer, was the opposite. He occupied the lower tier of a bunk two down from O'Keefe's, and it had been impossible for O'Keefe or anyone else to escape his attentions. It had taken no time for Spud to pry out of O'Keefe a scattering of personal information including his hometown. "Well, I'll be a God-dahm mid*wive*," Spud said. "That's my hometown too."

They went on comparing notes about that, Spud overcoming O'Keefe's taciturn minimum-word responses and never put off by O'Keefe's failure to care enough to seek similar information about Spud (though Spud supplied it nevertheless).

O'Keefe did inquire about the origin of his new friend's nickname. That turned Spud's face red.

"Okay, I'll tell ya, but I'll hunt ya down and saw off your dick with a butter knife if ya repeat it or tell anybody."

He cocked his eye, lifted his chin, and said, "Notice anything peculiar about me?"

He did look peculiar, but O'Keefe wasn't sure exactly how and wouldn't have ventured an opinion on such a delicate topic even if he had one.

"Mr. Fucking Potato Head. Some smart-ass came up with that in boot camp, and it spread like liquid shit down a baby's leg."

His head did have that shape.

"And I was clearly gonna be stuck with it. I couldn't bear that no how, so I came up with 'Spud' as a preferable substitute and started even introducin' myself that way "ta *head* off"—winking his right eye— "the other. If somebody asked about it, I'd point to my misshapen noggin and wink and whisper, 'Potato Head, Idaho Extra Special.' So, ya see," he said with a look of solid self-satisfaction, "I embraced the infernal damn thing that way, and Spud was a damn sight more acceptable of a nickname. Took the sting out of it mostly. Hell, if people weren't closely lookin' or thinkin' too hard about it, they might think I got it peelin' taters in KP."

Now, as they moved through the auditorium to the café, O'Keefe wasn't surprised that Spud was on enthusiastically friendly terms with nearly every vendor they passed.

It wasn't mealtime, but the café was nearly full, men in pairs or threesomes mostly, most of them wearing ball or hunting caps, some in military fatigues, others looking ready for the hunt, talking low and earnest. Surely most of the talking was innocent enough—gun and hunting talk spiced with the occasional eruption of militant opinionating—but he guessed there were likely a few dodgy transactions, schemes, and conspiracies in the process of hatching.

Spud let O'Keefe buy the coffees, then they made their way through the throng, Spud all the while hello-ing and joking with those he knew and those he didn't.

After they sat down, Spud looked around as if to make sure he hadn't missed anyone to wave at, greet, or banter with, and took a sip of the exceedingly hot coffee. "Careful," he said. "Damn scaldin' stuff'll strip your tongue down to the raw flesh."

"Thanks for the warning. Hate when they make it that way."

"We never did hook up after the Corps," Spud said. "Called ya once but no return back."

"Really? I didn't know," O'Keefe lied.

They talked for a bit about when Spud had called, who he'd talked to and left his message with, and speculated on how it must have gotten lost.

"That wouldn't've been unusual for me in those days," O'Keefe said. "I lost a lot and *was* lost a lot back then. Sunk very low. They say it was PTSD. Trauma from the war."

Spud twisted his whole body into a scoff. "That's bullshit. The PTSD was from how they treated us after. They sent us over to that infernal suffocatin', oozin' shitswamp of a place, tellin' us how we was fightin' for freedom against the Commies but *didn't* bother to tell us the people over there didn't give one bird turd about bein' free. Then they wouldn't let us fight to win the way we damn well knew how, sendin' us out wanderin' around in the jungle every day for no purpose, except to serve as human bullet magnets. Sufferin' and dyin' for God dahm nothin'."

O'Keefe nodded. "Perfect description."

"But that wasn't the half of it. However stupid those politicians were that sent us there and the dumbass generals in charge, I was proud to serve my country. But then I come back, get off the plane, and there's a crowd of long-haired, scroungy-lookin' so-called peacenik, make-love-not-war motherfuckers spittin' on us and screamin' at us, callin' us 'baby killers.' I never killed no baby. Did you?"

"Not that I know of."

"Nobody stood up for us. Nobody gave a shit. In fact, it was like a badge of shame to be a veteran. And the whole shitty country's only gotten worse since—"

O'Keefe was afraid Spud might never stop. "Hey, I'm with you all the way, but spare me the details, okay? It hurts too much."

"Yeah. I do go on … and on."

"Is that why you hooked up with these Ark people?"

"Yeah. I wouldn't go down there and live with 'em … too damn rough …but I'm like a ambassador for 'em out here in ZOG-land."

"ZOG?"

Spud looked around suspiciously. "The Zionist Organized Government."

"Do the Ark people pay you?"

"It's mostly volunteer. They do give me a referral fee if I send a payin' customer down there for the training. But that's it. I'm in it for the cause. I like their thinkin' and plannin'."

"Planning?"

"For the Apocalypse. They're armed and they're trained and trainin' others to take back our country and the world."

"I thought it was just to defend themselves from marauders when the world collapses," O'Keefe said.

"That's how they started. But they came to see that ain't enough. The flood waters is risin' and risin', always on the rise, gonna engulf us soon. It's got to be stopped. We can't, by the Lord God in the vault of Heaven, wait for the waters to be a'lappin' at our feet."

"Takin' It To The Streets, eh?" O'Keefe said.

"Exactly. You got it, man. Doobie Brothers."

And he began to sing the song about a "brother" living in hell, invisible to the smug eyes of the upper world now, but soon there would be, as the song title promised … a reckoning.

He sang it loud enough that people at some of the nearby tables began to join in, cheer, clap, and stomp their feet. Spud couldn't have been more pleased, nodding and basking in the attention as if he were on a stage before a packed house of screaming fans.

"Yep, O'Keefe. You come to the right place." Then, as pleasantly as if he were Santa Claus handing out Christmas gifts to children, he said, "You and me may not quite live to see it, but someday there won't be even one remainin' kike, spearchucker, raghead, faggot, lesbo, commie, pinko, or hippie left in this world."

And with his sunniest sunbeam of a smile he slowly drew his index finger across his throat.

CHAPTER 14

O'KEEFE ALSO IMMERSED himself in the geography and topography of the Ark property and surrounding area including the 40,000-acre man-made lake with 800 miles of shoreline. On a map its many coves made it look like something other than a lake, more like an extraordinarily detailed puzzle piece. It had been created by damming a wild river, supposedly for the primary purpose of flood control and secondarily for recreation, but the flood-control aspect had faded in memory as boaters and water skiers and fishermen descended on the place in the warmer months. Still, the lake was so remote, and almost all of the land along the Ark's lakefront so thick with forests of oak, hickory, cedar, and other pine and fir, that approach to the Ark compound by water was daunting.

Once ashore, trespassers would confront tangled underbrush through which copperheads, water moccasins, and, it was said, even a few timber rattlesnakes slithered and the occasional wild boar snorted and snuffled. Fishermen occasionally approached within a few yards of the Ark shoreline, but there was no reason other than cat-killing curiosity to be venturing into that wilderness. If they did brave that, they would soon discover that they had stumbled upon an armed camp.

"It would seem smart for us to take a look at the lakeshore," George said as they hunkered over the large map spread out on the conference table, adding, slyly, "You guys might have to swim out."

"You're quite amusing," O'Keefe said. He looked at Sara. "Can you swim?"

Of course she could.

"It's a good idea to take a look," he said to George, "even just from a reconnaissance point of view, swim out or not. Think we can get close?"

"We can be fishermen," George said, then looked at Sara and corrected himself. "Er, fisherpeople?"

"I've got no fishing gear," O'Keefe said.

"Figures," George said. "I do. Enough for all of us."

"Figures," O'Keefe said.

O'Keefe's Wagoneer was both spacious and comfortable for highway driving and the most suitable available vehicle for rougher country, so he drove. At George's request, Karma came along for the ride. The German Shepherd jumped into the back seat, and Sara began to climb in after him, but George insisted that she take the front seat instead. Sara looked shocked. O'Keefe was also shocked until George said, "Rough night last night. I need to saw some Zs and hang with my buddy Karma." But O'Keefe wondered if that wasn't a cover for a slight concession to a possible world in which women weren't always expected to volunteer for the back seat.

Spring was now fully sprung and warming rapidly into summer, and the landscape had responded with a profusion of greenness, interrupted only by occasional patches of yellow, red, and purple wildflowers, no brown left to the eye other than tree trunks, which were themselves obscured by the luxuriance of the green leaves.

O'Keefe used the cruise control to stay five miles above the speed limit. "Ever been down this way?" he said.

Sara shook her head. It seemed impossible that she could have lived in this area for very much of her life and not traveled down to the lake country. One more facet of her mystery. He was reluctant to probe, always waiting for her to volunteer, but she never did.

"It's fairly ugly for a while," he said, "but gets near spectacular after that."

George sawed his Zs noisily in the back seat, Karma quietly asleep beside him, the top of his head against George's leg, the very image of man and his best friend.

"Sweet," Sara said.

"The dog anyway," O'Keefe said.

Even Sara, Ms. Vigilance, drifted off during the dull part of the drive while O'Keefe drained what remained of a thermos of coffee. When the first line of hills appeared (some people called them mountains, but he didn't believe they deserved such an exalted noun), he didn't immediately wake his companions. He was trapped in memories of the last time he'd come this way.

It had been autumn then, the millions of leaves that would then soon die and fall presenting an exquisite palette of colors. That trip had plunged him into the strange world of mink farms and Ponzi schemes with a Christian evangelical overlay; the beautiful Tag Parker; a confrontation with Mafia boss Carmine Jagoda and his soldiers; and a reckoning with choices he'd made and failed to make.

As he'd done then, so he did now, following a route that would mostly avoid the crowded northern side of the lakes where hordes of visitors invaded in the summer to swim and boat and water ski, and, in many cases, get wild and sloppy drunk.

This other side had its share of drunks too, but it was more a visit to an older world that had once seemed to be disappearing. Extremely rural in the most unprosperous rural form. Increasingly poor and slipping further downward all the time. Still the Bible Belt. Churches everywhere. On this cool spring Sunday morning the people stood outside, being neighborly after the service. Big men in eyeglasses and inexpensive suits, string ties, and cowboy boots, many of the women almost as big as the men, looking weary and drained out in their knee-length dresses and light cloth coats. Assembly of God, Church of Christ, Pentecostal, Free Will Baptist, First Baptist, all proclaiming the certainty of salvation and immortality. Yet the churches themselves and the towns they ministered to seemed like nothing if not monuments to the futility of hope.

And yet they seemed to be not only holding on for dear life but springing toward a new life. Was this New Ark a mere throwback, like a corpse still dead but suddenly sitting up on the embalming table? Or was it a vital resurgence of a world that not only refused to die but intended to rise again—and, incredibly, to prevail—by violence if necessary? Early signs long ago: George

Wallace's 1968 presidential campaign and Nixon's Silent Majority appeal in that same campaign, both triumphant in different ways. And Ronald Reagan had brought all of it back to the fore in the early 1980s.

O'Keefe kept thinking about their first conversation with Maxwell. In the 1979 Iranian revolution, the most radical fundamentalism and patriarchalism had shockingly proclaimed itself as not only undead but still flaming in the human mind and heart and soul. Not dead at all but triumphantly resurrected and furiously intent on asserting dominion and decisive reversal of what had seemed to be the inevitable continuing encroachment of two centuries of the Enlightenment glacier—spreading, sometimes slowly, sometimes receding though only before pressing forward again, relentlessly, seemingly inevitably burying beneath it the old world of magic and miracles; the worship of gods or God; rigid family and societal hierarchical structures; stern codes of conduct, deviation from which would be punished in ascendingly painful ways from scolding to shunning to imprisonment and even to death. Was it possible that here, in this obscure backwater of the world, as Yeats had predicted long ago in another pregnant historical moment, the stony sleep of the New Babylon would soon be vexed to nightmare by another rough beast in a rocking cradle, slouching toward Bethlehem to be born?

"We've reached the good part," he said, his voice loud enough to wake his companions as the Wagoneer swooped down into valleys, around tight curves that suddenly disclosed startling vistas, and up onto the higher points where they could see for miles more valleys and hills, a patchwork of fields, meadows, and forests. Often there was no hint of man-made structures, the only evidence of human intrusion the occasional grazing cattle, horses, sheep, or great wheels of harvested hay in the pastures. But the pastures were themselves evidence of the massive human invasion and obliteration of the ancient primeval forests that had covered this land and much of the rest of the country as well.

George made an occasional travelogue sort of comment. Sara was quiet, intently absorbing the passing scenes, until she said, "Are we near the lake?"

"Yeah, it's out there," George said, "but you don't see it often because the roads don't get close to it and the big trees block it."

They wanted to drive at least a part of the rough road that led to the Ark compound's entrance, but the risk of encountering someone on the way who might later recognize them was too great.

Norbert had said that fishermen often got fairly close to the lakeshore side of the Ark property, so there was little risk in that approach provoking even curiosity. George guided them through a small town, more prosperous looking than O'Keefe would have thought, where the road plunged down and ended at a marina full of motorboats and signs advertising boats for rent, fishing guide services, and a "full-service" store. Fishing gear in tow, they descended on the marina. George did the talking while Sara stood by him, avidly following the conversation, and O'Keefe wandered around checking out the boating and fishing supplies.

George chatted up the proprietor nicely, identified some items to purchase, signed for a boat for the afternoon, and inquired about fishing spots including in the area where the compound was located.

"Be careful around there," the proprietor said. "That's Ark territory."

Ever innocent, George repeated, "ARK territory?"

"Survivalist nuts. They've got a whole community up there. Armed to the teeth. Get too close and they might send a load of buckshot your way."

As they motored away from the marina, George began a running stream of instructions and advice on how to handle a boat. "Who knows? One or both of you may end up having to drive one. Someone's life might depend on it."

Karma's usual Zen-like equanimity abandoned him as he tried to keep his balance and evolve an understanding of this strange situation he'd been thrust into by these friends he had no prior reason to distrust. He staggered around a bit, then George guided him to a platform at the rear of the boat, where, anticipating Karma's likely discomfiture, he'd spread out a blanket, a bowl of dry food, and even a chew-toy. He ordered the dog to sit and then lay down. This seemed to reduce Karma's anxiety, though the look he cast the way of the humans remained somewhat skeptical.

O'Keefe studied the landmarks on the water and the shore as George skillfully guided them through the maze of coves to a spot about twenty yards offshore from what he said was the Ark's property.

They cast their lines, just as George had shown them how to, awkwardly in O'Keefe's case, and observed what they could, which was not much. Except for a thin strip of rocky, muddy beach no more than ten yards long and wide, they faced a jagged wall of trees, formidable and forbidding.

"Be thankful for that dinky beach," George said. "The water's too shallow for a motorboat, so we'd have to anchor out here and either swim in, or, if we're humping weapons or other heavy stuff, paddle a little rubber dinghy in. Even simple sit-on-top kayaks might do."

"I wonder how much the Ark people patrol it," O'Keefe said.

"Won't be able to find that out until you get inside," George said.

O'Keefe said, "How about our own boat at the ready instead of having to rent one if we have to get into the place from here? We can't know what time of night or day we'll need it."

"I'll have it sitting in one of the slips in the marina," George said, "ready if ever needed. Now let's catch some fish, so we've got something to show the marina guy when we get back."

O'Keefe groaned.

CHAPTER 15

Two more things before he could leave.

A visit to Ginny.

And the other, an even harder thing: Kelly. He wasn't sure how to explain it or how she would take it. Ditto for Annie, his ex-wife, who he'd recently and unsuccessfully tried to persuade not to be ex any longer. She was more friendly to him these days, her polar ice slowly, slowly melting, but she was still wary, avoiding any kind of intimate contact.

It had been only a few months since he had re-proposed to her. She had rejected the offer. It wasn't an interest in another suitor, though that could develop any day. Some of it was surely once bitten, twice shy. He thought he could overcome that. But the seemingly insurmountable complication, for both of them, was his high-risk work, not intentional but seemingly unavoidable. It had earned him violent enemies and put him in the hospital and near death three times in the last few years. Far worse, on a couple of occasions, Kelly's just being around him had exposed her to danger. While things had cooled down lately, Annie had at one point insisted that he arrange an armed chaperone to accompany Kelly on her visits with him. That understandable fear, if that indeed was the thing that kept her away from him, was something he couldn't and wouldn't try to overcome because that fear was fully justified. He shouldn't have impulsively re-proposed to her in the first place.

Much as he'd tried to develop more "peaceful" lines of business and reduce his personal exposure to risky situations, he couldn't guarantee that some ogre from the past wouldn't re-emerge:

an enraged parent who wrongly but fanatically believed he was in league with the "child molester" and "witch" Virginia Montrose; or a vengeful mafioso blaming him for the Outfit's local demise; or serial killer Wayne Popper, in prison but likely having nothing to do but spin plots of escape and retribution to all who had put him there, especially O'Keefe.

And here he was now, like a moth hypnotized by the dancing flame, about to embark on this new exploit. He had resisted but knew he could have insisted.

No, he had done enough harm to them both already, emotionally anyway, and would only compound the harm by unnecessarily exposing them to physical danger in living daily with them. So he'd quickly halted his reunion campaign. Of course he couldn't eliminate all contact with her, but he minimized it and took care around every encounter lest he be tempted to try again to entice her. But he had become that man of constant sorrow, his emotional life now carrying a constant undertone of longing that often erupted into a sudden spasm of anguish.

He called her and said, "I'm heading up to see Ginny this weekend. You and Kelly maybe like to go?"

He expected a refusal, perhaps a bit of a thorny one. She and Kelly were frequent visitors to the prison, but without him. After a long pause—Surprise!—"Okay. It's been a while. We need to get up there and see her."

He brought copies of Harrigan's recently filed brief for them to read on the drive to the prison. Both, though primarily Kelly, peppered him with questions about various opaque legal concepts and oddities of legal procedure, many of which he understood only vaguely or not at all. Annie laughed at his occasional discomfort trying to answer the questions, and Kelly asked more than once, "Can I call Uncle Mike and ask him?"

They all wanted to hug Ginny, but that was forbidden. On the first couple of visits, appalled by the prison environment, Annie and Kelly had spent a lot of their time in tears, until Annie sat Kelly down and said, "Hey, pal, we've got to quit all this weeping and gnashing of teeth. It can't be helping her. We don't have to be stupidly cheery, but at least let's try not to cry."

Ginny always looked physically better than O'Keefe feared she would. She exuded a deep sadness but never complained. Today she brightened momentarily when she saw them all together. "Such a beautiful family."

At that, Kelly brightened too, Annie blushed, and O'Keefe had to stifle tears. *Not exactly.*

He handed her the brief and other legal papers. She rubbed her hand over the bundle in a kind of caress, then pressed it to her chest as if it were a Magi's gift.

"Thank you so much. Please thank Mr. Harrigan and give him my best. You know, *he* comes to see me sometimes too."

Which pleasantly surprised O'Keefe. It showed that Harrigan wasn't simply grudgingly going along with an old friend who'd made him feel too uncomfortably guilty about sitting on the bench, making money tending the very legal machine that had crushed this innocent woman.

"You know," she said, "he told me he almost ended up in here. I guess it can happen to anyone."

She seemed to accept that, even take comfort from it. O'Keefe felt the opposite. It was just another example of the unfairness of the system, the larger world, and life and fate itself that had to be endured but not shrugged off or rationalized.

On the way home, no time left to delay it further, he said, "I have a new thing that'll take me away for a while."

"Really?" Kelly said, a mixture of excitement and concern in her voice. "Something fun?"

"Not fun. Work."

"How long?" Kelly said.

"I don't know. Could be several months."

"Can I come see you?"

"Sorry, but no."

"What in the world is it?" Annie asked.

"It's an undercover thing."

"Like a spy?" Kelly said.

"Well, yes, something like that."

"What is it, Dad?"

Hard part coming. "Sorry, but I can't tell you."

"You're kidding," Annie said. Crossly.

He wanted to tell them it was for their own good, but that would be about the worst thing he could say to Annie. In fact, he couldn't think of a useful response.

"Is it dangerous?" Kelly said.

"Not in the slightest," he lied. "I mean that. *Not … In … The … Slightest.*"

"Then why can't you tell us?" Annie said, growing angrier by the sentence.

"I agreed to absolute secrecy. My client insisted. Very sternly too. It's in the contract."

"So what?" she said. "There's not a family exception or something?"

"I asked, but he was adamant," he lied again.

She shifted in her seat and stared straight ahead.

Kelly grasped onto the front seat and pulled herself up closer to him. "What about tennis and swimming and softball?"

"I'll sneak away for a visit any chance I get."

"You better."

When he pulled up to their house, Annie said, "Scoot along, kid. I'll be there in a second."

Kelly exited the back seat, came to the open window on the driver's side. They kissed, and she said, "Bye, Dad. I mean it. You better come. I'm gettin' good."

As Kelly made her way up the walk to their front porch, Annie said, "You might be able to get away with lying to her, but not to me."

"I'm not," he said with a sharp edge.

She climbed out of the car, slammed the door, and started walking way.

Quick calculation. Which would be worse—telling the truth or persisting with the lie and acting righteously outraged about her refusal to believe him?

"Come back," he said.

She returned, stooped slightly at the open window, and leaned in. "Well?"

"I'm not really lying. It *is* confidential."

"But it's dangerous, isn't it?"

"It shouldn't be. I'm not lying about that. It really shouldn't be."

"I don't know whether I want to know or not."

"You don't."

"I suppose you're gonna tell me"—and her tone turned acidly sarcastic—"'it's for my own good.' Save it."

She started to walk away again, then turned. "Goddamnit, be careful."

"I love you guys," he said, when what he really wanted to say was just "I love *you*."

Driving away, yet again involuntarily, the recurrent thought: For his arrogance and folly the Flying Dutchman was doomed to wander the seas in his ghost ship, never able to make port, until he found a woman who declared herself faithful to him for life.

But what if he'd already found that woman—and had cast her aside?

She watched him drive away. Only after he had disappeared out of sight did she allow her tears to come.

CHAPTER 16

A HUNTER'S DOG SNIFFED out her body. It lay in a scrubby thicket at the end of a short trail of drag marks through the dirt and grass not far off the side of a sparsely traveled country road. Despite the deterioration of the corpse, they could see that she'd been badly beaten and her throat viciously slashed, nearly decapitating her.

Nothing gave any clue to her identity. A photograph, the wound to her throat blacked out, was shown around town, with no result. But Deputy Riggins kept thinking he'd seen the woman before.

Eventually, he mentioned this to the sheriff. "A while back I stopped an old station wagon for a bad taillight. Those cult people. Frankly, I was hoping I could catch them with some illegal weapons and get a warrant to search their whole place. Two men with a tiny bird of a woman sandwiched between 'em. If she wasn't our corpse, she was her twin sister."

"Not what I'd call probable cause," the sheriff said, "or even a reasonable suspicion. You're always looking for an excuse to harass those people. Stand down. We don't need to provoke a fight with 'em."

"It's another Jonestown waitin' to happen," Riggins said.

"Lay off."

As he left the office, Riggins wondered whether the sheriff was simply afraid of those people, or if there was something deeper at work. It seemed he would likely be risking his job if he made a visit out there to see what he could turn up or provoke.

CHAPTER 17

THE NEXT SESSION of the Ark training regime was scheduled to begin soon, and no one involved in Maxwell's project wanted to miss that date. But they had to be careful. When Sara called to inquire about signing up, she was asked for a lot of information that they were nervous about giving up, worrying that the Ark people might have some way of doing background checks. While the new identities should be hard to expose as fakes, they wanted to minimize the lead time for investigation of their bona fides and had developed a strategy they hoped would avoid an investigation altogether.

They had become Peter and Sara McBride from Los Angeles, a place far away from the Ark location—geographically, culturally, and just about every other imaginable way. This would decrease the chances that any of the other training participants or the permanent community residents would either hail from there or know anyone who did.

Maxwell had grown up in Los Angeles and still had family, friends, and business relations there. He put the "McBrides" through an intensive course in LA neighborhoods, high schools, and other information about the city that they hoped would be sufficient to allow them to pass as Angelenos, at least in casual conversation. He also arranged for an old friend, whose family had owned a small warehouse operation in Culver City for decades, to be ready to vouch that Peter McBride had worked for him as a forklift operator until a few months ago.

George had also conjured up credible-looking faded and dog-eared California driver's licenses. They acquired an old Buick, licensed in California, with thousands of miles on the speedometer and looking like it had traveled a lot of those miles on rough roads.

Their story was that they'd gotten puking sick of the whole LA scene and hit the road, looking for the "real" America. In case they were questioned about their recent wanderings, they picked places between Los Angeles and the Ark where O'Keefe had spent time or at least visited. Sara, as usual, was not forthcoming about any similar experiences she may have had.

They knew that all this was a pretty thin camouflage to protect themselves from suspicion and discovery. There were LA addresses on their driver's licenses, but if someone searched the real-estate records, they wouldn't find the McBrides in the ownership chain. They believed they could cover that by claiming they could only afford to rent given California's notoriously inflated housing prices. But if someone knocked on the doors of those residences and asked whether the McBrides had once lived there, adamant denials might ensue, and then there would be some explaining to do. Yet that was the best they could accomplish in the short time available, and odds were good that the Ark people, though they might be wary and make a few inquiries here and there, lacked the resources to undertake anything sophisticated in the way of investigation.

Sara and O'Keefe worked on what to wear, what attitudes to adopt, how to talk, what appearances to present.

Sara showed up one day in a patrol cap, combat boots, camouflage pants, and a green military-style T-shirt. "I figured gung-ho but still attractive."

"I think you achieved it," he said.

That was as close as they got to a conversation around the pimp-bottom girl theme.

O'Keefe decided that for the first encounter, when they presented themselves for possible enrollment, both of them appearing in military dress would be too much. He decided that "cowboy"—a western shirt, white with some blue and red decorative stitching and the usual snap buttons, tucked into honestly faded jeans—would best fit his tall and mostly still-thin frame. Plus, he had cowboy boots stored somewhere, a relic from one of his previous personas. Like the jeans, the boots looked and legitimately were long lived in, with worn but still discernible red, blue, and green leather on top and banged-up suede on the bottom. No cowboy hat though. No way.

He also found a box containing the final set of Marine Corps fatigues he'd worn in Vietnam: pants, camouflage shirt with his lance corporal insignias clipped to each collar, field jacket, jungle boots, and his patrol cap with the USMC insignia on the front. He would save the rest of the outfit for the actual training. Except the cap. Much as he disliked headgear of any kind, he liked the idea of using that to "cap off" the cowboy duds. A mixed message but a good one.

Not that he'd kept those Corps items out of any fondness for his military days. He wanted no souvenirs from it, wanted only to shed the whole experience like an old dead skin. He remembered unpacking his sea bag after arriving home and throwing away almost everything, including his khaki "service" uniform, which was one formal step above the camouflage fatigues, to be worn at certain on-base functions and when in uniform off-base. But that final set of combat clothes had seemed like something to keep, he didn't understand why. Now he'd found a useful purpose for them. Maybe it would give him some extra "cred" with the paramilitary warriors at New Ark.

After much resistance, he decided his hair was too long. It had been that way since his discharge. When on the first night of boot camp they'd buzzed off every hair on his head, he'd felt like Samson shorn and in the mirror beheld not Peter O'Keefe but Knucklehead Smiff. He'd vowed never again to look anything close to that and so now instructed his barber to clip away just enough hair to reveal most of his ears and move the hairline above the collar.

Sara laughed. "I suggest not making that look a permanent one."

"You could have lied to me."

Before dawn on a Saturday, "D-Day" as they'd taken to calling their scheduled departure date, O'Keefe opened the steel locker in his garage and extracted other relics from his warrior days: the M16 rifle, its ammunition, and three hand grenades. The M16 had full-automatic capability. Congress had banned fully automatic weapons manufactured after 1986. This one was therefore legal—or it would have been if it were also registered, which it wasn't since he'd acquired it from the Marine Corps by theft, smuggling it piece by piece out of Camp Pendleton, his last duty station post-Vietnam.

Though the M16 had become notorious in Vietnam for jamming and had to be cleaned and maintained with special care—difficult to accomplish in that rainy, steamy, muddy world—he thought it was perfect. Light and easy to carry, shoulder, and aim, they called it a "toy" gun. So much better than the cursed M14.

Hard to believe, but the three grenades were legal. Originally, there'd been four, but one had blasted a Mafia gunman to pieces in the Arizona desert near the end of an episode that had also begun here in the lake country.

An unfortunate thought and ominous coincidence. That had ended badly for a woman he'd fallen in love with at first sight at the onset of the adventure, or more accurately, misadventure. Surely this one wouldn't also end badly for another woman he loved though in a different way.

In his first couple of years as a private detective, he wouldn't have admitted it, but he'd thought of himself as a sort of Rambo type (poet version: M16 in hands, tattered copy of Wordsworth or Yeats in his fatigues pocket). He'd stored the rifle and grenades in a secret compartment built into his customized van until someone had unkindly blown the van apart. After the mink farm lake country and Arizona misadventure, he shed what remained of his Rambo skin and stowed the M16 and grenades in the locker and hadn't opened it since.

Lately, he'd been trying to swear off firearms altogether, though that didn't seem entirely possible given his profession. But it seemed right to retrieve them now. Like the combat fatigues, the M16 might give him powerful "cred" with the Ark people, and a guy toting around hand grenades had to be good recruiting material.

He packed the items carefully but loosely so they could easily be shown to any interested parties, then loaded everything into the trunk of the Buick. Backing out of his driveway, he thought how odd it was to be leaving without having any idea when he would return. He was also leaving behind that prince of beasts, Karma, who in O'Keefe's absence would be eagerly shared (as he often was anyway) among George, Dagmar, and Annie and Kelly.

Sara stood waiting for him in front of her apartment building, by her side a big duffel bag. She hoisted it over her shoulder in a single smooth move. He went to take it from her, but she marched cheerfully to the rear and tossed it in the trunk.

A few miles down the road, he said, "I hope this junker can make it all the way. We may have gotten a little too authentic on this one."

On the long drive they discussed whether they'd be allowed in. He'd called down two days before and been told that the upcoming training was not full yet, but the phone was "ringing off the hook" from callers like him.

They reviewed everything they thought should be reviewed and shot each other questions about how they should handle hypothetical situations, everything from his military career to their "marriage" history, how they'd behave in church services, the views they'd express on Christian Identity teachings and Jesus Christ and his enemies including the evil ZOG, Jews, Communists, liberals, and homosexuals.

Finally, as they turned onto the narrow, pot-holed road up the mountain to the Ark, with its hairpin turns and stunning vistas that a driver had to be careful to no more than glance at for fear of plunging over the side and becoming one with nature in a decidedly unromantic way, he brought up the tender subject they had so far avoided and what he'd hoped Sara would initiate but disappointingly had not—the husband and wife thing, especially the sleeping arrangements.

Norbert had said that the few women who attended the training, whether their husbands were with them or not, always slept in separate tents, and there would be stern warnings about "extracurricular activities." In short, *don't do it*. Not in the tents, not off in the piney woods, not anywhere. This was war, not fun and games.

But if they were accepted into the community…

"They'll give us a house," O'Keefe said. "Or a trailer. Or at least a tent. Might be a double bed."

"We'll find a way," she said, and left it at that.

"You don't have to worry about me," he said. "You've advanced too much further in the martial arts than I have."

She laughed.

"But," he said, "there was once a time…"

A pause, then, "Yeah. For me too."

That was a shock, both that she had felt that way and was admitting it. He kept silent, not wanting to say the wrong thing after she'd just taken what seemed like a big risk, and glanced briefly at her as she stared forward intensely. Dark lady. Olive skin, eyes of deepest brown, brown hair almost black, cut rather short now, full lips, unlikely small sprays of freckles on both sides of her slightly sharp nose. She had a Gallic look about her, like some French actresses whose images he could vaguely recall but not their names. And dark even beyond her appearance. Herself a secret, her entire life before coming to work for O'Keefe a mystery. And she apparently intended to keep it that way.

O'Keefe had honored that, vowed not to pry and ordered George not to either, refused to learn and to know, avoided searching and discovering; not so much afraid of what he might find, but respecting her privacy, trusting that she would tell him if something in her past might affect their work together.

Finally, she spoke. "When I first came to work with you, I was star-struck. You were pretty much my hero. Divorced, yes, so available in that sense, but my boss. The last thing I wanted to do was take the risk."

Same here, he thought.

"And then I discovered you were kind of a mess."

He laughed. "Truer words never spoken."

"And then you got to be even more of a mess. I can't imagine what it would've been like if we'd complicated all that with some kind of…" Her voice trailed off, avoiding naming the thing. "Those boss-secretary things almost never turn out good anyway. So I made myself hold back."

Well, at least she'd wanted it—*Why does that give me solace?*—and he was glad he hadn't known that at the time.

"Lucky you did," he said. "One slight move from you, and I'd have been there."

"Yes, lucky. I'm sure if we'd let something happen, we'd have ended up just more broken and unhappy."

Well. Sara, he thought, *I'm not as sure as you are about that.*

CHAPTER 18

WORN-OUT, BROKEN-UP ASPHALT became dirt. The Buick jounced and bounced, leaving a cloud of dust in its wake. Around noon they approached a clearing that turned out to be a road off the main one. They conferred and agreed to try it. Not far along a lone guard blocked their way. He held an ancient-looking rifle and looked ancient himself, dressed in combat fatigues far too large for his shriveled frame, as if he had shrunk but not his clothing along with him. O'Keefe stopped the car about ten yards away, turned off the engine, and opened the door. He'd half climbed out of the Buick, his left foot planted on the dirt, when the old man lifted the rifle to his shoulder, aimed it at O'Keefe, and commanded in a cracked, tremulous voice, "Stop … er … I'll shoot."

O'Keefe later wondered why he took the risk of pulling himself fully out of the car to stand on both feet. But he did, and quickly thrust his hands into the air. "We're friends," he yelled. "We mean no harm."

The rifle barrel danced wildly in the old man's nervous hands. O'Keefe knew that fear could be even more dangerous than rage. *Keep talking.*

"My wife and I—"

Sara opened her door and emerged, also with hands in the air. The old man waved the gun over on her, then back on O'Keefe.

"We're just here for the training," O'Keefe said. "We're your friends."

"That don't start for two days."

"Can we talk to Mr. Lomax?"

"Turn around and lay flat on the ground on your stomachs, both 'a ya."

They did as ordered. O'Keefe, prone on his stomach but propped on his elbows so he wouldn't have to eat dirt, glanced under the car toward Sara across from him. She looked more amused than afraid. He heard the crackle of static, which he guessed was some sort of walkie-talkie device, and the guard saying, "Kenny, it's Larry. I need you out front. Can you come quick? Couple of strangers out here."

A few minutes later, footsteps crunched on dirt, and he heard low voices talking. He looked back over his shoulder. Two men had joined the guard. They walked toward the Buick, then split off, one heading for Sara's side, the other for his. A pair of black military boots and brown and tan camouflage fatigue pants stopped beside him just out of reach, and a voice said, "You armed?"

"No."

"No firearm, no knife, no other weapon of any kind?"

"Not on me. In the trunk, yes."

"Okay. You can get on up."

O'Keefe now stood looking at a smiling man in his forties, less than six feet tall, muscular, a rifle in a sling hanging from his shoulder. This must be Kenny. Sara was directed around the back of the car, her escort behind her, until they circled around and she stood next to O'Keefe. The old man remained at his post, rifle thankfully not pointing at anyone.

"No problem with her," the escort said.

A mild protest was called for at this point. O'Keefe pitched his voice a little high. "Helluva welcome for two people that came a long way to join your outfit."

"Join us?"

"The training. We've heard great things about it, and seen your ads."

Staring at the license plate, Sara's escort said, "*California?*"

"All the way."

"Land of fruits and nuts," Sara's escort said.

"Did you call … sign up?" Kenny said.

"Didn't know we needed to. We thought we'd just show up and start whenever we could."

Sara batted her eyelashes and nodded eagerly.

"It's not happening right now," Kenny said.. "New session starts in a couple days."

"Any room for two more?"

"Maybe. It'll be a thousand apiece, cash." Looking skeptically at the their Buick, he said, "Can you swing that?"

O'Keefe reached into his pocket as if to pull it out right then and there.

Kenny's head reeled back slightly. "Whoa. Not yet. I noticed your cap and your collar there. Marines. When?"

"Vietnam."

"MOS?"

"Door gunner."

From Sara's escort, "Cool."

Looking at his comrade, Kenny said, "What say, Dwight? Think it'd be okay with the General?"

"Oh, yeah. I don't know if we've got any ladies signed up yet."

"Mind if we look in your trunk?"

They stood slightly back as O'Keefe opened it. He showed them his pistol and Sara's, the grenades, and, finally, the M16.

Staring appreciatively at the rifle, Dwight said, "Cool. You should take better care of this thing. Can I hold it?"

O'Keefe certainly wasn't going to say no. He nodded, and Dwight brought the rifle to his shoulder, aimed at the sky, then tucked it up against his body, all lithe and skillful.

"Where'd you get it?"

"Let's say it insisted on being discharged from the Marine Corps along with me."

They laughed at that, then O'Keefe's keeper formally introduced himself and his colleague: Kenny Graham and Dwight Scott.

"So you've had it that long," Dwight said. "I see it's clean, but, like I said, you should take better care of it than just tossin' it in your trunk. It's worth a lot of money now, after the '86 ZOG ban."

Kenny told them to leave the car where it was and accompany them into the compound. Thinking he should respect Dwight's feelings about the M16, O'Keefe laid it gently on the back seat instead of the trunk.

Dwight led the way, through a covering thicket of scrubby third-growth trees and bushes beyond which the road quickly ended in a graded parking area occupied by vehicles of various types and degrees of operability, everything from pickup trucks to campers, to vans, to jeeps, to sedans, to motorcycles. When O'Keefe remarked on that, Kenny said, "Yeah. Some of them are even drivable."

They passed a second and more formal guard post kiosk, currently unmanned, and joined a wide and well-groomed dirt path.

"Sorry about ol' Larry there," Kenny said. "He ain't used to the guard duty. We're a little shorthanded this weekend and had to put him on. The responsibility's got him kind'a spooked. And we really do have a problem with the Feds. They're trying everything they can to put us out of business."

"I'm with you on ZOG," O'Keefe said, "but I hope you don't actually let him put bullets in that thing."

Kenny laughed again, Dwight too.

They crowded into a hut at the end of the path with a lush grassy area to the right and two large stone and wood structures straight ahead and to the left. The "General" was unavailable, but Kenny took their money and signed them up anyway.

"Everything'll be shown to you and fully explained on opening day, which is Monday. Be here bright and early. 8 a.m. start. Show up late, and you'll be on General's bad list and might never get off it.

On the way back to the Buick, O'Keefe heard something odd, and asked, "Is that singing I'm hearing?"

"You bet. It's Sabbath service," Kenny said.

"On Saturday?"

"Yep. We follow the Bible, not the corrupted modern Sunday thing."

"Did we get you out of church?" Sara said. "I'm so sorry."

Dwight laughed. "There'll be plenty more today. All day on Sabbath and sometimes into the night, and some weeknights too. We ain't lackin' for the opportunity to pray." Then he added, as if remembering what he ought to have said, "I wouldn't want it any other way."

Back at the guard kiosk, O'Keefe and Sara shook hands with the old man.

"Sorry about that welcome," Larry said. "But we have to be careful. They're after us. They really are."

As they made their way back down the road, O'Keefe said, "Quite a welcome. Did you notice they didn't answer when I asked if they let Larry have bullets in that thing?"

Sara nodded. "They liked that M16, though, and your money."

"And my wife."

"Glad I'm performing a useful function."

"I was hoping," he said, "that they'd give us a tour and maybe even a place to stay until the training starts."

In a deep voice, mimicking Kenny, she said, "You must wait until opening day when General will reveal all to you."

Approaching the outskirts of town, he said, "I hope we can find a motel."

"If not," she said, "you can have the back seat, I'll take the front," beating him to the punch.

The town had two tiny motels. One was full. "It's a weekend, ya know," the desk clerk said, but at the other motel an early checkout had opened up a room.

O'Keefe unloaded a sleeping bag from the trunk. "I'll use this tonight."

"We'll flip for it," Sara said.

For dinner, they stood in line at a diner that was the only option on a Saturday night. Several people remarked on their California license plate. They said they'd come to join the Christian Soldiers Survival School program at the New Ark and received polite but unenthusiastic head nods and shoulder shrugs among occasional subdued "good luck to ya" mutterings. The townspeople didn't seem overjoyed about sharing their spot of God's country with the Ark folks. One fellow said, "I hope you can shoot straight. Someday, I swear, one of their stray bullets is gonna kill someone out on the lake."

On Sunday they filled up the gas tank, hoped the Buick would hold out for one more day of hard driving, and reconnoitered as much of the surrounding area as they could, identifying everything from the location of pay phones to lakefront spots that looked good for possible put-ins and takeouts, even places for hiding if somehow they ended up in flight and on foot.

In the late afternoon they called George and had him tie in Maxwell for a report.

"Damn near got blown away already," O'Keefe said, and told them about Larry and the rest. "But we're in. First stage of the mission accomplished."

"You're great people," Maxwell said.

O'Keefe hung up, thinking, *Not exactly.* It was a long way from here to greatness.

CHAPTER 19

Early on Monday they braved the road again, this time in the dark, multiple times more terrifying than the daylight ascent. "Glad we won't have to do this again for a while," he said.

They arrived at a sunrise struggling to break out as if unsure whether it really wanted to. Many trainees had arrived overnight. Some were still asleep in their vehicles; others were cocooned in sleeping bags in the open air; yet others had erected single-person tents in the parking lot. There were several camper vans, lots of pickup trucks, one sports car. O'Keefe parked the Buick somewhat away from the rest. They remained in the car for a time, watching the earlier arrivals, some still keeping to themselves, others gathered in small groups. Almost all wore some form of military or hunting dress. A few were making coffee over heat-tab flames and wolfing down C-rations or MREs in a rehearsal for what would likely be a month of horrid food.

Watching the gung-ho types he was about to spend a month with, O'Keefe cringed inwardly. Bad memories began crowding in.

"I only count two women so far," Sara said, "and it looks like they're together. I think you and I are the only male-female couple."

"I guess we'd better get out and sort of present ourselves," O'Keefe said.

They positioned themselves in front of the Buick, O'Keefe perching on one side of the hood and Sara leaning against the front bumper on the other. Newcomers continued to arrive every few minutes, each of the vehicles churning up a cloud of dust that didn't have time to fully subside before another vehicle arrived to make its own contribution to the haze. The air began to taste of it.

"Better go introduce ourselves?" Sara asked.

"Go ahead," O'Keefe said, "but I've found that if you stand in one place, everyone eventually gets around to *you*."

"I'll at least go talk to the ladies."

The first to come to his perch were new arrivals who'd parked close by. A couple of them lingered, which attracted others. Soon a group had gathered around him, and he was wishing he'd gone with Sara. He felt both shy and nervous, afraid he might reveal too much in light conversation or have to answer questions that uncomfortably probed into the weaker elements of their identities and backstories. They'd discussed how important it would be to tell each other about every exchange they had with anyone at the camp so their stories would stay consistent.

One man, showing off his muscles and tan in a wife-beater undershirt, cut-off raggedy jean shorts, and rubber thong sandals, gestured toward Sara and the two other women. "Even got some of those, eh? I'm surprised they let 'em in."

O'Keefe said nothing, but another of his new acquaintances said, "One of them's yours, eh?"

O'Keefe nodded.

"Drop you off, I suppose?"

"No. She's here for the training."

"Really?"

Another man in the group rolled his eyes. Damned if he wasn't losing face fast, but he reminded himself of his vow. Not now, not later would he let shame take over and make him strive to look "manly" in the eyes of any of these characters.

Staring at O'Keefe's cap, the skeptic said, "You were in the Marines?" as if that just couldn't be true in view of the previous disclosure.

O'Keefe nodded again.

"So was I," another said, and rattled off his unit and years in service—years when the country had enjoyed an interlude of peace. "You look Nam era," he said to O'Keefe.

"True."

"Real sorry I missed all that."

Again O'Keefe didn't respond. He knew he needed to adopt an ultra-patriot persona, but he intended to keep it to the minimum required to seem bona fide.

Sara's return led to a fairly quick dispersal of O'Keefe's new companions.

"You're the cat that got their tongues," he said.

"They might use a different word."

"How about your lady friends over there?"

"I think they're more than friends, but they're not saying so."

"They'd better not," he said, "This is no place to be coming out of any closets."

"Or," she added, "any black ghettos."

"Or," he added, "synagogues."

"Yeah," she said, "no kikes for sure."

O'Keefe couldn't help it, he flinched a little, but that was the way they'd need to talk until the job was done.

At 8 a.m. sharp, two stern-looking gentlemen with AR-15s slung over their shoulders arrived from the interior of the compound and ordered everyone to gather close around for roll call. A few names weren't answered, and O'Keefe wondered what might happen to the tardy ones. One of those bad memories, still so vivid after all these years, surfaced. "Get down and give me twenty." Or a grab of your collar or even your throat. Or even "Down on your knees, puke," followed by a side-thrust kick in the solar plexus.

One of their new keepers shouted, "We're goin' to see the General now, and we're gonna present ourselves in an orderly manner." He lined everyone up in marching columns. "Surely you veterans remember how to march. We expect you to be an example for the others."

More boot camp thoughts crowded in. On arrival, stampeded out of the buses, formed up in ragged columns, screamed at for having no idea what to do: Welcome to the Marine Corps Recruit Depot, San Diego, California.

Here at the New Ark they formed up and moved along, some but not all in proper military alignment and cadence, rendering the presentation of the new recruits to the General comically disjointed. O'Keefe was certain that the eyes behind the General's dark glasses were sparkling with contempt for the rabble raggedly arrayed before him.

"My name is Leon Lomax, but they've decided around here to call me 'General,' and so you too will address me in proper military fashion either as 'General' or 'Sir'. I understand that some people didn't show up this morning. They won't be getting their money back. And you won't either. You're in this for the whole program. You can quit. We won't imprison you here. But you won't get a refund. I don't care what your excuse is—sickness, injury, emergencies at home— makes no difference to me. Well, maybe death … that is, *yours*. If it's an honorable one. A heart attack, or one of those copperheads out there in the woods gets to you … something like that.

"It's not that we're greedy. We don't need your money. But your money is your promise to us that you're not here for a vacation … not here to play soldier in the woods for a few weeks and go home with a puffed-up chest, bragging about it. That money you paid is your promise to us, and to your family, and to your fellow Christians that you're just as serious about this as we are. God's people can't afford any more lazing and lollygagging around.

"Because you'd better understand something. We're in the final days, even the final hours now. The End Times are upon us. We're on every edge of every steep cliff, every yawning gulf imaginable. Nuclear holocaust is coming. Race war is here and more's on the way. Our Zionist Organized Gov'ment has trained the niggers in their ghettos and in their prisons to kill us. They're taking away our guns, rendering us defenseless, naked among our enemies.

"Their abortion mills are killing our babies. The Jews and their allies are assaulting Christianity and all morality at every turn, whether by banning prayer in schools or flooding the movie and TV screens with filth. They're killing Jesus Christ all over again. And when it all collapses, parents will be eating their children. Witches will roam the land, killing and sacrificing the weak to Satan. The niggers will be raping and killing white women first, then the rest of us. The homos will be sodomizing anyone they can. Even what were thought to be good Christians, but were really only lukewarm ones spat out of God's mouth, will be rampaging, desperate for food, water, and weapons.

"The Lord has promised us salvation … but only if we earn it! Only if we fight for it when the End Times and the Final Battle come! We cannot and we will not tolerate half-measures. We can only win with the discipline we Americans followed in World War II, not the debacle that our Gov'ment subjected our boys to in Vietnam. The purpose of military boot camp is to instill that discipline, and that's the purpose of our training here.

"They won't even leave *us* alone, those of us here at the Ark, just trying to live out here in nowhere according to God's will and laws, not bothering anyone. They've sent informers to spy on us and report back to them. A couple have probably gotten away with it, but a couple haven't. We've dealt with those people, you bet, and if you're one of them, we'll deal with you when we catch you. And we've got ways to find out…"

CHAPTER 20

WHILE THE GENERAL preached, two men emerged from the tree line behind him. Keeping a respectful distance, they scanned the recruits. O'Keefe recognized them from photos Maxwell had provided: David Dodd, the Prophet himself, and Caleb Nathanson, not so much the Prophet's second-in-command (that was more the General's role) but the "Chaplain," the man in charge of "religious training" as the General was in charge of the military instruction.

Noticing the recruits looking upward and beyond him, the General turned around, but once it was clear that the newcomers intended to advance no further, he turned back to the troops and explained that he was a former Army drill instructor. This training, he said, would in certain respects mimic Army boot camp, but in many ways it would be even tougher because they had less time and "Most of you have likely grown soft even if you haven't always been soft. We don't expect to make all of you into marvelous physical specimens in your few short weeks here, but we do expect to take you to your limits, so you can assess where you stand in terms of physical readiness and what you need to do to prepare for what's coming."

O'Keefe could assess nothing other than that he might piss his pants—talk about soft—but he was also afraid to ask to be excused. He recalled the first days of Marine boot camp, after their heads had been shaved and their spirits broken from a night of marching in their civilian clothes around the parade ground in the February monsoon rain of Southern California. He had lamented silently at the time, *It was so easy for them to break my spirit.*

The next morning they had stood for hours, waiting to be fitted and issued uniforms. One "boot" or "private," or "puke," as they now were called, meekly asked if he could go to the bathroom. Nothing doing. Not long after, the guy shit his pants. They forced him to sit on a bench outside the barracks, his soiled underwear displayed on the bench next to him, as O'Keefe and the rest paraded by, grateful even for their current plight; it could always be worse.

The General began an inspection of the ranks. When he came to O'Keefe, he nodded toward his cap and insignia. "You're pretty proud of yourself, are you, Marine?"

As he had been taught in boot camp, O'Keefe said loudly and fawningly, "Sir, yes, sir," and hated himself for it.

"Well, we don't think *all that much* of the Corps around here. You think you're better than us Army?"

"No, sir."

"Well, that's a good enough start, I guess. But you can be sure I'm gonna prove, especially to you, that Marines aren't any tougher than anybody else."

He kept staring at the cap. "Lance Corporal. Was that your final rank in the Corps?"

"Yes, sir."

"And you did a regular tour in Vietnam? Thirteen months?"

"Yes, sir."

"And managed to advance only from an E-1 Private to an E-3 Lance Corporal?"

"'Fraid so, sir."

"I guess you weren't much of a Marine after all."

So the Marine Corps get-up had backfired. O'Keefe wondered how much else he would be getting wrong during this ordeal and what the consequences might be.

The General moved to Sara. "You with him?"

"Yes, sir," she said, not loudly but firmly.

The General stepped back and addressed the crowd. "We welcome women here, and we expect all to respect them as long as they remember their place and don't forget what their primary duties in life are. But we welcome them because, believe me, when the End Times come and you're defending your limbs, lives, homes, families, and everything else you cherish, you'll be grateful when that sweet thing by your side can blast away and mow down the heathens right alongside you."

When he finished the inspection, he said, "We'll meet again right after lunch. Those of you with your own weapons, you'll present arms in formation, and we'll check them out to see if they'll serve our purpose here. If yours doesn't qualify, we'll issue you one of our AR-15s. Then we'll do some target practice at our firing range."

Lunch was "served." Right out of the military. Meals Ready To Eat. Not really. Ready maybe, but not to eat. O'Keefe picked at his and thought how these MRE's were only a slight improvement on the nasty C-rats that had gagged him two decades earlier.

Sara, to O'Keefe's amazement, scarfed hers right down and said, "Not that bad."

"You must've left your gag reflex back home."

She laughed a little and lowered her voice. "I'm nervous about this target practice. I've learned to handle a pistol pretty well and shot some with an AR-15 in the past few weeks, but I wasn't all that good at it."

"I'm a little nervous myself," he said.

"You're kidding."

"The last time I was on a rifle range I didn't do so well."

He wished he hadn't blurted that out. Now he had to tell her…

Everything about Marine Corps boot camp had seemed to build toward the grand climax of "qualifying" on the rifle range. He'd never shot anything like a rifle, other than occasionally a friend's BB gun. His parents wouldn't let him have a rifle of his own, not even a BB or a pellet gun ("You'll put someone's eye out!"). Yet O'Keefe had felt no *special* anxiety about the rifle range because every single thing about boot camp was something to be fearful of in equal measure. He was coordinated, athletic. This shouldn't have been a big deal. But the drill instructors kept ratcheting up the pressure, implying that a "nonqual" on the rifle range was the lowest form of life in the Corps and would be made to suffer a grim fate.

Then, when he lifted the M14 for the first time, it was so much heavier than he'd imagined. Plus, the target was so far away, and he couldn't keep the damn thing's barrel still. It kept jumping up and down or to the left and right in his shaky arms. Even before he fired it, despite his jaw-clenched determination to keep it still, which in hindsight had probably only made things worse, the barrel came to rest on the bullseye only for the briefest moment before circling around and outside the magic bullseye circle. And when he pulled the trigger, the recoil had pulled the shot toward the outer edge of the target, the "nonqual" edge.

They tallied his final score. He'd come close but had failed to qualify. Since the drill instructors couldn't be sure that the shame of that status was sufficient punishment, back in the barracks they called the four "nonquals" into their quarters, which had a long horizontal window so the instructors could observe their charges but pull down the shade when they wanted privacy. Of course they left the shades up for this session so the superior warriors watching would learn a salutary lesson from the spectacle.

The UnFab Four were made to kneel while two drill instructors took turns planting well-placed side-thrust kicks into the solar plexus of the slimy pukes until they were bent over gagging, slobbering, and in one case actually puking. Of course the puker was made to clean it up. "We oughta make you lick it up," one of the DIs said.

"They could do all that?" Sara said. "They could get away with that?"

O'Keefe shrugged. "I think it was expected of them. Unwritten, unspoken, but expected of them by the top brass, and those tough guys in the Smokey the Bear hats with absolute power over us were only too happy to oblige. And what were we gonna do, tell our mommies? The theory was that we'd get our buddies killed in combat because we couldn't adequately perform the basic function of a soldier, and we needed motivation to do much better next time."

"Did you?"

"Luckily, that was almost the last M14 I ever saw. After boot camp, we got M16s, like this baby. They called it "the toy gun." And better yet, when they randomly assigned MOS ... that's Military

Occupational Specialty … Sounds impressive, doesn't it? Mine was machine gunner. My initial weapon was an M60 machine gun that you didn't have to be quite so precise with, and you fired it most of the time when it was mounted on a tripod, which took most of the nerves out of it. I qualified fine with that."

"And," she said, "that toy M16 worked for you out in Arizona … Mr. Canada's crew."

"Yeah, I wasn't a 'nonqual' out there."

Except, he thought, *for that one shot, the most important of them all.* It had found its target. But wounded, exhausted, he'd hesitated. For no more than two seconds, making sure his wavering aim would be true.

True it had been.

But one second too late.

For her.

One second—ripe, vibrant life … the next second … in that tiniest of intervals … silence … forever.

At the post-lunch gun check, the General paced up and down in front of the ranks, a small whip in hand that he used for punctuation by pointing fiercely with it at the trainees.

"Those without their own weapons make ranks up here, and we'll be issuing you AR-15s. Be careful, because they're fully automatic. Illegal, you say? How they got that way, *I* sure don't know. A miracle, I guess," pointing to the sky, which brought scattered laughter from the group. "If you've never fired one, tell us. Be honest about it. Don't be a danger to others. We'll show you how on the range."

Sara sent O'Keefe a look of mock dread and joined the AR-15 group. O'Keefe stood at attention in formation with the others who'd brought their own weapons.

The General smirked and said, "Let's see how many of you know or remember your Manual of Arms." He commanded, "Order Arms."

O'Keefe managed to remember to place the rifle butt on the ground, the barrel pointing upward and resting against his right leg. Which turned out to be mostly correct. The variety of other responses from the hapless crew were comical. The General laughed out loud at the miscellany of clumsy responses from his hapless crew and said, "Oh, Lord Almighty! But don't worry about it. We'll shape you up. That's what you're here for. Now try this one. Parade Rest!"

The General was staring at O'Keefe, whose recall wasn't so sharp this time, other than to prompt him that the maneuver required doing something with his left hand. He put it behind his back at his waist, palm outward. That also turned out to be correct. From the other troops, again a fumbling miscellany of responses that brought a derisive smile from the General.

One man dropped his rifle.

"Oh, my," the General said. "Now, when I come to you, you need to automatically 'Present Arms.'"

He took a rifle from the man in front of him, demonstrated how to do that, and set about his inspection.

When he came to O'Keefe, he took the M16 from him. "Kenny and Dwight told me about this. Pre-1986, I guess?"

"Actually, sir, pre-*seventy*-six."

"Where'd you get it?"

"On my release from the Marine Corps, I released it too."

Marine, I might even be able to tolerate you after all is how O'Keefe interpreted the General's smile.

On the firing range O'Keefe sensed the General watching him and worried he wouldn't be able to handle that pressure. But he managed to perform respectably, not an expert marksman but by no means a "nonqual." *No side-thrust kicks today.*

CHAPTER 21

Aꜰᴛᴇʀ ᴛʜᴇ ꜰɪʀɪɴɢ range, they were introduced to their sleeping quarters—for the men, large tents on raised wooden platforms, accommodating sixteen cots. There were four such tents, able to accommodate up to sixty-four male trainees. Only forty-seven had signed up for this round of training, so they spread the men out over the four tents. They were assured this was a great windfall and they should be grateful for the "luxury."

The three women shared a smaller tent, only eight cots, and it was said that it had been full only once. Some of the men joked that they'd be willing to move in there for the women's "protection."

There were outhouses, one dedicated to the women and placed at a modest distance from the men's. As outhouses went, these weren't bad, but they provoked more bad memories. O'Keefe had become intimately familiar with that particular contrivance when, for reasons never explained to their five-year-old son, the family had moved onto a farm where they remained for two years. No running water in the house, no inside toilets. Outhouse only. Of course it always stunk most powerfully. Though it seemed impossible, he worried about somehow falling in. But he suspected that the real danger lurked below, what might be swimming around down there. A standard feature in a high corner was a wasp nest under construction. *Be very quiet, try not to move at all, and maybe those two stingers at work up there won't notice you.*

Worst of all, the outhouse had been placed a long way from the house, for understandable reasons, but it challenged him on too many nights: the coyotes howling; in his imagination the snakes slithering along the dark path; the existential dilemma whether to brave the terrifying journey or, worse, wet the bed and face the unpleasant consequences for that offense, including a shaming, a whipping, and an overall bad next day.

Saturday night was bath night on the farm. Haul buckets of water from the well into the house, heat them up in big kettles on the stove, dump the hot water into the tub. Here at Ark II a wooden building with a tin roof had been furnished with six showers. That triggered another memory because the roof was almost identical to the one at the airbase in Nam where the copter crews returned each night from dodging shrapnel while hauling troops and supplies to and from Landing Zones and ferrying out the suffering wounded and the beyond-suffering dead. Here the *Ark*itechts had devised a system that captured rainwater in a large tank above the building and distributed it downward so that a lightning-fast arctic plunge of a shower could be experienced. In Nam the water was always too hot, here too cold.

Buckets near the sinks were available to wet their faces for shaving in the tiny mirrors above the tiny sinks along the wall (mandatory for all males in the community since Yahweh, through the Prophet, had forbidden, though only recently, all facial hair).

While a second such building was under construction, for now, precision scheduling was required. The ritual began in early-morning darkness. The women went first and were allowed no more than ten minutes total. The men in flights of six were given fifteen minutes because of the need to shave, a series of sprints causing numerous shaving nicks and cuts and much grumbling, bickering, jostling, bumping, and on one occasion actual fisticuffs.

At least it was early May. O'Keefe had been told that these training sessions were also held in the early and late weeks of the winter season. Imagining what that might be like, he tried to take chilly comfort in the notion that things could always be worse as he slapped at the mosquitos, some the size of houseflies, attacking in swarms even before summer had arrived in earnest. Was it King Lear whose line was, "It's never the worst as long as we can say 'this is the worst.'"? Didn't quite make sense to O'Keefe, but he knew this was likely not the worst, only its beginning.

Every morning they assembled for PT, which O'Keefe managed reasonably well, grateful that he'd gritted his teeth and continued with a more or less daily exercise program all these years. It was exceedingly tough on some of the men. A few reached a point where they refused to continue, and the instructors, including even the General, seemed to know they had to tolerate this form of malingering, looking the other way with occasional barked warnings like, "This stuff isn't hard, people. If you don't get yourselves in shape, you won't survive what's coming."

After the early morning struggle with all of that, the actual training, though rigorous, provided welcome relief. As Norbert had said, they'd erected what looked like a rudimentary movie set, a false-front urbanscape of streets and buildings. The would-be guerrillas crept through and into it, firing at human-size cutouts representing stereotypes that the Ark people despised so much: a Shylock figure to represent the stereotypical Jew (Golda Meir for a female version); a black man with huge, razor sharp teeth and not one but two knives to match; a policeman with a badge on his chest in the form of a Star of David; and for the Vietnam vets, photos of Ho Chi Minh and Jane Fonda.

They were trained to carry and use gas masks. Occasionally, real tear-gas canisters were exploded inside the "buildings," and the students had to rush to don a mask before the worst effects of the gas were felt. Some didn't make it and had to be led out and administered to. O'Keefe kept waiting for someone to get seriously hurt.

Next to the pretend city a large field was dedicated to blowing up and burning things. Using a live grenade, instructors explained how to pull the pin, hold down the safety lever until ready to throw, then toss it into an already blast-damaged shell of a vehicle positioned at what O'Keefe hoped was a safe distance away. One fumbled grenade or bad throw and...

After the instructors demonstrated the technique to show how simple and safe it could be, they brought Sara to the front. She'd quickly become the instructors' favorite because she was gung-ho, a quick study, and attractive even in oversized fatigues. She expertly showed everyone how to do it (though taking no chances, the instructors had rehearsed it with her the night before, using a dummy grenade).

The same vehicle was used to demonstrate the effect of other explosive devices. After receiving lectures on general bomb-making with an emphasis on simple expedients like booby traps, Molotov cocktails, and pipe bombs, presented by an intense young man named Rudy Acuff who was referred to mostly as "the Bomber," they set off various explosive and incendiary devices until there was nothing left of the vehicle to further bomb or burn and a replacement was towed in.

They also crammed into the course a broad range of other ways to harm their fellow beings: knife fighting; garroting and strangling; "Christian" martial arts, which they were encouraged to take up in earnest when they returned home; arson techniques; and on the firing range, everything from rifles to handguns to submachine guns and machine pistols. Provoking another in the streaming cavalcade of O'Keefe-boot-camp memory prods, they were made to don helmets and pound each other with long pugil sticks padded at both ends while the onlookers roared with a bloodlust likely not outdone by the Romans in the Colosseum.

The topography furnished a prime setting for wilderness survival training. Among other things they were shown how to rappel, and each person, except a couple of wimps who were too afraid of heights to try it, actually did so from a large bluff. This considerably racked O'Keefe's nerves. With the rope tied around his waist, leaning back on the ledge, his boots sinking into and slipping slightly on the soft dirt crumbling beneath the weight of his body, knowing that a fall would at least break his back if it didn't kill him, he thought, *I wonder who tied this fucking knot, and did they know what the fuck they were doing?* And when he could tolerate the suspense no longer and they were yelling at him to "Go! Go! Go!", he leaped backward, let the rope slide through his gloved hands, dropped a few yards and swung back into the bluff, jamming his feet into it, then dropping again, and just as he seemed to be getting the hang of it, he hit the ground hard—mercifully, feet first.

The training continued even into nighttime, with frequent emergency drills, sirens calling them to bound from sleep, rapidly dress, then assemble in formation. After a few of these heart-thumping disturbances, one night when the sirens went off, two buddies who'd traveled there together failed to appear at formation and were found packing their gear, announcing they were "DONE." They headed out to the parking lot and drove into the night down the treacherous access road. O'Keefe couldn't help but envy them. If he wasn't being paid for this…

It had seemed like a small fortune at the time he negotiated it with Maxwell, but now it seemed not to be nearly enough to compensate for enduring this insanity. He found his own breaking point during an exercise in a jungle-like area of the forest, apparently chosen to somewhat replicate the Vietnam experience.

They were crawling through a thicket of weeds and vines when he came face-to-face with what was unmistakably poison ivy. He was so allergic to it that he feared even a slight breeze might blow enough of the stuff his way to cover him with an invisible oil that would later erupt into an abominable blistering crud, tuning his face to lizard and causing him to suffer days and nights, sometimes for weeks, in an agony of itch-but-can't-scratch.

Poison ivy had either not existed in Nam, or he hadn't encountered it in his short period of grunt duty in the jungle—or maybe the Agent Orange had killed it, delivering a then unknown but eventually much worse fate to those who absorbed it. During the few days he'd spent in the bush, he'd lived in near mortal fear of it or whatever its Southeast Asian equivalent (probably even a worse thing) might be. His certainty that he'd ultimately crawl through it was one of several reasons why he'd impulsively volunteered for door-gunner duty despite everyone saying it was the second most dangerous job in Nam right below first lieutenant in charge of an infantry platoon.

When he came upon the evil weed at the Ark, he scrambled up, walked slowly amid the gaping stares and the "where you goin', Marine?" and similar mutterings, reported to the General and told him he would not do this unless the Ark had a cortisone supply and someone willing and able to inject him with it.

No such thing. Only a low growl. "Get back there, Marine, and make the Corps proud of you."

O'Keefe knew he wouldn't quit, given the importance of his mission here, but he would risk calling the General's bluff.

"No way," he whispered (so as not to risk the consequences of the General losing face). "Please don't try to force me."

After a brief hesitation, the General snorted in disgust but said sotto voce, "Okay. Fall out. But just tell everyone you were sick, not that you were afraid of a damn leaf. And this is it. Don't test me again, Marine. And you owe me, and you can bet I'll collect."

O'Keefe returned to the tent area, ashamed but relieved, and knew he'd have to perform at some near heroic level for the rest of the training to make up for his cowardice.

CHAPTER 22

Depressingly, the effort to recreate a true military experience extended even to the food: MREs for breakfast, lunch, and dinner. O'Keefe could feel himself losing weight. Not a bad feeling that. Leaner and meaner was good. He'd been getting a little tight in his trousers and shirts, so this thinning out was one byproduct of the misery of it all that he could be grateful for.

The only thing to look forward to came in the form of big metal containers of hot coffee that Kenny or Dwight or other of the General's assistants lugged down to the training camp for breakfast and dinner. (One of them would usually stay on, making small talk and joking with the trainees. O'Keefe suspected one of the motivations for these chat sessions was detection of any ideological or religious waywardness or mutinous impulses within the group.) Otherwise, the would-be soldiers had to satisfy themselves with packets of instant MRE coffee, a concoction that, according to one man recently discharged from the Army had "the aroma and taste of mice piss." Someone asked him how he'd become so intimately familiar with mice piss.

Breakfast this morning was the far too frequently served MRE referred to as Omelet with Ham. After his first encounter with the dish, O'Keefe steered far away from it and tried to satisfy himself with the welcome fresh morning coffee and dreams of an apple or a banana or a bowl of berries. He envied his fellows, most of whom, including Sara, managed to suspend or otherwise overcome their gag reflexes and wolf the stuff down fast enough to keep from actually tasting it.

The recently discharged Army man said that this meal was known by the troops as the "Vomelet," which provoked an unusual outburst from O'Keefe. "The horror of this thing can't compare to the C-rations they used to serve us."

Another Vietnam vet joined in, and they expounded at length, riffing like a two-man jazz group with great energy and much laughter all around on the horrors of the C-rat offerings, especially Beans and Frankfurters ("Beans and Baby Dicks") and Ham and Lima Beans ("Ham and Mother Fuckers").

"Nothing but that out in the jungle?" someone asked.

The other Vietnam vet, an infantryman, answered, "There was one time we slogged out there for twenty-three days with nothin' but C-rats. By about the thirteenth day, you were hopin' for a grazin' wound to get you the hell out of there. By the twentieth day, death seemed like a better deal than a wound."

"How 'bout you, Marine?" the General's man said.

"I had it better. After a short time in Grunt World, I became a helicopter door gunner. A lot of the time, after missions, we got back to base in time for a hot dinner in the mess hall."

"*Had it better?*" the Army vet said, opening his eyes wide. "They said that door-gunner job was the most dangerous job in the whole Goddamn war."

"None of that cursing," the General's man ordered. "That's blasphemous."

O'Keefe said, "Put it this way. It was better if you managed to survive until dinner."

"Well, buddy," the infantryman said, "we were eternally grateful to guys like you. You saved our asses so many times."

"The least we could do," O'Keefe said. "You guys took the worst of it twenty-four hours a day and night."

And he found himself not playacting then, but meaning exactly what he had said…

The brain-rattling whomp of the chopper blades … the oppressive weight and poor fit of the helmet … the bulky pack's straps digging into his shoulders … the twenty pounds of the M60 on his lap …

the two bandoliers of ammo hung around his neck and rubbing it raw … the choking heat of this steam bath of a country, magnified to the max in the close quarters of the tightly packed helicopter interior full of sweating male bodies exuding their own intense heat—all of that almost stifled O'Keefe's rising terror, as he waited his turn with the other grunts, about to plunge into his first combat mission, wondering if he'd survive even the first few seconds of it. And hoping for injury instead of death.

He watched the men before him struggle up and out of the open rear door of the hovering copter and drop several feet, hitting the ground with thuds, many stumbling, some falling, one spraining his ankle and hopping and limping to catch up with the others. O'Keefe wasn't sure he'd be able to lift himself from his seat even if he wanted to. He didn't want to. What if he just stayed put? Why did he think now of Bartleby the Scrivener? *I would prefer not to.* He felt himself smiling. Had he lost his mind? Surely they'd pry him up and drag him out. Somehow the very momentum of the process, and the ever-reliable fear of the guaranteed public shaming that such cowardice would earn, overcame his fear of an early death.

He too stumbled, nearly toppling over the man in front of him, and fell to his knees. Someone grabbed him and pulled him up. *Thank you.* Gunfire and mortars on their right. Everyone had run past him. He was the last one.

The sergeant was waving him on. "Get behind that fucking berm or you're dead meat."

It seemed ill-fated from the outset. They hadn't even arrived as a complete platoon. There were only eight of them, all of them replacements for men of the existing platoon who'd been killed or wounded. They didn't even rate a lieutenant to lead them, only a sergeant to substitute for the dead one from the platoon. Since O'Keefe was as green as the jungle itself, he wouldn't be operating as the machine gunner but as the lowliest member of the three-man gun team (gunner, assistant gunner, and second assistant, aka "ammo-bearer"). The assistants each carried M16s and also humped at least 400 rounds of extra ammo (24 extra pounds) and extra gun barrels, guided the belt of bullets into the gun as it fired, and stood ready to replace the gunner when he was killed or wounded.

The "killed or wounded" was an especially high risk for an M60 man. He was the most attractive target on the ground except for that marked-for-death lieutenant and maybe the platoon's radio man, who had to stay too close to the lieutenant and attracted the enemy's special attention because it was he who summoned death from the sky above. Similarly, the gunners, popular with their fellow grunts because their firepower could avert disaster, were also highly valued by the enemy—as targets. In this case, the first assistant gunner had been the one to attract that enemy attention, and it had killed him. The ammo-bearer second assistant had replaced him. O'Keefe was there to fill in that final dangerous space as the new ammo-bearer.

By the fifth day it was clear to O'Keefe that their function was not to conquer territory, as one might expect in a war, but to float around in the jungle like worms on a hook, human bait to attract enemy fire and provoke a battle that would hopefully tote up a higher enemy body count than their own. The burden of lugging the extra ammo … the bugs … the sweat, always soaked in sweat … boots soaked too from wading through paddies and puddles … death lurking everywhere, the jangled nerves on constant edge until they wore down to a possibly fatal indifference.

By the sixth day it became clear that this was going to kill him. It might kill him in any number of ways: bullets, mortars, landmines, friendly fire, but mainly it would kill him because he'd likely stop caring as much as he ought to care about staying alive in his plodding sweaty misery and seething anger at what they were doing to him and at himself for putting himself in a position for them to do it.

So, despite his exhaustion as he sprawled in camp at dusk at the end of the sixth day, wanting to fall asleep but afraid to fall asleep because it might only last a few moments and make him more tired than before, when the lieutenant read the circular requesting volunteers to train and serve as door gunners, and when nobody else immediately spoke up, perhaps because they'd heard that it was the most dangerous job for an enlisted-man in the war, after taking dangerous seconds to measure and calculate one possible form of misery, danger, and likely doom versus another—the one right here surrounding him, the other conveniently far away—he jumped to his feet and uncharacteristically yelled, almost screamed, "O'Keefe, Sir! PFC O'Keefe volunteers!"

A couple of other shouts followed his. The Lieutenant conferred with the Sergeant, and then the Captain, who'd collected volunteers from the other two platoons (there were only three in this typically shorthanded company in 1969). No way would he have the good *luck* (irony there for sure?) to be chosen. But it became decisive that he was the only volunteer from his platoon who was already trained as a machine gunner. And better yet, he wasn't the real thing right now anyway, only a sort of pack mule for the real gunner and first assistant, both of whom would remain, and the ammo-carry burden could be spread around to the regular grunts.

That night, as he straightened up his gear and got ready to be picked up in the morning, people said things:

"Damn, O'Keefe, I wouldn't've figured you for having the balls to do that."

"Dumb fuckin' move, O'Keefe. You're dead for certain now."

He made himself look even more clueless and glum than usual and said nothing. If they thought it was about balls, okay. If they thought he was an idiot for volunteering for maybe the most dangerous enlisted man's job in the war, okay. But it wasn't about any of that. It was because he was certain that remaining here would mean death for certain.

CHAPTER 23

Once a week or so the Ark treated them to a barbecue dinner, usually chicken, game of some sort, or beef ribs—no pork allowed here. Ironically (he was pretty sure that slippery concept applied here), the antisemitic Ark II community observed certain Hebrew customs and rejected traditional Christian ones such as celebration of the "pagan" holidays of Christmas and Easter and eating pig. A couple of times, with much fanfare, steaks were served. Small, tough, gristly steaks ("to help build our jaw muscles apparently," O'Keefe said), corn on the cob, beans, and salad.

As each of the intervening "MRE days" dragged on, they pined for barbecue night but even more for the feasts they would gorge themselves on once out of this place. They became versions of the characters in one of those old movies, stranded in the desert, crawling toward an oasis only to find it was a mirage. In this case the mirages promised everything from pitchers of beer to chocolate milkshakes, but always just out of reach. Back in Marine boot camp, he'd longed not for booze or sex but a cheeseburger and fries.

The post-dinner campfire conversations, usually with one or more of the General's men present, were sometimes quiet, at other times friendly disputations over professional and college sports, but at other times they ignited or stoked the simmering rage that had brought so many of them to the New Ark—litanies of grievance, already present but further inflamed by the literature they'd been furnished during their stay, such as *The Protocols of the Elders of Zion,* the hoax text purporting to reveal a centuries-old conspiracy of the Jews against the Christians.

One farmer had lost his farm, another was about to lose his: "The Jew bankers took my land. They're taking people's land all over the country. But they've gone too far. We're not taking it anymore. They'll pay. That's why I'm here … Make 'em pay."

Another: "And their ZOG with its unconstitutional income taxes and gun laws. They're already rounding us up. It's now or never."

Another: "Ya know, most of the liberals are Jews. It's the libs and the Jews that got the niggers all riled up. Now it's only white men that don't have civil rights."

Another: "It's like the Mafia. It's really not the Italians. Not in the main anyway. The Italians are just stooges for the Jew money pullin' all the strings."

There was also the Vietnam betrayal, the stab in the soldiers' backs courtesy of the traitorous politicians, the "Jewsmedia," and the chickenshit, yellow-bellied hippie antiwar draft dodgers.

"How many died over there for nothin'?" someone asked.

"A helluva bunch," the Army vet said. "I bet you know, Marine … how many?"

O'Keefe knew. "Fifty to sixty thousand," he said. "And how many others blown to pieces, ground up to dogmeat but not dead, crippled for life … and the Agent Orange guys … and how many went crazy, into a deep black hole, shattered forever?"

One of the vets, who'd been quiet until now, erupted angrily. "When I came home in '69, I wasn't expecting a ticker-tape parade down Fifth Avenue, but I thought I might at least get a little respect, an occasional 'Thank you for your service.' Instead, a mob of them were waitin' for us when we landed, spittin' on us and callin' us war criminals and baby killers … when all we did was what our country asked us to do. I had to skulk out of there like a dirty, beaten dog."

A younger man said, "Well, I'll say it now, soldier. Thank you for your service."

O'Keefe raised his coffee cup. "To *everyone* who served. To the crippled and the crazy and the insulted and the disrespected. And especially to the sixty thousand who died … for someone else's sins."

"Amen to that, Marine." And that became a refrain, repeated all around the circle, along with near shouts of "Make 'em pay," "Down with ZOG," "Take it to the streets," and a final "Apocalypse *now*."

Later, when they were alone for a moment, Sara said, "That was quite a thing tonight."

"Quite an angry bunch, eh?"

"I mean you."

"For the benefit of the General's man. Maybe it'll help us get in."

"Quite emotional though. There were tears in some eyes. Even mine. Didn't seem like a performance. Seemed like you meant it."

"Some of it I probably did." Recognizing the import of the look she gave him, he said, "Don't worry. Not drinking the Kool-Aid…"

She nodded.

"Not yet anyway," he added.

She rolled her eyes. "Don't leave me all by myself as the only sane one in this place."

"If you were sane, you wouldn't be here."…

Like so many of the other men around the campfire, O'Keefe could, if he tried, get himself worked up and hateful over all that, but he didn't regard what had been done to him and others as traitorous or criminal, at least not criminal at the beginning—just tragic folly, deeply flawed leaders. He couldn't flatter himself to think he'd have done better in the same circumstances, stumbling into playing God. But it was the boys, mostly lower-class boys, who'd paid for that folly with their lives, and at that point the folly perhaps did become a crime—against humanity if not "the law." That folly or crime, combined with his own personal folly, his lazy drifting into troubled waters, casting his fate to the wind like one of his favorite songs, a wind that proved an ill and wayward one, sweeping his pathetic little dinghy into a maelstrom of pain and death.

Bucking against authority and orderly proceedings as he had done, it seemed, from kindergarten on, continually getting into disciplinary scrapes with every kind of overseer, still he'd been a B, sometimes an A, student and a decent athlete, the sixth man on the basketball team with his share of shining moments on the court. Then 1968. The Summer of Love. Sort of. That was the summer when he and Annie had fallen into their sometimes celebratory and uplifting romance that too often devolved into tormented melodrama for no discernible cause. In September, he entered the university. Later, he came to understand that he was simply too immature to handle the freedom of it, all the temptations. Plus, it turned out he'd read too much of a certain kind of literature or, more likely, had just absorbed many wrong lessons from it. He wasn't antiwar in anything other than a surly, private way. He wasn't political at all, just alienated.

He looked around and thought he saw clearly that the whole college thing, still in thrall to the snobby fraternities and sororities, was merely the same old bourgeois bullshit. He refused to play that game but found no better game to play except to drink and smoke weed and listen to folk and rock and Delta blues, maybe in the haze write a few lines of navel-gazing poetry until well beyond the witching hour and in the morning sleep late and cut classes.

There'd been nobody in the world to regulate or even influence him. Certainly nobody at home. They didn't believe in his college-boy pretensions anyway. The student loans that paid for his initial tuition and books and room and board had run out after a few months. By then, he was gone anyway, flunked out. You really needed to do something more than show up for the final exams.

Now lacking a student deferment, he was quickly summoned to report. He did give some thought to an escape to Canada, or staying in the U.S. but not reporting for duty, going fugitive and daring them to catch him. But he wasn't quite brave enough for that, and he even discovered a surprising faint patriotic impulse, leading him to think, *What the hell. All those guys went to World War II. I'll do my duty. Maybe it'll be interesting.*

What he had *not* planned on was standing in line at the induction center, the Army guy leaving the room, and a dude he didn't even recognize as a Marine (and he didn't really understand what the Marine Corps was all about anyway), marching down the line and ordering every sixth man to take two steps in front. He was the eighteenth man.

The dude said, "Okay, all you gentlemen in the front row, your asses, elbows, your swingin' dicks, and everything else are now the property of the United States Marine Corps."

He sensed something unpleasant had just happened as he shuffled with the other hapless "every sixth" out the Army door to a fate not quite worse than death, but, as he would learn, certainly a higher likelihood of death in combat due to the Marine banzai "take the hill" frontal assault jarhead suicidal bravura.

The jeering and spitting on returning from Nam had happened to some, but not to him. His flight back to the U.S. had landed after midnight to an essentially empty airport. A few airport employees had even applauded, as the boys—none of them were more than twenty years old—plodded into the terminal from the tarmac.

He spent a few weeks at Camp Pendleton, hanging out and drinking with Spud and keeping Annie from visiting him to ensure that the wildly anticipated homecoming would be all the more charged.

The day of his discharge she and only she met him at the airport, each of them pulsing with relief that he'd managed to survive, and each of them full of erotic longing and believing Fitzgerald's orgastic future awaited, would unfold endlessly before them. They got only mildly drunk, managed to avoid their usual disputation, and made love most of the night. He still looked back on that night as one of the magical moments in his life, and he guessed she felt the same when she could bear to allow herself to recall it. If only they had known then what would happen later, could they have done something to change it? Or should they have just given it up right then and spared themselves a lot of good times but ultimately, it seemed, "more pain than gain," as the saying went. But that was not a choice they understood to be open to them.

On that homecoming night, he'd been so sure he'd left Vietnam behind, had managed quite literally to dodge the bullet. Not quite. They ascertained only much later that he was suffering from PTSD. But he knew it wasn't solely or even primarily Vietnam that ailed him. He also hadn't left behind that strange, inexplicable existential stance of churlish lassitude that had contributed so much to sending him there.

Drinking almost every night in Nam after they returned to base had pushed him over the final edge of what he later learned was alcoholism. Not understanding it, he kept staggering from one mess to another, vowing to "handle" it in the future. Then cocaine came along and offered a temporary cure for the alcoholism. But that stuff soon began to make things even worse. Even having a daughter he cherished failed to reform him. He rationalized the divorce as inevitable. After all, they'd fought with each other from the beginning, hadn't they? Doomed from the start. Both of them had to be better off now.

Finally, the possession arrest and jail. Nowhere left to go that morning Harrigan appeared like an angry Archangel Gabriel with a different kind of Annunciation, one that, amazing to both of them, O'Keefe actually listened to. Not that that he had any real alternative but to listen since he'd finally hit bottom and all rationalizations and escape routes had vanished, all doors closed except the one to a cell.

CHAPTER 24

Except for the General and his assistants, occasional "guest" speakers, a folksy and funny weaponry wizard explaining how to convert an AR-15 from semi-automatic to automatic and equip various types of weapons with silencers, demonstrations by Rudy "the Bomber" Acuff on bomb-making and booby traps, and a few visitations at a distance from the Prophet and the "Chaplain," Caleb, there was minimal contact with Ark II residents. Those few who had some function within the training operation were tight-lipped to the point of rudeness.

As a condition of their permitted early-evening walks, always confined to the deep woods away from the living and community areas, Sara and O'Keefe were instructed not to "interfere with or distract" (which clearly meant "engage with in any form") people dedicated to a simple life of worship and work. On the rare occasion that someone crossed their path or came into view, they quickly disappeared.

The sole exception to the no-contact policy was a soft invitation to join the Sabbath religious service, observed on Saturdays at Ark II, according to the ancient Hebrew custom, "directly ordained by Yahweh Himself,", as Kenny had told them on that first day and Caleb reaffirmed when he delivered the invitation to the assembled trainees.

O'Keefe and Sara welcomed the opportunity to mix and try to lay the groundwork for a request to join the permanent community. Otherwise, there were few takers among the trainees, especially after the first weekend. While they were overwhelmingly professed

"Christian people," they showed little interest in devoting their one day of R&R to hours of being cooped up listening to sermons, prophecies, and hymns.

He wondered if Sara was feeling the same mix of anticipation and anxiety as he was, as they walked up the gentle slope on an unpaved but lovingly groomed and tended gravel path with occasional random bursts of flowers along the way. As they later learned, this was called the "Pilgrim's Path." To their right as they climbed were the residents' houses, not lined in a straight row down the slope but spread around in a more interesting way that maximized privacy and views. Other Pilgrims climbed with them on the Path, making their way to the service, most of them friendly, waving or bidding them "good morning."

The Path ended at a small plateau with a flat grassy space large enough to accommodate outdoor assemblies of the full community, named by the Prophet the "Gathering Ground." To the right was a complex consisting of the Prophet's house attached to the most substantial building in the community, "Yahweh's Fortress," or simply, the "Fortress." The front section was a simple chapel with plain wooden chairs with cane backs and thin, lively yellow seat cushions. On either side of a central aisle were rows of chairs facing a small, slightly elevated platform on which two chairs were placed. An ancient-looking piano on wheels stood in one corner.

Behind the chapel there were bathrooms and classrooms for their community school. The second floor was divided into rooms used for classes or meetings.

After an opening hymn, the Prophet took the stage, followed by Caleb. The Prophet stood and Caleb sat. It was O'Keefe's first close-up view of the man. *Physically imposing,* he thought. He was slightly taller than O'Keefe's six feet two inches. His thick, dark hair was not quite Marine Corps short but sharply trimmed all around. O'Keefe guessed that years of hard manual labor before he answered the call to mount the pulpit was partly responsible for the powerful upper body that was starting to show some midlife heaviness and sagging in the chest and belly. His prominent jaw and chin reminded O'Keefe of one of the action heroes in the Sunday comics, but he was getting puffy, jowly, and slack there too. His physique and bearing and manner suggested power and dominance.

But for one thing. His eyes. Light blue, soft and gentle, they spoke the opposite of the rest of him: "I understand. Trust me. I'm here to help."

Caleb had wispy and thinning blond hair, a curly lock of it squiggling a couple of inches down onto his forehead. He exhibited a surfeit of nervous energy, his legs bouncing slightly as he sat. He leaned forward often, elbows on knees, but soon straightened back up, his hands rubbing his face or clasping each other as though he were forcing himself to refrain from cracking his knuckles. He was scarecrow thin, as if the energy burning inside him had hollowed him out.

Caleb's frequent nervous movements didn't distract from the Prophet's hold on the congregation, who listened raptly as he spoke, and O'Keefe had to admit there was something close to mesmerizing about his rising and falling, rhythmic rhetorical delivery, sometimes mighty roar, sometimes whisper soft. The substance, *not* so mesmerizing, a down and dirty version of the Christian Identity dogma, the evils of ZOG and all the modern "Babylon" world, and the imminent End Times that would obliterate all those evils.

"As we know," he preached, "our Israelite forbears were kidnapped and held as slaves in Babylon for centuries during what became known as the Babylonian Captivity. We modern Christians have also been seized and imprisoned in a New Babylonian Captivity. But it was not from an *outside* force like the ancient Israelites suffered. For us it was an *inside job.* Our politicians and media and teachers, even many of our preachers, turned rotten and spread their rot and corruption everywhere. We few here, and a few others around our country, have managed to escape to places like this, but *they* will not permit us even that fragile refuge. *They* will not let us be. *They* are doing everything they can to re-enslave us, until they've left us with no choice but to arm ourselves to prepare for the Final Battle.

"Jesus told us that the rising in the world of what He called the Abomination of Desolation would be the first sign that the

End Times, the Tribulation, the Apocalypse, the Great and Final Armageddon Battle between Jesus the Risen Christ and the Antichrist are at hand.

"The Abomination of Desolation. What does that mean? Big words there, for sure." He chuckled and the people followed. "But it means this simple though horrible thing: the whole world engaging in or surrendering to the grossest and most foul blasphemies and blasphemous acts in desecration of all that is sacred.

"We all know that day is already here. Our times *are* the Abomination of Desolation. Such a disgusting spectacle it is too. Thankfully, we were able to flee from it, but the sewage is everywhere out there, everywhere, rising and spreading all the time, fouling the whole world. And today it's lapping at our very thresholds and threatening to drown us in filth.

"But none of that is cause for despair or even sadness. Just the opposite. *Rejoice* that you have the privilege to live in these times, the greatest in all history—when, yes, there will be the period of Tribulation, the war of all against all. But that will, as Jesus promised, lead to the Final Armageddon Battle when He will return in triumph and all His glory. It's not far off, people. It's close. Maybe right around the next bend on our Road to Calvary.

"And then, the most beautiful thing, so far beyond our mortal imaginations it's almost impossible even to conceive it. God's Chosen, who've given themselves to Him with their whole body and soul, and armed themselves, and prepared and trained, and then fought and destroyed the Jews and the Gentile Philistines … those Chosen *shall* survive. Not only survive, but they shall have the Dominion promised to humankind all the way back in Genesis … until Adam and Eve broke and violated their covenant with God. But that horrible act of betrayal still, thanks to an ever-merciful God, did not deprive the human race forever of its original promised birthright. It only suspended it … until a future day.

"And that day is now. But make no mistake. We'll have to fight for it, and some of us will have to die for it. Just as Christ died for the sins of the world, so may some of us. We're going to die anyway. Why not die for the greatest Cause of them all—the Final Triumph of the Risen Christ, when all of us, we Children of Light, will beam right through the gates of Paradise and sit at the feet of the Father and His Son for all time and beyond all time."

This last, as it was certainly intended and expected, even required to do, "brought down the house." But when the shouting and clapping and screaming and Hallelujah-ing finally died down, it was unfortunately followed by an *extended* recital and *further* detailed explication by Caleb of the relevant Bible passages mentioned in the Prophet's sermon. That shut the eyelids of a few of the Ark people, and O'Keefe felt his own lids drooping too.

But, mercifully, they were jolted back to attention by the Prophet's intervention, recounting certain interpretative revelations divinely vouchsafed only to him.

That was followed by specially gifted congregants speaking in tongues, a form of incoherent babbling that O'Keefe had no doubt was phony but still often impressively creative.

"Prophesying" followed (each concluding with the pronouncement, "Thus sayeth the Lord") from two congregants momentarily "struck" by God to deliver a message. Both essentially amounted to complaints about a particular citizen's rude behavior or other deviation from the good of the colony that turned the service into a sort of group therapy session, a lesson in civics Ark-style, and undoubtedly a means of social and mind control of the flock.

CHAPTER 25

Rudy Acuff rose from his chair at the back of the room and waited to be recognized.

At first the Prophet didn't notice. When he did, he was clearly taken aback. Not only was this not the usual order of proceeding at services, this was the young man known not just as "the Bomber" but as "the Hermit," always keeping to himself, not saying a word, even his response to "Hello" or "Good morning" a reluctant nod of the head.

"Has the Spirit moved you, Rudy? Do you have something to tell us?"

"With permission, a prophecy."

Opening his arms wide, the Prophet said, "Please, Rudy."

Rudy rested his hand over his heart. "I ask that all of us bow our heads in remembrance of the Holy Innocents … the babies that have been violated, tortured, destroyed this very day and for so many years now, year upon year, month upon month, day after day, minute by minute. Mass torture and murder. Tiny things, but the little creatures"—rising to a near shout here—"DO FEEL PAIN. CHOPPED TO PIECES OR JERKED OUT WHOLE FROM THE WOMB AND TOSSED IN A TRASH CAN. Animals cannot be treated so cruelly under our laws. But these tiny humans *can* be. How many thousands, how many hundreds of thousands, MILLIONS, have been tortured, then slaughtered in this barbaric way? What did these Innocents do to deserve this horror? What was their sin, their crime?

"Inconvenience. We made these little beings, but we don't *want* them. They're inconvenient and unwanted. *So massacre them!* In the most brutal way imaginable.

"Where does *that* logic lead? It justifies killing anyone who's inconvenient, unwanted, helpless.

"A prophecy then. The Lord sayeth: *ALL* those who've done these horrible deeds and are doing them now and will do them in the future, *ALL* those who've cheered it on, *ALL* those who've stood by and allowed it to happen and are standing by today and allowing it to happen, making no protest, babbling like Cain—'Am I my brother's keeper?'—*ALL a*re guilty.

"The end of this evil world cannot arrive soon enough—when the torturers will be tortured, the killers killed, and all the guilty bystanders along with them. Anything we can do to bring that on we must do … without fear, without pity. Thus sayeth the Lord."

Rudy's speech had been punctuated with a few outcries and a couple of startling shrieks from the crowd. Some were weeping.

"Thank you for that, Rudy," the Prophet said. "It reminds us all of the divine justice of our cause and the holiness of the war we'll soon be waging."

Then he guided the flock from a final prayer to a solemn hymn and from there into many songs—not the usual barely melodic Protestant hymns, but rousing folk-style numbers, some of them original compositions of Ark people, accompanied by guitars, an old out-of-tune but effective piano, bongo drums, and tambourines. The final one was called "Keep Your Rifle By Your Side," with lyrics that warned of sinners coming for the children of the Chosen … why they must always have their weapons at the ready.

Everyone was singing. O'Keefe realized this was an opportunity for them to show their enthusiasm, make their mark. He forced himself to clap and hum enthusiastically, even joining in with the words when he could anticipate them. When he couldn't, he made word-like noises, his own version of speaking in tongues, and even caught some of the genuine spirit of it. He made a face to Sara that urged her to join in. She outdid him, imitating some of the other women—eyes closed, a rapturous expression, both hands raised high above her head, offering her voice and life to Yahweh.

O'Keefe caught the Prophet staring at her. At first this pleased him. Then it shamed him. *Yes, like a pimp, offering a woman as bait.*

As they made their way back to their tents, she said, "How brutal was that? Another people claiming they're 'Chosen.' Big mistake. Tragedy follows."

"Yeah," he said, "I guess it hasn't done so well for the Jews."

"You bet it hasn't," she said. "And the two seeds impregnating Eve and the rest. How can they believe that stuff?"

"Absurd," he said. "But it occurred to me in the middle of all that … my own Catholic church taught, and I think still teaches, something called transubstantiation—that during the Mass, the priest turns the bread and wine into the *actual* body and blood of Christ. Later in the Mass, we *consume* that body and blood. At one time I believed all that. Didn't even question it."

Still staring at the ground, she shook her head. "Where do they … we … come up with this stuff?"

"The hell of it," he said, "is that I bet some people got burned at the stake over that. They come up with this stupid shit like the Adam and Satan two-seed theory, or transubstantiation, or all kinds of other dogmatic idiocy, and they'll kill you over it."

"How about Rudy and his prophecy?" she said.

O'Keefe hesitated, then said, "Troubling."

She frowned, not understanding. "Rudy … or abortion?"

"Well, actually, both."

"You're against it?" she said, a sharp edge to her tone.

He was quiet for a few seconds, then: "I don't know what I think. I can see both sides of it and don't particularly like either of them. I'm bothered by the logic of saying you have the right to kill something just because it's yours. Where do you draw the line? What's the difference in something inside the womb one minute and outside the next minute?"

"Viability," she said. "Ability to survive outside."

"No more than inside. Not on their own anyway. And what's the difference between the moment before viability and the moment after?"

"Is this some lingering Catholic thing with you?"

He was quiet again for a time. "I don't think so. I haven't held on to any of the rest of it. And when I was a believing kid, I don't recall anyone ever even saying the word 'abortion.' I guess it was beyond the pale. So I never had it in the first place for it to linger."

"But," she said, "it must have been happening, even to some Catholic girls."

After another brooding silence, he said. "I can't remember anyone even saying the word. I guess Annie and I were lucky. It went with the territory for teenagers back then, worrying constantly about getting knocked up or knocking someone up. But the girls at our college found a friendly source for birth-control pills, and she got on that train. We planned it out and rehearsed it like it was for a play or a trial. She had to come up with some sort of 'feminine problem' that the pills were supposed to help with. I've always wondered whether without those pills there would ever have been a sexual revolution … So she and I were never faced with having to make a choice. But where I came from, there really was no choice. Forget being a Catholic. That was the '60s. Couldn't even conceive of such a thing, no pun intended. I'm sure we'd've gotten married whether that was good for us or not … But the thought that Kelly might have been aborted…"

He realized he was rambling on with no idea where to go next or where to stop. After several more steps in silence, he said, "I've always thought I was probably a good candidate for it."

Her look said she didn't understand what he meant.

"I mean that everything I can put together suggests that my mother got knocked up. They were still kids. I never could find out their wedding date and how that might have matched up with my birth date. Within a couple of years he took off. Gone forever. I never saw him again … have no memory of him at all. Two years old. So if it *had been* an option for her back then, little Zygote or Embryo Pete was a perfect candidate for it. Not that it really mattered … or matters…"

"Pretty dark thoughts," she said."

"It sort of gets worse. What if it *had* been available to her? What if little inconvenient and unwanted Zygote/Embryo Pete *had* been chopped up or vacuumed out of there? A stab of searing pain maybe … Can you even feel pain then? … But anyway, over quick. Better all around? He ended up bringing a bunch of suffering into his little world. His mom was a mess the rest of her life … and he didn't exactly bring joy to the rest of his world either—"

"Stop," she commanded.

Neither of them said anything more until they were almost back at the tents. Lots of looking at the ground for both of them.

Finally, lifting her head, she tried to smile, almost but not quite got there, and said, "And give him time. Seems to me he's making progress."

That closed the conversation, leaving him to his confusion. And he was grateful for that.

CHAPTER 26

A GIANT BOULDER ON his shoulders—or was it a cross?—the weight of it pressing down on him more and more as he stumbled along, afraid that any minute he would trip and fall, never able to rise again. He remembered from his altar boy days that Christ fell three times on the road to Calvary. Not that he had anything in common with that worthy gentleman, especially his virtues, and certainly wanted to avoid a common ending. But thinking like that, he must be getting *really* desperate.

He'd done a great sales job on Maxwell, but now he was having to perform—day and night, every minute and second of every twenty-four hours—and he was afraid that he'd oversold their capabilities, especially his own. If he wasn't up to this task, Maxwell—or God forbid, his wife—or don't even think about it, his kids—could pay with their lives. Every minute a life-and-death situation. And no time to stage for it, prep for it, do anything but throw in the troops he had or could grab.

He'd built their security operation from nothing, had landed a number of good plain-vanilla security assignments (guards walking around at night in warehouses or office buildings) and had up to now only a few low-level, low-risk bodyguarding ("executive protection") jobs. He had a bunch of flatfoot security guards, mostly paunchy and creaky of joint and weak of muscle, not really qualified for anything more than the "watch and listen and don't fall asleep" aspect of the job. He had a couple more guys on the bench, qualified to do the bodyguarding, ready to start work, and he'd gritted his teeth and tightened his jaw and offered them generous bonuses to begin right away.

Even more teeth-gritting and jaw-tightening had been required to even contemplate the dollar amount and other benefits necessary to overcome the reluctance of his prize prospect, Jack Shaughnessy, to start immediately on a "part-time" basis (meaning four to six hours a day on top of his cop shift) and go full-time as soon as his required notice of termination period expired. The other benefits included a promise to consider in good faith designating Jack as his second-in-command, not just on the Maxwell project but the whole security operation. No problem with that part. George was eager to get the help.

George's current situation was the opposite of what he'd had in mind when he accepted his old buddy O'Keefe's offer to work for him in his startup PI business. He thought it would be sort of a lark. And for a while it was. Compared to the regimented and thankless police officer's job he'd happily left behind, O'Keefe was so easy. George took to calling O'Keefe "Boss," but his friend didn't much act like one, didn't even make George come to the office much, trusted him to do whatever job it was without hardly ever having to write reports, fill out timecards, or suffer through any of that other bureaucratic baloney.

All proceeded wonderfully, except for O'Keefe's troubles with mood-altering substances, which he'd seemingly managed to get under control, plus some magnetism within the Boss that attracted the very personal attention of various life-threatening objects like bullets, bombs, and even venomous snakes, that particular problem seeming beyond O'Keefe's ability to solve.

But it was none of these disturbances that had led George to his painful present. Surely O'Keefe had not, with diabolical deliberation and full intent of the will, conceived then spun the sticky web that had finally trapped George—the offer of a partnership, and the really tempting thing that went along with it—the assigned mission of starting up "your own" security and executive-protection operation.

He had become that infamous frog, the one that would've leaped right out of the water if he'd been thrown in at boiling point, but instead had been gently placed in lukewarm water and the heat turned up a degree at a time until the frog suddenly realized he was at boil with no escape.

And now, there was no escape for George. The lives of Maxwell and his family depended not only on swimming in the scalding water but doing so with perfect strokes.

He was working sixteen to eighteen hours a day, setting up the protective shield around the Maxwells, establishing and maintaining a training regime for the protection team, often filling personnel gaps by doing driver or bodyguard duty himself.

Maxwell himself was cooperative, accepting the rigid restrictions on his personal freedom the protection required, worrying most of all about his family and the long-term effects on them, coming up with every idea he could to make it easier, especially for the children.

At first the children had been excited, accepting the "fun" new world of the bodyguards coming and going, driving them around in their big cars, taking them to movies, serving as new playmates, often more enthusiastic in play than the kids themselves, and who could be called on and then dismissed at any time. But soon they realized they were isolated from the rest of the world. Their friends' parents didn't want them anywhere nearby. No play dates anymore. They couldn't even play by themselves in their own yard. So things with the children began to sour.

With Mrs. Maxwell things were sour from the start. Sitting at the modern-design showpiece of the Maxwells' dining room table, George had explained how things would need to work for all of them to be safe. She looked at her husband. "This isn't life. This is prison. And do you know, they've told us we're going to have to home-school the children until this is over … if it's ever going to be over. All the money wasn't enough for you. You had to become Mr. Save the World. And look what it's brought on us."

Maxwell squirmed. So did George. She broke out in sobs and excused herself.

"I guess she's right," Maxwell had said. "The world's been good to me, and I was just trying to give back some. It seemed like all the money was pouring into the worst causes and Limbaugh and ilk absorbing all the oxygen on the air waves. Who knew there were people so insane they'd want to kill you for a pretty tame social and economic program? I'm not exactly even Marx, let alone Lenin. I'm a dyed-in-the-wool capitalist, for Christ's sake. Please do what you can for her. Make it as easy as you can for her. But protect her whether she likes it or not."

When Jack Shaughnessy arrived, George spent half a day with him painstakingly laying out the plan for protection and asked Shaughnessy to look for gaps and holes.

Shaughnessy looked hard but couldn't find any.

That felt good, though it was hard to believe. George watched Shaughnessy as he engaged in solo brainstorming until Shaughnessy looked up and said, "The hardest thing is protecting him against a well-placed sniper. Somehow we'll need to keep him from occupying any chunk of space in the world that would allow someone to get a clear shot."

CHAPTER 27

"**W**E NEED YOU now," Matthew said with his usual gravelly gruffness, leaning across the table and, disconcertingly, because it was untypical of him, engaging her eye to eye while Darby, as always, sat silently next to him, showing no emotion other than an occasional nod of affirmation.

"We should've just killed the scum when we had the chance," he continued, "instead of painting useless crap on his front door. But the Prophet wasn't quite up to it. Now he is. But now Maxwell is up to it himself … loaded up with security. We can't risk exposing ourselves until the day of reckoning. Which'll be soon. You said once that you'd help us if you could. Here we are. This is a direct request from the Prophet. He said, 'Tell her this is her chance to earn a special place in God's kingdom.'"

"I'm ready, Matthew," she said, addressing Matthew Sinclair by his first name, which she'd done from the beginning despite the grimace of displeasure it produced in him then and now. "Show me how."

With his coaching she came up with a number of ways to make occasional forays into Maxwell's territory. She took occasional walks past his house, alternating that with slow car and bike rides, but she knew she couldn't do much more without arousing suspicion. No doubt a security man would be stationed inside the house, eyes on the street. Still, she was able to ascertain that Maxwell had a regular pattern when it came to leaving for work, usually around 8:30 in the morning, not always by the same route, though there were only so many that the bodyguards could conveniently take without foolishly wasting the time of an important man like Maxwell. And so she came to believe that the best place to "terminate him," in Matthew's words, would be on one of these established routes on his way to work.

Maxwell's building was locked up tight. She tried to get access and wander the hallways by claiming she was visiting a business in the multi-tenant building, but the men at the security desk in the lobby told her she must be pre-approved by the business she was visiting or provide identification so they could call up and verify she was expected. Same problem when she'd tried to drive into the parking garage. Even if she could manage to get in and start wandering around on her own, the elevators and the hallways were probably covered by cameras, and if she tried the staircase, the doors to Maxwell's floor would likely be locked … and if she got caught in that staircase…

The wife's comings and goings had proved desultory and unpredictable. She was either driven around in a Lincoln Town Car, or when driving her own car, never did so without a bodyguard in the passenger seat.

If the Maxwells ever had a social life, it had disappeared. The couple, and sometimes the entire family, went out to dinner occasionally, but that seemed to be it. On one occasion they'd all piled into a big limo and gone off somewhere for several days. Other than that, the whole household seemed to be in a virtual lockdown, the family members venturing out only when essential and only under heavy guard.

After she felt like she'd done all she could and might be on the verge of creating suspicion—if she hadn't already done so—she arranged for a message to be sent to Matthew's pager..

He came to her apartment. With Darby. Always with Darby.

She was so alone. She wondered what it would be like to live at Ark II. Maybe even as, someday, *his* wife, legal or common law, it didn't matter. He wore no ring, didn't even have the telltale white circle around his finger revealing a ring's temporary removal. She'd dropped numerous hints, prompting no invitations.

She'd taken detailed notes and frequently referred to them as they sat sipping from glasses of the sweetened iced tea she'd poured for them and listening to her report at the tiny, round, linoleum-covered kitchen table, a scratched up and stained but treasured hand-me-down from her mother.

"Seems like the office is a no-go," Matthew said.

"Yeah. Seems like it'll have to be in the car on his way to work." So Darby could talk after all. "How 'bout the wife?"

"If we have to," Mathew said, "but that wouldn't make a lot of sense. Plus bad, bad publicity that."

"The kids?"

"Really?"

I can't believe they would harm the kids.

"I meant grab … kidnap. Same with the wife."

"Too much trouble," Matthew said. "Too much danger. It would be all over the news, day and night. Somebody'd see something. We'd probably end up having to kill 'em in the end anyway."

Surely they wouldn't do such a horrible thing.

The men sat there for an uncomfortable time in silence. *Like cows chewing cud,* she thought.

Finally, Matthew said, "Seems like there's only one possibility."

"Yeah, I think I know. Sniper?"

"Agree. Let's see what the Prophet says." Turning to her, "Anything else you can tell us?"

"One thing. I don't know if it matters or will help, but the boss of the bodyguard bunch is a big man. Very recognizable. What if I followed him?"

They chewed on that for a bit until Matthew said, "Not a bad idea. We'll discuss that with the Prophet too."

They got up to leave. This might be her last chance. "I'd like to meet the Prophet," she said, "and see where y'all live. I might even want to live there myself."

Unpleasant reaction from Matthew. Not hostile, but not welcome either.

"We'll also consult the Prophet on that. But you're doing an awful lot of good for us right here."

"But someday…"

"Yeah. Maybe."

"When will I hear back?"

"Not sure," he said and stood up, Darby following. At the door he turned back, "Let me have your notes. Need to burn 'em."

CHAPTER 28

O'Keefe decided to make their plea during the third Saturday worship service, which would leave one more weekly worship service and most of the following week for whatever qualification process the Ark people might undertake, and if they initially rejected him, there would still be time enough to adjust course, correct errors, and try one more time.

The Prophet sermonized. A couple of men and one woman prophesied. A woman spoke in tongues, and the Prophet translated the words that the Holy Spirt had elected to deliver in this odd way. O'Keefe couldn't help smiling and thinking, *He couldn't have just spoken English? He has to be multilingual.*

Then came a couple of rousing hymns. Rousing even to O'Keefe. These hootenannies were the high points of his Ark experience. Well, the *only* high points if you could even call them "high," the bar being pretty low.

There were rustling movements among the flock. Had he waited too long? Was it too late? A serious miscalculation. *Go. Get up.*

He stood, nervously, humbly clearing his throat, which he had to do twice, failing to gain attention the first time. He could almost feel, physically, the concentrated focus of the congregants on him, this exotic creature, a stranger.

"May I ... I really don't know how to do this, or even whether I should ... but I'd like to say something—"

"Of course, Peter," the Prophet said.

"It seems like my whole life has been a drifting, waiting for a wind to blow me somewhere, and not always to good destinations. One place it blew me was into the war in Vietnam."

He described in sometimes exaggerated detail the horrors of that: the heat, the foul smells, the incessant rains, the slogging through water and mud and monsoons, until there was no part of your being that *wasn't* soggy, drenched, and molding; the venomous snakes and other dangerous animals, small and large (one soldier had been devoured by a tiger, which was true, not just some soldier's tale). He told them how, as a door gunner, he'd witnessed almost daily the gruesome stream of casualties hastily jammed into the helicopter; how if they stayed too long on the ground, the aircraft and all its occupants would soon be torn to pieces by bullets and shrapnel, or so much worse, engulfed in flames from an exploding fuel tank. He recalled for them the men's groaning, cursing, begging for anyone, anything to ease the pain—except for those beyond pain, enshrouded in the infinite silence of death.

"But worst of all was what our so-called leaders, the politicians and the generals, did to us … sentencing us to wandering around—whether in the air like me or, so much worse, on the sodden ground—in that God-forsaken jungle … *Not* to win a war. *Not* to take territory. *Not* really even to defeat the enemy in any decisive way, but to kill enough of them that a body count could be reported back home … as if, even if the numbers weren't fudged, they really mattered. It seemed then and still seems now like an actual human sacrifice to some kind of vicious, inscrutable pagan god.

"And speaking of God, Yahweh, our Lord, I had no dependable religion to fall back on. I was born and raised a Catholic, and as a boy I was as devout as one could be. I was an altar boy and seized on every chance I was given to rise before dawn and track through the cold, the rain, the snow to church to serve at the daily Mass at 7 a.m. I said prayers in the morning on waking and again at bedtime. I wanted to be a priest, even a missionary, and if some heathen savage butchered me, then good, I'd become one of the Holy Martyrs.

"But once I got to college and absorbed the philosophy and message of the modern intellectuals … anti-Christian, anti-all religion, anti-all morality, I discarded pretty much everything the

Church had taught me. And anything left of it was thoroughly drowned in the monsoons of Vietnam and obliterated by the cries of those wounded and dying soldiers and the constant terror of constant battle that deadens your very soul after a while. And then only to return as an unwelcome stranger in my own land."

So, he explained, given the weakness in his character, his absence of belief, it was probably inevitable that he would surrender to alcoholism and eventually also to cocaine addiction. His poor wife, Sara, a blessing he hadn't recognized as a blessing at the time and certainly didn't deserve, had stood by him through all of it. And he couldn't explain what happened to him one day. A bolt from ... well, literally from the blue. Like Saul on the road to Damascus.

"But Saul knew what to do next. I didn't. I struggled every day with the impulse to return to the darkness ... until one day, aimlessly trolling through the TV channels as usual, I paused for a few moments on a sermon, one of the television preachers, talking about what Jesus said to his disciples: 'If anyone would come after me, let him deny himself and take up his cross and follow me.'

"Somehow that got through ... all the way down, down, down ... to some wisp of smoldering ember deep, deep, so deep down in my soul ... and it flared, just a little. So I kept watching those television preachers, even attended a few church services, read a lot, and in the course of that I discovered why all these terrible things had happened to me. I didn't know what to call it then, but I was living in the New Babylonian Captivity that the Prophet preached about here recently. It had corrupted me to the core, as it has with almost everyone in the whole world, and even now it was pulling me back into its vicious, bloody maw. I'd been too ignorant before to resist it, but now I had this spark of insight ... God-sent ... that's the only explanation ... because, like Saul, I was all the way in Satan's grasp without knowing it.

"And it made me angry. Full of rage. I wanted to strike out at what it had done to me, what it was doing to the whole world and everyone in it. But I didn't know how. I only knew I had to somehow find out how. And"—he looked at Sara now with as loving a gaze as he could muster, hoping she wouldn't laugh as she had done every time they'd rehearsed this—"I said to Sara, faithful and fearless handmaiden that she is and always has been…" And she smiled, but it looked like something beatific, not mocking as in their rehearsals. Nice move that. The smile, he thought, must have been a way for her to stifle the laugh and produce the opposite effect.

"…I said something like, 'Sara, we have a little savings, enough to support us for a few months. Jesus, our Lord and Savior, said, "Seek and ye shall find" and "take up your cross."' And of course she agreed, without hesitation, and we set out from Los Angeles, the very citadel of the New Babylon, and began wandering. But not a purposeless wandering. A real pilgrimage … to all the spiritual places we could find within our reach. And in the course of that we heard about this place, and we made our way here, and I have no doubt it was the hand of God that guided us here. And we want to stay. We've heard your call to arms. I was once a fierce warrior for a perfidious kingdom in an unjust cause. I want now to be a warrior for Yahweh. And Sara is a warrior too, a warrior fiercer than I could ever hope to be. Just ask the General, who's seen her in action for these many days now."

The General nodded slightly.

"So, as the psalm of David says, 'Lord, hear my prayer.' People of the Ark, hear *our* prayer. We pray you, take us in … Thank you."

The ensuing painfully long silence was finally broken by the Prophet. "And what does your Sara say?"

She was either a great actress or genuinely moved. O'Keefe thought he could see tears in her eyes.

"My prayer is exactly the same," she said. "Every word. I'm here to give everything I have, my entire being, my entire life to this community."

Usually, there was some level of callout when a congregant spoke. He'd expected at least some excited utterances. Instead, silence. They were all staring ahead, eyes on the Prophet, waiting for a cue from him, his judgment.

After another short but portentous delay, the Prophet opened his arms wide, then brought them together, his hands steepled in prayer. "Please know," he said, "that many of those here have suffered the same trials and tribulations that you have, Peter, including the earthly hell of alcohol and drug addiction. And low as they may once have fallen, they've been saved. I can promise you that I and the other Elders of the community will give full and prayerful consideration to your request."

He lifted both hands, palms up, pumping his arms, an instruction to rise up. The congregation exploded in applause, shouts, even screams of "Hallelujah!"

It lasted a long time. The McBrides beamed their gratitude.

CHAPTER 29

ON RAZOR'S EDGE, no word from the Prophet, only two days before discharge from the training program, Caleb appeared after dinner, retrieved O'Keefe and Sara from their tents amid the raised eyebrows and exchanges of "what's-going-on?" looks among the other trainees, and keeping unusually silent, escorted them to the Prophet's house. They weren't sure whether to be relieved or regretful.

Above the front door was a plaque:

ADULLAM

David therefore departed and escaped to the Cave
of Adullam. And every one that was in distress, and
everyone that was in debt, and everyone that was
discontented, gathered themselves unto him. And
he became a captain over them.

Caleb explained. "David, the slayer of Goliath, who ultimately became our great King David, incomparable warrior and poet of the psalms, escaped to the Cave of Adullam from the insanely jealous King Saul, who was trying to kill him because the people loved David so much." He pointed to the inscription. "And this describes exactly what happened with our Prophet and his first followers. I wasn't here then, but they even considered naming our community Adullam, but then"—he chuckled—"they thought it was a bit hard to pronounce and took some explaining, while the Ark was not only easy to pronounce but known to everyone in the world, needing no explanation at all."

O'Keefe wondered whether David was the Prophet's original first name or he had adopted it to fit this Scripture.

They entered into a spacious room with comfortable furniture. To the immediate left was a large dining area that served also as a meeting room where the Prophet met informally with his congregants as individuals, couples, or small groups. He now waited at his dining-cum-conference table, and they were directed to sit across from him. Caleb took a chair beside him.

After a few perfunctory pleasantries, the Prophet got to the point. "One thing we ask anyone who seeks to join us is to take what's called a VSA, a Voice Stress Analysis test. Ever heard of that?"

Sara clearly had not. O'Keefe thought he might have but wasn't sure. "You mean a lie detector test?" he said.

The Prophet cocked his head back slightly as a gesture for Caleb to take over, who said, "Not exactly. You're not hooked up to any wires. Just a microphone and a computer."

A shocker that.

Sara didn't respond, leaving it all to O'Keefe.

No way to say no. Don't even hesitate. "Sure," he said. "Never heard of it. Hope it's accurate."

No comment from the men of the Ark except Caleb's "Who'll go first?"

Hesitant, O'Keefe looked at Sara. No hesitation from her. "Me."

As she followed Caleb toward a hallway leading to the back of the house, O'Keefe guessed she must have decided it would be best to give him time to gather himself. But he wasn't sure that more time would help him stifle his thumping heart and quell his clamoring monkey brain. Meanwhile, the Prophet was making small talk. What had he just said?

"Sorry, sir. I missed that."

"Please ... not 'sir.' Call me David."

A good sign?

"I was lost in thought there for a moment," O'Keefe said, "considering that our heart's desire, really our entire future, might depend on some computer producing accurate results."

"We think that in this house Yahweh is likely to guide the computer to the right answer. I hope you can understand why we need to protect ourselves. The ZOG is always trying to plant spies in our midst. We've had some very unfortunate situations."

Unfortunate situations? Such as that informer who was probably caught out and killed and buried on the property? But go the other way now. Suck up.

"David, I understand completely. I support you one hundred percent in that. What scares me right now is there's so much at stake. I'm afraid I'd exhibit stress if you asked me my name."

The Prophet chuckled. "And that will probably be one of the control questions."

Great. First answer will be a lie. Or maybe I'll be asked to deliberately lie. They do that in polygraphs. "Is Peter McBride your name?" "No." That's the truth. Or supposedly the truth. But you were supposed to lie. We're in the deepest shit here.

The Prophet was saying, "I understand your discomfort. But we have to do it. I'm glad you understand *our* discomfort. Would you like a few moments alone? She'll be done soon."

"Not really. But I *would* like to visit the bathroom."

In the bathroom, no way he could actually *go* under these circumstances. All bodily functions were suspended. Except the chattering monkey brain. *Zen time. No strategy except STIFLE … QUELL. Answer in a monotone. Answer as soon as you understand the question. Don't judge it or your response. Que sera. Crazy Horse: It's a good day to die. But surely they won't kill us if we fail it … not with all these trainees here … just expel us … acceptable outcome. Yes, acceptable. STOP THINKING RIGHT NOW. THERE IS NO RIGHT ANSWER..*

She came out smiling. Was it fake? It looked real. But STOP. He didn't need to be entertaining troubling thoughts about that or anything else.

Caleb, smiling sweetly, beckoned O'Keefe to join him. They proceeded down the hallway that O'Keefe had traveled on his way to the bathroom. At the end of the hallway they came to two doors. The one to his left was open, the one to his right closed.

Pointing to the closed door, Caleb said, "That's our conference room. Or as we call it these days, the 'War Room.'"

Farther to the right, past the War Room, down at the end of the hallway, another closed door. Caleb noticed him looking and said, "Down there is another wing that's about as large as the entire rest of the house. That's the family wing for the wives and children. From there is an attached direct entrance to the Fortress, where you've been for Sabbath service."

Caleb guided him through the open door to the left. Each of the room's four walls was lined with shelving on the top half, and below the shelves, sturdy wooden tables that served as workspaces loaded with computers and accompanying monitors, a police scanner, fax machines, a large TV, and what O'Keefe guessed was a ham radio. On some of the shelves and the floor underneath were stacks of publications, some of them Ark-authored, on Christian Identity, survivalism, the coming Tribulation and End Times, the Illuminati, and perfidious Jewry including *The Protocols of the Elders of Zion.*

"You watch much television?" O'Keefe asked.

"Seldom. There's nothing and no one out there we want to see, communicate with, or even know about. But it comes in handy sometimes."

A wire led from a computer on one of the worktables to a monitor sitting on a smaller table, a chair on each side of it. An open notebook lay on the table on the screen side of the monitor and a wire led to a microphone on the back side. Caleb took the chair facing the screen and gestured for O'Keefe to sit opposite.

"Have a seat there, Pete. You'll be speaking into that mic."

He took a pen from his shirt pocket and let his writing hand hover above the notebook. "Please state your name."

The buttons on Caleb's shirt. "Peter McBride."

O'Keefe avoided looking at Caleb's face so he wouldn't react to any changes in the Chaplain's expression as he registered whatever he might be seeing on the monitor.

"What type of car did you drive here?"

Buttons.

"A Buick."

"Pete, on the next three questions I want you to lie … Ready?"

The slightest affirmative nod.

"Is your wife named Sara?"

Buttons. Woops. No monotone now. Be agitated.

"No."

"Did you grow up in Los Angeles, California?"

"No."

"Did you serve in the United States Marine Corps in Vietnam."

"No."

"Okay. Back to the truth now."

Did you grow up in Los Angeles, California."

Monotone … Buttons … I'm a mannequin. "Yes."

"Was your job there in a warehouse?"

Twenty more minutes of questions ensued, including a detailed exploration of the story he and Sara had been telling. *I hope her answers weren't different. Stifle.* Any prior arrests, prosecutions, jail, or prison terms? "None." *True, at least for Peter McBride.* Recent drug or alcohol use? "None." *True. But don't get proud about it. A day at a time.* His religious beliefs? *Uh oh. Really tricky. Deep breath.* "I know so little. I'm searching. That's why I'm here. That's why I want so much to stay here." *Mostly true. A little excited? Too sincere? May have lost the monotone. What the hell is that computer chart saying?* Finally, of course, a series of questions focusing on whether he was working for or with the "gov'ment."

At the end, O'Keefe had no idea how he'd fared, and Caleb wasn't providing any hints, saying only, "Okay. We'll be printing out the results and studying them, and you'll have a final answer, maybe as early as tomorrow morning."

Back in the dining room, Sara and the Prophet were chatting away like good buddies. O'Keefe tried to look relaxed but knew he wasn't pulling it off.

"So, how was it?" the Prophet said.

"Simple enough, but like I said, so much riding on it. Scary."

He wanted out of there. To Sara he said, "Ready?"

She was. They gave them a flashlight so they could make their way back in the dark.

"Well," she said once they were on their own, the flashlight beam bobbing in front of them. "How'd you do?"

"How would I know? For all I know, Caleb was staring at a blank screen on that monitor. How about you?"

"Like you. Can't say. I just hope all they do is reject us. Nice as this little Garden of Eden is, I'd prefer not to end up in an unmarked grave here."

"Look at the bright side," he said. "Maybe they'll honor a last request for a lakeview plot."

CHAPTER 30

Tʜᴇ ɴᴇxᴛ ᴍᴏʀɴɪɴɢ, after the showers but before breakfast, Caleb, looking something between noncommittal and grim, came to fetch them.

Following a step behind Caleb, they exchanged looks of curiosity and portent.

More than the Prophet were waiting. The Elders, most of whom they didn't know, except Sinclair and Darby, who they'd met briefly during the training, and the General. All were gathered around the dining room table, most of them stern of visage, the Prophet sternest of all. *A firing squad?*

"We've given the most prayerful consideration to your request to join us in our great mission here," the Prophet said, "and we must convey to you our deepest regret…"—O'Keefe's mind veered between regret and, oddly, relief—"that we haven't met you long before now. Please accept our most blessed invitation and welcome."

O'Keefe tried to muster tears or some other visible expression of fake joy, but he couldn't. He could only place his hand over his heart and say, "Thank you. This fulfills our most heartfelt dreams."

Sara's eyes danced, and she lifted her face to the sky. It looked real, and maybe it was. This seemed to have become some kind of holy war for her, though a much different one than the Prophet was waging.

"Don't thank us," Caleb said. "Thank He who brought this to pass."

This irritated the Prophet. "Through *us*. Brought this to pass *through us*."

"Yes," Caleb quickly agreed. "Of course. He depends on us to work His ways."

O'Keefe noticed a couple of the Elders smiling, but the General sat stone-faced, and Sinclair and Darby looked downright hostile. He wondered if there'd been dissension over this. Maybe they suspected, as he did, that this was a mere scheme of the Prophet's to lure into his web the blessed prize of a luscious new concubine.

"We must have a toast," the Prophet said.

His two wives brought in trays with small glasses of what looked like wine. The first wife, Naomi, seemed pleased; the second, Linda, did not. Naomi went directly to Sara and presented the tray to her.

Sara shook her head. "Thank you, but no ... Please serve the others first."

"I insist," Naomi said. "You two are the guests of honor today."

Sinclair refused a glass and left, Darby trailing. O'Keefe noted that both the Prophet and Caleb looked after them with concern, darting troubled glances at each other.

O'Keefe eyed his glass uneasily. The Prophet noticed and said, "Don't worry. Grapes only. No spirits. The Spirit of Yahweh is plenty enough for us."

O'Keefe wondered how careful they were about that but saw no alternative but to chug it down. *For the cause,* he thought, *but is it worth it? Doubtful.* He couldn't detect any alcohol and hoped the slight buzz he began to feel was from the sugar.

As they prepared to leave, the Prophet said, "Best to keep this among ourselves until the training ends. We wouldn't want anyone to get jealous of you or mad at us because we didn't invite them. But if they wanted to stay with us, they should have done what you did and announced themselves. We don't want the half-baked or the indecisive here. We have the greatest possible tasks ahead of us."

The General approached, unsmiling but not hostile. (*He's just that way ... always a badass.*) He nodded politely at Sara and shook O'Keefe's hand. "Welcome, Marine."

That lifted a burden, but the abrupt departure of the Sinclair-Darby duo still gnawed.

On their way back Sara was almost bouncing with joy. "We did it. Damn it, we did it!" For a moment, O'Keefe thought she might hug him, but instead she grabbed his shoulder and squeezed hard. Such an outburst of delight compared with her usual gritted-teeth determination to move on to whatever was served up next surprised him. It seemed out of character for the person he thought he'd come to know so well. He considered saying, "Be careful what you wish for," but held back, not wanting to spoil her special moment.

"I wonder," he said, "if that voice test was worthless, or even a deliberate, elaborate ruse, a way to scare us off if we were government spies."

Or a thought he kept to himself: Maybe neither of them had passed it but the Prophet wanted Sara badly enough to ignore the test results … Or maybe only Sara had survived it by telling them whatever truth there was about her past that she hadn't volunteered to her business partners.

The next day O'Keefe found Caleb and asked him about the General and Sinclair-Darby.

"The General's okay. He doesn't get happy about anything. His only comment was, 'Glad to have a machine gunner on board.'"

"But the other two sure didn't act okay," O'Keefe said.

"No, Sinclair's not. Never is. And Darby does what Sinclair does and doesn't do what Sinclair doesn't."

"Can you tell me what he said? I'd like to find a way to mollify him somehow."

"Sinclair is not a man to be mollified. A bad man in so many ways. When I came here, it was a gentle Christian community of devoted people, most of them ex-addicts of one kind or another, grateful that the Prophet had led them out of Hell. Look around at what they brought forth … out of a rough and tough wilderness … the very peaceable kingdom that Isaiah prophesied."

"I see that. What you've all done here is astounding."

"But the place has changed over the years. Necessarily so, I'm sure. First, the Prophet received the revelation that we must arm ourselves to defend against the hordes of starving marauders that'll be thrown up by the imminent Great Tribulation before the End Times. But the ZOG would not and will not leave us be. Harassing us with their unconstitutional gun laws. Trying to infiltrate and undermine us with their spies. Under the Prophet's guidance, we concluded that we were probably going to have to strike first … ignite the Great Conflagration ourselves. That brought along another kind of man. The General, for example. And Sinclair and people like him, including his sidekick Darby. They represented yet another evolution … or devolution … or an escalation … but, unfortunately, a necessary one. As Christ said, 'From the days of John the Baptist, the kingdom of Heaven suffereth violence, and the violent bear it away.'" So, Jesus told us that we must answer force with force.

"Sounds like you regret those evolutions."

"I certainly do regret them. But I see no way to avoid them. I believe that David Dodd has a special relationship with God Almighty and that the revelations and prophecies he experiences are real. I know they can be. I have had them myself … that closeness … that certainty that the Divine is speaking to you and through you. Some really are the Chosen, and some more Chosen than others. These days I just try to be … I guess you'd call it … maybe … a softening influence … Sometimes anyway."

O'Keefe took the risk of exploring a bit further.

"Is there something brewing I should know about?"

A long silence … until Caleb said, "Trust the Prophet. If there's something 'brewing,' as you say, it will be brewed in due time and ready to quaff in due time."

Keep going. "That voice test was so weird. I'm surprised we passed."

Smiling paternally, Caleb said, "What makes you think you passed?"

"We didn't?"

Caleb's smile deepened, and he brought his index finger to his lips. "Trust the Prophet."

CHAPTER 31

ONCE THE OTHER trainees had left for home, the "McBrides" were moved to an area of the compound closer to, though still away from and out of direct sight of, the main residential area. It was Ark II's version of the other side of the tracks, containing three house trailers, mostly used to accommodate visitors to the compound who were expected to remain for only short periods of time. But since their neighbors included two skinheads in one trailer and a scruffy single man in another, and there were two unoccupied timber-and-stone homes available, it likely signaled that their admission was probationary.

The new quarters immediately raised the issue of sleeping arrangements. The bedroom was predictably tiny, with a dinky bed topped by a thin, beaten-down mattress that two people were too many for anyway. The "couch" in the living room seemed more like a medieval torture device than a place to sleep. They set up an air mattress and sleeping bag in the front room and made sure to roll it up and stow it anytime one of them wasn't sleeping in it, so a visitor, entering surreptitiously or otherwise, wouldn't become suspicious and start some gossip about this unusual marital arrangement.

As usual, Sara insisted on scrupulously observed equality in regard to switching places daily, to which O'Keefe acceded with the comment that "the bed is actually more uncomfortable than the floor, and who knows who's slept on that mattress before."

At least they'd been sufficiently "admitted" to the community to receive several "welcome" baskets of food and an allotment of food stamps, and O'Keefe was issued the daily uniform of all the men: standard fatigues with special Ark II shoulder patches.

He was instructed to keep his M16 and expected to carry it slung on his shoulder everywhere except when working or at worship. Even at worship their firearms were lined up against the wall, close to hand. Sometimes, at the church door, the Prophet led them in a gun-salute, firing their rifles in the air without apparent concern that a bullet might come plunging back down and lodge in someone's noggin, which caused O'Keefe to brave the contemptuous looks and maneuver up against the side of the building as soon as the guns went off, guiding Sara along with him.

Sara retired her fatigues and combat boots in favor of long dresses with high collars and loose bodices with tight bras underneath. They "asked" her to help out in the school, which occupied a section of the Fortress building, a room for grades one through four, another for five through eight, and the third on the upper level for grades nine through twelve. The curriculum was a form of homeschooling utilizing few books beyond the Bible, the Protocols, and similar, all of them militant Christian, creationist, and racist.

One of Sara's duties was the supervision of the youngest ones in the small outside play area during recesses and lunch breaks. He sometimes visited her there. Watching and sometimes interacting with the children gave him a mental boost, little creatures not yet entirely corrupted by the Prophet's or any other ideology. As far as he could tell, the kids were just as happy as Norbert had claimed them to be, though he didn't think they looked any happier than Kelly and her friends at that age. One little girl especially delighted him. She didn't simply walk or skip or run but *bounced* as if her every step was charged with joy, her blondish mane bouncing along with her.

For the boys, a substantial part of each day was devoted to weapons training. Each was assigned and responsible for the cleaning and care of his own firearm. Twice a week, one of the men marched the boys to the shooting range while the girls read aloud from the Bible or other religious texts. According to Sara, the emphasis was primarily on passages describing their biblically determined role of dutiful submissiveness. In addition, the girls were schooled in Ark II's approach to home economics, most of which seemed lifted verbatim from a nineteenth-century primer on the subject.

The women, never the men, acted as teachers, except for Caleb's Bible classes and occasional visits from the Prophet or the General to make sure the children were being sufficiently fanaticized and militarized.

Naomi, the Prophet's first wife, was the unofficial principal of the school—unofficial but nevertheless holding absolute power, always subject to the men, but definitely over the women in her charge, which she exercised judiciously and with kindness to both students and teachers. Most of the other women failed to exhibit those traits. The Prophet was not the only gentleman in the compound lecherously ogling the new woman, who was younger than most of the others, as smart or smarter than almost everyone else, male or female, and blessed with a tomboy's athleticism in an ample female shape.

Sara was quick to register the hostile vibrations, understood their source, and tried to overcome them with sweetness and deference, a constant turning of the other cheek. Forget it. Most would have shunned her, or worse if Naomi hadn't protected her by staring them down whenever she overheard a catty comment or witnessed a snide stare, an unnecessary bump-into, or hostile snatch of a paper or book or crayon out of Sara's hand.

The women submitted meekly, at least in public, to the rule of their husbands, but the Prophet's recent taking of a second wife had been profoundly unsettling. The Prophet hadn't allowed the practice to spread beyond his own household—yet anyway—but the women seemed to suspect that many if not most of their men believed they would ultimately enjoy the "duty," as the Prophet phrased it, citing Scripture, to implant their superior white-man seed into as many deserving females as possible. And this new interloper, Sara, might turn out to be a reincarnation of Jezebel, tempting David and the rest.

Sara understood this was a special challenge for Naomi and Linda. Linda's hostility made sense. Being the new girl on the block, the woman had more to lose than the wife who'd already lost once, but she couldn't quite understand why Naomi was the essence of saintly, especially after having already been pushed aside for Linda.

They put O'Keefe on night patrol, which was a little scary at the start as he tried to remain alert to the possibility of stepping on a snake in the dark. Or worse, a land mine. But they had shown him how to recognize the mine placements so he could avoid them, and the mines supposedly could explode only after being "activated" from somewhere in the Prophet's house. He never got comfortable with that, worrying he might fail to remember one or more of the placements at the same time someone accidentally hit the activation switch. He made sure to keep his flashlight on and his attention sharply focused so he could detect the disturbed ground where the mines had been planted, thinking how this mine-sweeping was not exactly the kind of "detection" he'd anticipated to be a feature of his new Harrigan-decreed career.

His disquiet notwithstanding, the job quickly became excruciatingly boring. Sometimes he had a partner, which allowed them to take shifts, one dozing, the other presumably staying awake. But often he was alone. It was hard to stay awake on guard duty. In Vietnam, where so many lives had depended on a guard's alertness, it had been easier, but here, any intrusion seemed a mere long-shot, the night watch a foolish melodramatic precaution. Still, he wanted to prove himself to be trustworthy to the maximum. As soon as drowsiness descended on him, he'd shake it off and begin moving again.

He hung out near the lakeshore as much as possible. There he could splash water on his face or hope to catch an occasional cool breeze. The summer heat had arrived, accompanied by excessive humidity, reminding him, as so much here did, of Vietnam, but only vaguely; nothing could compare to that suffocating air. Mosquito swarms continued to attack, along with smaller pesky no-see-'ems that caused even more trouble because they couldn't be observed, felt, slapped, and killed. He could only console himself with the idea that this was the best way to learn the layout of the compound intimately, especially the placement of the mines, which might come in very handy someday.

The daylight hours also dragged on. The men were an impressively talented group in their way, far different creatures than he, and he envied them their skill with their hands and inventiveness involving seemingly any form of gadgetry. Many of them went out to work for hire on lumbering, agricultural, or general handy-man jobs in the local area. They hadn't encouraged O'Keefe to do that, and he saw no benefit to his mission in working off-site. Instead, he thought it best that he hang around and learn what he could. During the day, he worked as a construction laborer on Ark projects or attended to gardening, animal husbandry, basic landscaping, and clean-up type chores around the grounds. They also assigned him a number of tasks supporting the training operation, everything from lugging the coffee containers down in the morning to cleaning up spent shells on the shooting range.

They kept the place orderly and well-tended, the "peaceable kingdom" that Caleb had described, and O'Keefe had to admit that the residents, both adults and children, seemed content living this simple life. It made him think of the whole hippie "back to the land" commune movement of the '60s and '70s. And, indeed, many of these people were ex-hippies who'd fallen into addiction and had found a way out of that misery under the Prophet's ministrations. O'Keefe understood how desperate that affliction could be and that a person might do almost anything, embrace any solution, however delusional, as long as it removed the temptation to relapse. Creating all this from nothing was a testament to what ex-addicts could accomplish in recovery.

But here it was a Faustian bargain. Life in this Edenic peaceable kingdom required the surrender of their minds, bodies, and souls to the Prophet and his beliefs.

O'Keefe and Sara continued their late-afternoon and early-evening walks. Only during these sessions did they discuss their evaluations of the developing situation and struggle to figure out next steps. "Seems like everybody in the world is listening to each other," he said. "We shouldn't assume that they don't have some device hidden in our trailer. I've looked hard and couldn't fine one but still don't trust it."

Now allowed to roam more freely, they focused on the area deep in the brush thickets and woods at the farthest southern and western end of the compound bordering the lake, the area they'd observed from the motorboat with George and Karma. Using alternate entryways from the compound proper, alert for not just reptiles but also anyone following them or already concealed there for the purpose of spying on them, they often worked their way to the small strip of beach via various routes with varying degrees of difficulty, observing possible landing areas for a motorboat, a canoe, a kayak, or a swimmer.

"We should create a map," he said, "but I can't draw for shit. How about you?"

She could, but what if someone searched their place and their belongings and found it? How would they explain it?

"You're right," he said. "If we need it later, we'll have to produce it from memory … That is, if we ever get out of here. Garden of Eden it may be, but I'm beginning to understand why Eve was so tempted by that apple."

CHAPTER 32

Digging a ditch, apparently for the purpose of building yet another bunker that they always seemed to be feverishly constructing, wondering whether he was about to collapse from heat stroke or heat exhaustion (he'd never quite understood the difference, even though they'd lectured on it in boot camp), O'Keefe looked up to see Caleb approaching with a definite purpose to his step.

"Looks like you could use a short spell in the shade."

"You offering that? You might've just saved me from an early death."

"Yahweh provides."

They found an Ark-crafted wooden bench under some trees.

"Sara mentioned to Naomi," Caleb said, "that she's done a lot of work with computers and software programs and such. You may not be aware of it, but we've got a pretty darn sophisticated operation in that regard. For instance, we're tied into a modem network with other groups, and we've set up computer bulletin boards that let us all communicate with each other … without prying eyes and ears if you know what I mean. I'm in charge of all that; plus, I try to do word processing for the literature we publish. Even tried spreadsheets. David's come to *love* spreadsheets. But I'm no good at any of it, and it takes time away from my Bible study and meditation and writing, teaching, lecturing, sermonizing, which are the only things I really want to do. Being able to devote most of my life to those things is why I settled here in the first place and one reason I love it so much. I'd so cherish getting freed up from all that computer nonsense, but nobody else here'll volunteer to help even a little, let alone take responsibility for it."

"So Sara might help with that?" O'Keefe said, trying not to seem as eager as he felt.

"Not only might she. If she's really good at it, she'd be a miracle sent straight from Yahweh as far as I'm concerned. I'd *beg* her to help. I've spoken to David, and he's all for it."

Of course he is.

"Have you talked to her?"

He looked shocked. "Of course not. We'd never do such a thing without the husband's permission."

Since it seemed like a giant step closer to the inner circle and its secrets, Sara had no hesitation. O'Keefe had a little. "I guarantee he'll be pawing at you, and have you noticed he's big, looks strong?"

"I can handle it."

"Do I have to show you again how easy it is for a strong man to pin a strong woman?"

"That was when I was just a white-belt beginner. Now I'm a three-stripe blue and heading to purple. Want to try it now?"

He thought better of that. Little upside to winning, big downside if he lost. Not that he would be ashamed, but that she might be too proud of herself, enticing her into ever more daredevil undertakings. Smiling, he said, "I don't want to embarrass you again. Just be careful and not so damn cocky."

That evening Caleb came to the trailer. "We'd like Sara to come up and check out the operation."

O'Keefe thought about inviting himself, but Sara seemed to have anticipated that and stifled it with a quick shake of her head.

Caleb and David (he'd insisted she call him that, as he'd done with O'Keefe) escorted her to the same room where she'd taken the voice-recognition test, which they called the "Evangel Room."

After first proudly pointing to a switch on the wall ("That activates the landmines"), Caleb turned on one of the computers and nodded toward the monitor. "Here's a spreadsheet I've been working on. It's like pulling teeth for me … my own teeth."

"You're still using Lotus," she said, in a slight tone of disapproval.

"There's something else?"

"Ever heard of Microsoft?"

"Maybe."

"Ever heard of Microsoft's Excel?"

"Don't think so."

"It's the future … *and* the present. What's your word-processing software?

"Word Perfect."

"Now there's something called Microsoft Word. It'll dominate before long."

She sat down in front of the computer. "Tell me something you'd like to do on a spreadsheet. I'll work with what you've got until we can get Excel installed."

Caleb seemed uncertain how to respond, but David volunteered. "Let's say I want a list of every miracle Jesus ever performed with the name of the evangelist and a reference to the chapter and verse."

"Is that all? That's too easy."

"Well, how about estimated chronological order?"

"Give me some passages."

Easy for Caleb, who'd committed so much of the Bible almost to memory. David tossed in occasional suggestions as well.

Soon they beheld on the computer screen an exquisite spreadsheet with all the information clearly presented, as ordered.

"Jumps right out at you this way," Caleb said. "Almost more powerful even than reading the Good Book itself. Miraculous."

She showed them other ways the material could be quickly reorganized and presented. "With Excel you could do even more, and even quicker and more easily."

"I have a terrible time trying to print a spreadsheet," Caleb said.

David nodded. "You can say that again. What a mess."

Shortly, each of them held a printed spreadsheet.

"Now *this* is a true miracle," David said. "Loaves and fishes."

All felt the light in the room shift. A sudden new presence. Naomi stood in the doorway.

"I still need her at the school," she said. "I had first dibs."

"This *here,*" David said sternly, trying to squelch her, pointing to the spreadsheet, "is a *lot* more important."

"More important than the education of the children? That's foolish. Downright sinful."

Caleb rode to the rescue. "But this here isn't any full-time thing. She could do both."

Sara rose, bowed her head and spoke in reverent tone. "I'm here for you, night or day, twenty-four seven. It would be a privilege to help as much as I can."

On the spot they negotiated a sharing arrangement, Naomi holding her own in the negotiation with her two "betters." .

The next day, on returning from her duties at the Prophet's house, looking anxious and determined, Sara said, "Got to talk. Let's walk."

They headed for the lakeshore. "I thought these people would be a bunch of yokels," she said, "but they're far from it. That whole bulletin-board operation is cutting edge. They share all kinds of things and plan and plot with other groups. Some of the stuff these groups spew out … makes you very afraid."

"The usual targets?" he said.

"What else?" she said. "Jews, blacks, liberals, everyone and everything that isn't themselves. And it's not just that junk. It's more sophisticated than that. It's not just for propaganda, but to sell their literature and advertise their training program … and scarier … to scheme, conspire, plot, plan. They're close to achieving almost real-time two-way communication instead of having to wait hours or days for a response. That'll be coming soon, you can bet."

"I wonder," he said, "if they communicate with anyone in Southern California, specifically Los Angeles … maybe specifically looking for some help checking on the backgrounds of a married couple named Peter and Sara McBride."

"If so, we'd certainly know it by now. If they'd found anything, they wouldn't've asked me to do this work right there in the heart of things."

"Or," he said, "someone at that end hasn't found anything but isn't finished looking."

They were standing on the little strip of beach, the troubled water lapping at their feet as if trying to claim them.

"We know there's some bad people here," O'Keefe said. "And doing bad things and planning more, but we're not sure exactly what, or when."

Hints, signs, portents. But those wouldn't do. What they needed was *evidence*.

Looking out in the distance, his ruffled gaze matching the wind-ruffled waters of the lake, he said, "I can't let you be the only MVP on our team."

CHAPTER 33

O'KEEFE TURNED THE ignition key with trepidation. It was Sunday, and they were going to town.

The Buick's engine turned over twice without catching.

"Don't flood it," Sara said.

"Thanks for the sage advice."

He waited a minute, then tried again.

Both sighed with relief when it caught.

In town he found a pay phone and managed to roust George, whose first words were a worried, "You guys alright?"

O'Keefe said they were and briefly explained the current stalemate and his plan for breaking through it.

"They might follow you. What about that?"

"I've got a plan for that too."

"Be good to see you guys. What's it like there?"

"Terrible."

"Really that bad, huh?"

"First, go turn on the television and watch a few hours of one of those TV preachers. And it's eighty-eight degrees today. Turn off your air conditioning. I know you don't read much, but tonight try it by kerosene lamp, sort of Abe Lincoln style. And make sure to take a cold-water bath … outside, on a chilly morning—"

"I get it!" George said.

"And you?" O'Keefe said.

"Just hell trying to make sure these people stay in one piece. Hurry up and get those bastards."

"Tell Maxwell he's gonna have to get out his checkbook again."

On the way back they discussed the next step. The story would be that he'd called home to check on things. His mother, who was showing the first signs of senility, was having some issues including a recent fall. They needed to go back to LA to arrange some homecare for her.

"I shouldn't go directly to the Prophet," he said. "I'll go to Caleb first."

Caleb was sympathetic. He headed for the Prophet's house while Sara and O'Keefe waited for news in their trailer. When they heard the Chaplain's footsteps on the gravel path, they went out to greet him.

Looking around, Caleb said, "You know, we need to give you some better accommodations."

"That would be so nice," Sara said.

"I'll work on it. As for your problem, he asked that you come to dinner at his place tonight."

"Can you give us any hints?"

"I would if I had one. But I couldn't read him. He did ask if *both* of you needed to go. I told him I thought that's what you were asking."

Dinner was by candlelight even though the Prophet's house had electricity. Despite the hot and humid evening, the two wives served roast turkey with dressing, mashed potatoes and gravy, green beans, and dinner rolls.

The Prophet was cheerful. "It's Thanksgiving in this house every day."

Naomi seemed strained, embarrassed, Linda smugly triumphant and hostile toward Sara.

After some tortuous small talk—the Prophet again admonishing them to call him "David"—he got around to the issue. "So tell me about your mother."

O'Keefe told him the lies he and Sara had worked out.

The Prophet thought for a moment, then said, "It's very unusual to do something like this. When people come here, they leave all that out there in Babylon behind. Forever. Jesus himself said, 'I have come to set a man against his father, and a daughter against her mother, and a daughter-in-law against her mother-in-law, and a person's enemies will be those of his own household.'"

"I can understand that," O'Keefe said, "but our decision to stay here was so abrupt. We left everything behind in LA without any idea we'd end up here permanently. I feel, under the circumstances, I just have to go."

Scowling, the Prophet said, "I guess I can understand *your* need to go, but does Sara really need to? She's become invaluable at the school … Right, dear?"

Naomi, after a pause of reluctance, seeming well aware she was being drafted on the spot to serve in a manipulation, said, "Very much so, but—" David interrupted. "And we also desperately need her on the computers. I'm speaking more for Caleb than for me."

O'Keefe plunged in. "But she's always been very close to my mom."

The Prophet's scowl deepened.

"I mean," O'Keefe persisted, "like a daughter—" Now Sara interrupted. "Let Pete and I talk about it. Can we give you an answer on that tomorrow?"

The Prophet brightened. "Of course."

"Since it's an emergency, we'll get back to you first thing," she said.

"What was that about?" O'Keefe said. "I don't want to leave you marooned here."

"I think I need to stay. I think it might really hurt the cause if I don't."

"The horny bastard."

"True, but I don't think that's necessarily it, or all of it anyway. I think I'm sort of a hostage for your return."

"Or maybe he thinks my plane'll go down … or some other fatal harm'll come my way."

"You forgot one thing."

No guess from O'Keefe.

"Maybe I've just become indispensable to them."

He made a face. She made one too. "And not in *that* way."

Speaking of "that way," in that respect he welcomed a short separation. Living celibately in close quarters with an attractive woman was beginning to weigh on him heavily, inflicting on him unwelcome thoughts about "letting nature take its course," or even helping it along. *I mean, what's the big deal anyway? We've made this "that way" thing far more complicated than it ought to be, right?*

CHAPTER 34

Now O'KEEFE WAS certain they were following him. They weren't very good at it. One of the dented-up old vans in the parking lot kept appearing in his rearview mirror. Fortunately, his home city (his real one) was also the closest city with a major airport, the obvious place for him to take off for Los Angeles.

Halfway there he stopped at a pay phone and called George's car phone. "Is the ticket arranged?"

"Done. And the return too."

"And I have a cover story if someone checks on me in LA?"

"You do."

At the last exit before the airport off-ramp, he stopped again, this time at a gas station, and called George again. "Where are you?" O'Keefe said.

"Put it this way, Boss, you should be ashamed of that grossly wrinkled black shirt you're wearing."

"Do you see the dumbasses in the van?" O'Keefe said.

"Yeah. Those geniuses just pulled to the side of the road right across from you."

"I'll call you from LA."

The van followed O'Keefe, and George followed the van. O'Keefe pulled the Buick into the airport parking lot. The van stopped at the parking lot entrance, and a man jumped out and headed in O'Keefe's direction. George wished he could warn O'Keefe but wasn't sure how. He concluded he'd be better off sticking with the van, which U-turned from the parking lot entrance and followed the terminal access road until stopping at the doorway that O'Keefe and the amateur gumshoe behind him had entered.

George drove past it, pulled over a few yards in front of it, and watched in his rearview mirror.

The phone rang.

"Plane's on time," O'Keefe said.

"You've got a companion."

George did his best to describe the man he'd seen only from afar.

"There's a guy talking to the gate agent. Damn, I hope he's not gettin' on the plane with me."

"We've anticipated that possibility," George said. "If he does, call me from LAX, and I'll tell you what to do. When do you board?"

"Thirty minutes supposedly."

About forty minutes later, the man who'd followed O'Keefe exited the airport and climbed into the van. George trailed the van until it took the highway heading south in the direction of the lake country and Ark II.

Later that evening she watched a man carrying a small bag hurry out of the terminal and climb into Peter O'Keefe's car.

Just before he'd returned to the Ark, Matthew had said he'd consult the Prophet about her idea of tracking the one she had called the "big man," but she'd not heard from Matthew about that or anything else.

So she'd decided to seize the initiative.

Keeping up with the big man hadn't been easy. He moved around frequently, mostly going to Maxwell's house and office building, but to other places as well. On many days he ended up at his office in one of the former warehouse and light industrial sections of the town, now a "cute" area of old brick multistory buildings, but human-size, not even close to being skyscrapers. While a few stragglers from the old days were still being used for warehousing or distribution, many of the buildings had been renovated into offices, loft apartments, restaurants, coffee shops, and bars.

Sometimes, the big man would stay in the office for most of the day and often into the night. After a while, she felt she could sneak away at times, especially in the middle of the day, and go about her other business, though she didn't have much of it, only household errands, and could still drive by a couple of times a day to check that his car was still in his office building's parking area.

She even found a way to make godly use of the hours of waiting this duty entailed, having resolved to start at the beginning, Exodus 1:1 ("In the beginning God created the heaven and the earth") and read in precise sequence the entire Bible. In this way she had turned what some might call a fool's errand into the worthiest of pursuits. Charged with inspiration, she also bought herself a portable tape player. As she drove around trying to keep up with the big man, she listened to teachings of some of the leading evangelical ministers of the day. Even the Prophet himself had produced a few tapes.

One day she left her car and entered the building, but there was a security guard even at this older and smaller building. She approached a wall next to the guard, looked at the building directory and asked, "May I look? I'm not sure exactly where I am."

There were a number of names listed, and she asked if there was a security company in this building.

"I think you mean O'Keefe & Associates," the guard said.

She turned back to the directory and read the names listed under the company's name:

Peter O'Keefe

George Novak

Sara Slade

Kevin Shaughnessy

Dagmar Sibelius

"Should I call up?" the guard said.

She didn't know what to say but managed, "Oh … I'm not sure … thank you so much" and scooted out the door.

The big man had a commanding presence. He was there more than anyone else except for the young red-haired woman who was there even more of the time, sometimes bringing along her dog, a scary-looking German Shepherd, though sometimes the big man also brought what looked like the dog's twin. She concluded that he must be the boss, Peter O'Keefe, and she began referring to him that way.

On this day O'Keefe hadn't left until well after dark. It would probably be the usual. He might go to Maxwell's office or house, apparently to check on things, then to a restaurant or bar, the same one most of the time, or straight to his apartment. But this time her pulse quickened as he drove in another direction, and she realized he must be heading for the airport.

That was how she had come to witness the stranger with the small bag hustle out of the terminal and slide into the passenger seat of O'Keefe's car.

Since there wasn't much traffic on the highway or streets, she lagged behind as far as she dared, so far that at one point she lost them. O'Keefe was probably taking the stranger to some motel or hotel. She didn't know what to do other than to drive to O'Keefe's apartment complex. She arrived just in time to see the two men leave O'Keefe's car and disappear into the building. This was intriguing.

Well before dawn the next day she returned to the apartment complex so she wouldn't miss them if they left early, and she was rewarded for her initiative when the two men left the apartment right after sunrise.

They headed to O'Keefe's offices. A while after they'd gone in, one of the big black Lincoln Town Cars that shuttled the Maxwell family around pulled into the parking lot. That wasn't unusual. The Town Cars arrived there often. They would park, and the driver would get out and go into the building, probably routinely reporting in since this was the headquarters of the whole bodyguarding operation, meeting with the boss to discuss whatever bodyguards discussed with their bosses.

But this time seemed different. After the Town Car drove around to the rear of the building, she left her own vehicle and walked through the lot, hoping she looked like a wandering tourist and wouldn't raise the curiosity of anyone watching.

The Town Car was parked, its motor not running but the driver still there, sitting at the steering wheel. Someone must have left the car and gone in the back door of the building. It was first thing in the morning, the beginning of the workday. It occurred to her that it may have been Maxwell in that car. A meeting among Maxwell, O'Keefe, and the stranger that O'Keefe had picked up at the airport?

This may not have been a waste of time after all. Rather, it might be a special blessing on her efforts. The Lord *did* work in mysterious ways.

Driving away, her excitement overcame her. She found a pay phone booth, pulled over, and called in a page to Matthew.

CHAPTER 35

"There's definitely some bad people down there, and they've likely already done some bad things and likely planning some more bad things," O'Keefe told the small group around the conference table—George, Jack Shaughnessy, and Maxwell. "But until recently we haven't been able to get close enough to get any specifics. I know they're assembling an arsenal of everything from hand grenades to other explosive devices and automatic weapons. One of their big initiatives is to take semi-automatic AR-15s and turn them into illegal automatics and sell them. They've got a guy there named Rudy Acuff who's an anti-abortion zealot and expert bomb-maker. He's teaching them how to make every kind of simple booby trap, pipe bomb, and other exploding thing. It's worth looking him up if that's his real name, which I doubt."

Shaughnessy, taking notes, said, "I'll check."

"I think they've robbed a bank or two and done some experimental sabotage stuff like they did to you, Richard, including at a gay church in a town down in that area.

"Locals probably applauded that," George said.

"I'm sure," O'Keefe said. "And there's been dark hints that not long ago they 'disposed of' an informer they caught out. I paid special attention to that one. But it's almost all rumors, nothing specific, nothing evidentiary. And for all I know, they're cooking up something major and could strike anytime while I'm sitting there twiddling my thumbs.

"There's two classes of citizens. The old-timers, the people who were there at the beginning, most of them former alcoholics and drug addicts, so desperate to escape the hell they were living in they were willing to grab on to any piece of flotsam floating by. I know because I've been both. A few especially devout Christians have joined over the years, including a guy named Caleb Nathanson, who's not exactly second-in-command but sort of spiritual adviser, Bible study leader, religion teacher, and in-house author. Seems like a decent person in his heart, but he's the Prophet's lapdog and ventriloquist dummy.

"I'm not kidding when I tell you they've built something pretty special down there with their bare hands … put up sturdy wooden houses and other buildings, some with stone foundations, dug wells for water and ditches for electric lines, cut timber and raised crops and gardens, worked outside the place to bring in money they put in a communal pot. They're birthing their babies all on their own with just a couple of midwives, and educating the kids right there, if you can call it an education. Antigovernment, anti-entire-outside-world, it's all Babylon to them.

"And they believe what the Prophet's told them … that they're being attacked … that the government and all the forces of evil in the world are conspiring to destroy them. They're basically decent people who unfortunately believe a lot of nonsense, so they're always in danger of approving evil deeds and even doing them. Let's call them the Devout Dupes. Except for Caleb, the lapdog, they're mostly not in the inner leadership circle, the so-called Elders.

"But over time others have joined, especially as the Prophet's become more militant and more famous and increasingly admired in racist, survivalist, neo-Nazi circles. Very different characters than the Devout Dupes. I'd call them the *Unholy* Warriors. Not only do they hate blacks, Jews, and the whole government … the Zionist Organized Government, ZOG as they call it. They think it's their duty as God's Avengers to destroy it and all the related enemies along with it, starting with Jews and moving on through black people and people of any color other than pure white. They hate Mexicans, 'Indians,' whether American Native people or East Indian, and of course *A*-rabs who they refer to as 'sand niggers.' Even most white people won't be spared … the Communists, the 'nigger lovers,' in their phrase, and anyone who doesn't practice and believe their particular version of Christianity, which they may or may not faithfully practice themselves. Some are likely actual criminals but not yet caught.

"One of these Unholies, the chief one in fact, is a guy named Leon Lomax, but everyone calls him the "General.""

"I'll look *him* up too," Shaughnessy said.

"I'll give you every name I can remember. This General character is helping the Prophet whip everyone into a frenzy. He's the one who designed the training Sara and I attended."

"What makes you think they'll do anything other than talk, talk, always talk?" Maxwell said.

"Maybe you should get out those photos of your house and radio station and study them again … Rumors, but not just rumors. Slips of the tongue. Recent newcomers like Bomber Rudy Acuff. Lots of visitors from the local army base."

"Fort Maddox?"

"You bet. I think some of the soldiers are stealing weaponry for them. They're installing more landmines around the perimeter right now, probably fresh out of the Fort Maddox armory. But I can't claim I've come up with anything more than suspicions and speculations. And here's the bottom line. We don't want to hang around there for months, wasting your money and driving ourselves crazy."

"Speaking of my money," Maxwell said, "George tells me you're here because you want me to spend more of it."

O'Keefe nodded. "Sara's managed to find a good situation there, actually running their computers, bulletin board, and general communications operation."

"Bulletin board?" Maxwell asked, now even more alert.

"Yeah. It's a sophisticated network that lets all these groups around the country stroke and inflame each other, share intelligence, and plot their revenge on the world. So she's well positioned, but that's not enough. They won't let a woman, no matter how smart, into the inner circle. She probably got that opportunity mostly because the Prophet has the hots for her. Like his two existing wives aren't enough. But right now I'm stuck in the Devout Dupes group. There's no time for me to slowly and patiently try to work my way into the inner circle. We'll all hate ourselves if they do something terrible, whether it's to you, Richard, or someone else, while we're dawdling around down there. I need to do something heroic. I want to go back there with a decent pile of money and present it to them. I think that might get me where I need to go."

"How much?"

"Thirty thousand dollars."

Silence.

O'Keefe broke it. "I'm sure I don't have to point out to a numbers man like yourself, Richard … that's nothing compared to what you're paying us every month for spinning our wheels, plus all the protection required up here."

"What if it doesn't work?"

"It'll be time to pivot and try something else. At some point we'll have to just go to the police."

"You bet," Shaughnessy said. "You can't sit on stuff like this."

George laughed. "Spoken like a man with one foot still in the Department."

"No, not that, no way," Maxwell said sternly. "Sorry, Mr. Shaughnessy, but I don't trust the police to not screw it up. I'm afraid they'll decide they don't have enough to move. I want to get enough on our own and publicize it and make them look bad, or threaten to, so they won't have any choice but to move. Otherwise, I'll end up having to create my own witness protection program for my family … who's hating me right now by the way."

"I agree with that," O'Keefe said, "and this plan is the best chance of getting us exactly there."

"Okay," Maxwell said. "You've got it."

"Mixed bills," O'Keefe said. "Large denominations are okay, but not too much large. As much variety as you can give me. It needs to look like it's been assembled over time."

"That may take a couple of days."

"Hurry, please. I need to get back to Sara."

"How's she doin'?" George said.

"Fed up with it but soldiering on, exactly like you'd expect."

"How's she doin' with the Prophet?"

"If you mean, is he lusting for her, hell yes. He's moving slowly but moving. My plan was for her to come here with me. But he put the squeeze on, no pun intended, and she felt she had to stay. I'm worried about her being there too long without me there. Not that I'd do much good outnumbered and outgunned. If they ever find out what we're up to…"

Then, as he remembered Spud doing that day at the gun show, he slowly slashed his forefinger across his neck.

CHAPTER 36

In the classroom, concentrating on the too-tall pile of coloring books and crayons precariously balanced on her outstretched palms and forearms, she collided with the woman. It would have to be Martha, one of the worst—hardly ever any more than two or three words muttered through clenched teeth and never a friendly one, no expression other than scorn.

"Watch where you're going, you!"

Naomi intervened. "Martha, your manners."

"Yes, jump to her side. She's been your favorite ever since she got here. And *his* too. Everybody's favorite. You'll regret that. She's wormed her way in. She's smarter than all of us. Look at her. She doesn't even look like us. I think she's a damn Jew."

Sara shoved the woman hard and sent her stumbling backward, reeling until she fell flat on her back.

"Help me," the woman said, struggling onto her side, trying to rise. "Look what she did."

"No violence here," another woman scolded.

"How about verbal violence?" Sara said. "How could you say anything worse than calling me a kike?"

Naomi barked, "Stop it now. Martha. That was a horrible thing to say. And Sara, we mustn't resort to violence. Turn the other cheek, as Jesus said."

"Not for that. Not for calling me the worst thing she possibly could."

"Worse?" Martha said. "Oh, I can do a *lot* worse. How 'bout Jezebel? How 'bout Jew whore?"

"Martha!" Naomi shouted.

Sara turned and hurried out of the room and the building. Outside, she paced back and forth.

Naomi joined her. "You need to come back in. The children need us. I'll deal with Martha."

"Do they all hate me?"

"No. Not all. Some are jealous and mean. It's the smallest of small towns."

The situation offered Sara the chance to tell Naomi something she'd been wanting to share but hadn't found the right moment. "I would never do anything … not anything … to try to seduce your husband or respond to any advance he might make toward me. I don't want you to ever suspect me of such a horrible thing. I love my husband. I love you. I love—"

"Enough, child. I believe you. Now let's go back in … And hold your head up high when we do. You've got nothing to fear or be ashamed of."

O'Keefe arrived in the early afternoon, unloading from the Buick the bag he'd left the compound with, plus a new smaller gym bag. He was sure the guard would report his arrival to headquarters by walkie-talkie, and he headed directly there.

Wife Linda opened the door for him and led him to the back of the house to a door to the room next to the Evangel Room where the Prophet, Caleb, the General, Sinclair, and the other Elders were gathered around a table studying some intriguing looking papers including a map.

Caleb smiled. The others didn't register much, except Sinclair's expected hostility.

"How's Mom?" Caleb said.

"Stable, for now, but I don't know how much longer she's got." *Might need another trip soon. Poor Mom.*

"We were wondering," the General said. "It took you longer than we thought it was supposed to."

"I decided I needed to make a more substantial offering to the collection plate."

He set the gym bag on the table and reached to open it.

"Stop!" Sinclair yelled, leaped up, grabbed O'Keefe by the collar and thrust O'Keefe's head down and over the bag. "Unzip it. If there's somethin' nasty in there, you're gonna get ugly fast."

"Matthew!" the Prophet said.

Sinclair wouldn't be brooked. "Unzip it."

O'Keefe resisted the impulse to physically resist and did as he was told.

Looking down into the open bag, Sinclair's expression changed to disappointed chagrin.

O'Keefe shook off Sinclair's grip, turned the bag over, and dumped the contents onto the table.

Eyes widened and smiles followed as the greenbacks cascaded out.

"Where in the world did you get it?" the Prophet said.

"Let's just say I know a fool and his money, and now he's just a fool."

"Is anyone on your tail?"

"Not a chance. The fool won't know who did it and is guilty himself, so he can't even report it to the cops."

The joy continued unabated, each of them, aside from Sinclair and Darby, approaching and vigorously shaking his hand. A couple of them hugged him tight. Even the General thanked him with, miraculously, the whisper of a smile.

But not Sinclair. He remained aloof, ignoring the Prophet's disapproving glances. As the meeting broke up, he drew O'Keefe aside and said, "I think you're a fraud, asshole." He pressed his finger below O'Keefe's collar bone and drew an imaginary vertical line down his chest. "If I catch you, I'll gut you … slowly … until you're squealin' like a pig. Your woman too. Count on it."

Caleb walked with O'Keefe back to the trailer. "You can't know how important that money is to us right now. It gets us where we need to be. We're beyond grateful."

"I'm afraid not everyone is." O'Keefe told Caleb what Sinclair had said and done.

"He only speaks for himself, no one else … except Darby."

"Are you sure? Not the Prophet?"

"Sometimes. But not always. Unfortunately, we need some people like him. And the General too. A necessary evil in these terrible times." He walked along, looking down, pondering, then lifted his eyes to heaven. "To protect what's been created here. A city on a hill. A re-creation in the evilest of evil times of what the Pilgrim and Puritan fathers, fleeing, like us, from persecution in their own country, originally envisioned for the new land of America."

His comparison seemed eerily apt. They held much of the same belief system as the Puritans 250 years earlier. Both had embarked on an errand into the wilderness, to carve out a new world for themselves, in flight from a world they rightly or wrongly believed persecuted them and denied them the right to their beliefs, repairing to a far-away land where they themselves could, without interference, do to others exactly what they believed had been done to them—zealously persecute and deny the rights of anyone with beliefs different from their own.

Caleb continued, "We need those kind of men because the ZOG will just *not* leave us be. They're always nosing around, trying to find something we're doing wrong, sending spies in here to frame us. And there's that so-called Brady Bill moving through Congress, which refuses to die. They're gonna take our guns from us, the last line of defense. They'll have us at their mercy."

"We won't let that happen," O'Keefe blurted, wanting to dam up the flow.

"Yes," Calebe said. "I still have unshakable faith in God Almighty … that his promises to us will be fulfilled, and that David, our Prophet, is one of his special instruments. During these End Times there will be the Great Tribulation, but the elect will triumph amid the carnage. I'm so glad you and Sara have come here and become our partners in our holy mission."

Mission, yes, O'Keefe thought. *But a different kind of holy than yours, Caleb.*

CHAPTER 37

THE FIRST SIGN that their status had changed was the move from the trailer to a house in the residential section of the compound, the same house that Linda's elevation and Norbert's departure had left vacant. *Same house, new Linda, new Norbert. Hopefully not.*

The next sign was the General's early-morning knock on the door. "I'm taking you on a special tour."

He first showed O'Keefe several impressive bunkers dotted around the residential area. "There are a few more of these near the front entrance and at various other access points around the property. Imagine the fields of fire, the devastation we'll be able to wreak on them when they attack us."

In what the General jocularly called "the machine shop," one man was busily converting AR-15s to full automatics, equipping machine rifles and pistols with silencers, and assembling homemade grenades. Another man worked at a table dismantling and adding something to individual bullets. The General stopped and looked on the work with obvious pride. "We're treating the tips of those sugar babies with cyanide. So no wounding. If they're shot, they die … very painfully."

They walked to a separate shed deeper in the woods. "This is Rudy's place," the General said. "We keep him well separated, so if he makes a mistake, he'll only blow himself up … or"—he chuckled—"those unlucky enough to be visiting him at the time."

Rudy was working underneath an especially bright overhead lamp. He looked up from the device he was attending to with a go-away grimace. Clearly, the usually dominatingly arrogant General knew his man, adopting an entreating tone far from his usual one.

"Come on, Rudy. We won't bother you for long. Give Mr. McBride here a look at your handiwork."

With a sigh Rudy complied. Laid out neatly on several tables were various types of pipe bombs. Rudy identified other more mysterious items as types of booby traps and other explosive devices. Some were "time bombs." Others could be triggered by remote control.

On another table, land mines. The General seemed especially proud of those. "We're considering burying more of these around the perimeter. They'll explode when stepped on, but harmless until activated, which we control from headquarters. That way we make sure our people don't get accidentally hurt. But when *they* come for us, we'll blow them into Hell where they belong."

"So I'm not in danger from those when I'm walking guard?"

"Not until we set the trip on them." He smiled. "We'll likely let you know. Better behave yourself."

But O'Keefe still had his doubts about whether all that was foolproof. He planned to continue, as he walked, to carefully scan the forest ground in front of him to ensure he'd never step on one, supposedly inactive or not.

They moved out of the deeper part of the woods to a padlocked shed.

"Now a final and special treat for *you*, Marine."

The General unlocked the door and flicked on a light bulb. "This is our arsenal of very special weapons."

AR-15s resting on hooks, presumably converted to full automatic, lined the walls along with grenade launchers. Below them sat several washtubs brim-full with grenades.

"And there's more where those came from. We've got direct lines into the armories at more than one Army base. It's amazing how sloppy their procedures are. They haven't even missed these yet."

In one corner stood a large metal barrel with a padlocked lid. "And that?" O'Keefe asked.

"There's enough cyanide in that barrel to poison a small town, maybe even a big chunk of a city. We're trying to figure out the best plan for it. If you have any ideas, the suggestion box is open."

In the middle of the room, directly under and spotlighted by the overhead bulb, were items he couldn't fail to recognize as the ones he himself had wielded as a machine gunner in Vietnam—the M60s he'd humped in his early days as a grunt and, in the center of the array, three M2 Browning .50 caliber machine guns, the terror-inflicting "Ma Deuces" or "50 cals" from which he'd fired what seemed like millions of rounds as a door gunner in CH-46 helicopters.

The 50 cals boasted far more firepower than the M60s, but they were too heavy to hump around in the jungle. They were not even used in lighter helicopters for fear of knocking the aircraft off course or even shaking them to pieces. Though mounted on a sturdy tripod attached to the floor of the helicopter, the monster still had rattled his bones as he'd fired it. He'd taken down trees with it. Anyone trying to shield themselves in the jungle had little hope of surviving concentrated fire even from 300 yards above.

"Can you imagine the massive wall of fire that we'll greet those ZOG bastards with when they come for us? And if we take it to the streets, think of one of these 50 cals blasting out of each of the windows on both sides of a van and a couple of 60s pouring lead out of the open rear doors."

"Slaughter," O'Keefe muttered, more to himself than to the General.

"You're the first actual machine gunner we've had here. I'd like to set up a couple of these and get you re-acquainted with them."

"Love to." But it was about the least appealing thing O'Keefe could imagine.

CHAPTER 38

S UCH A DIFFICULT trip. She couldn't remember traveling for this many hours in a car since she was a motion-sick, bored-to-death kid in the back seat with her sister and brother while her parents worried aloud and bickered over whether they would run out of gas before the next service station or the engine would overheat or a tire blow—the two longest days of her life up to that point as they slogged along on summer vacation to somewhere not even close to worth the trouble.

Here, today, she bickered similarly, with herself, as she made the long trip to the New Ark. The two-lane roads down here in the lake and hill and forest country, up and down and winding around, had been, improbably, simultaneously terrifying *and* boring. Much of the time she'd been stuck in a line of cars that stretched not just ahead of her but also behind, because no way was she going to risk passing another car only to face some daredevil bearing down on her from the other direction. So drivers behind her had to risk passing her in order to overtake the car in front of her, one of them shouting and flipping the bird as he heedlessly zoomed by in his pickup truck with a rifle in a gun rack visible in the truck's rear window. She slowed down even more, hoping he'd get far away. Who knew what violence a crazy person like that might inflict for even the most minor and unintentional slight?

Even more worrisome were the long stretches on obscure roads. What if her crappy little car broke down? She was alone. What would she do? What kind of nuts were roaming around out here? Would she just end up as scattered bones in the woods that some hunter or hiker later stumbled upon? ("Damn, Bill, that looks like a piece of skull there ... Human, ya think?")

Much worse had been these last miles bouncing along the merely bulldozed, rutted, dirt and rock sort-of-a-road through the forest, rocks bouncing up and smacking against the bottom of the car, nothing but curves, most of them blind ones, though it quickly became obvious that no one would be coming the other way. If one of those rocks punctured a tire, she had no idea how to deal with that or how far she'd need to go for help. Would there even be a house out here? And what might await her when she got there?

But she had no choice. She had to brave it. Matthew hadn't answered her page, and the news of the strange visitor picked up at the airport and the meeting at the O'Keefe offices with Maxwell seemed too potentially important not to convey to Matthew and the Prophet.

Suddenly it was upon her. No sign or other identifying marker, only a well-graveled side road maintained far better than what she'd just endured. Was this the place? Didn't it have to be?

She took the turn but began to wonder as the road kept going and narrowed even more, shrunk narrower and narrower. Overhanging tree branches brushed against her car.

So much relief when, after a particularly narrow stretch, it finally opened up into a clearing with cars and trucks and vans parked in a graded area.

Beyond the parked vehicles two men popped up, apparently from sitting positions. As she approached them, she could see the rifles slung over their shoulders, which made her a bit anxious, but only a bit, because that must mean she was in the right place and that these were good Christian soldiers.

She pulled the car around. One of the men, leaving his rifle shouldered but looking hard, mean, and menacing, thrust out the palm of his hand to halt her. He gestured wildly and shouted for her to put the car in park, turn it off, and *"Exit The Vehicle!"*

Now scared so much that her cheeks and lips were quivering, she blurted out she was a friend of the Ark, particularly of Mr. Sinclair (what if he wasn't here anymore or had gotten himself in trouble here or...), and she had important information for them.

The guard turned to his companion and said, "Go tell them at headquarters. If they wanna talk to her, tell 'em to send a lady out here to frisk her before we let her in."

After the other man left, she was told to "leave your car and have a seat." The guard gestured to an empty chair. She did as instructed and tried to engage the gruff fellow in small talk, but to no avail. Time crept slowly, her mind skipping between fear of rejection and the anticipation of … could she dare to hope? … a new life with these good people.

The second guard returned with a woman who introduced herself as Linda and said, "Sorry, but I need to inspect you."

The gruff guard watched carefully as Linda gave her a gentle but thorough going over while the second guard modestly looked away.

Finishing, Linda said, "Come," and led them on a path into the compound.

Looking around as they walked along the edge of the Gathering Ground, taking in the Prophet's house, the Fortress, the houses sprinkled below, she gasped. "It's so wonderful … what you've done here."

"Thank you. We've worked very hard … You'll be meeting with David, the Prophet."

She lost some of her breath and put her hand over her heart as if to muffle its beating. "How wonderful. And … Matthew … Mr. Sinclair?"

"We've sent someone to find him."

They entered a large house built in the style of a log cabin. The furnishings looked soft and comfortable. A man sat at the head of a large table with only a glass of water and what she assumed was a Bible, battered and worn as if from long and frequent use. He didn't rise to greet them but gestured for her to sit down. Linda faded away.

He reached his hand out to her, and she realized he was offering to shake hers, which she proffered limply as he said, "I'm David."

"It is so wonderful to be here … to meet you."

"And it's wonderful to meet you. What can I do for you?".

As it all came pouring out, he didn't interrupt, just engaged her with his captivating deep blue eyes. What she had done for

Sinclair and Darby earlier. What she had done all on her own since. What more she thought she could do. The big man, Peter O'Keefe. The strange visitor. The meeting at O'Keefe's offices.

After she could find no more to tell him, he reached across, took both her hands in his and said, "So wonderful. A gift from God Almighty. Thank you."

A noise came from behind. She turned. Not Linda, a different woman, and behind her—*him*—his face stern, impatient, disapproving. But she was used to that. He exuded strength, power. She dared to venture a glimpse up at him. He said nothing but strode confidently forward, hardly looking at her, and stood in front of the Prophet.

The Prophet said, "Naomi, give this wonderful lady a tour while Brother Sinclair and I have a talk."

This was not a request. Even a perfunctory "please" had been omitted. It was a command, though not an unpleasant one, easy to accept without question, from a man worthy of being obeyed. She quickly stood and followed Naomi.

"Sorry," Sinclair said, taking a chair. "I can't believe she showed up here."

"So *that*," the Prophet said with a sly grin, "is how you were so successful in surveilling Maxwell."

Sinclair's head jerked slightly, a defensive flinch. "Yeah, I thought she'd be less conspicuous. Not so smart, I guess. A silly woman—"

"Quite smart actually."

The Prophet told him about the work she'd undertaken on her own. "Matthew, this is more than a piece of information. It's a sign from above, blessing our work, bestowing on us a new and potentially powerful weapon, however humble seeming at first look … this veritable Judith, reborn and sent to us by Yahweh."

Sinclair didn't look convinced but did look relieved that the negative reaction he'd seemed to expect hadn't manifested.

"It's coming to me from Yahweh like a prophecy. You need to go on up there and work with her, coach her, direct her."

"I need to be here for the planning, the preparation. Don't exile me."

"We'll bring you to us down here when it's time. But don't be a stubborn, blind fool. You'll be playing the most valuable role of all. Embedded"—winking at his pun—"up there with her as our eyes and ears. You'll be in place, poised to strike the first blow. As at midnight on the very first Passover, our own Angel of Death, putting to sword the firstborn of Pharoah's Egypt. You've been anointed, Brother. Don't refuse the call."

"Is that an order?"

"No. It's a call from Yahweh to do his work and fulfill his prophecy. Refuse it at your soul's peril, and maybe peril to our mission as well."

Sinclair nodded grimly.

The Prophet smirked, and in case Sinclair had missed his point, said, "And I do mean 'embedded.' Don't tell me you haven't dipped into that pot of honey."

Sinclair frowned and shook his head. "No way. Darby was there the whole time. And I'm not sure there's honey in that pot. Might just be shards of old dried-up pottage."

"The prophecy reveals to me that it will be otherwise, A true reward for your devotion. She's obviously hungry for you."

Sinclair's face said he wasn't convinced or even interested.

"But you won't refuse the call," the Prophet said, his blue eyes probing.

"I'll do your will."

"Not my will, Brother. *His* will."

Walking down the path to the parking lot, hearing the powerful soothing crunch of his boots close behind her, after so many years of faithful but feckless devotion to the Lord, unrequited longing, unanswered prayers, now an inward SHOUT of joyful thanksgiving. The triumphant words of the Psalm came to her (oh, how her immersion in the Psalms had given her comfort on so many lonely days and nights):

I prayed to the Lord, and he answered me.

He freed me from all my fears.

Those who look to him for help will be radiant with joy.

No shadow of shame will darken their faces.

In my desperation I prayed, and the Lord listened.

He saved me from all my troubles.

She'd hoped they would take her into the community immediately. That was not to be. At least not yet. But this could be even better, so much better. He'd taken less than an hour to grab some things and load up his car. He would be following her home. He would be there, living with her, in her second bedroom; at the beginning anyway; but surely they wouldn't be separate for long; surely that gift would not much longer be withheld from her. And this time, no Darby. She would now have the chance to show him in so many ways what a soft and useful handmaiden she could be.

Her leave-taking was so much more wonderful than her entrance. The lapse of only a couple of hours had made all the difference. Those hours had changed her life. The guard who'd been so nasty, now so much more respectful, virtually stood at attention as she passed. His colleague, the second guard, rushed to open her car door for her (she couldn't remember the last time anyone had done that).

"Safe travels," he said.

"Thank you so much," she said, then smiled and looked him directly in the face.

He responded in kind with the nicest smile. A thought passed through her mind. This second guard looked somehow familiar. Had she seen him before? And if so, where…

But here was Matthew, pulling his car up behind hers and blinking his headlights, prodding her to move on.

Yes, go on. She had a purpose in life now and the promise of reward for her devotion to it. *Get back on the paved highway before darkness falls.*

CHAPTER 39

"MARINE, REPORT TO the firing range at dawn tomorrow," the General said, somewhat jocularly but with a serious edge.

O'Keefe wanted to tell the General to stick it, but this was a necessary move in the game he'd agreed to play.

The early morning was cool, with even a light breeze—a moment to be enjoyed in the peaceable kingdom. But no lingering allowed. The General stood at the rear door of a van they'd placed on the firing line. O'Keefe joined him there. The General yanked the door open, and O'Keefe was staring into the barrel of a Ma Deuce mounted on a tripod.

The General turned and pointed behind them. At the far end of the range they'd parked one of the more decrepit old cars he'd seen in the parking area. With the broadest smile O'Keefe had ever seen on that stern visage, the General said, "We've already thoroughly pirated that junker for parts. Nothing useful left of it. You get to provide it an honorable execution, Marine. Get up there and have at it."

O'Keefe climbed up and knelt behind the gun. The carpet that had once covered the bed of the van had been worn down to almost nothing. "This" he said, "is gonna tear up my knees."

"We can get you some knee pads … next time."

O'Keefe maneuvered to make himself as comfortable as he could and looked through the sight, though pinpoint precision had almost never been required in this job.

His job … the first time looking through that sight in twenty years…

The most dangerous job in the war for an enlisted man? Maybe. But maybe not quite so much in this particular version of the job. Not as dangerous as some. When they showed him the weapon he would wield and the aircraft he'd be firing it from, he couldn't immediately absorb the implications for his own life, its length and the possible date of its termination. But it turned out that he wasn't fated to be a true "shotgun rider," the guy seen in so many photos and films, entire body exposed and unprotected at his perch in the entry door on the right side of his relatively small, slow, thin-skinned and highly flammable CH-34 helicopter, feet dangling out, vulnerable to whatever fire might be directed at him from below, a bungee cord wrapped around his waist to keep him from plunging to the ground—that is, if he wore it, many didn't, risking free fall to their deaths in exchange for more freedom of maneuver—shells clattering on the deck behind him as he fired hundreds of rounds in a sweeping, traversing field of fire down onto the LZ while their flying tin can attached to a 300-gallon gas tank bomb descended into a maelstrom of enemy mortar and automatic weapons fire concentrated on nothing other than blowing them out of the sky. Their primary—well, really, their *only*—defense against that fiery funeral—the shotgun rider's M60 and his ability to fire enough rounds in great numbers and in the right places to keep enemy heads down so they couldn't fire at all or at least couldn't effectively aim when they did.

Maybe, O'Keefe thought at the time, his was only the *second* most dangerous job in the war for an enlisted man. His weapon, it turned out, wouldn't be the M60 of the shotgun rider, but the Ma Deuce, weighing eighty-five pounds without tripod (one hundred and thirty with) to the M60's twenty pounds. Not a weapon you carried. No hanging out of the door with feet dangling. This was a weapon set on a tripod firmly affixed to the aircraft, a weapon you stood, or crouched, or sat behind, gripped the handle with both hands and triggered a flood of death with bullets six times more powerful than an M60's and that could travel three times farther, sweeping the tree line with fusillade after fusillade, sometimes taking down entire trees.

This monster gun, so powerful they were afraid it might shake a smaller aircraft to pieces, required a monster helicopter to match. Thus, the recently revamped and reintroduced CH-46.

It was an odd-looking thing, nicknamed the Phrog because it resembled that awkward-looking amphibian, especially when bouncing down the runway in a series of what looked like frog jumps. It had not one but two motors and attached propellers, one in front and one in rear. The Marine Corps, the poor relative of the armed forces, as usual having to make the best it could with limited resources, employed this one chopper for almost every function in helicopter warfare: dropping troops, evacuating troops, medevac, flying hearse, supply ship. It could carry thirty troops (forty-five if they were the much smaller and lighter South Vietnamese ARVN soldiers). It could carry heavy equipment, entire vehicles. It could rescue far more wounded and dead than its predecessors.

Still, like the others, it was only a flying tin can. Bullets penetrated it too easily, as they often discovered once they landed back at base and inspected it. But for the door gunner it provided a marginal but real increased hope of a longer life expectancy, mostly because it could accommodate that terror of a beast, Ma Deuce, but also because the side opening was only half as large as the one that framed the shotgun rider; and only the top half of the aperture from which the Ma Deuce was fired was open, the bottom still only the thinnest metal sheet but at least providing a modicum of additional protection, and, more important, offering a smaller target. It was a window more than a door (and O'Keefe often thought that *this* job should be called "window" gunner).

Luckily, it was a job for the deficient soldier he knew himself to be, the dunce of the ship, the inferior by uncountable degrees of the other three crew members. The crew chiefs, men not to be envied but certainly to be admired, only enlisted men but the real "owners" of "their" aircrafts, the wizards who lovingly cared for these machines and understood them enough so that under the most intense stresses those machines wouldn't go haywire and kill their occupants, and accomplishing all that while also often doing duty as a second gunner on the left side. And then the pilot and co-pilot, who had to actually be both brave *and* competent under fire, improvising life-saving solutions to problems flashing in their faces at dizzying pace.

Every moment in the air he was glad that his life was in all their hands and not his own.

As door gunner, O'Keefe almost never had to actually think, only observe and report over the radio to the pilots as they approached an LZ. The handles of this weapon he gripped with both hands, one on each side of the barrel, allowing him to steady those hands, no M14 rifle barrel nervously circling around a bullseye. Just find the most likely enemy hiding places and unleash traversing, devastating curtains of fire accurately enough to keep enemy heads down and ducked, or up and fucked.

When he thought about it, which he tried not to, it seemed so much safer to be flying high above in that tin can strapped to a gas-tank bomb, which a bullet or piece of shrapnel could ignite and fry all of them like hot dogs over a campfire, than to be a grunt below, with his feet firmly on the ground but with hardly any field of vision, no view of anything but the impenetrable green of the jungle, no idea where and what, hidden in that jungle darkness, would soon bring death or maiming to you as it had done to three of your fellow grunts yesterday and two others that morning.

Not that he wasn't still terrified, but the mind-numbing noise of the motors was enough all by itself to drain out some of his sanity and some of the fear with it, until he somehow managed to think of nothing but the current moment; not the next moment or the next after the next, just that immediate one, as they swooped down in an adrenaline-surging whirligig swirl of flashing images amid the roar of motors and machine guns.

Hovering a few yards above the ground, they avoided landing whenever possible, avoided even touching the ground at all whenever they could keep from it. And if they did have to land— *Quick! Get the fuck in and out of there! Get those boys! Live, wounded, dead. Fast! Fast! Fast!* Because a stationary helicopter on the ground was the essence of the fundamental existential concept of the Sitting

Duck—the pilots always saying things like "Don't fly low, slow, and stupid" and, most bracingly of all, "On the ground more than thirty seconds, you're dead."

Moreover, the closer they were to the ground, the more the gunner lost the edge that elevation had given him, and things equalized or worse. He would love to know precisely how many bullets he'd dodged—well, more accurately, had dodged him—but he knew it was a high number because he could hear them pinging off the side of the aircraft or penetrating and bouncing madly around the interior until gravity triumphed. They would often find the spent rounds from the enemy's weapons on the floor when cleaning up back at base, along with bullet holes in the sides of the aircraft that they worked late into the night to repair.

Only once in all those missions was he hit. Not by a bullet. A flying razor blade of shrapnel. He would later swear to himself that he saw it actually zing by his right eye to slice his upper cheek, putting him in the infirmary for a day with stitches and bestowing a two-inch scar that some people admired, some envied, and almost all respected. People would sometimes suggest he get a plastic surgeon to "fix" it. No chance. This was a treasured badge, not of honor but of remembrance. Remembrance of a certain price that he had paid and that could have been a price so much steeper, and most of all, a reminder of the damage that fools—small (him) and large (the politicians)—could inflict if you failed to live your life in such a way as to steer clear of all the fools, especially the fool in yourself.

Only back at base at the end of the mission did the fear come on strong, when he might hear about a crash miraculously avoided, or—not daily but not infrequently either—an entire crew roasted in a ball of fire, or the death of a gunner when a bullet or a spike of shrapnel found a spot a few inches to the left of the one that had sliced O'Keefe. Those news bulletins were fully sufficient to keep him always poised on that razor's edge that was probably a necessary condition to continuing survival.

And when he wasn't drunk enough, when he flopped into bed and lay awake trying but too often failing to think about anything but those *moments* that had passed so quickly then but were now suspended in unanimated imaginary time; when he couldn't drop off to sleep fast enough and the terror really grabbed hold and wouldn't let go for seemingly all night, it was on those early mornings-after that he pondered how he might concoct a good enough excuse, one he might even manage to believe in himself, to stay glued to the bed, convinced he was deathly ill, so he could pull off a credibly self-deceiving malinger and avoid the mission that day, which would doubtlessly be the one destined to kill him. But then his mind would conjure up a potent mix of guilt and shame for even thinking that way, because the poor grunts who had it so much worse really did need him, or someone like him, and if he wasn't the one there to help them, he would be putting some other hapless schlub in danger in his place in that side door-window…

And here it was again, all of it and all at once, the same feelings even after almost twenty years to the day. Here on the firing line, with the General watching and no doubt judging him, O'Keefe got used to the gun quickly, wasting only a few rounds trailing up to and a little to the side of the junker until he had it dead on. After all, what was there to master? Point and fire. Minor adjustment here and there, nothing to bother him except his knees bumping and scraping on the metal floor and the damn van shaking like it might tip over. Goodbye, old junker. In a few seconds, hardly even there anymore. What this monstrous, evil device would do to human bodies, especially at close range, was an atrocity he resisted even imagining, but it appeared that these crazy Ark fuckers were actually planning to do that very thing and were expecting him to be the one to do it. Was it an irony that despite blasting away with it daily over a year of war, he couldn't say that he had the witness of his own eyes to inform him whether he'd ever actually killed anyone with that Ma Deuce, so far away he'd been from the consequences of the devastation he unleashed, yet here in Caleb's peaceable kingdom he was rehearsing for a massacre of human beings at close quarters?

The General was waving both arms above his head in a crossing pattern, telling him to stop.

"Good job, Marine. I wasn't sure you had it in you."

General, there's no "it" to be in me.

"Hey, fire a single round, will you? See if you can hit one of those pieces that are left."

He did. He missed. Figured.

The General looked disappointed in him. "I heard this was actually a *preferred sniper weapon* over there."

True for some. There was a Marine that a couple of years before O'Keefe's tour had supposedly used the Ma Deuce as a single-shot sniper rifle to achieve the world record for the longest kill.

"Not by me for damn sure," O'Keefe said. "I fired from at least 300 feet above the ground and mostly at trees. I didn't hardly have to aim the thing. I probably did hit something human sometimes, but never that I saw or knew of."

A lie? No. Truthful if his memory was truthful. It may have been convenient memory, or a void of memory, a phantom in the shadows, but he held firmly onto that absence, that void. Questioning that void, venturing into those shadows, foolishly searching for that phantom could lead him into the darkest of corners, from which there might be no return.

CHAPTER 40

Tʜᴀᴛ ɴɪɢʜᴛ O'Kᴇᴇꜰᴇ couldn't fall asleep, speculations birthing more speculations pinging around in his mind. Sometime after midnight he surrendered to the insomnia and headed to the kitchen to make coffee when he heard what he thought was engine noise and distant voices. And was that a bumping, squeaking sound along with an engine revving up to a whine? Out the window he could see lights up toward the Prophet's house, brighter than the usual house nightlights. He put on a jacket, pants, shoes without socks.

Moving slowly upward to the Gathering Ground and the house, he saw a large flatbed truck pulled up onto the grass in front of the Fortress and a van parked behind it. Two men stood on the truck bed and three men below. He sensed movement out of the trees behind him. One of the night guards on his rounds.

Maybe he wasn't supposed to be seeing what he was seeing. To avoid making noise, he slowly lowered himself and lay flat on his stomach.

He carefully raised his head. The guard had stopped to watch the men at the truck but soon resumed his patrol, heading directly for O'Keefe. If the guard continued on that course, he would certainly stumble over O'Keefe, who could do nothing but plant his face in the grass and dirt and hope for the best. He started to construct a story he could tell when he was discovered.

As the footsteps sounded closer and closer until they were almost upon him, he held his breath and resisted the urge to spring up and run or try to overwhelm the guard. No percentage in that. Better just to tell the sort of truth (couldn't sleep, heard noises, worried maybe there was trouble, maybe from law enforcement, didn't know whether the approaching guard was from the Ark or an invader).

He felt a small whoosh of air from the guard's boot stepping down and heard the crunch of twigs and grass next to his left ear. The sound drifted away. First, he only listened. Then he raised his head, more sensing than seeing the man move on through the dark and out of sight. Staying close to the tree line, O'Keefe crept around toward the rear of the truck, stayed upright for as long as he dared, hit the ground again and crawled forward, then propped himself on his elbows and watched the men unload several crates from the truck and carry them into the building.

No cover here, he was exposed. When the men's backs were turned, he seized the opportunity to scramble around the back and to the other side of the van parked behind the flatbed truck, which gave him concealment and a good viewpoint. The flatbed was empty except for two crates and something under a canvas covering. Stenciled on one of the crates: *U.S. Army.*

He remembered Norbert saying, and the General had only a few days ago confirmed, that active-duty soldiers stationed at the local Army base and sympathetic to the Ark cause were stealing weaponry from the fort's armory.

When the men returned, one jumped up on the truck, ripped the canvas off and lifted the first item from the pile and handed it down to the man waiting below.

And O'Keefe was in Vietnam all over again.

The LAW rocket. Light Antitank Weapon. Not used often in the tankless jungle warfare of Vietnam, but with an awesome reputation. It could take out a tank or blow the front of a bunker or a building to pieces. Weighing only five pounds, it could be quickly whipped to the shoulder and fired. Were there more of these that they'd already unloaded and taken into the Fortress?

Talk about a secret weapon. Perfect for urban warfare.

CHAPTER 41

THE NEXT MORNING the truck had gone. Perhaps only a few of the Ark denizens were aware that it had been there the night before and of what had been unloaded from it. Still, the atmosphere in the compound rippled with the flutter of anticipation usually associated with the arrival of a special visitor. O'Keefe always tried to lay eyes on every newcomer and, if he could do it unobtrusively, learn as much as possible about them and the purpose of their visit.

Attracted by movement and noise at the front entrance, he wandered that way and positioned himself along the path that led from the parking lot to the Prophet's house.

And behold! Before he could flee or even turn away, he was staring … at Spud.

Spud spotted him, his eyes wide and bulging, and he reeled back slightly. O'Keefe could think of nothing to do other than give a quick shake of his head, hoping that nobody but Spud had seen it. Spud got the message. He averted his eyes and kept walking. But after Spud had taken only a few steps, O'Keefe decided he had to risk acting immediately.

"Wait," he barked at the backs of Spud and his escorts, and as they turned toward him, he moved forward, his hand outstretched, knowing he had to get there before Spud said his name—his last name anyway (*good choice, keeping our first names*). The escorts seemed not to know what to do. Neither did Spud.

"Pete *McBride*," he said, pronouncing the last name distinctly, louder, slower. "You remember me? We met at that gun show. You told me about this place. Great to see you."

"Yeah … I *do* remember," Spud said, cautiously playing along.

"Let's catch up," O'Keefe said.

Spud frowned, obviously trying to understand the import of what he was seeing and hearing, and said, "Yeah … that'd be interesting … *for sure.*"

O'Keefe took Spud by the elbow, gently led him a few steps away from the escorts, and said softly, "I'm living here now … but not in my own name. Please don't out me. I got in some big trouble back home. All you know about me is we met at a gun show, and you told me about this place."

O'Keefe winked.

Spud looked unsure but slowly nodded.

"Let's go," someone commanded.

With a last befuddled glance back at O'Keefe, Spud moved on with his escorts.

Could he trust Spud? Should he stay put or try to crowd his way in with them?

Sara had continued to work at the school, subject to being summoned for computer work at the Prophet's house. Today she'd been summoned. If he didn't go in and Spud outed him, they would be separated. Not just trapped but separately trapped. She had no idea of the danger. He did, but he couldn't make his own escape and leave her at their mercy.

By the time all that had passed through his mind, it was too late to go in except in a kind of headlong fools rush. He retreated to the house and sat down, rifle lying across his thighs, pondering what he should do now.

Here I am in my own private Alamo. If he took the initiative, he might provoke an avoidable crisis. If he stayed holed up here, they could grab her, and all they had to do was threaten to kill her to force his surrender. Or they could keep her for other uses, surround the house, and burn him out or up.

It took what felt like hours to decide that he couldn't tolerate one more minute of suspense and was afraid he'd already lingered too long in indecision. He should have immediately followed Spud and his escorts in.

Maybe he could take the Prophet hostage. Worst case, he could do some serious damage. *They'll wish they believed a little more in gun control.* Best of all, grab Sara and make a rush for the parking lot. He pocketed the Buick keys.

The Prophet's house wasn't specially guarded, no danger being expected from *inside* the compound. He knocked on the door. Naomi opened it. Her face registered no surprise, no fear, no trouble at all. If something was wrong, she didn't know about it.

"Looking for Sara?" she said.

"Actually, can I bother David for a minute or two?"

"Come right in."

She escorted him through the hallway he'd followed when he'd taken the voice stress test and where Sara now did her work. That room was to his left. The door was closed. Seemed ominous.

"Can I just stick my head in to say hi to Sara?"

"Of course."

The door opened, and Sara turned from the computer screen with a frown of interrupted concentration.

"Hi," he said. "Everything good?"

She seemed taken aback, but he tried to look like he was supposed to be there and knew exactly what he was doing.

"Everything but this damn program," she said and turned back to refocus on the screen. Still facing the screen, she said, "And you? What's up?"

"Just meeting with David for a bit. See you later."

So far, so good.

Naomi took him a few more steps down the hallway to the War Room, knocked at the door, cracked it open a bit, and said, "May I interrupt?"

"What is it?" an irritated voice responded.

"Pete's here. He'd like to speak to you."

A muffled voice said something he didn't catch but that Naomi interpreted as permission to enter.

The Prophet, the General, and Caleb sat at one end of a large conference table, the Prophet at the head, the others, one on each side. A large map was spread out before them on the table. On an easel behind the Prophet was a whiteboard with writing on it. They looked up. Curiosity. No hostility.

The Prophet abruptly stood as if to block the view of the whiteboard. O'Keefe said, "I was looking for Spud."

"Gone," the Prophet said.

O'Keefe hesitated, not sure which card to play next. "I just wanted to catch him … thank him for telling me about this place."

"He didn't come find you? We encouraged him to do that. But he was in a hurry."

"Too bad. Thanks."

They looked at him expectantly, waiting for him to leave. He got the hint, bowed and backed out of the room like the most obsequious servant.

Naomi led him back down the hallway. As they approached the front door of the house, he asked if she'd been there when Spud left.

"I showed him out myself. Seemed in a big hurry." She shook her head. "Comes all the way down here, then hustles right back out again."

CHAPTER 42

"WE'RE SO VULNERABLE," O'Keefe said to Sara on their walk that evening. He'd told her about Spud and his uncertainty about what he should do now. "Next thing you know, *Norbert's* gonna show up here."

They arrived at the shore. The orange-red sun seemed to perch on the lake as if reluctant to leave the scene.

"I have some news of my own," she said. "They decided to suspend the militia training."

O'Keefe stopped, still looking out at the lake. "That's amazing."

"The sunset?"

"No. Stopping the training program. Are you sure?"

"I helped them word the bulletin and sent it out for them. It's done."

"It can't be. They need that money to keep this place going. Let's stop at Caleb's on the way back."

"You go," she said. "I had to spend most of the day with John the Baptist. He gets old quick."

He laughed. "You ever wanna just slap him upside the head and say, 'Wake up, Caleb, Goddamnit?'"

"Often … Well, always."

He found Caleb in his recliner chair, serenely studying the Bible while his wife scooted around finishing the dishes and wrangling the kids into bed.

The Chaplain looked up from the Good Book, folding his face into a look of irritable impatience, apparently to make sure O'Keefe understood that he was barging in on the deepest of spiritual contemplations, even, perhaps, divine revelations.

"Sorry to bother you, but I had to ask. Sara tells me there'll be no more militia training."

"Yes, sir, at least for a while, thank the Good Lord."

"But don't you need that money to keep this place going?"

"Yahweh will provide. In this case he provided one Peter McBride."

With a look of bemusement at O'Keefe's reaction, he said, "You seem … chagrined."

"I am. Because that little treasure chest won't last long. I can't keep that up."

"Maybe it won't need to last long." Caleb cupped his hand around his ear and smiled. "I think I might hear in the distance the faint but steadily growing rumble of the End Times coming near."

They said a mind was a terrible thing to waste. There sat Exhibit A, an inverted paragon, the utter waste of an intelligent man. *Yes, Sara, you want to punch this idiot, beat him to a pulp. Or maybe lift him up and shake him until he's gagging,* and say, "Wake up, Caleb, Goddamnit. Get your fucking head on straight."

He spent yet another day trying to figure out what to do. If Spud had revealed O'Keefe's true identity to the Ark men, they were the best actors in the world. But one way or the other, his cover was blown. He had to get to Spud. Or get to someone else who could get to Spud. Plus the LAW rockets. Plus the suspension of the training. *Welcome to End Times?*

He told Sara, "I've got to alert them up in the city about Spud and all the rest. I'll try to convince the Prophet to let you come too."

"Forget it. There's no way he'll let me, and it'll only make them suspicious. And if I stay, instead of arousing suspicion, it might have the opposite effect. They might trust us even more."

"I'll get back as soon as I can."

My poor mother, he thought.

To help it go down easier when he broke the news of his mother's condition to the Prophet, he sweetened the deal. "And my poor fool is still there … and likely the rest of his money too. I'll be trying, shall we say, to 'borrow' some more."

The Prophet said, "I think we have enough now."

"Enough?"

The Prophet looked at the General, and the General gave one slow shake of his head, a command to keep quiet

Take a risk. "What's the deal? What do I have to do to get you people to trust me? I might be able to help with whatever it is you're planning."

The Prophet squirmed, about to say something, but the General put his hand on the Prophet's arm in gentle but unmistakable restraint, and said to O'Keefe, "When the time's right, we've got a very special role for you, Pete, but everyone is on a need-to-know basis. We'll get you involved in due course."

"'Fraid not, General. This ain't the Marine Corps. I'm not gonna charge any hill unless I've been consulted on the battle plan."

"Congratulations, Marine. Smart of you. Especially for a Jarhead. But you're also smart enough to know how important security is, and how loose lips sink ships—with lots of Marines on board. You want us to trust you. Same here. Trust us. We'll let you in on it as soon as it's smart for *us* to do that. What if you get caught during your little caper with your poor fool?"

"You assume I'd give you up? Squeal?"

"Better men have done so. Everyone's got their weak spots."

The Prophet nodded. "Yes. In your case maybe it would be your beautiful wife and what they could do to her."

"Can you at least tell me *when* something's gonna happen?"

"Let's just say"—again the General tried to interrupt but failed and could only lock his jaw and look on disapprovingly—"you'd better get back here quick, or your little lady'll get all the glory."

At first O'Keefe had thought she would need to die. But that would mean a funeral, and him attending the funeral, something that was too difficult to stage, especially on such short notice. Plus, if she managed to keep clinging to life, she might still be of use to him later. *Sorry, Mom. I'll have to prolong your suffering.*

Same drill as last time. Airport in the city, fly to Los Angeles, fly right back. Might they have someone watching him in Los Angeles? They hadn't last time, he was certain, or they'd've known he'd never left LAX, and this particular adventure, and maybe his life too, would be over now. And they certainly weren't competent enough to manage a successful tail in that situation. A huge and crowded airport, then out into a gigantic, traffic-choked city. They couldn't even manage to follow him competently right now.

CHAPTER 43

"THEY WOULDN'T GIVE me all the details, but they're gonna strike … and soon."

"What's 'soon'?"

"I don't know, but damn soon for sure. Could even be tonight for all I could tell."

"Where?"

"I think right here. This town."

"What do you mean, 'strike'?"

"Bullets and bombs for sure. Maybe grenades. Multiple targets."

"Any idea what the targets are or what specifically they plan to do?"

"No. They wouldn't tell me anything specific, just vague stuff like 'the Lord's vengeance is at hand' and 'the arm of the Lord is prepared to strike the Philistines.' Shit like that. Fuckers are goofier than a pet coon."

"We need more."

"Not from me. I've held up my end of the bargain. No more. This ain't a bunch of nut cases playin' war games in the woods no more. It's the real thing. Too scary. They'll chop me up and sprinkle me on their Cheerios. You know what happened to the last guy you put down there."

His interrogators stared at each other, seeming to accept that he wouldn't do more and it didn't make sense to try to pressure him to.

"One more odd thing," he said. "I don't know if it's worthwhile info or not, but you ever heard of a guy named O'Keefe … Peter O'Keefe … private investigator up here?"

"Oh, yeah," one of them groaned.

"He's joined 'em … livin' down there with 'em. Says he got in some trouble up here and he's hidin' out down there under an assumed name … Peter McBride."

"Sounds crazy, even for O'Keefe. Are you sure?"

"Sure as I'm sure I'm sittin' here wantin' to cut a giant fart and send you boys scurryin' right out of the room."

Another one said, "Kevin, can you check that out?"

"I will. One of his partners used to be on the force."

"So, we're square as Pat Boone now, right? I've held up my end. Those gun charges'll disappear?"

"That's the deal."

After the door closed behind him, one of the agents said, "You ever noticed the shape of that guy's head?"

"Yeah. Potato."

CHAPTER 44

SHE'D FOLLOWED SEVERAL of them. The red-haired girl. One of Maxwell's drivers. A couple of the other bodyguards. But all that had led nowhere. Matthew had been getting more impatient by the day, then seemingly by the minute. He kept saying he needed to get back to the Ark. If he did, would he take her with him?

He'd appeared at her bedroom door on the second night as she was reading in bed. Just standing there, saying nothing. It was his saying nothing that let her know the blessed moment had come. She also said nothing. She only nodded, folded back the covers, turned off the lamp, and moved over to accommodate him. He took her more gently than she'd expected he would, almost disappointingly so.

In the ensuing days, he'd lost some of his gruffness, smiled sometimes, even joked occasionally, showed her a gentler side of himself. But then he'd grown restless, muttering, "I can't believe they sent me up here for nothin'."

She'd come home one afternoon after another round of fruitless surveillance, and he was sitting on the couch, his duffel bag at his feet. She took the big risk of asking him to take her back with him. He said, "No. There's a big job to do right here, and you're still an important part of it. The Prophet strongly believes that. We need you right here."

He stood. Giving him no choice, she went to him. He half-heartedly allowed her to hug him. She rubbed her hand up and down on him, felt him harden, tugged at his belt, whispered, "I'll give you something to come back for."

The longer he'd stayed away and she'd heard nothing from him or anyone else from the Ark, the more she doubted that she could depend on him to return. She needed to make sure, elevate herself as high as possible in his mind, accomplish something important to the mission, whatever the mission was.

She decided to focus solely on the big man, Peter O'Keefe. And once again he was leading her, she was sure, back to the airport.

The last time she'd followed him here, he'd picked up the man who was clearly someone "special" and somehow involved in the Maxwell situation. And her adrenalin spiked when she realized, *There he is again,* hustling out of the airport with what she thought was a fugitive sort of look about him and into O'Keefe's waiting car.

It soon became obvious they were heading, as before, to the office building. They pulled into the driveway at the side of the building that led to the surface parking lot out back. She slowed the car, inching along, trying to figure out what to do.

A car behind her honked loud and long. Panicked, in flight from that horrible horn and the exposure it threatened, she hit the accelerator too hard, the car lurched forward, she jammed on the brakes, her tires squealed. Something within her prodded her to choke down her fear at the risk she was running. She continued, navigating slowly now behind the building.

They were just getting out of O'Keefe's car. She moved close, taking it slow—*don't alarm them*—stopped to let them cross her path. The man from the airport hesitated, halted in front of her, unwilling to cross, looking at the door while curtly waving her on. She complied. Hurrying into the building, they paid her almost no attention. *Story of my life, but it comes in handy now.*

That moment when they'd stared at each other, before he'd impatiently waved her on, she'd realized something. She *had* seen him before. Not just that first time at the airport … some other time…

Out on the street, she pulled over to the curb, left the car running … thinking … trying to remember … A man had opened the door for her and closed it. Smiled at her … Now he'd impatiently waved her on … The same man?

CHAPTER 45

DAGMAR JUMPED UP, held out her arms, skipped to him, embraced him. O'Keefe was surprised by her strength.

"Is Sara okay?" she asked.

"Last time I saw her, yes."

"So scary. I've been reading about all that, those people. Bring her home safe." Then, blushing, "Yourself too. Kelly's called here a couple of times worrying about you. Annie called once too."

George interrupted. "Are they here?"

She nodded vigorously, and they left her smiling after them.

Maxwell seemed just as happy to see him. He shook O'Keefe's hand and grabbed him by the shoulder. "Glad to see you. I worry about you guys every day. And every night. I lay awake and think, *Why did I send them into that madness?*"

"Feel better," O'Keefe said. "You may've saved not only yourself but a bunch of other people too."

O'Keefe spilled it all out quickly. The armed camp with its fields of fire. Bunkers. Landmines. Dozens of rifles converted to automatic. The M60 and, so much worse, the Ma Deuce 50 cals. Homemade grenades. The barrel of cyanide. The LAW rockets, three of them, spirited away from the armory of the local Army base, possibly more of them to come. And the final straw, the cessation of the militia trainings.

"They haven't quite let me in all the way, so I've got no details, but they're planning something big, and not only against you."

Maxwell leaned back in his chair. "A Saint Bartholomew's Day."

O'Keefe remembered something about it. George looked clueless.

"1500s," Maxwell said. "The Wars of Religion. France. In one day and night, on the feast of Saint Bartholomew, the Catholic authorities engineered a wave of targeted assassinations and incited lynch mobs that virtually wiped out the Protestant population.

"Four centuries later," O'Keefe said, "Some things don't change. Kill people because they believe in a different fairy tale than yours."

"When?" Maxwell said.

"I can't tell exactly, but soon."

"What do we do?"

"We can't keep this to ourselves anymore," O'Keefe said. "We have to go to the authorities. Now."

"No shit, Sherlock," George snorted.

Maxwell thought for a few moments, then said, "No. You have to find another way. They'll fuck it up. They fuck everything up."

"Richard, it's not our play any longer," George said. "If this was ever really a private matter, it's not anymore."

"When you agreed to take my money, you signed up for a private matter."

O'Keefe leaned across the table toward Maxwell. "What? What are you saying?"

"You'd be breaking the contract … forfeiting the right to the money."

"Your money in my bank isn't worth innocent blood on my hands, you jackass."

Maxwell stood and began pacing back and forth, brought both hands to his temples and pressed as if massaging something into or out of his brain. When he lowered his hands, he looked ashamed.

"I'm sorry. Momentary insanity. How did I get myself into this? But let's think it through first. Is there an alternative? You talk about innocent blood. There's women and children down there. What about their blood? Those G-men will storm that place with who knows how much firepower."

"They might have to," George said. "You heard that about fields of fire and landmines. Hell, the kids and women'll probably be in the bunkers, praising the Lord and blasting away with M60s at the ZOG demons."

That made O'Keefe think about the little girl, her hair flouncing at her shirt collar as she bounced along wherever she went. No M60 in *her* hands.

A sharp knock at the door. Dagmar slipped in without being invited, closed the door behind her, pressed her back against it, flummoxed, near breathless.

"There's some fierce-looking men out there. They showed their badges. One's from the FBI, the other from ATF. They want to talk to George."

"Not me?" O'Keefe said.

She shook her head.

"Goddamnit, George," Maxwell said. "Did you already tell them?"

"First thing I heard about this was in the car on the way over here from the airport, and the rest here at the table, just like you."

"You?" Maxwell barked at O'Keefe.

"Hell no."

Dagmar's back seemed glued to the door. "I'm afraid to go out there. I don't know what to say."

"I'll go," George said.

"Don't spill it," Maxwell said. "Buy us some time to think."

O'Keefe was temporarily paralyzed, feeling only that events had moved beyond his feeble ability to control or even influence them. "Yeah, George," he said. "Keep 'em at bay for now."

George knew the FBI agent, Kevin Doolan, from joint local-federal investigations in his police officer days. Doolan was young, dark-haired, handsome. And angry (and George recalled Doolan had looked that way and was that way almost every time he'd ever dealt with him). The ATF guy introduced himself as Calvin Brewster. He was small and stout with a bushy mustache pasted on a disdainful countenance. He had an ex-military look about him, like he wasn't comfortable out of uniform and probably never would be.

"Where's O'Keefe?" Doolan said.

"Am I my brother's keeper?"

"Not amusing. The last guy who said that *murdered* his brother. What are *you* guilty of?"

"Not of that."

"Give it up. Where is he?"

"I assert my Fifth Amendment right not to answer on the ground that my answer may incriminate me."

A confused frown from Doolan.

"Because," George said, smirking, "I'd then be committing the crime of lying to the FBI."

Doolan flickered a whisper of a smile. "So you're obstructing justice instead. Let me give you a little help. We know he's down there at the Ark. I'm sure his mother and his priest both warned him not to hang around with people like that. What's he up to?"

George kept mum and dumb.

Doolan turned to Dagmar, of flushed face and the widest of eyes. "How 'bout you?" he growled. "Want to spend some time in a jail cell with your boss here?"

She couldn't seem to get any words out, just vigorously shook her curls.

"One more chance, George. And I'll give you a little more help. We think there's some very nasty stew being cooked up down there. O'Keefe is either willing to talk to us or he's a co-conspirator."

George tried to look contrite. "I'll see what I can do."

"Twenty-four hours. We can't afford to fuck around. Excuse my French, young lady."

"What the..." George said when he opened the door to the conference room. No one and nothing in there. Except a note on the table in O'Keefe's handwriting.

> We decided not to take any chances.
> See you soon.

And they did soon return after watching the G-men drive off in their separate government blandmobiles. O'Keefe said, "It's not that we didn't trust you, but we sure as hell didn't trust them not to bust in here."

They deputized George to negotiate the conditions of O'Keefe's appearance.

Doolan tried to strongarm George into producing O'Keefe at the FBI offices, but George insisted that O'Keefe refused to meet anywhere but at his lawyer Michael Harrigan's office.

"Your partner," Doolan said, "seems bound and determined to get himself sent to prison, and I'll be more than glad to put him there."

CHAPTER 46

THAT EVENING DOOLAN and Brewster entered the conference room at Harrigan's office and sat down. No pleasantries, not even hellos. The two sides eyed each other for a few moments, until Doolan said, "You make me sad, O'Keefe. Lawyering up so quick. You must be in deep."

"Not at all. Just want to even the playing field. I was planning to come to you with the whole thing, but I needed to at least warn my client that I intended to do that. He thinks you're likely to fuck the whole thing up."

"You waited too long. We found out about you first. We came to you first. Caught you. So before you say anything more, 'You have the right to remain silent. Anything you say…'" He recited the remainder of the Miranda warning.

O'Keefe looked at Harrigan. Harrigan shook his head.

"That means my lawyer thinks I shouldn't say a word to someone who's dunce and prick enough to pull a stunt like that. You're already proving my client was right about you guys fucking everything up if you get half a chance. If you'd known when you gave me that idiot Miranda warning what the consequences of my silence might be, you'd've choked on it, you dumb shit."

Doolan jerked upward as if he intended either to walk out or lunge across the table. But then he caught himself and settled back in his chair.

O'Keefe said, "But I don't see any alternative for the good and innocent people of our city but to talk to you anyway."

Doolan relaxed a little, though his jaw remained tight, his eyes glinting like broken glass in sunlight.

O'Keefe continued, "You know who Richard Maxwell is, I'm sure. He's our client."

Doolan looked at the ATF man. "One pain in the ass hires another."

"Flattery will get you nowhere." He told them everything he could recall about the Ark—its inhabitants, its worldview, its weaponry, its grievances, and the little he knew of its battle plan. They furiously took notes and asked questions until there was something close to a tensely precarious atmosphere of truce in the room.

O'Keefe concluded, "I haven't quite earned their trust enough for them to let me in on the details of what they intend to do, or when and how, but whatever it is seemed to be getting close enough that I didn't feel I could wait any longer. If they moved before I could get the word to you"—he made a shuddering gesture—"say no more. They say they don't need any more money, which is scary enough all by itself, but I think if I go back with another pile, I'll get all the details."

"Jesus Christ," Doolan said. "Automatic weapons, M60s, even a Ma Deuce, fucking LAW rockets—"

"And more a'comin'," O'Keefe said. "They're helping themselves at the armory at the local Army base."

Doolan gawped, incredulous, then said, "Sounds like you're planning to go back. When?"

"Now. Our partner, Sara, is down there all by herself."

"Don't. Not yet. We've gotta go upstairs with this. *Way* upstairs."

"Sorry, fellas. Can't dance with that. Maybe you didn't hear me. She's all by herself."

"I hear you. And I hear you say you knew what you were doing when you left her alone down there, and she knew what she was doing when she agreed to stay. You've been supporting, even financing, a seditious conspiracy. Her too."

Proving he could also threaten, Brewster said, "And if Doolan doesn't get you, I will. All those illegal weapons. That's a lot of jail time all by itself."

Doolan added, "You're vulnerable as hell. Her too. And, by the way, so is Maxwell. So just wait until we can figure things out and coordinate something."

"How long?"

"That's for us to know and you to find out. It's whenever we decide to tell you."

"One other thing," O'Keefe said. "Who told you I was down there? You got an informer in there?"

"You know we can't disclose that."

"But," O'Keefe said, "we could easily trip over each other somehow … both end up dead."

"No. You can't trip over each other because you're not going to be down there."

Watch me, Mr. Doolan.

After the G-men left, O'Keefe said, "Anyone think I'm not gonna go back until they give me permission?"

"That," Harrigan said, "would be entirely too sane a thing for a guy like you to do."

"I'd've told them to shove it right then and there, but I was afraid they'd arrest me on the spot. Could they have done that?"

Harrigan laughed. "How the hell do I know? You know I'm no criminal lawyer. You might as well've had a mannequin sitting here. I won't charge you for it. I'd be disbarred."

"Alright," O'Keefe said, "here's the deal. You guys tell them they've got forty-eight hours, and then I'm goin' back whether they like it or not. And between you and me, I'm layin' low, not even telling you guys where, so they can't snatch me."

"Big risk," George said. "They really might have enough to persuade a grand jury to indict you. I doubt you'd be convicted, but you're an obvious flight risk, so maybe no bail. In jail for a long time waiting for the trial. Good defense counsel would bankrupt you pretty quick."

"I think," O'Keefe said with a smile, "I'm looking at a lawyer who'd do it pro bono."

Harrigan smirked. "Then the fool of a client would have a fool of a lawyer."

CHAPTER 47

Things were getting dicey for her in every way. The activity on the computer message boards had intensified. The Ark and the other groups kept their communications obscure, all subtext, never any discussion of details. But clearly some major scheme was afoot and speeding along, and the Ark was at the center of it.

Finally, hoping to invite a disclosure without directly asking for it, Sara said, "Seems like something important's going on."

But the Prophet only smiled and put his index finger to his lips. "You know what loose lips do, I'm sure."

He kept finding more things for her to do in the headquarters office. Caleb was there some of the time, but mostly she worked alone. Naomi and Linda seldom ventured into that corner of the house. If either wanted or needed to report something, she used the walkie-talkie. And then, increasingly, Sara wasn't alone, and it wasn't Caleb accompanying her.

Initially, it had been a "special project." The Prophet would dictate Bible passages to her along with his hate-filled sermonizing—delivered soothingly, hypnotically, she had to admit—which she then transcribed and printed out for him. After that, he would mark up, and she would type, a revision. This had coalesced into a "Declaration of War" against the whole of "Babylon": publicly the government (privately "ZOG"), publicly militant pederast homosexuals (privately "faggots" and "lesbos"), publicly the news media (privately "the Jewsmedia"), publicly Muslims (privately "towel heads"), publicly Negroes (privately "spearchuckers" was the kindest of the appellations), race mixing miscegenators and other "mud people," and, of course, the all-powerful Jews, their string-pulling always behind every evil their father Satan had let loose in the modern world.

But after the Declaration was completed and published to rousing acclaim on the message boards, the Prophet kept finding other and increasingly more trumped-up reasons to be there, just Sara and David, engaged in their own little pas de deux.

It came as he bent over her shoulder, reading something on her computer screen.

The day before, he'd rested his hand on her shoulder. Only briefly. It could have been mistaken for an accidental touch. But the next day, again the shoulder, then slowly, perhaps as the Serpent had slithered toward Eve in the Garden, the palm of his hand creeping down and gently cupping her breast and remaining there, gentle but firm and with no intention of moving.

She locked her hand around his wrist, not angrily, not a violent rejection, not immediately yanking the hand away, just maintaining control, perhaps a mere pause while she considered but continuing a slight upward pressure that countered any further advance.

Without anger or fear in her voice, she said, "This can't happen."

"Why not?"

"Naomi."

"She would understand."

"I don't think so."

"Your husband hasn't given you a child. I could do that for you … fulfill your purpose in the world. Naomi would understand."

She'd rehearsed a number of scenarios portraying how such a moment might go. This was not one of them.

"I don't think so. She's already hurting enough … after Linda."

"No. She knows the Lord has revealed His Will to me."

"This, you with me, she knows that?"

Sufficient answer was his hesitation before saying, "She will accept this."

"What about my husband?"

"He's failed you, and thus failed his race and God's plan for his race. And he needn't even know. You could make him believe the child was his."

There seemed nowhere to go with that. She waited, maintaining that slight counter pressure.

He withdrew the offending hand and took a step backward. She swiveled her chair to face him. He said, "I would take you as my wife. It would make you a queen, *the* Queen.

"So, David, I'm to be your Bathsheba? And Naomi would approve of *that?*"

"Just as she did Linda."

"Acquiescence isn't approval. She seems wounded to me. I would need her approval … stated to me … directly … just she and I."

His face flushed. Entreaty had turned to anger. He looked ready to pounce. *That* scenario she *had* rehearsed. Several possible martial arts moves might now come into play. She couldn't be sure they'd work, but she'd learned well and practiced much.

But he subdued himself. "You're making a great mistake."

Soften it. "I realize what a privilege it would be, but even if I could betray my husband, I couldn't do that to Naomi."

"You're mistaken," he said, and abruptly turned and left the room.

She thought, *Is he going to get her? What if she gives me her approval?*

When she'd rehearsed the several ways he might approach her and what her reaction might be, she'd mainly anticipated attempted rape, but she'd failed to appreciate the immensity of his ego. He had apparently assumed that no force would be needed, that she would ecstatically welcome the implantation of his consecrated seed within her. Now, what if he did ask Naomi and Naomi was as crazy as her husband? Sara had left herself an out ("even if I could betray my husband,"), but if Naomi was insane enough to approve, was Naomi also insane enough even to help him rape her?

He didn't return that day but did the next and acted as if nothing had happened. She thought it best to keep silent. But had he given up? She doubted it. He didn't seem the surrendering type, especially to a creature who was, after all, merely Adam's rib and Satan's dupe and accomplice in engineering the Fall of Man.

Maybe he was developing another strategy. Or, the worst possibility, Naomi was considering his proposal. She'd already endured, and apparently accepted, the ignominy of Linda. What was one more? She was already crushed. And she was fond of Sara. Could Sara be an ally against Linda, and more subtly, against David himself, the kind of manipulative intrigue that probably often developed in a polygamous family, the modern harem?

CHAPTER 48

Dᴀᴠɪᴅ, ᴛʜᴇ ɢᴇɴᴇʀᴀʟ, Caleb, Sinclair, Darby, and several others had once been called the Elders, but lately the Prophet had taken to calling them the War Council. Their meetings had once been irregular and infrequent. Now they met almost daily. Probably cooking up something terrifying. And there Sara was, on the other side of the wall, her ear pressed against it, hearing only garbled speech when she could hear anything at all.

It was the best she could do. There was nowhere for her to hide and eavesdrop in the meeting room. She'd considered somehow drilling a hole through the wall, lower down, along the baseboard, where they might not see it, and crawling under her worktable to listen. But it would take only a random roving of the eyes of any one of several men … and if they spotted it…

Bad odds, too risky.

The solution she'd adopted was also risky. Risky as hell.

She could nimbly operate computers but knew little about how computers and monitors actually worked in an electromechanical way. She removed the cover and examined the wiring and tubing. *Can't risk pulling a wire out, might not be able to restore it.* Then she removed a tube. Nothing obvious happened. When she replaced that tube and removed another, the screen went black. She restored the tube. The screen blinked back on.

She called in David, who called in Caleb, and showed them the blank screen and then the tube. "This is the problem. It needs a new one."

If Caleb had simply asked her to put the tube back in and see what happened, *Goodbye plan.* But he showed no interest in that.

Alarmed, the Prophet said, "*Now* of all times for it to break. We have to get it fixed."

Caleb's face scrunched in perplexity. "How? Where? Not in our little town down the road, you can be sure of that."

Sara said, "I'm sure there's a Radio Shack in Lakeview. I'll get it there."

Heading for the door, the Prophet said, "We can't do without it. We need every single one of the computers working. I'll get the car keys."

Bingo. "I need to get a jacket," she said. "Be right back." She hurried to the house, grabbed the jacket and the stash of folded bills they'd hidden for needs such as this.

Caleb was waiting on the Prophet's doorstep, keys in his hand. She reached out for them.

But not so fast.

"He wants me to go with you. I'll drive."

"Are you sure about that Radio Shack?" he said as they emerged with jangled nerves from the too-long and too-bumpy road from the compound to the highway.

"I don't know. If not, we'll have to go on to Ironton. College town. Only a junior college, but I'm sure there'll be something there."

"You think we could get all the way there before closing time?"

"We'll have to. Go fast but go the speed limit. Can't afford a ticket."

On the outskirts of town they passed a locally famous ice-cream shop.

"You know," Caleb said, "I've been delighted to leave civilization behind … except for one thing … Chocolate milkshakes."

There were no parking places on the street. He drove slowly and uncertainly along the line of parked cars until he was in front of the store. "Maybe I'll just let you out and I'll go find a parking place."

"I don't need any help. Why don't you go find that milkshake instead?"

Through his expansive smile he said, "You sure?"

"Surely, my leader, you don't doubt me on such an important matter."

The smile turned into an embarrassed laugh. He handed her a wad of dollars, and she scooted out the door before he could change his mind.

They didn't have the exact part she was looking for. No problem. She only had to buy something that looked similar and put the existing functioning one back in.

Now for her real purpose.

Good news. They carried what she wanted.

She purchased their most expensive microcassette recorder/player with voice-activated recording (earphones and carrying case included); five microcassette tapes, each with three hours of recording time; batteries; and a roll of black electrical tape to attach the recorder to the underside of the conference table. Fortunately, the recording items were "micro," so she was able to carry them in the pockets of her pants and jacket.

"You don't want a bag?" the clerk said.

"Just a small one for the tube."

The small bag with the tube was the only thing in her hand as she hustled out to the street, hoping she hadn't kept Caleb waiting too long, perhaps turning him at least inquisitive if not suspicious. He wasn't there. She paced up and down the sidewalk until he drove up five minutes later. Flinging open the door and jumping into the front seat as if she'd just robbed the place, she dangled the bag with the tube triumphantly back and forth. "Got it."

Caleb pumped his fist, smiled broadly, and sucked fiercely on his straw, loudly extracting the last bit of liquid from the milkshake cup.

He pointed to a paper bag beside him. "Got one for you too."

"No thanks. Crazy, but I've never cared much for ice cream."

"Oh, no," he said in mock horror. "Don't force me to drink this second one."

He laughed guilelessly, and she hoped hers was guileless too.

CHAPTER 49

Thel NEVER BOTHERED to lock the conference room, giving her easy access when no meeting was in progress. She ducked in, closed the door and locked it. If they caught her, she'd say she'd been overcome with exhaustion and had used the empty room to take a short nap, hoping not to be interrupted. The story wouldn't stand up to much scrutiny but would likely be accepted given the level of trust she enjoyed (or hoped she did).

The Prophet always sat at the head of the table, Caleb to his immediate right and the General to his left. She guessed that the Prophet and the General would be doing most of the talking. She turned on the recorder, set it for voice activation, and taped it under the table closest to where the two men usually sat.

She wasn't sure how long the batteries would last but had bought an ample supply and planned to change them every day so every recording would start with a full battery. If she ran out of batteries and couldn't obtain new ones, she would recycle the existing ones, which would hopefully have ample life left in them. It would mean regular visits to the conference room and associated risk, but that wasn't her biggest worry about this scheme. Her biggest worry was that the voice activation wouldn't work properly. *Stop!* she scolded herself. She could only do her best and hope that was good enough.

She didn't have to wait long. Several hours later on the same day she heard several of them moving in the hallway. She stood close to her open door but out of sight, listening for their movement into the conference room.

She waited a few minutes after she heard the door close, then moved to the closed door. *Quick knock. Open the door.*

They looked up, startled.

She said loudly, almost a shout, "Anything I can do?" she said. "You need anything?"

She'd spoken so loudly to make as sure as she could that the voice activation turned on.

Loud it certainly was. Disconcertingly so. Taken aback, their faces registered their confusion.

Recovering, the Prophet said, "No, thank you," and waved her away.

Hours later, the meeting long over, the recorder removed from the table's underside, she made an excuse to leave work early and headed to the house. She listened to the recording through the earphones in case anyone walked in on her they wouldn't hear anything they (or she) weren't supposed to.

She recognized the first voice as Sinclair's cranky, "What's with her? She goin' deaf or what?"

"Strange," the General said.

Then the Prophet: "Just trying to be helpful, I think. Let's get started. Big day."

The Prophet led them in a prayer to the "Lord God and His only begotten son Jesus Christ" and asked blessing on "our great undertaking in Your Name and for Your Purposes in this time of the Great Tribulation before the End Times, the Final Battle, and the Second Coming, which we faithfully welcome, seek, and endeavor to hasten in accordance with and obedience to Your Will."

A rustling of paper. Then the General's voice: "As we agreed, we've reduced our Abomination Targets to five. There were so many to choose from. We selected these five, the ones with the red circles around them…"

Rustling paper, likely a map. Sounds of movement, a squeaking chair. She pictured the men standing, gathering, leaning over, examining the map, as the General continued, "…because we think they're best geographically situated for coordinated attacks and the easiest, smoothest escapes. We've selected a primary escape route and a secondary for each Target. All our soldiers have been thoroughly drilled."

"Remember," the Prophet said, "we aren't planning for a firefight up there. We're planning to do the damage and get back here alive to fight another day. If it goes as we've planned, and of course if the Lord wills it, they might not even know it was us."

"And if we can't accomplish that?" Sinclair said.

"Do what you have to," the General said. "Fight it out, whatever, but no matter what, if you're captured, don't lead them back here. Don't give us up. Not a word. Fifth Amendment all the way. Actually, scratch that. Best not to say even those two words. Best to say nothing at all. Not One Word.

"So," he continued, "there's Maxwell of course. Mr. Sinclair and Mr. Darby will be handling that. Matthew?"

Sinclair said: "Our lady friend up there,"—Sara could hear both the Prophet and the General chuckling, Sinclair raising his voice to overcome it—"*tells* us that his security has tapered off some lately. Only one bodyguard at the house on weekends. They change eight-hour shifts regularly: 7 a.m. to 3 p.m. etcetera. We'll go at 7 a.m., right after the new guy comes on and the other one's gone home.

"We'll keep it simple. We'll pull up. Fake license plate of course. Three of us on the assault team, the driver and Darby and me. Full-face masks, etcetera. They haven't done anything to reinforce the big front windows of the house. It appears they've chosen to station the bodyguard mainly in the front room behind that window. Blow the window out with our AR-15s, toss in a grenade, and enter right after it blows. Find Maxwell. Kill him."

"Wife and kids?" Caleb asked.

"We don't intend to kill them. But if they're in the way, they'll have to pay for the sins of the father."

Then a voice Sara couldn't identify spoke: "They'll be going to a better place, and to a lot better place than their father."

The General took over. "Then there's The Gay Blade."

"Open on Sunday?" another unfamiliar voice asked.

"Not until nine. We plan to get there at ten. Ought to be pretty isolated from regular traffic at that hour. But the homos flock in there from opening time on. They offer," he lisped effeminately, "*the most wonderful little brunch on Sunday.*"

Laughter.

"It's located on the far edge of the main business district in a block of little businesses, all of them except the Blade closed on Sunday. All we'll need there is one guy and a driver. The guy walks in the front, sprays the place with automatic fire, tosses a grenade and a Molotov cocktail right after it. Good morning, homos. Have a sweet little brunch. See if Jesus really loves you like you say He does.

"Number Three. This one's a special gift for Rudy and all he's done for us. Planned Parenthood. We'll use the Ma Deuce. It's a cheesy little building, so we might be able to knock down one of the front walls with it. Follow with a grenade or two. But no matter what, they won't be killing any babies in there for a while after that."

"Will Rudy do that one?"

"No. He says that's not his style. Says he only works alone. He's done enough for us with the bombs."

Caleb's voice: "Strange bird. Not really our kind."

The Prophet: "But a good, dedicated Christian man. And he's been enormously helpful. Yahweh works in mysterious ways. Brought him to us out of nowhere at exactly the right moment. One of the many signs of blessing to our project."

Mumbled affirmations.

The General continued: "Fourth. B'nai Israel Jewish Community Center. See here … the front building is a big general-purpose structure that'll likely be closed that early on a weekend morning. But the back building is a multi-purpose athletic facility that opens at 7 a.m. every day but Saturday, and there'll likely be a few sweaty Yids in there.

"We'll first thing drop one guy off at the rear building, then go back around to the front building, drive on the grass right up to the front door, do whatever damage we can with some quick hits with grenades, AR-15s, and an M60 on the building and anyone that might be in the front there.

"Too bad it won't be Saturday," someone said. "It'd be full of 'em then."

"We can't let the perfect be enemy of the good. Meanwhile, our guy in the back is planting one of Rudy's specials in the shrubbery next to the front door of that building. The car comes back around and picks him up. They drive a block or so away and press the button. BOOM! Welcome to Apocalypse. You're the Chosen alright. *Our* chosen. "

"Number Five. The Federal Building. Ten stories. All those ZOG offices. It's on a street that's basically deserted on Sunday morning. We're devoting two of the LAW rockets to it. The third one we keep back here for when they come for us. We back up the van over the curb and onto the sidewalk immediately in front of the entrance. One rocket goes into the entrance, the other up to the sixth floor. That will take out most, if not all, of the front of the building, and who knows what collapses it might trigger inside. Whole floors might crash down, one after another."

"Is the FBI in that building?"

"No. They're in a heavily fortified and guarded building out near the airport. Too far away."

"Too bad."

"But guess what's on the sixth floor?"

Silence.

"ATF."

Someone clapped. "That's even better."

Sinclair again: "Too bad there'll be no employees in there on Sunday. Have we considered doing that one on a weekday, maybe the next day, Monday, while the cops are scrambling around all over town dealing with the rest of it?"

"No," the Prophet said. "It's foolish not to do all of it on Sunday morning. And we don't need to be too bloodthirsty. Not all by ourselves. We intend to ignite a chain reaction of firestorms. Our good friends around the country will be inspired to act on their own. But no matter what, we'll make one thunderous remonstrance and demonstration of Yahweh's wrath, hopefully without also making too many ZOG martyrs. And there'll probably at least be a few dead homos and Yids along with Richard Maxwell and his bodyguard."

Caleb's voice: "Exodus. The Pharoh's Egypt. The Angel of Death."

Again, a voice she didn't recognize: "Did we ever consider doing it on that very night … First night of Passover? That would be perfect."

"We thought about it," the General said. "Talked about it. Seriously talked about it. The Gay Pride parade too. But we weren't ready this spring, and the next Passover and Gay Pride are too far away. We'll never be in a better position than we are now."

Someone said: "We left out a very important target."

"What?"

"NAACP."

"Not enough there. It's a pissant little office a long way from everything else."

"Why can't we do a sixth?"

"We're already stretching ourselves thin."

"A shame we can't make use of the cyanide."

"Too hard," the General responded. "Can't figure out quite how to get it into the city water supply. And then it might get too diluted to do any damage. We've tried to get someone on the inside at the water department. No luck yet on that, but a bunch of our bullets are tipped with it. Even a grazing wound'll produce a writhing, painful death."

Someone laughed and said, "Let's do somethin' simpler. Why couldn't we sneak some into the NAACP … put some of it in the water cooler maybe?"

Laughter. "The bunnies would all be coming to work on Monday *so* happy they didn't get hit. Woops, boys and girls, you're wrong … you're screwed again."

"Enough fun," the Prophet said. "Let's move on. We shouldn't get greedy. Need to give ourselves every chance of getting away clean."

They reviewed in detail the "fire teams" for each of the targets.

Again an unidentifiable voice: "Where's our Vietnam machine gunner in all this?"

"He's way late getting back from LA. Mom's dead or something."

"Not yet. Just real sick, I think."

"Too bad. He could'a been helpful on a Ma Deuce.

"I guess he didn't know about the plan?"

"Nah," the General said. "Too new. Couldn't be sure enough about him. I might've been mistaken on that. You're right, he could've helped a lot."

"*You* make a mistake, General? Can't be."

"He seemed all-in to me," someone said, another voice she couldn't put a name to. "Brought us that money. You got his missus in the next room. You must trust her."

"That's different," the Prophet said. "She doesn't know about any of this." His tone definitively closed that subject. "And one more time. Drum it into everyone involved. If you're caught, say nothing. Complete silence. Maybe they won't be able to trace you here, and no matter what, *evade* as long as you can. We'll need all the time we can get to prepare."

The General added, "We'll mow 'em down like Andy Jackson did the redcoats at New Orleans."

They closed with a prayer entreating Yahweh to bless the great work they were undertaking in His name. Then the Prophet read Matthew 10:34–39:

> Think not that I am come to send peace on earth:
>
> I came not to send peace but a sword.
>
> For I am come to set a man at variance against his father, and the daughter against her mother, and the
>
> daughter-in-law against her mother-in-law.
>
> And a man's foes shall be they of his own household.
>
> He that loveth father or mother more than me is not worthy of me:
>
> And he that loveth son or daughter more than me is not worthy of me.
>
> And he that taketh not his cross, and followeth after me, is not worthy of me.
>
> He that findeth his life shall lose it:
>
> And he that loseth his life for my sake shall find it.

CHAPTER 50

Sara pressed the "Off" button with a slow, precise, deliberate movement designed to bring her somersaulting mind and drumming heart under some kind of control. The attack could be imminent. Maybe even this Sunday.

She jumped up from the table, ready to dash to the parking lot and somehow figure out how to commandeer one of the vehicles and get the hell to a phone and call O'Keefe, George, or anyone else who could alert the authorities to the planned attack. But one skill she hadn't yet mastered was how to hotwire a car (and she vowed on the spot that if she survived all this, she would learn), and the only keys she knew about were in a cupboard in the Prophet's house.

She could swim out, but she didn't know whether she could make it all the way to a place where she could make a call. There might be neighbors somewhere near the compound, but she didn't know which way or how far or whether they would bid this stranger welcome. If she could get past the guards, she could break out and take the road out to the highway, maybe flag down a ride to a pay phone. But there was a phone right there in the room she'd be working in tomorrow after she got things started at the school.

Still unsure what she would end up doing, she felt she had to do *something,* at least move in the direction of a possible action. It was well past dark now. She left the house, recorder in one pocket of her field jacket, cash and identification in the other, and walked toward the parking lot.

No guards were visible as she approached the entrance. Maybe they were asleep or somewhere else on the grounds. They were supposed to patrol the entire compound at various points during the evening, not just park in one place and stay there.

"Halt!" someone screeched, his voice breaking. "Who is it?"

Shit. "Sara. Sara McBride."

Just one man. Older. Not exactly a tough guy. Maybe she could overpower him. But that still wouldn't get her into a vehicle she had no key to start.

"Couldn't sleep. Taking a walk."

"Careful, honey, you could get shot. At least use a flashlight."

"Thanks. I'll go back now."

That decided it. Tomorrow.

She hadn't lied to the guard. She hadn't slept … and wouldn't sleep the rest of the night.

Another was also unable to sleep that night.

The silent second guard. It had to be him. Yesterday, after seeing him at the back of O'Keefe's building, then thinking, thinking, thinking so hard about it, that was her conclusion. But a bit of doubt lingered. And if she was wrong, what would Matthew say?

By late that evening, she had convinced herself. She needed to tell Matthew. She called in a page. "I have important information. Urgent. Please call right away."

That night, no call.

Next morning, no call.

Maybe he didn't even carry the pager anymore. She hadn't seen him use it the whole time he'd last stayed at her apartment. But she needed to get to him somehow.

That brutal trip. Again.

It was mid-afternoon already. She thought she could probably make it down there by midnight at the latest. But no way would she brave those scary last few miles in the dark. Get a little sleep now if she could somehow manage to sleep. Leave at midnight or a little after. Arrive down there at dawn.

If that second, kindly guard wasn't there at the community, she could be near certain who she'd seen at the airport and in that parking lot.

If he *was* there, she'd have to explain herself. It would be a severe mistake. Could be the doom of any possibility of happiness for her. Disgusted, he might turn his back, banish her, never speak to her again. But if she did nothing, and something terrible happened to the mission—whatever the mission was that was so important to Matthew and the Prophet—then something terrible might happen to Matthew. Not only would she lose him, maybe forever, but her failure to warn him …

She wouldn't be able to bear that. What reason would she have left to live at all?

CHAPTER 51

Sara took one measured step after another to the Prophet's house. She'd been due to help at the school but had told Naomi she'd have to miss that morning because there were important things to be done for the Prophet and Caleb.

She opened the door and received her first surprise. Linda sat knitting on a couch in the living room.

"Is he here?" Sara said, affecting casual and keeping on the move.

"No. They called him down to the entrance for something. I don't know what, but Caleb's back there."

The key cupboard was in a room off the hallway that led to the Evangel Room. She could simply retrieve a few keys, then turn around and breeze by Linda and out the front door.

But if the Prophet was down at the entrance, there would be others down there. Not the right time for this.

In the Evangel Room Caleb was scribbling on a notepad. Without looking up, he said, "I'm drafting a bulletin for you to send out."

"Does he have to see it first?"

"No. We've agreed on what it'll say."

"Where is he?"

"Not sure. I think he went down to welcome some visitor."

"Someone important?"

"I doubt it. If it is, nobody told me anything about it."

"When will yours be ready?"

"Maybe thirty minutes."

Then she'd have to type it up in bulletin format and post it. By then the Prophet would have returned, and there would be further delay. She wondered if she could jump Caleb, immobilize him somehow, make the call and light right on out into the forest or get to the parking lot with a key. Seemed like another goofy scheme. *Be cool.*

After an excruciating forty-five minutes, Caleb laid his pen on the notebook, stood up, and said, "Need to go to the head. Might get a cup of coffee too. Want one?"

Of course she didn't.

There she was, alone in the room, staring at the phone. Caleb was well known for long stays on the toilet and the unpleasant emanations lingering after those sessions. But what if he was just taking a leak? What would her story be if he returned while she was on the phone? But before she could make up a story, he was back, cup of coffee in hand.

He picked up his notepad and read what he'd written, frowning. "Just isn't quite right. This one is so important. Got to be right."

"I need to go myself … bathroom."

He looked puzzled when she grabbed her jacket on the way out.

She passed the bathroom and ducked into the cupboard room. Well organized. Chains or strings threaded through the holes in the key tops, a tag attached showing which vehicles they matched. She stopped herself from rushing, examined them carefully, took three that matched cars she was pretty sure were in good condition. Into the pocket, out the door, down the hall, past the kitchen, through the living room … there was the door…

People in the living room. *Breeze on by. Don't look.*

The commanding voice of the Prophet. "Sara."

The Prophet, the General, Sinclair, Sinclair's pet pit bull Darby, and a woman she'd never seen before.

"I forgot something at the house." She slowed but kept moving toward the door, toward the path to the parking lot … a car … escape.

"Sit down."

CHAPTER 52

To the woman the Prophet said, "This is Sara, ma'am. Tell Sara what you saw."

And while the Prophet, with that troubled look and Sinclair with his contemptuous stare, more hateful than ever, watched intently, observing Sara's every twitch, blink, flush, tremble, or tremor, the woman spoke.

She told Sara about the solicitous gentleman guard she'd taken particular notice of on her previous visit. He'd opened her car door for her, smiled at her, wished her safe travels. At that time she'd sworn to herself that she'd seen him before while working on her special mission observing Richard Maxwell and his top security man, a big blondish fellow named Peter O'Keefe of Peter O'Keefe & Associates … or at least she thought at the time he was Peter O'Keefe.

Sara, her face impassive up to this point, now frowned, deliberately, hoping it looked like confusion, not concern.

The woman continued. She'd followed the big man who she at that time thought was O'Keefe to the airport as she'd done once before, "and it was like … what's the word for that? Day…"

"Vu," Sara said. "Déjà vu." The perfect embodiment of innocence. Except she felt her upper lip pulsing. Had they noticed?

The woman was talking. "Yes, that's it. Déjà vu. A man came out of the airport, got in the big man's car, and they drove to a building where Peter O'Keefe & Associates has its offices. I followed them into the parking lot. I drove up to them as they were getting out of the car. It was the same man who'd come out of the airport. Then I was almost sure I'd seen him before. Twice in fact … when I followed the big man to the airport the first time, and the second time was right here at the Ark. It was the guard who was so nice to me."

The Prophet said in his gentlest sermon voice, "Are you sure now? Such a coincidence is, well—"

"I couldn't be more certain of my own name."

Sara wasn't sure which would explode first, her head or her heart, but she managed to pull off a calm tilt of her head and the best expression she could muster of shock and confusion.

Sinclair took over. No gentleness there. "You're acting like you don't know that was your husband."

"What?"

"Don't give us that phony crap," Sinclair said. "*Your husband.*"

"It had to be," the General said. "There's no other explanation."

She tried to unlock tears but couldn't coax them out, the panic stifled them. "It's unbelievable. Some crazy coincidence. A double."

"No. A spy. An informer. And what's that make you, Mrs. McBride, or whatever your name is? Interesting that your husband's name is Peter, the same name as Peter O'Keefe's, who has a business partner named Sara."

Shouldn't've used our real first names, she thought, and said, "I still don't believe it. You must be mistaken, ma'am, or there's some other terrible mistake. A look-alike, a double maybe … a doppelganger … People have them, it's a true thing, it happens. But I'll tell you this. If it's true somehow, give me the chance, and I'll be the first one to put a bullet in his head or a knife in his heart."

"You really think you can make us believe you know nothing about this?"

"I understand completely. But just get him in front of me, and I'll show you."

Sinclair spoke directly to the Prophet. "Let's not be fools. She needs to go the way of the last one."

"At the moment," the Prophet said, "we need her … to help us with the network."

A movement behind her. Caleb. His notepad in hand. "I'm ready, Sara. Sorry it took so long, but I'm ready now. It's so hot it's burning my hand."

"Stay here with us for a bit, Caleb," the Prophet said. "Mr. Darby, could you accompany Sara back to the Evangel Room?"

As they made their way down the hallway, Darby, his tone soft, said, "Any trouble and I'll be happy to break your neck."

Caleb sat down. The Prophet asked the visitor to go out for a short while. "Have a nice little walk on a fantastic Indian summer day. Thank you for your assistance. It's been of the greatest value. God is with you because you're doing His work. You're an angel He's sent to us."

As soon as the woman was gone, the Prophet explained the situation to a flabbergasted Caleb. "Never would I—"

"Nor I," the Prophet said, "but it would appear we've made a great mistake. The question is how to rectify it."

"How can you possibly believe she doesn't know?" Sinclair said. "Let me have her for a few minutes, and you'll know for sure what she knows."

"I only know three things, Matthew. One, we can't be one hundred percent sure that she or even her husband is an informer. There could be something else going on that may not be so damning. Second, he's likely to return, if for no other reason than to retrieve her. We might be able to extract some valuable intelligence from him. Third, most important of all, we need her for the messaging operation until we've completed our mission. It's just a few days away now. We can keep her under guard until he gets back, if he does get back. And we'll get to see whether she'll really plunge that knife into his heart."

Sinclair started to argue, but the General intervened. "He's right, Matt. Eliminate her now, and we potentially lose a lot for little gain other than the short-lived satisfaction of taking revenge. We have to transcend that impulse. Sacrificing something so large for something so small would be a downright sin."

"What if she won't help?"

"I think she will," the Prophet said. "And if she doesn't, you can have her."

Sinclair leaned back in grudging defeat. "Matthew," the Prophet said sternly, "I was not flattering or exaggerating. That lady is an angel sent to us from on high. Yahweh is speaking directly and strongly to me on this. You've been anointed, Matthew, as God's instrument in finding her and bringing her to us. She can be miraculously useful to us up to the final moments and beyond. You need to go up there with her and help guide her to her destiny, which is now *our* destiny. They have no idea about her. Right in front of them she is, but they cannot see her. She's invisible to them."

"A cipher," Sinclair said contemptuously.

In a sort of trance, with visage beatific, the Prophet engaged Sinclair with utmost holy earnestness.

"Oh, Matthew, you must remember:

> God moves in a mysterious way,
> His wonders to perform;
> He plants his footsteps in the sea,
> And rides upon the storm.

"Nothing could more poignantly demonstrate that we are doing God's own, true work than the gift of this humble cipher, as you call her, that He has sent us … through you, Matthew. I prophesy it. *He* prophesies it *through* me, His servant. The walls of Jericho will collapse. The Philistines will be smote. Babylon will be destroyed utterly, with sword and fire. You need to go up there with her now. Guide her. Help her help us. You've been anointed, Matthew."

"So well said," Caleb intoned. "Nay, wonderfully said. Beautifully said. It is surely the Word of the Lord."

Even the General was moved. "The Word of the Lord."

Sinclair nodded, churlish but accepting. Again, the Prophet: "Take Darby with you. We'll send Garrett Thiel up the morning before in the van loaded with the weaponry. You'll be perfectly placed for the Day of Wrath. Go now."

Sinclair rose from his chair and said, "I'd like to go over a few things with the General."

"We're done here anyway," the Prophet said. "Go on, Matthew. Please get right up there. Today."

"How about the McBride woman?"

"Caleb and I and Leon can handle her. Trust us."

The General accompanied Sinclair out the door. On the front stoop Sinclair said, "Can I trust you to do what needs to be done?

I can't trust those two. Caleb's a jellyfish and the Prophet wants to fuck her."

"I'll do what's necessary."

CHAPTER 53

THE G-MEN SCOFFED at O'Keefe's two-day ultimatum. Doolan told George, "If he wants to get himself indicted for sure, and maybe get himself and his girlfriend killed in the process, tell him to go right ahead."

O'Keefe himself wasn't sure whether he was bluffing or not, but if it had been a bluff, they'd called it. Toward the end of the second day they contacted George and said they needed a little more time, maybe one day, at the most two. O'Keefe reluctantly decided to go along with it. What gave him most pause was their jibe about him getting himself and Sara "killed in the process."

The third and fourth days came and went. On the morning of the fifth he sent George with a message: *Time's more than up. No more delays.*

George called back and said they'd asked O'Keefe to come in and meet with the Supervisory Agent who'd flown in from headquarters to execute the takedown of the Ark.

"Yeah," O'Keefe said, "so they can arrest me on the spot."

George arranged a telephone call instead. O'Keefe initiated proceedings from an obscure part of town, hoping that by the time they traced the call, there'd be no chance of finding him anywhere nearby.

The agents were on a speaker phone. Doolan spoke first. "O'Keefe, I'm about to turn the phone over to Charlie Redmond. He's in charge of the task force. He's a modest guy so he probably won't tell you that he's a former Green Beret, a decorated war hero, an experienced hostage negotiator, and an expert on these right-wing hate groups."

"Task force?" O'Keefe said. "You taking an army down there?"

"And hello to you too, Mr. O'Keefe." A new voice, presumably Redmond's; not like Doolan's in-your-face voice; unexpectedly more on the gentle side. "The safest thing for everyone involved is to make a demonstration of overwhelming force so they understand they have no choice but to surrender. We need to convince them right from the start that they won't even be able to make some vainglorious Alamo last stand … that it will be over in minutes if not seconds."

"You can't just go storming in there," O'Keefe said. "Hasn't Doolan bothered to tell you there's a bunch of little children in there?"

"That's their parents' doing," Doolan said. "It'll be on *their* heads, not ours."

"If that's your approach, I'll let them know you're comin'.

Doolan, blurting, apparently to Remond, in a low voice but not low enough: "See what I told you. We need to arrest this asshole right now."

Redmond intervened. "I'm sure you don't mean that, Pete. Hope I can call you Pete. We won't do that. We would if we thought we could do it with complete surprise … if we could get in there before they could even pick up a weapon. But we don't think we can keep it secret long enough given the size of the force we've assembled."

"Why," O'Keefe said, "can't you just grab the killers and their assault teams when they leave the place? You know the day."

Doolan made a scoffing noise. "That's real genius, O'Keefe. It leaves too much to their initiative, too much to them possibly changing their mind. They might already have teams in place up here. I could go on.

"So you'll at least give them a chance to surrender?"

"Of course," Redmond said. "But to be completely honest with you, Pete, not much of one. The more chance they have to prepare, the more my men are at risk."

"And," O'Keefe said, "more of those children too."

"If they're determined to fight us, it'll be better for the children if we give them the least possible time to prepare."

"When?"

"Not exactly sure, and you know I couldn't tell you even if I was. The task force is on its way down there right now. I'll be heading there myself as soon as I hang up this phone—"

Click.

"I think he just hung up on us," Redmond said.

O'Keefe immediately called George. "The bastards snookered me. I shouldn't have given them the extra time."

"What now?" George said.

"I'm on my way."

"They'll have every access blocked, including the highway itself."

"Maybe not. Do they know about the boat?"

"Not from me," George said. "Can I tell you not to do this?"

"And leave Sara to everyone's tender mercies?"

There was nothing for George to say to that except "I want to go too. Where can I meet you?"

"No. You need to stay with Maxwell, like white on rice."

"I don't remember you being much good at navigating a motorboat. I'm not even sure you know how to start the thing or even back it out of the boat slip."

"It's a long drive. You can get on the phone and drum it through my head over and over again."

"Wonder if they can intercept the call."

"Shit."

"You need some other things."

"No time to go shopping."

"I've got them."

"Meet me at I-70 and 10th Street."

CHAPTER 54

Aт A TRUCK stop on a highway leading out of town, George handed over a small flashlight, a loaded pistol in its holster, additional bullets, a buck knife in its scabbard, two pairs of swim fins, two wet suits (one significantly smaller than the other), a pair of thick-soled sandals, and a dry bag with straps so it could be worn as a backpack.

"Really?" O'Keefe said. "You got a warehouse of this stuff?"

"Be prepared. I don't recall little Petey being in our Boy Scout troop."

"'Fraid not. One of my many errors in life."

"Probably mooning around with Harrigan, writing poetry or some such shit."

"Why flippers?"

"You can't drive the boat all the way up to the shoreline. You'll make too much noise and probably get stuck. You'll have to swim in. Thus, the flippers. And you need to be functional when you get on shore, not loaded down with sopping-wet civvies or having to stop and put on dry clothes. Leave the wet suit on."

"I could go nudist."

"I shudder to think. They might die laughing, but I wouldn't count on that. The second suit and flippers assumes Sara's with you when you return to the boat. I had no time to get some sandals for her. Yours here are my size, but they'll work for you in a pinch if you need them. You may not have time for her to put the suit on. Then she just discards it, strips, and dives in."

O'Keefe looked something between confused and daunted.

Picking up on that, George said, "You sure I can't come with you? Why do I have the *strongest* feeling that you desperately need me?"

"I always need you. But Maxwell needs you more."

"Shaughnessy's a good man. He can handle it."

"Not like you can, Boy Scout."

A hug was out of the question, but George plunked his big paw onto O'Keefe's shoulder and tightly gripped it. "Be careful, buddy. You've exhausted all your nine lives already. I'll be by the phone day and night. Call me right away on the road. If there's any coverage down there at all, it'll be spotty. We'll go over every possibility I can think of for you to get that boat from the marina to the Ark. And don't let me forget to tell you how to drop anchor. You'll be wanting that boat still available if you're high-tailing it out of there, not floating around the lake unmoored."

"And how about the keys?"

"See what I mean about needing help? There's a little lock box under the lid of the storage unit. Combination is 7452."

"What's that relate to?"

"Nothing at all. Random. Like your life."

On the way down, George had drilled him on the boat startup ("Lucky for all of us, it's electric, so you don't have to prime and yank the cord and all that shit") and how to back out of the boat slip and maneuver out of the small harbor. O'Keefe had just managed that and was now on the water and struggling to remember the details of the original trip from the marina to the Ark shoreline with George and Sara and Karma. But that had been in daylight. Now he was burdened by the darkness of a cloudy, starless night.

He used the front light until he reached what he thought was the inlet that led to the Ark property. He needed to cut the engine but couldn't be sure he wouldn't kill the motor if he pulled the throttle back too far. He'd barely been able to start it at the marina. He was probably still moving too fast and too loud. *Should have brought George.*

He could roughly make out a shoreline and stayed as far away from it as he could while keeping it in blurred, uncertain sight. Out in front of him somewhere was the inlet's end, and the water leading up to it would get increasingly shallow the closer he approached the shore.

The farther he moved into the inlet, the more the darkness seemed to deepen. He was now relying more on sense than sight and more on guess than calculation. *Screw it. Worst case, I beach the damn thing and find another way out.*

And, indeed, the next meaningful sense he experienced was the boat scraping the lakebed. *Shit. Stuck in the mud?*

Instinctively, no conscious intent, he immediately pulled back the throttle and reversed. The boat lurched backward and found water instead of mud. *Miracle.*

He shut off the engine and went for the anchor at the rear, almost tumbling overboard when his movement caused the boat to rock angrily. He regained his balance, grabbed the anchor, and tossed it over the side.

In wet suit and flippers, dry bag strapped on his back, ready to enter the water, he noticed that the boat had no ladder. *Not like George to miss that. Must be a good reason.* Striving to make as little splash as possible, his back to the water, he tried to ease himself over the side but slipped and plunged too hard and noisily into chest-high water much shallower than he'd expected. He almost laughed when he realized his flippered feet had hit the lake bottom hard and anchored themselves in the mud so firmly that he wasn't sure he could move.

Imprisoned, panic rising, he squirmed back and forth and sideways struggling to free himself. No luck. He managed, barely, to reach up and grip the rim of the boat with the tips of his fingers and slowly pulled then jerked himself upward.

One of his feet had lurched halfway out of its flipper.

He was going to lose the Goddamn flippers.

So what.

In two pulls, one large and one small, he managed to get himself part of the way up and into the boat, his belly on the rim and his feet freed from the mud, one flipper still firmly on, the other still on but dangling precariously from his foot. He lunged forward and awkwardly and again too noisily flopped into the boat. He remained on his back for a few seconds, wondering if he was really up to this task. Several more mistakes saved by more miracles had just occurred. His quota had to be more than up.

Move.

And fuck these things. He wrenched off the flippers, stood, and again eased himself backward over the side, keeping his knees tucked so he wouldn't get stuck again. *Would have been so much easier with a ladder.*

Bobbing in the water, treading, unsure what the varying depths would be as he got closer to shore, wanting at all costs to avoid getting stuck again, he tried to make out the shoreline in the moonless darkness—*What now? What next?*

Once he thought he could see the shoreline, he breaststroked forward until he knew it was land he was seeing. He remembered the Ark property didn't extend to the inlet's end. It would be to his right, maybe thirty yards away. He continued his breaststroke toward the shore until he knew he was close, then extended his right leg downward until just his toes touched bottom. He would need to keep his feet out of the muck until he was almost on shore. Adjusting to keep what he hoped was the profile of the land in the corner of his left eye, he resumed his breaststroke, occasionally muttering curses as his feet rose and noisily splashed the water.

And then his hand touched the bottom. Less muddy here, even sandy. He hoped it wasn't his imagination telling him that right in front of him loomed the small sort-of-beach where he and Sara had stood and admired so many sunsets.

When his chest hit bottom, he climbed out of the water.

Sitting on the tiny strand, wet and shivering, he put on the sandals, stood, wrapped the pistol holster around his waist and strapped the buck-knife scabbard to the side of his right calf. With the bulb of the flashlight pressed against his chest to block the beam, he switched it on to make sure it worked, then moved into the woods.

In the woods, all was dark, all quiet. If the G-men had already descended on the place or even made their presence known, there would have been more activity, lights, commotion.

Now to elude the guards. He'd performed patrol duty many times. They had lately begun deploying three guards at night to ensure that the front entrance was always manned while the other two made occasional forays around other parts of the compound. They were supposed to patrol the perimeters two or three times a night, and mostly did, but they weren't gung-ho about it. They never, in his experience, struggled through the brush and brambles and snakes to reconnoiter this little beach. They just beamed their big flashlights in its direction and, never seeing anything close to an invader, moved on.

But the landmines … Supposedly they could be tripped only when activated at headquarters, but he could never convince himself to trust that the workmanship was competent and trustworthy or that somehow the activation switch hadn't been flipped on. Anticipating a situation like this one, he and Sara had tried to memorize all the placements in this area, but O'Keefe wasn't that confident in his memory. If the Ark people had learned the Feds were on their way, the kill switch might already have been flipped. It would be hard enough to remember in the bright of day, much less in this darkness. A flashlight would expose the disturbed ground, but that wasn't an option now.

And then the snakes…

Fuck it. Cast fate.

The sandals protected the bottom of his feet but not the tops. He trod as lightly as he could through the underbrush, but the brambles and burrs inflicted considerable pain.

A flashlight switched on. The beam bounced around until it stopped a few yards in front of him and began slowly moving in his direction. He planted his face in the thorns.

Voices.

"Wonder what that was?"

"Boar maybe?"

"Nah, I think we killed 'em all. Hope it is though. I'd like to blast one of 'em."

"Some other kind of varmint maybe."

"Not hearing anything now."

O'Keefe inched up his head. The beam bobbed along and away from his position.

What would he say if the patrolling guards or someone else confronted him? One patrolling guard usually carried an AR-15, the other a shotgun, and both had pistols.

Something like this might go down.

"McBride, you scared me, man. Almost blew you away. Thought you were away for your mom's funeral."

"Got back"—*what time would they have come on duty? Usually not until five*—"around three."

"What's up?"

"Doin' a little exercise. Trying to get my night vision back."

Was that even close to believable? If not, then *BOOM.*

He passed Caleb's house. A light was on.

He could see that a light was also on up at the Prophet's house, not a usual thing at this time of night.

No light on in their own house. No surprise. She liked to get a good night's sleep.

He'd better be careful going in. If he scared her enough, she might be the one to shoot him dead. *Would 'ironic' be the right word for that?*

He knocked on the door. No answer. Opened it. "Sara."

Not a shout but loud. "It's Pete."

No answer.

He used the flashlight to guide him to the bedroom they'd posed to look like a real married couple used it.

Not there.

What the…

CHAPTER 55

Trapped. under guard. Caleb writing furiously, reading his draft aloud to the Prophet and the General; the Prophet and the General dictating riffs on Caleb's text; Sara transcribing Caleb's oddly looping, feminine handwriting and reading the typed text aloud with all the verve she could muster, still the good soldier despite the noose of suspected treason around her neck; Caleb and the Prophet making occasional corrections as she spoke but mostly beaming with satisfaction on hearing their fulminations; Sara transmitting the screeds, several a day, to the maniacs at the end of the wire. Calls to arms. Annunciations of the Apocalypse. Invitations to a holocaust.

She'd been at it for days now—four, maybe five—feigning enthusiasm until she almost hated herself, hoping she could convince them of her unshakable loyalty, lull them into carelessness, take advantage of a momentary lapse to make that break for the parking lot. Amazingly, they'd failed to search her. She still had the three sets of car keys in one pocket of her jacket, the recorder in the other.

Caleb and the General watched scrupulously as she worked with the computer, trying, she guessed, to prepare themselves to perform those functions in case she was "no longer available," as they phrased it.

If only she could be alone with Caleb or the Prophet, each of them vulnerable to her in their own ways—Caleb due to his physical weakness, the Prophet due to his hunger for her body. But she was never alone with either of them for more than a few minutes. Both were usually present. Worse, the General, especially vigilant and stern, often joined, making a formidable trio.

When she wasn't doing something that required her hands free, she was cuffed. Linda accompanied her to the bathroom, left the door wide open, and stood in the hallway, watching her the whole time, one of the men stationed a few feet away to come to Linda's aid if necessary.

There'd been no sign of Naomi. Sara was left to wonder whether that was because Naomi now detested her so completely that she couldn't stand to even look at her.

When she wasn't working, they deposited her, still handcuffed, in a small room along the hallway, windowless and empty except for a sleeping bag on top of an air mattress and, mercifully, a comfortable chair and a small made-from-scratch portable toilet.

They fed her twice a day, first thing in the morning and then in late afternoon, sandwiches or other handheld food items that could be consumed without utensils. Two of the men brought her meals, violently kicking the door open and staying in the hallway until they knew where she was in the room (in case, she supposed, she'd been able to maneuver herself into a position to pounce on them when they entered).

Through it all, she suffered in silence, although with facial expressions and other body language she tried to convey that this was the martyrdom of an innocent person who graciously understood why it was necessary to subject her to all this until she was vindicated.

Where was O'Keefe? She had to hope he was—and would stay— far away. Otherwise, he'd waltz into the compound unsuspectingly, and they both would be trapped—and likely doomed.

Where is she?

Something had to be very wrong if she wasn't in the house in the middle of the night. Maybe they'd drafted her for guard duty? Maybe someone in the compound had been injured or fallen seriously ill, or one of the women was experiencing an especially difficult labor and she'd gone to help?

Or maybe they'd found him out somehow. That informant of Doolan's … maybe a double agent? Or maybe Spud had betrayed him. Why wouldn't he? His ties to O'Keefe from a time long ago seemed a lot weaker than his allegiance to the Ark.

He had the M16, the pistol, the knife. Plunge ahead, go find her?

Foolish.

Or wait? Gamble that she was in no trouble, would return soon, maybe even in the next few minutes.

Or her situation could be worsening by the hour, the moment, and any chance to come to her aid was disappearing.

He decided to wait. If that choice turned out to be a mistake, he knew he would forever wonder, once the layers of calculation and rationalization were peeled away, whether it was, at bottom, a decision made by a coward—not a failure of physical bravery but fear of making the wrong choice.

And when dawn came, and the morning ambled too slowly toward afternoon, his mistake became clearer and more painful by the minute. There was no good explanation for her continuing absence. Despite his contempt for their bungling surveillance efforts, maybe they *had* managed to follow him and Sara was paying—or had already paid—the price for his arrogance

He spun out in his mind how he might play it, how it might go. He returns, innocent as a child. How? Circle around and walk up the road and into the parking lot. If they've already found him out, it's all over right there. If they haven't, why has he arrived on foot? How to explain that? Car broke down on the nasty road from the highway. He's had to hump the rest of the way here. That had some sense to it. The guards would probably offer to get someone to drive him back right away to get the Buick working, but he'd tell them, "No, I have some important news for the Prophet he needs to hear right away." He goes toward the Prophet's house but deviates to his own. Retrieves his weapons. To the Prophet's house. He busts in. "Where's Sara?"

All that risk when he'd already managed the feat of actually getting here and hiding, undiscovered, behind enemy lines. Much as he was cursing himself for the previous night's procrastination, he knew that darkness was his friend, and the only reason not to wait until nightfall on this day was to impulsively try to remedy the mistake he may have made the night before.

Sara was also waiting for dark. She would beg them to let her take a bath while Linda observed, first escorting her back to her house so she could retrieve clean clothing and a few toiletries.

She wished for luck. Maybe they would send only Caleb with her. She felt confident she could subdue him. Even if it was the General, even if it was both Caleb and the General, she had to try.

CHAPTER 56

IT WAS TO be the last posting of the day. Sunday, two days from now, would be the greatest of all days, when David and his warriors would strike the blow against the Philistine Goliath in accordance with Yahweh's revelations. Theirs would be the spark to the ultimate conflagration. The End Times. The Tribulation. The war of all against all. The return of Jesus Christ. Armageddon. The Final Battle of Christ and his angels against the Antichrist and Satan and his demons. After that carnage, only the elect, God's Chosen, would remain. Jesus would rein and God's promise of blissful eternal life would be fulfilled for the deserving few who had shouldered the cross and followed their Savior.

They heard, at first faintly, some ruckus, a stomping, a shouting—from the front of the house—growing louder, coming closer.

The guard flung himself headlong into the room, almost falling down, terrified, panting, face flushed, eyes wide and burning. "They're here, they're here."

"Who? What?"

"The ZOG. The Feds. Multitudes of them. They say they have us surrounded. They have arrest warrants. Weapons violations."

The General turned to Sara. Pulled his pistol out of its holster. "Your husband did this."

Somehow, she wasn't afraid. "Don't dare point that at me, you pig. If he did, I'll reject him, renounce him. I've made that clear. I'm innocent..."

She turned to the Prophet. "I'll be your hostage."

"Leon. Stop," the Prophet commanded. "As she says, she's a hostage, voluntary or not. There'll be negotiations. That'll buy us time. Go rouse the men. Get the defenses ready. If they attack, we'll slaughter them."

The General walked over to the switch that activated the mines, flipped it, then left.

The Prophet turned to the guards. "Let's go."

Caleb had seemed dumbstruck but now managed to blurt, "You can't. They'll arrest you."

"I won't show myself," the Prophet said. "I'll just instruct the men what to tell them. Meanwhile, post an emergency bulletin. Under no circumstances will we surrender. It's time for the Armies of Christ all over this country to arise and strike."

Caleb's voice quivered as he dictated. Sara's hands trembled as she typed.

EMERGENCY BULLETIN

BATTLE CRY!

THE MOMENT HAS ARRIVED!
ZOG'S BRUTAL ENFORCERS
HAVE ARRIVED AT OUR DOORSTEP,

WITH THEIR UNCONSTITUTIONAL LAWS

AND THEIR ILLEGAL, UNHOLY
ARREST WARRANTS.

WE WILL FIGHT TO THE LAST!
JOIN US IN OUR GLORY!

GOD'S WARRIORS, ARISE AND STRIKE!

"I think that's enough," he said. "Post it."
She hesitated.
"Post it!"

She posted it. He was behind her, bent over her right shoulder, examining the screen. She crooked her arm, swung it back and jammed her elbow into his Adam's apple. Gagging, he rose up and brought his hands to his throat. She swiveled, thrust herself up from the chair, and kicked him in the groin. As he folded over, she brought her knee up hard against his nose. He fell to his knees, face to the floor. Blood dripped onto the carpet. She kicked him in the back. It knocked him prone. She bent over him, snatched his pistol from its holster.

Why am I enjoying this so much? "You stay right there. Don't come after me. Don't think I won't shoot you. I'd love to shoot you."

Face still pressed to the floor, he only groaned.

She headed for the door, stopped, stepped over to the landmine-activation switch and flipped it off, then rushed into the hallway.

Startled, frightened, she halted, took a step back. It was Naomi, standing but a few feet away from her, the strangest look on her face. Not fear. Not anger. What was it? Not knowing why, Sara muttered, "I'm sorry," and ran past Naomi through the family area and out the rear door.

She wouldn't see Caleb rise to his feet, pain still etched on his face. Wouldn't see him lurch over to the landmine-activation switch. Wouldn't know that he'd switched it back on.

The darkness seemed to welcome, enfold, and protect her. She composed herself and walked calmly behind the other side of the community building and around to the front. The lights of the Prophet's house and the Fortress had been turned on. On his bullhorn the General was summoning the men to assemble for battle and the women and children to shelter in the Fortress, but so far only a couple of people had emerged. She needed to get to the house for the M16. If she could avoid the General, she should be clear. The others likely knew nothing about the suspicion she'd fallen under.

As she closed in on the house, a figure, unidentifiable in the darkness, moved up the path toward her. She aimed the pistol, said

"Stop!" and hoped the figure would obey. If it came to shooting one of these people, at least the more innocent ones, she wasn't sure she could pull the trigger.

A movement. Hands going up? "It's Pete!"

She ran to him. They embraced awkwardly, quickly separating.

"Where'd you come from?" she said.

"The lake. The boat. What's the ruckus?"

"The Feds just showed up out front. The General's calling the men to battle. They found out about you and put me under guard. When all hell broke loose, I took off, but they're probably coming after me right now."

"What about the kids?"

"They're gathering with the women in the church and school building."

They heard what sounded like Caleb yelling from the top of the hill.

"Let's go," O'Keefe said. "To the beach. A short swim from there to the boat."

They ran, dodging a few people who'd come out of their homes and were heading up the slope to answer the General's call. One man saw them and said, "Where you goin?" They didn't answer, but both understood what was likely to happen next. The man would encounter Caleb. Pursuit would commence.

CHAPTER 57

I**N THE DENSER** part of the woods, O'Keefe stopped and grabbed her arm. "Stand still." He switched on a flashlight, panned it over the ground ahead, then shut it off. "How well did you memorize where the mines are?"

"I just deactivated them up at the house."

"Better not trust that. What goes off might go on again. Do you remember?"

"I think I can remember."

"Between the two of us maybe we can remember them," he said. "We'll walk abreast, keep on the same line, grit our teeth and go slow even though they're after us. I'll hold the flashlight, shine it a few yards ahead."

"They'll see the light. They'll catch up to us," she said.

"Better they catch up than we trip a mine. At them we can fire back."

They picked their way through the woods, watching out for the bare or disturbed patches that would reveal the placement of a mine, trying to ignore the growing clamor of voices and flashlight beams to their rear. In spurts as they moved along, she recounted recent events including the plan of attack revealed on the tape in her pocket. To each succeeding revelation he would respond with a "No shit?" or "Unbelievable" or "Insane."

Through the last stand of trees the moonlit lake came into view. "That's it," she said. "No more mines here to the beach."

In seemingly direct and startling contradiction to her statement, EXPLOSION.

It sent them diving to the ground as if it wasn't already too late to protect themselves. Behind them a scream. Then yells. Apparently one of their pursuers had stepped in the wrong place.

He helped her up. She cried out, fell back down, clutched her lower leg.

His flashlight exposed the snake, coiled and ready to strike again. Not knowing what else to do, he jumped straight up as high as he could and landed on the snake with both feet, flinching in anticipation of a bite.

No bite. He bounced up and down, making sure he crushed every flicker of life out of it. He looked down. He might need to show it to the medical people. He picked it up by its tail. He'd stomped its head flat. No worries about another bite.

"What is it?" she said.

He chose not to tell her it was a timber rattlesnake.

"I don't know, but let's go. We need to move faster than the venom."

"*Venom?*"

"In case there's any. Probably isn't."

A hospital seemed so far away. A swim to the boat. A struggle to get into the boat. Would it start? Would he be able to navigate it? If he screwed it up, would she be in a fit state to help? There was a radio on board, but George had said it probably wouldn't help. "It has hardly any range," he'd said, "one or two miles at most. Assuming you're in range, you can push the button and say "Mayday" and hope someone's listening *and* is in a position to actually do something."

Once they made it back to the marina, it would doubtless be closed, nobody around. He could try the radio from there, but that limited range and random possibility of reaching the right person might just be a waste of valuable time while the venom continued to rapidly take its toll. Hopefully, they hadn't towed the strange car that had been mysteriously parked there for days. Hopefully, he hadn't left on an overhead light or something else to drain the battery. From the marina, up a steep hill and what amounted to a few blocks down a winding road to the town. But he couldn't just randomly start knocking on doors. If the car phone worked, how to call an emergency phone line down here? Did they even have an ambulance service down here? How long would all that take? Just take her straight to the hospital if he could figure out where one was. How far away in this sparse country might a hospital be? Even if they made it in time, would they have an emergency room and properly trained personnel?

O'Keefe knew all about venomous snakes. The hard way. Once bitten, twice shy. He'd even checked out the situation in this part of the state before their trip. But it hadn't seemed that dangerous then. Copperheads and water moccasins abounded, but while their bites could lead to severe consequences if not treated within a reasonable time, fatalities, even permanent disabling injury, they occurred seldom if ever. But what was "a reasonable time"? And a rattler's bite would be far more dangerous and maybe faster acting. If not timely treated, the consequences of a rattler's bite went from bad—swelling of limbs, sometimes to elephantine proportions, the tissue becoming "necrotic" (doctor talk for "dead"), the complications including disability and amputation—all the way to lethal. Death was a possibility.

There was another option. "We could go back," he said. "Give ourselves up … get you taken care of." *Should I tell her it was a rattlesnake?* Instead of that, he said, "I can't tell you how it's gonna develop, if there's poison in you, how much, and how long it will take to move through you. But the exertion will speed it up—"

"Stop. Let's go."

When they reached the beach, he could see in the distance what he thought was the outline of the boat, but it was far out enough and dark enough that he wouldn't have been able to detect it if he hadn't known it was there. Or hoped it was there … if his night vision wasn't deceiving him. Someone could have found it and figured out how to drive or tow it away.

He looked at her. She looked stricken.

"How are you? Can you swim it?"

She nodded vigorously. "Yes."

Hurry, he thought. *Forget about wet suits and swim fins and all the rest of that shit … Except maybe for her.* "Would fins help?"

"No. Let's just get going. I'm feeling sick."

He took the recorder from her pocket and stuffed it into the dry bag pack with the pistols, flashlights, and snake corpse. No way to break down the M16 and get all the parts into the already bulging pack. He put the 20-round magazine in the pack and positioned the rifle in its sling across his chest and back, leaving his arms mostly free for swimming. It might not fire properly until he had the chance to dry it out after reaching the boat, a risk he had to take.

"Stay with me to my right," he said. "Grab me or hit me if I'm going too fast."

He surged forward, occasionally freestyling but mostly breast stroking so he could keep his eyes on the boat, his right hand occasionally reaching back to check for her placement beside him. She fell back a couple of times and he adjusted. By the time they got to the boat he felt exhausted, unsure if he'd be able to haul *himself* up and in, let alone help her. He cursed himself for not staying in better shape, especially fudging on the strength training, but cursed George even more for the missing ladder. *Well, Georgie Boy, I guess even Boy Scouts make mistakes.*

How to do this? Go first and help lift her in? No, he thought it better to use his shoulders as a platform for her to plant her feet on and lift herself in.

"No ladder?" she said, struggling to catch her breath.

"'Fraid not."

He went under, placed her feet on his shoulders, grabbed her ankles, and heaved upward. But she floundered. *Bad choice. Try the other way. Looking grim. Should've surrendered back there on the beach.*

He surfaced, reached up, grabbed the side, and struggled upward, making it only halfway before wondering if his puny forearms could take him the rest of the way in. He envisioned both of them bobbing around by the boat, unable to get in, her survival at the mercy of how much venom the snake had been able to inject and the quality of her body's resistance mechanisms … if she didn't drown first … *Should have at least put the life jackets on … at least hers.*

One more lunge. If it didn't work, he'd get her back to the beach and hope those freaks didn't put a bullet in their heads right there.

Last chance…

He thrust himself upward and got his chest as far as the boat rim, wobbled backward but managed one more thrust, and he flopped over and in. He scrambled onto his knees and leaned over. Grabbing her hands in his wasn't going to work. "Can you grab the rim?"

She tried but couldn't quite make it.

All for the want of a ladder.

He put all his weight against the side of the boat, leaned over the rim, and pushed down hard. The boat tipped slightly toward her. He grabbed the back of her collar and pulled her up. She got purchase on the rim with both hands. He reached under her arms and pulled her in, toppling backward as he did so, and they both flopped like caught fish.

Breathless, he managed to say, "You alright?"

"Yes." But there was a moan in her voice now.

Every movement from there on felt like a fumble and took time they didn't have … *she* didn't have. He misdialed the combination the first time. Breathe. Go slow. Got it on the second try. Key in hand, he crawled back over to her where she lay huddled and shivering in a heap on the deck Nothing to do to help her except get this thing going. Up on his feet, willing himself, as the boat rocked, not to fall on his ass and break his arm or knock himself out.

Now the moment he'd been most dreading. His whole life had been a failure to subdue things mechanical.

Turn the key. Push the button. A sound. But not a start.

Another sound. A chug. Another chug.

Another type of sound. Gunfire. Bullets hitting the side of the boat. AR-15 on full automatic.

"Get down," he yelled, but she was already there.

He ducked as low as he could and gave it another go.

Another chug, but not a start. *Don't flood the bastard. Could a boat engine flood? Sure it can, rockhead.*

He seemed pathetically ill-equipped for everything he needed to do in this moment.

But third time, it started; more than a charm, another miracle.

Something whizzed too close. Something pinged off the side of the boat. AR-15 again. *Can't turn on the lights.* Seemed like only one shooter.

How close was the boat to the lake bottom? Going forward even a little seemed like the wrong choice. He reversed and felt the boat scrape bottom. *Fuck it. Power it out. Don't pussy around and dig it in deeper.* He snapped it hard into reverse and the boat jerked back, almost knocking him down, and he heard her mutter an agonized "Fuck," but the steering wheel had been positioned so the boat swerved around until he was almost facing away from the shore and out into the lake.

He'd normally have gone forward slowly, carefully, fearfully but for another burst from the AR-15. He throttled it all the way. The front of the boat lurched up. He staggered but managed to hold onto the steering wheel. Soon he was out of the cove and into the lake. As they sped along, he waited for the bullet that would rip off the back of his head. All the bullets fired at him in Vietnam. All had missed. Maybe his number was finally up. If that happened, Sara was low enough not to be hit. If she had the strength to take the wheel and avoid his fate, she might make it.

Slamming up and down, struggling to keep control, he glanced back at her. She was hunched, holding the lapels of her jacket shut with both hands against the wind.

The AR-15 went silent in surrender.

He grabbed the radio and called "Mayday" a couple of times, but at full throttle he needed both hands on the steering wheel. At this speed, and with this level of abandon, hitting a floating log or a shallow spot would likely mean disaster, probably the boat flipping end over end in a wild topsy turvy, but it was a risk that had to be taken against the relentless march of time and spread of venom.

CHAPTER 58

T HE SHORE SEEMED to be getting closer. It turned out to be a peninsula jutting out into the lake. He swung left to avoid it and steered back toward the main part of the lake. Rounding the peninsula's end, he faced a row of boat lights and the noise of powerful engines coming fast at him. How strange that seemed, until it occurred to him that it might be the G-men-become-Marines heading toward an amphibious assault on the rear of the Ark compound.

He swung farther to his left to avoid them, but they adjusted to their right, as if they intended to run him down.

A bullhorn-amplified voice confirmed that precise intention. "Halt! Shut off your engines. Stop! Stop or we'll blast your ass out of the water."

He brought the throttle back and puttered toward them. He heard, then looked back to see Sara vomiting over the side as the lead boat approached, Agent Doolan at the prow, looking angry and fanatical, like the demented Ahab himself.

The lights almost blinded O'Keefe as Doolan's boat pulled up alongside.

In stunned recognition Doolan said, "O'Keefe! Talk about a bad penny. What the fuck are you doing?"

"My partner's been bitten by a timber rattler, and the venom is surging. She's getting sicker and sicker. We need to get her to a hospital or at least a doctor."

"Assuming I even believe you, I never heard of a rattler bite killing anybody except in a cowboy movie. Did you suck the poison out like they do in the movies?"

"All that proves is you don't know shit."

"And *you* are under arrest. Your snake-bit partner too."

O'Keefe lowered his voice, hoping Sara couldn't hear him. "She could die. Even if she survives, the complications could be horrific. Let us go. You can arrest us later."

"You took off last time. Can't be trusted."

O'Keefe staggered over and grabbed the throttle. "I'm goin' to the marina."

"You hit that throttle and I'll blow you out of the water. Your partner'll have a lot more than a snakebite to worry about."

"You know we work for Richard Maxwell, right?"

"So what?"

"He's got lots of money and controls lots of media. If you kill my partner or even make her suffer unnecessarily, we'll chase your dumb ass to the end of the earth. There won't be a hole left for you to hide in."

"Maybe you need to see my badge. It says *FBI* on it."

"And when we're through with you, your stupid fucking badge will say *Ex-FBI Dunce.* You think Redmond would approve what you're doing? He'll be the first one to make you walk the plank, Captain Bly. Listen to this and believe me. We have valuable information that could save some of your FBI buddies' lives. For both our sakes, yours and mine, call him. Ask what he would do."

"I'm the one in charge right here."

"That's only until I hit this throttle and you blow me out of the water ... and then you'll have the biggest scandal on your hands you can imagine. First thing I'll do is ram your ass. Better grab somethin' right now 'cause you're goin' overboard, dickhead."

O'Keefe shifted into neutral and raced the engine to a loud whining roar. "Just like that. And I and this boat'll be a double decker with yours and you a flat little mud-and-blood pie underneath it."

The standoff lasted another moment or so. Then Doolan seemed to get himself under control enough to say, "Stay right there." He went over to the radio and talked into it, his back to O'Keefe.

"Your wife and kids'll thank you for that," O'Keefe yelled and swung his boat enough away from Doolan's so some hero type couldn't leap across and board him.

He went to Sara and knelt down beside her. "How is it?"

"Not good."

"Is it getting worse?"

"I can't tell. It's just bad."

O'Keefe glanced back over his shoulder. Doolan was finished with the radio and standing at his prow. O'Keefe left her and wobbled his way back to the front. Doolan signaled to his driver to move closer to O'Keefe's boat. His attitude had been adjusted. "One of our boats will escort you in. They're calling an ambulance to the marina."

No time to gloat. "Thank you, sir," O'Keefe said, without sarcasm.

"Don't fuck us around anymore, okay?"

"Come close. I've got something for you that's the opposite of a fuck-around."

Doolan looked mistrustful but said, "Can you toss it?"

"Don't want to chance it ending up in the lake. This is major stuff, my boy."

Doolan offered up a skeptical grimace, then motioned to his driver, who brought the FBI boat even closer to O'Keefe's.

O'Keefe clambered back to Sara. "I'm giving him the tape."

A sudden burst of energy. "You sure? How can you trust him?"

"I can't. But it's their job now, not ours. Our job is to get you to a hospital."

O'Keefe handed over the recorder. "You'll be the Big Shit for a minute or two when you show up with this, Doolan. Remember me a little more fondly next time … You have a medic over there or someone good at first aid?"

"Not good enough. Let's just get her to the marina as fast as we can."

"Doolan, one more thing. They've got landmines planted all over the area where you're probably planning to land."

Doolan looked shocked … and grateful.

CHAPTER 59

 The General paced back and forth on the Gathering Ground, AR-15 slung over his right shoulder, bullhorn in hand, nervously and impatiently watching below as the people seemed to be taking their own sweet time making their way to him, despite his repeated urgent calls for haste and the fiercest scowl he could muster, as if the blazing concentration of his gaze might itself hurry their steps.

At first he sensed more than saw or heard a commotion toward the bottom of the slope. Then he heard raised voices, indistinct but disturbingly urgent. *Now what?*

One of the men, Lester Vance, came running up the path. "The McBrides are running away!" he sputtered.

McBrides? Plural? He's not even here.

Behind him came the clomp of heavy running footsteps. He turned. Caleb.

It was Caleb, out of breath and sweat soaked. A near scream. "*She's escaped!*"

"How?"

Caleb didn't answer.

"She was with *him,*" Vance said.

"Who?"

"The husband. Pete."

The whole world seemed to be going insane, and that was before he heard the explosion. It could mean only one thing. One of the mines had detonated. Had the ZOG soldiers already infiltrated? The perfidious bastards had proposed peace talks at the front gate while sneaking around the back for an amphibious assault.

"I'm telling you," Vance said, "Pete was with her."

Good, he thought. *That means the mine got 'em.* Unless it was the ZOGs that had tripped it. Hopefully the ZOGs, but good enough either way.

What should he do now? He'd always expected an attack from the front. That's where he'd laid out his fields of fire. The mines were there to protect them from a relatively unlikely assault from the rear. A couple of the men were setting up the 50 cals. This war would be lost, but the glory would be in how long they could hold off the ZOGs and how many they could kill while they did. More men were arriving while their wives and children peeled off toward the Fortress.

He kept asking the men what they'd seen. Some had seen the McBrides, but none had spotted any ZOGs.

Shouts in the darkness below. He could make out what at first seemed like one large object struggling up the path. It turned out to be two men carrying a prone third. *One of the McBrides,* he thought … hoped … a bloody, gory, chewed-up version.

But as they came into the light, he saw that the person was one of theirs. Mark Johnson. He shouted at the rubber-necking men around him: "Get a stretcher. Get him into the Fortress. Is Naomi in there? Find Naomi. And where's McConnell?" Then, to no one in particular, he said, "What the hell happened?"

"We went after the McBrides. We didn't think the mines were on."

And there'd been no reason for them to believe otherwise. He'd summoned them on the bullhorn but hadn't thought it smart to announce why. He was the one who'd impulsively flipped the switch in anger after the Prophet had chastised him in front of the McBride woman. But it had made utter good sense to do that. The ZOG barbarians were at the gates. Who knew how deeply they'd already infiltrated or were about to? He was not unwilling to blame himself for other things, but not for this. Yes, he should have remembered and warned them when he'd called them to assemble, but the McBride traitors were the ones to blame.

Now he heard gunfire. His head snapped around to the front entrance. He wondered if the ZOG attack was underway but then realized the shots were coming from below, and it was an AR-15.

"That's Lucas," one of the men said. "He was after them too."

He imagined Lucas and others down there in the trees or on the beach, paralyzed, afraid to move. Or worse, foolhardy enough to move despite having heard the explosion.

Caleb was standing there, so unusually and strangely quiet. "Caleb, get in there and turn off the switch."

Obeying without hesitation, Caleb headed back to the house, deciding on his way there that it wouldn't help anyone's cause for him to report Sara turning the switch off and he dutifully turning it back on.

The General sent one of the men back down the hill with the bullhorn to announce the all-clear to Lucas and anyone else down there. Defensive preparations resumed. He ordered the precise placement of 50 cals and soldiers equipped with M60s and AR-15s to create a devastating mass of firepower that would decimate the invaders. He ordered others to bring up boxes of grenades, then positioned those men at intervals behind the front line of automatic-rifle power—"To cover the gaps," he said. He decided to initially keep the LAW rockets in reserve but ready to pulverize any armored vehicles the ZOGs might use to try to overrun his defenses.

Lucas and one other straggler arrived, reporting that the McBrides had managed to escape by boat, and that lights from a flotilla out on the lake had been spotted. A couple of the boats appeared to have turned back, but others remained.

The General ordered one of the men to climb a tree and observe any further movement by the flotilla. The front-entrance guards, who'd be the first line of defense and would warn of an attack from that direction, received additional ammunition and a supply of grenades.

Surveying his arrangements, he had to admit that his army could only be described as "ragtag." Some were obviously too old to be fighting a war. Some looked like they might shit their britches at any moment. But they'd been well trained for this, and most seemed to be resolutely stepping up to do their duty despite the real and imminent possibility of injury or death.

Satisfied that he'd established a decent perimeter, he decided to rouse David. It was time for the Prophet to fortify his people.

Then he heard the screaming from the Fortress.

CHAPTER 60

THE WOMEN AND and children had gathered in the chapel as instructed. The children were thrilled and boisterous. Most of the women, except a few of the more fanatical ones, verged on the edge of hysteria. Gossip and rumors were mushrooming. The traitorous McBrides were the main topic. Naomi had no idea what to tell them. Instead, she set about assigning chores to the women and organizing diversions for the children, drafting one of the women to gather the young ones and read them Bible stories, starting with Daniel in the lions' den.

When the mine exploded, it was not particularly loud. The reaction wasn't hysterical, more an anxious curiosity.

Until the damn fools brought in the mangled, bloody mess that was Mark Johnson.

Women and children gasped and gawped, terrified. Weeping and wailing broke out and spread quickly.

"Get the kids out of here," Naomi ordered two nearby women.

"Where?" one asked.

"Anywhere but in here. Take them upstairs."

When Connie Johnson realized that the injured man was her husband, she screamed, then collapsed into a near faint. A couple of the women propped her up and guided her over to him. She knelt beside him but couldn't bring herself to touch him.

McConnell, the Ark's "doctor," was ministering to Mark. McConnell had never attended medical or nursing school or even worked in a hospital, but he somehow knew more about medical things than any of the others. Naomi had been a nurse a long time ago and performed midwifery and first-aid services in the community. Connie asked McConnell if Mark was going to die. He said nothing, but big tears squeezed from his eyes, confirming to Naomi what she could see for herself—that Mark was going to die soon, if he wasn't dead already, from blood loss and shock. They made feeble efforts to staunch the wounds and treat him for the shock, but soon there could be no pretending.

Naomi understood that she would need to be the lead actor here. "Take him into the big classroom on this floor," she whispered to McConnell. "Take Connie too."

Moments after they carried Mark out, the General stomped in. Naomi pointed him in the direction of the classroom, saying nothing. Let him find out for himself, *I've got to keep these women calm.*

She turned to Jenny Morgan. Ignoring the tears smearing Jenny's face, she said, "Sing something … Something rousing … Get them to clap their hands and join in."

Jenny took a deep breath, then launched forth with "Mine Eyes Have Seen the Glory" (likely unaware of its abolitionist origins), her exquisite soprano immediately soothing the clamor of distress pervading the room.

Naomi turned then to dependable Alice Robley. "The men, the children, the rest of us need to eat. We need to get something going."

The General returned. He seemed to have lost his usual clench-jawed composure.

Yes, General, what are you thinking now about your war talk and war games?

She drew him aside. "Have you thought about all we're going to need to do? Like meals? I can organize something, but I'll need some help from some of your *warriors.*"

If he'd noticed the sarcasm she'd loaded into the final word, he ignored it, looked startled, then nodded. He should have thought of that long ago.

A commotion outside. They went to the door. The Prophet had emerged from the house.

"I have to go," the General said. "But we'll get to work on that right away."

Naomi followed him out, watched him jog to where the Prophet was standing. They conferred.

David's face, bathed in the floodlights, changed.

She knew him so well after all these years. He was afraid, close to panic. He turned around, his back to the General and the soldiers. It looked for a moment like he might walk or even run away. But he turned back, and when he did, she knew he'd overcome that moment of fear and doubt. It almost made her proud of him again. Maybe he would change his course, rescue them all from this horrible situation.

The Prophet nodded to the General.

The General issued a command. "A-tten-*TION*."

They quickly came to order.

The Prophet began.

"Do not be afraid. You have nothing to fear. I've prayed to the Lord, and we are exactly where we belong. In His hands as always, where He has led and precisely steered us. If you know your Bible well, you know the story of Jehoshaphat, a King of Israel in the olden times. A gigantic army of Moabites and Ammonites surrounded the people of Israel. The odds against the King and his people were overwhelming. Jehoshaphat lost all hope. All human hope, that is. One last hope was left to him—his hope and faith in his Lord God Yahweh.

"The King stood before the men of Israel"—the Prophet gestured toward the soldiers standing before him. Then he gestured toward the Fortress—"and he stood before their women and children as well.

"And before all of them the King humbly begged for God's help. And the Spirit of the Lord came unto one of the multitude, who said, 'Jehoshaphat and all of Israel, do not be afraid. Take your positions. Stand firm. Do not cower. The Lord will be with you.' And Jehosaphat's hope and faith were renewed. He ordered his people to sing God's praise."

The Prophet cupped his hand behind his ear, calling attention to the rising swell of Jenny Morgan and her choristers that had been building from inside the Fortress during his speech. "And," he continued, "lo and behold, the huge multitude of enemies began to quarrel among themselves and then even fight among themselves, until they slayed each other, to the last man! When the warriors of

Israel came to the battlefield, there was nothing before them but enemy dead … all of them … to the last man!

"Let's all join now our brave women folk and our beautiful children in this inspiring hymn in praise of the work of the Lord, the work we are doing, trampling out the vintage where the grapes of wrath are stored."

The Prophet, joined quickly by the General, then by the assembled soldiers, sang in full voice.

Caleb, hand over heart, sang as loud as his lungs would allow. He thought it seemed that everyone in the community was singing.

Except for one. At some point Naomi had turned and walked away.

The singing continued until one of the guards at the entrance came running up to the Prophet and the General. As they conferred, the singing slowly petered out.

The winded guard could hardly get the words out. "They said we're cut off, that they have overwhelming numbers and even more overwhelming fire power. Said they can't and won't let us resist much longer. They asked if it's worth having a talk before they come in here with everything they've got."

As the Prophet considered this, a look sly and even a touch triumphant spread across his face, and he said to the General, "It's a sign of weakness. Tell them we'll respond in the morning."

CHAPTER 61

Trying to keep up with the FBI boat, O'Keefe struggled to keep his craft steady at high speed in the surprisingly rough water. He risked a look back to check on Sara. At first he couldn't see her at all. He called her name. No answer. The boat rose up and slammed back down against the water, at times so hard he thought he might topple over. Ducking to keep sprays of lake water from dousing him, he managed in a series of over-the-shoulder glimpses to see her lying on the floor of the boat, curled into a fetal position. He called her name again. No answer. The sprays of lake water from the rollicking boat must be inundating her. He was cold, drenched, shivering. As she must be. He considered slowing to idle and going back to tend to her, but what good would that do? Best to keep blasting along.

Just as he was thinking they must have gotten lost, he saw lights in the distance at what he hoped was the marina. Moving up alongside the FBI boat, he spotted on shore a pickup truck with an overhead camper shell. Was that the "ambulance"?

The maneuvers required to gently slide the boat sideways into the dock proved beyond his competence. He banged hard into it, almost upending a couple of the helpers waiting on the dock, but they kept their feet and yelled at him to cut the engine. Two of them clambered into the boat and picked Sara up. O'Keefe lent a fifth and sixth hand to prop up her body as they lifted and passed her onto two others on the dock who laid her on a stretcher and struggled to keep their footing as they made their way along the madly teetering dock.

They installed O'Keefe in the back of the "ambulance" with Sara and three other people disturbingly *not* dressed in medical garb. They had stripped the wet clothes off Sara and wrapped her in a blanket. The vehicle had been minimally outfitted for its amended purpose, worrisomely lacking the contraptions and paraphernalia he would have expected. Certainly, it looked nothing like the ambulances that had transported *him* on too many occasions. He knew they had citizen *volunteer* firemen in these rural areas and hoped it wasn't the same with emergency medical personnel.

He felt better when one of them, dressed in a flannel shirt and blue jeans, introduced himself as Doctor Nugent. O'Keefe didn't ask the two questions that came to his mind. Did these people or anyone at the hospital have any idea how to treat the victim of a timber rattlesnake bite? And were they even heading to a hospital, or would it be to some farmhouse?

Sara was conscious, but her eyes were glazed, and he wasn't sure she could see. He said her name. The slightest nod.

"The doctor asked O'Keefe, "Where's the bite?"

"Her right ankle."

They cut her right pants leg. The leg was swollen below the knee, almost twice its usual size.

"I understand that's fairly typical," the doctor said. "It might spread on up to the top of her leg."

Understand? He doesn't know?

O'Keefe wanted to ask if amputation was a possibility but was afraid the best answer he could expect would be, "I don't know," and she might hear.

"How long ago was she bitten?"

He'd lost all track of time. "Not sure."

"Was it less than four hours ago?"

"Pretty sure."

"Less than three?"

"Not sure."

"How many times was she bitten?"

"Not sure, but twice at least, I think."

O'Keefe had his own question. "Are we heading to a hospital?"

"Yes." The doctor seemed to understand the concern in O'Keefe's voice. "A good one," he added.

Whatever 'good' means down here. "How far? How long?"

"Thirty minutes."

The doctor turned to Sara. "Can you talk?"

She didn't answer.

"Sara, can you hear us? Nod if you can hear us."

She did, and he asked her a series of questions. Some produced slight nods, some a flutter of negative movement, some nothing at all.

"Does it hurt?"

A slightly more vigorous nod. Twice.

"In your leg?"

Nod.

"Anywhere else?"

Nothing.

He gave her a shot of something. "Morphine," he said, answering the question on O'Keefe's face.

Her breathing seemed more labored, shallow, rapid, like she was reaching down deep to make it happen. O'Keefe looked imploringly at the medical people, and the two assistants looked imploringly at Nugent, who said, "She's likely going into shock if she's not already there."

O'Keefe didn't know exactly what the consequences of that might be and was afraid to ask. He couldn't—even during the war, even during his own near-death trips in ambulances in the past few years, even in the most boring of surveillances—recall time moving as slowly as it was moving now.

CHAPTER 62

IT WAS DIFFICULT to decide who should be the designated negotiator with the ZOGs. It couldn't be him. He couldn't trust those ZOGs, who were doing Satan's work whether it was intentional or not on their part. Ignorance was inexcusable when he and so many others had been warning them for years. Forever really, clear back to John in Revelation. What rules were those ZOGs required to observe in a situation like this? They might just arrest him on the spot despite giving their word not to. What would it cost them to break their word? Why would an accused criminal have any right to believe them? Then he would go down in the annals not as a great warrior for Yahweh, but as a damn fool. His people would be left not only leaderless but bereft, betrayed by the stupidity of their Chosen One.

He had long ago come to believe, on the basis of unmistakable signs, intuitions, and insights, that he had been called and anointed for the greatest mission since perhaps even the mission of Jesus Christ, the Savior Himself. After the long centuries of humanity's wandering in the wilderness while Satan and the Antichrists, so many Antichrists, leaped to triumph after triumph until they ruled the whole world, inflicting desolation after desolation, creating a world swimming in its own bodily and other waste and all other manner of vileness, he, David Dodd, had been assigned that holiest of missions—finally to light the spark that would in turn light so many other sparks and ignite the Great Conflagration that would finally bring forth the promised End Times, when Jesus Christ would return, and the infidels, every one of them, would be massacred, and the true Christians, and only the true Christians, not the lily-livered backsliders, would be rewarded for the hard road they had traveled, the cross of Christ they had willingly shouldered and suffered.

So then, who could be trusted to deal with the assembled ZOG killers? The General would be the obvious choice, but if they arrested him, what would be the fate of the resistance? With the General in charge, who knew how many of the ZOGs they could kill or wound before they succumbed? This was the Alamo of the warriors for Christ, so much more sacred than the Alamo battle itself, but that was the only comparison his mind could conceive, and they must acquit themselves as bravely as had Travis and his men, and as savagely too, killing far more of the enemy than their own small number, exacting a terrible price for this vicious assault on God's people … No, on God Himself. So the General must remain and be available for that final reckoning.

He wished he hadn't sent Sinclair away, the hardest of men. He'd been too overconfident that his soldiers would strike first, trusted too much in someone like Peter McBride (and he remembered with shame how often Sinclair had warned him about McBride). So perhaps God had used McBride to teach His David a lesson, as the Yahweh of the Bible had so often done with His Chosen People. Yet that surely was only a minor setback. He knew God would not let him fail in the end. He must muster the same unshakable faith as Jehoshaphat.

That left Caleb. A weakling, but he would be no more than a messenger, would not be allowed to exercise judgment in any way. He was an articulate man. If there were Jewsmedia out there with the ZOGs, Caleb would present a respectable face to the world, show the world that the people of the New Ark were not some halfwit cretins as they were so often portrayed.

He discussed it with the General, who agreed with his analysis but warned, "We've got to keep him on the shortest possible leash. He's a sloppy pudding at his best. He'll betray us without intending to, without even knowing it."

They found Caleb in the Evangel Room, hunched over and squinting at the computer screen, tapping away, frantically composing bulletins seeking to rouse the "network" of true believers and professed Christian warriors.

"What's happening?" the Prophet said.

Caleb turned from the computer, seemed about to weep, his voice squeaking. "Lots of tough talk but no action."

They had counted on their fellow warriors—not to come directly to their aid necessarily, isolated and surrounded as the Ark people were, and their fellow warriors spread out and far away as they were, but to be inspired by the Ark's glorious initiative to burst forth into local actions around the nation, even the world.

But that was when they'd planned to strike first, a devastating blow that would uncork the justified hatred that would erupt like boiling streams of lava from the hearts of all true Christians and spur them to take up arms and destroy the infidels once and for all.

That was before they'd been—here, at the last possible moment—thrown onto the defensive.

The McBrides. Treachery. Anger. But also a stab of regret. The woman especially. He would have made her Queen. He had been tempted so many times just to take her. All those times alone with her in a constant state of discomfited arousal. But he'd let the opportunities pass, confident that the charismatic divinely vouchsafed Spirit that had first seized him decades ago would bring her voluntarily to him, to that exquisite place, like several before her, their initial resistance always turning out to be a sham, they'd surrendered so easily and enjoyed it so much when they did. If only she'd been a true Christian instead of some scheming witch sent from Hell to tempt and confuse him. Yes, the End Times certainly had come, but it was no surprise that Satan would not go down easily, especially when the Beast knew this might be the final conflict.

Jehoshaphat. That's who he must become now with his entire being and infuse that spirit into Caleb who seemed to be wavering, and even into the General in case that stalwart was himself weakening. "Don't waver, Caleb. It will happen. It's only the beginning. We have a special mission for you."

They told him about the offer from the ZOGs, clearly a sign of weakness they could exploit, and none could be better at exploiting that weakness than Caleb.

Caleb wagged his head back and forth in disagreement. "No way. You two are the strongest men here. One of *you* should go."

"No," the Prophet said. "If I go, they'll have almost everything they want."

"You think they'd do that? Under a flag of truce?"

"Wake up, Caleb. Who do you think we're dealing with here? But that's not the important thing. This doesn't call for a so-called strong man. It calls for a wise man, a man of words, a trickster, soft-seeming on the outside but iron-hard on the inside. That's you, Caleb."

Which was all Caleb needed. His posture straightened, his chest puffed out.

His mission, they told him, was simple. Find out everything the ZOG leader was willing to disclose. Look around, assess their physical strength. Draw them out on what they might be afraid of. "Then convey our strength. They probably don't know all of our power. They may not know about the LAW rockets, the drum of cyanide, the cyanide-tipped bullets, the 50-caliber and M60 machine guns, all the grenades and other explosive devices we've managed to assemble for this very moment. But don't specify those things necessarily, just suggest them. You tell them, 'We knew you'd come, and we are ready, have been getting ready for years. Every man, woman, and child in this fort will fight you to the end ... to the death. You may ultimately prevail, but you'll never recover from the victory. Your cause will be lost. Our martyrdom will be your own downfall as surely as the crucifixion of Jesus Christ ultimately doomed Rome itself.

"But ... and this is the most important thing ... tease out their offer if there is one. Say you can't believe the Prophet will accept it but that you'll take it back and even try to convince me. Make them believe that you're sympathetic to them, that they might have nudged you, at least a little bit, toward their side."

"Why?"

"Because we need as much time as we can get before they attack, if that's what they really intend to do ... so we have the time to make sure the whole world knows what's happening here ... and let God's will work on the world and especially on our brother warriors ... who'll finally see with absolute clarity that this is *it!* Armageddon. The Final Battle itself. And only those who prove themselves worthy *now,* in that Final Battle, will earn eternal life and glory."

"I should send a bulletin out saying exactly that right now."

"Do it. Make it short and powerful. You need to get out there to the ZOGs immediately."

A flutter. A vibration. A slight change to the air in the room.

"Mark Johnson is dead."

They turned to the familiar voice, Naomi standing in the doorway.

"How many more of us have to die for you?"

CHAPTER 63

CALEB GAPED IN disbelief at her audacity. Even the General flinched as if he'd been slapped.

David wanted to punch her face, knock her down. He needed to reassert control—at once, not a moment's delay. He turned to Caleb. "Get that bulletin done now. Don't fuss over it. We need you out there."

Caleb turned to the computer. Capturing the General's eye and jerking his head toward Caleb, the Prophet's look said, *Stand over his shoulder. Make sure he gets it done right and fast.*

Naomi remained in the doorway.

"Woman, you and I will have a talk."

As he advanced on her, she didn't move. He grabbed her arm and squeezed. Hard. She winced in pain but stood her ground. He turned her roughly around and shoved her in front of him, not as hard as he could have but hard enough to hope she might stumble and fall. She stumbled but remained upright.

"Go." He pointed down the hallway toward the front of the house.

She obeyed, but her pace seemed deliberately, defiantly slow. When they reached the front room, she turned, still with that blazingly angry rebel's face.

Squelch that face. Humble her as she deserves.

"Woman, you seem to have forgotten your place, your God-directed duty."

"You're not playing soldier games anymore. Now someone's dead."

"God's will be done."

"No. *Your* will be done."

"God has spoken to me. You once believed that."

No response. But no change in her expression. Still defiant.

"I'm fulfilling the Biblical prophesies."

"You make the Bible say what you want it to … like taking a second wife."

"Ah, woman, now we know what this is about."

"It's not about that at all. That wounded me, wounds me now, wounds me always, in my every pore and cell, but I accepted that. Only you, in your delusion and self-justification, the madness I've seen slowly overtake you, only you could believe that God is speaking to you, telling you to do all these horrible things. But I can't and I won't go there with you. Not to the killing of innocents."

"I repeat. God's will. All of this is preordained. We're going to the place we were always going to anyway. It's an early and blessed release."

"We came here to create a new Eden. It's now a Hell on earth."

"Blasphemy."

He advanced on her. He'd choked her into unconsciousness once before and it had tamed her. But he sensed something different in the room. A movement in the corner of his eye. The General and Caleb standing at the edge of the hallway, watching, listening.

Had they heard everything? *Control.* His angry attention turned toward them. "What do you want?"

"I-I've," Caleb stuttered, "finished the bulletin."

The General to the rescue: "He's ready."

"Then go! You know what to do. Go!"

They hurried outside.

At least for the moment his impulse to choke and beat her had subsided. "Woman, your duty is to obey your master on this earth. Your duty is to trust that I'm doing God's will."

"No more. I'll stay to the horrible end. But not for you. I'm guilty too. I've stood by while you became a monster and led us to this Perdition. I owe only"—she raised her arm in the direction of the Fortress—"*them* … to stay and take care of *them*, to the extent I'm able. I owe them. *You* owe them too. You've led them here … to what fate?"

"I can't have you out there fomenting unrest and rebellion. Do I have to lock you in a room?"

"Do what you will, but out *there* I intend only to serve them. In *here,* I'll do whatever I can to touch whatever good is left in your heart."

"A traitor in my own house. You'll shut your mouth in here too."

"I'm ready to leave now. I want to go back to them … and out of this cursed house."

"You will apologize to Leon and Caleb, and in front of them apologize to me … take back … renounce what they heard you say."

She slowly shook her head.

"Then you'll not be welcome in our presence. Linda will take over everything in here. You've broken the covenant."

She turned and walked toward the front door of the house.

Above them a new sound.

Thwump Thwump Tthwump

Both looked up.

The helicopters had arrived.

CHAPTER 64

At the hospital a team, thankfully wearing actual medical clothing, greeted them and transferred Sara to a gurney. Dr. Nugent rapid-fire recited her symptoms. The hospital doctor looked at O'Keefe and asked, "How long?"

"Since the bite," Nugent clarified.

"I'm not sure. Around four or five hours, I think. Could be more."

"Let's hope it was four," the hospital doctor said. He clapped his hands twice and said to one of the nurses, "Is it ready?"

It was. "Let's go," he said. "Op Room One. Dr. Nugent, please join us." And to the anxious, befuddled O'Keefe: "We should know in a few hours."

Nugent remained behind for a moment. "She's a lucky woman."

"Doesn't look so lucky to me."

"We had one dose of antivenin. Been around for years. We had a hard time finding it. And the reason everyone wants to know the time of the bite … It's much more effective if it can be given in the first four hours."

O'Keefe wondered if he was an optimist or a pessimist. He'd always tried to think of himself as simply a realist. You didn't have to be an optimist to conclude that rattlesnakes almost never killed people anymore, especially if you got help quickly. But had he gotten her there quickly enough?

They were taking too long, and nobody had come out to reassure him. Alone in the tiny waiting room, the time dragged. His confidence dripped, then flowed out of him. Despite Sara's ambition and the whole culture virtually shouting at him that he was a male chauvinist, paternalistic, patriarchal pig to even consider holding her back, he'd tried to avoid letting her get herself into situations where she might end up in physical danger. He'd thought he had her safely buried in paper working for Harrigan where the only risk would be death from boredom. But he hadn't tried hard enough to stop her from undertaking this crazy mission. The cost? A life lost? Or a limb amputated? Or maybe the venom was frying her brain?

He shouldn't have left her there at the Ark alone in the first place. Then he should have surrendered there on the beach and begged them to help her. They might be demented and dangerous, might have executed them on the spot, would almost certainly have executed him, but surely the Prophet, with his ulterior motive, wouldn't have let her die. She had refused that solution, demanded to go on. But that was no excuse for him, he was the leader. Was it actually an act of cowardice *not* to surrender?

Nugent and the hospital doctor came into the waiting room looking exhausted and beaten. O'Keefe kept his seat. He wasn't sure he could stand without staggering.

"Man, I have to confess that was a little scary for a while," the hospital doctor said. "A little harder than I thought it would be … But she's fine. In fact, in a day, at most two, she'll be back to normal."

"No permanent damage? The foot? The leg?"

"None."

One less human sacrifice to the god of war.

It seemed like a reprieve for both of them.

CHAPTER 65

WEAPONS AT THE ready, the conspicuously heavily armed ZOG troops were arrayed on both sides of the path, a gauntlet ten or more yards and many soldiers long that he must now traverse to meet with the ZOG commander standing at the far end—tall, muscular, arms akimbo like a disapproving schoolteacher.

Behind the commander were numerous vehicles, large and small tents, equipment, what looked like cables and phone lines. He thought he could detect some sort of armored vehicle, not quite a tank, but all the same, a formidable-looking machine of war. If they'd arranged their assembled forces in this way to terrify Caleb, they'd succeeded. What he could see was bad enough. There were likely many more soldiers beyond. This was only the northern entrance to the compound. On the lakeside to the west sat a flotilla of ZOG boats possibly poised for an amphibious landing. And who knew what forces might be standing ready on the neighboring properties to the east and south of his beloved refuge?

He could only pray now, beseech Yahweh to bestow on him a special favor to still his pounding heart, tame his wildly racing thoughts, and tighten up his loosened bowels.

How would the Prophet handle this? How would the General? He must remember that this was the beginning of all they had waited and yearned for. Focus. Envision the Promise and its Fulfillment finally coming to pass, the Father and the Son welcoming him and his family and the whole Ark community through the gates of Paradise.

And, indeed, he managed to establish a sense of control, something bordering close even to calm, as he stepped firmly, almost proudly, down the path toward the surprisingly friendly and welcoming face of the commander, who smiled and shook his hand as if they were not the deadliest of enemies, introducing himself as Agent Charlie Redmond.

The worst they could do was arrest him … Across the sky of his mind a streaking plume of thought, quickly guiltily quashed. *Better than the fate that might await those remaining in the compound.*

"Please. Come with me," Redmond said.

He was led to a large tent crowded with tables with men at computers and on telephones. Around the sides of the tent were easels holding large maps of the general area and the compound. Some of the maps had handwritten markings on them. He squinted, trying to read the markings, trying to gather intelligence as the Prophet had instructed, but he felt all eyes on him and looked away. He had still managed to register that the maps portrayed in detail the neighboring properties to the south and east. This should be somewhat helpful information for the General. He felt a little pride knowing he was trying to fulfill as completely as possible the mission they'd assigned him.

Redmond sat down at a field desk and gestured for Caleb to sit across from him. Two men pulled up chairs at either side of Redmond; on the left, a handsome, dark-haired, fierce-looking young man who said his name was Agent Kevin Doolan; on the right, a balding fellow who introduced himself as Agent Calvin Brewster of ATF. *Yes, that's what it's all about. The guns. They want to take away our guns, strip us naked among our enemies.*

Redmond said, "I issued the invitation to David, your Prophet. It was to be one commander to another. I'm disappointed he refused to see me."

"He understandably doesn't quite trust all this," Caleb said, making a circling gesture. "Can you blame him?"

Redmond shrugged that off. "Seems like both sides unintentionally find themselves in a highly dangerous situation."

"We're only defending our God-given right to live according to our beliefs and our rights under the Second Amendment to the United States Constitution to keep and bear arms. We owe it to ourselves and the world and to Yahweh not to go meekly to your dungeons."

"It's a government of laws. You'll have lawyers to represent you whether you can pay them or not."

"Lawyers can't overcome unjust laws. What do you want from us?"

"We made that clear at the beginning. We have a few warrants to serve."

"On whom?"

"David Dodd, Leon Lomax, Caleb Nathanson, Kenneth Graham, Dwight Scott, Mark Johnson, and Peter McBride."

Mark Johnson. Hearing that name made him sad … and a little guilty too, which he didn't understand. That last name on the list confused him. Had they come to the wrong conclusion about the McBrides? *Is there some other traitor … or traitors?* "That's all of our leadership," he said. "You arrest all of us and it'll leave the women and children and elderly with no one to care for them."

"You underestimate your women. And that assumes you won't be able to make bail. And if you can't, we can get help for them."

"Why won't you leave us alone? You do nothing but harass us, all over a few weapons you claim are illegal."

"You think we've brought all this here just because you've illegally converted some AR-15s to automatic?"

Caleb shifted nervously. "There could be no other reason," he said, realizing he had sounded a bit uncertain there.

"Do you really mean that? As a devout Christian man, you can sit there and tell me there's no other reason?"

"I surely can."

"Lies can only lead to a tragedy here, Caleb. We hoped you'd come here to negotiate in good faith."

Redmond reached for something, then slid it into the center of the table. A cassette-tape player. He pressed a button. The tape began to play.

Caleb immediately recognized the conversation. The final planning meeting. Someone had taped it and put it into the hands of ZOG.

Things began coming together. The trip he and Sara McBride had made to Ironton. The milkshake he'd so greedily and stupidly fixated upon, letting her out of his sight into that store.

As the tape continued to play, his mind raced, desperately seeking an excuse, a rationalization, an explanation that would free him from the horrible responsibility of having brought this down on all of them. Maybe they could claim it was a fraud—doctored, manufactured—another of ZOG's evil machinations.

Redmond apparently intended to play the whole thing. Caleb had to admit that now, here, it didn't sound good. It didn't show them in their best light, some of it was almost to be ashamed of. The world might misunderstand. He stood up to leave. "I've heard enough."

"Sit down, Caleb. You're going to listen to all of it. You're going to hear all of the devastation you people intended to inflict on the innocent."

Once the tape ended, all he wanted was out of that tent. He stood again. "So what is it you want?"

"Each of the people I mentioned need to come out of there, unarmed, and surrender themselves. Then we need to inspect the entire compound."

"The Prophet will never agree, I can assure you of that. I haven't the slightest doubt."

"And how about the rest of you?"

"We'll follow to the end. To the glory and triumph of Yahweh in the End Times. We'll be martyrs. We'll inspire others. The Final Battle is on the horizon. It's you who'll perish and suffer … for all eternity."

"And how about the women and children?"

"You'd attack them?"

"Of course not, but if you use them as human shields … We'd like you to let the women and children leave the compound."

"They know what their duty is. They'll stand by their men."

"Then the men, if they're real men, should *order* them to leave."

Caleb had no answer for that.

"And the children?" Redmond said.

Silence for an uncomfortably long time, which Caleb finally broke: "Even the little ones know their duty. If you kill them, they'll have a special place in Paradise."

"We'd like you to order them to leave. If not the women, at least the children."

"We won't deliver them up that way. If they get hurt, it will be by your hands and on your heads."

"Caleb," Redmond said, no anger, matter-of-factly, "everything that's been said here between us has been recorded. You can be sure we'll let the whole world know exactly what happened here; that you and your Prophet knowingly and deliberately and cruelly used your women and children as human shields. It's the ultimate cowardice. I can't believe it. As a Christian man myself, I cannot believe that any true Christian would ever even consider such a thing."

"God's people won't believe you. Or it won't matter to them. The stakes here are the highest stakes in all history."

"We'll certainly find out whether that's the case, my friend, because the entire world will hear that tape. You put such an inflated value on yourself and this pissant little compound of yours. In the Christian tradition—my tradition, your tradition—Pride is the first and the worst of the Seven Deadly Sins. What unmitigated gall, what un-Christian, ungodly arrogance to call your compound the New Ark. Noah *saved* humanity, he didn't destroy it."

"I want to leave now," Caleb croaked. "If you're men of your word, men of the law, you'll honor that and let me go."

"Go. You have forty-eight hours to surrender. If you don't, then at some point … it might be minutes, or hours, or even a couple of days, but we'll come at you with full force."

As Caleb Nathanson walked back through the gauntlet, Doolan said in a lowered voice, "You didn't read him his rights."

"Kevin," Redmond said sharply, "we could be on the verge of another Jonestown here. I wanted to talk to him not as the 'ZOG' commander but more as one Christian to another, apostate though I may be. We've already got all the evidence we need anyway … Break down this headquarters tent and move it back."

Doolan and Brewster looked confused.

"He'll be able to tell them exactly what our position is. We might just be eating one of those rockets if we don't move the whole operation."

The three looked at each other, each having to acknowledge to himself once again the devastating fire power the Prophet had assembled and the slaughter it could inflict.

CHAPTER 66

CALEB DELIVERED HIS breathless report.

They agreed that it must have been Sara who'd taped the meeting, and they cursed her for it.

"Wonder where she got that tape recorder?" the Prophet said.

"Probably brought it with them," the General said. "

Caleb kept silent. The General might be right.

"If I'm ever able to get those people in my hands…" the General said.

Caleb moved on quickly with his narrative and ended with the thing most urgently on his mind. "They want us to order the women and children to leave—"

"Good," the Prophet interrupted. "They're worried about that … what the world will think of them if they attack and harm the women and children. We can use that to our advantage."

Caleb hoped he'd hidden his shock at that remark. Was David holding their own women and children as hostages? He ventured, "Why? What good would that do?"

"It will give us more time. More time for the others to rally and strike."

"There's been no rallies. No strikes. Nothing."

"There will be. I know there will be. Surely, Caleb, those ZOGs haven't caused you to lose your faith."

"Not at all. Not ever. But what if nothing happens? What if Yahweh doesn't come to our rescue and the true Christians remain silent and cowed?"

"Oh, ye of little faith … You two go on. I need to pray on this."

Caleb and the General left together. The General split off to mingle with his men. "Coming, Caleb?"

"I'll be there soon."

He waited until the General was engaged with his men, then headed toward the community building. In the distance he saw Naomi exit through the front door and walk around the side of the building. He followed her, thinking he might have a word with her; that is, if she'd even speak to him now.

She disappeared into a copse where they'd hastily buried Mark Johnson. He stopped and watched her standing, head bowed, hands folded together at her breast, in front of the rough wooden cross they'd hammered together and stuck in the ground on top of Mark in his shallow grave. Perhaps she sensed that someone was watching her. She turned and looked at him with that same sad-angry mask of reproach that seemed to have become a permanent feature of her face since Mark's death, reproaching them all, herself included.

What if she knew that he, Caleb, might be considered the primary cause of Mark's death, his killer in effect? He'd let Sara fool him into that trip to Ironton and the embarrassment of falling for her milkshake ploy. On this very day he'd let his guard down again and shamefully allowed a woman to overcome him and escape. Then he'd thrown that switch. The General had been the first to throw the switch. Sara had turned it off. Caleb had turned it back on, exactly what the General would have wanted and ordered him to do had he been there in the room. Yes, one could rationalize. Many things had come together to produce Mark's fate, including Mark himself, one of the Prophet's most militant followers, scurrying through the woods, bent on killing or capturing human prey. But if Caleb hadn't so miserably failed in those other ways … He had not come here for all of this. He had come here to pray and read and meditate on the Word of the Lord and translate it to the people in language they could understand and incorporate into their daily lives and very being. Could God have meant to let this happen to his devoted servant? Or was there some deeper message here…

He turned and made his way back to the community building where the women had organized a major cooking operation for the evening's dinner. His wife was stirring something in a large pot.

He forced a smile and hoped it didn't look forced. She went back to her pot. He asked one of the women where the children were. "Upstairs," she said.

The children regarded him with curiosity. Likely, none of the other men had visited them. They seemed to have already recovered from whatever trauma they'd endured when Mark had been brought in. He found his Rachel, Abe, and Jeremiah and told them to come with him.

The boldest one, Jeremiah, said, "What for?"

"Just come," he said sternly. "None of your lip."

They trailed along behind him as he made his way out the back door.

"Where we goin', Papa?" Jeremiah again, but less aggressively this time.

He led them behind the building to yet another grove of trees. At its center was a formidable rock pile where the children loved to play despite their parents' warnings to stay away or they might get hurt. Even the threat that "there's snakes in there" failed to deter most of them. He sat down on a large boulder and lined the children up in front of him.

> *And a man's foes shall be they of his own household.*
>
> *He that loveth father or mother more than me is not worthy of me:*
>
> *And he that loveth son or daughter more than me is not worthy of me.*

He embraced each of them in turn, hugging them so tightly that Rachel cried out, "Papa, you're squeezing too hard!"

CHAPTER 67

As he drove to the hospital, O'Keefe roamed around the radio dial. There were few stations in range. No doubt all of them were trying, with minimal staff and technology, to cover the biggest thing that had ever happened in this part of the world. Some of the national and regional television stations had sent reporters and camera operators to the area, but there were few special broadcasts locally, only the coverage during the regular morning, noon, and evening news programs. He gleaned little other than that the FBI and ATF had descended in force, taking over motels and any other available accommodations in the area, while additional agents and support were camped out in tents and sleeping bags at or near the Ark compound.

On this second day after the doctor had delivered the good news about Sara, the roar of the helicopters had become almost constant. O'Keefe couldn't escape vivid memories of Vietnam though now he was on the ground instead of up there above with his Ma Deuce trained on the landscape. By phone he stayed in touch with George and especially Maxwell, whose broadcasting stations had predictably taken a keen interest in unfolding events.

But all that was frustratingly remote. He had no way of communicating with any of the G-men gathered at the site. For Sara's sake, he'd resisted the impulse to drive there alone to try to convince them to let him through to see Redmond. Not that he had any realistic hope of accomplishing anything, but he felt he had to try. He couldn't get out of his mind the little girl with her hair flouncing along with her every bouncing step.

And another girl before her…

A medevac into a hot LZ, the firefight still raging, always the scariest of missions.

They loaded a lieutenant, "zipped up," meaning dead.

Another Marine was losing a lot of blood. Lucky for him, they'd taken off from base with a Navy corpsman, a "Doc," the Navy and Marine Corps fond term for a medic. He'd just happened to be available and volunteered to come along. Lucky for all concerned. O'Keefe and the crew chief wouldn't have to frantically, desperately fumble around trying their utmost but failing to help the man while he bled to death.

The third Marine had a more minor wound but a disabling one.

And then they brought in the girl.

Occasionally they picked up wounded civilians. O'Keefe was paying scant attention when they loaded her because the firefight was still going strong, and he needed to be pouring rounds wherever the enemy might be while making sure not to kill his own comrades. But they were soon off the ground and high enough that there was no further reason to continue firing.

He turned around.

She was right there in front of him, facing him. She couldn't have been more than seven, eight, nine years old, hard to tell exactly. The Doc was at her head. Luckily, she couldn't see Doc's face, because he was crying. Her arm was as good as gone, obviously unsalvageable. He'd surely given her a shot of morphine, but it didn't look like it had taken yet. She was looking directly at O'Keefe, her face twisted in pain, shock, agony, and, he thought, anger. *Who did this to me? You did this to me. Why?*

He couldn't bear it, turned away, grabbed the gun handles, aimed out the window though there was nothing left to shoot at. A Malignancy as ancient as humankind itself had descended on her village and torn her arm off and might now be killing her and might have already killed her mother, father, brothers, sisters, friends, neighbors. It didn't matter which side he was on or which side had the greater claim to the justice of its cause. He was an agent of the Malignancy, and by turning his back on her now, too squeamish to look on any longer, turning away from the accusation on her face, he would be abandoning her, unforgivably magnifying the atrocity perpetrated on her.

He turned back. Both he and the Doc were crying, and the veteran tough-guy sergeant of a crew chief was struggling not to. O'Keefe put his hand on her arm, but quickly withdrew it, realizing that she could no longer feel a squeeze of reassurance or anything else in that arm except phantom pain. His feeble gesture of pity and succor failing, he let go, withdrew the hand now stained with her blood and forced himself to look and keep looking, with all the commiseration, compassion, condolence, and consolation he could summon from within himself, into those eyes, until the morphine took effect and she closed them.

If Sara wasn't able to leave the hospital by tomorrow, O'Keefe thought he might just go on without her before something terrible happened without him trying to affect the outcome somehow. Maybe he could provide some inside knowledge to the Feds that could help avert a massacre, some special insight into the Ark people or information about the geography of the place that he'd traversed so many times, whether on the training maneuvers or guard duty or on his evening walks with Sara.

Entering her room, he did a double take. "What's this?"

She was smiling, sitting in the visitor chair at the foot of her made-up bed, a small bag at her feet. The room was clean and tidy, ready for the next occupant.

"I'm discharged. What's next?"

"No lingering side effects?"

"Nothing. A little tired is all."

"Get around okay? No leg issue?"

"Hardly even swollen anymore."

"Let's go. To the compound. I've been waiting for you. I knew you'd hate me forever if I went without you."

He noticed a slight hitch in her step as he followed her out of the room and wondered if she was really as restored as she claimed to be.

CHAPTER 68

"Roadblock" was too tame a word, "Blockade" a more appropriate one for what greeted them as they turned off the highway and onto the road to Ark II. The guard was in no mood to hear the story O'Keefe was telling him. "Sir, you would not believe the number of bullshit stories like this we've heard this week. Go away."

"If you'll just call Redmond, he'll tell you to let us right through."

"Yeah, I'm gonna bother Redmond with some tall tale. Turn around. Get out of here."

It was Doolan on the boat all over again, except this guy seemed even more unlikely to be persuaded.

"If you don't let me through, Redmond is gonna do a lot more than *bother* you."

"Turn around."

Apparently these bluff threats of his were no longer having the desired effect (if they ever had).

He squinted determinedly at the guard trying to show he was a man of utmost resolve. "I'm driving through. You'll have to arrest me, and sometime soon you'll be in the unemployment line, trying to figure out how you're gonna feed your wife and kids."

"You try that and we'll blow your ass off the road."

Seemed everyone wanted to blow his ass off or out of one thing or another.

"Get out, Sara. I'm going forward."

"No way. I'm in."

He pressed the accelerator. The car lurched forward a couple of yards. It took only a few long strides for the guard to grab the door handle. O'Keefe engaged the lock, but before he could get the window rolled down, the guard reached through it and grabbed him by the shirtsleeve.

"You achieved it, asshole. You're under arrest. Turn that engine off and get out. NOW."

O'Keefe obeyed.

"Cover him," the lead guard ordered another, who brought his rifle to his shoulder and aimed at O'Keefe who was hoping the guy had the safety engaged on that hair-triggered killing machine. The lead guard jerked him around to face the vehicle, slammed him up against the side, and began frisking him.

The other guard shouted at Sara to get out of the car and put her hands up. She shook her head in refusal. He gestured for another comrade to move around to the passenger side and deal with her.

"Now you're gonna have to manhandle a woman," O'Keefe said. "You think I'd put either of us through this if I wasn't legit? All you've gotta do is tell him Peter O'Keefe and Sara Slade are here to help. He'll tell you not only to let us through but to escort us there yourself."

No comment from the guard, who kept frisking.

"Just tell him that the guy who gave Doolan the tape is here to help."

Whether it was the inconvenience of having to break in and drag Sara out of the car, or that they'd found nothing in the frisk, or that the tape comment and the mention of Doolan's name had somehow rung true, the guard said, "You know what to do," to his comrades and stomped off.

After thirty minutes, O'Keefe asked if he could sit down.

"No."

It was more than an hour later when the lead guard returned, looking even angrier than when he'd left.

"Three questions. You have to get all of them right. First one: What's the General's first and last name?"

"Leon Lomax."

"Second: What's the name of the Prophet's wife?"

"Which one? He has two. Naomi and Linda."

"Third: What type of snake?"

"Timber rattler."

"Come on."

O'Keefe resisted the urge to gloat (visibly anyway).

CHAPTER 69

"**T**HE ARK. THEY have it surrounded," she said when he opened the apartment door after a long day spent scouting various escape routes out of the city. His abrupt entrance had startled her as she stood in the middle of her living room, staring at the television set. "The Prophet refuses to surrender. Says they'll fight to the death."

He called in a page to Darby, who called him right back.

"You in the motel room?" he said. "Turn on Channel 9. Watch it until they break, then call back."

When Darby called back, he said, "Come and pick me up right now. We have to get down there."

She knew he wouldn't like it, but she said, "I want to come too?"

"Of course not."

"I could be of use."

"What use?"

"In all the ways I've been of use already. Good use, I would say."

"No."

"What if they catch you?" she said.

"They won't."

"Do you intend to get in there and fight? They'll kill you."

He shrugged.

It was too risky to push him any further. She moved to him. At first, he stood there like a statue, but then relented and let her hug him, putting his arms weakly around her. She knew this was the best she would get. She hoped she might feel him grow hard against her. He didn't.

"But you can still be of good use," he said.

She was to stay glued to the television, write down every detail. "We'll have the radio on, but I don't know how good the coverage is. The signal is always in and out down there. We'll make several stops on the way and call you to get a report."

As she was trying to come up with something to ask or say that he might respond to, he turned and walked out the door.

CHAPTER 70

$\mathbf{A}$s they jounced up the road behind the escort vehicle to Redmond's headquarters, passing a long trail of assembled force, they kept exchanging portentous glances and shaking their heads in fear and amazement.

"Was that some kind of tank I just saw?" she said.

"I don't know. Could've been. The Prophet and the General wanted a war, and they sure as hell got it."

At the headquarters Doolan and Brewster looked wary, but Redmond was welcoming.

He shook Sara's hand. "So glad you came out of that okay, ma'am. Very scary. No serious casualties on our side."

"How about the other side?" O'Keefe said.

"Nothing we know about."

"I'm wondering about that mine that exploded behind us."

"If somebody got hurt," Redmond said, "they haven't let on to us."

Speaking softly, a near whisper, O'Keefe said, "What's the plan?"

"Let's go outside," Redmond said, gesturing with a jerk of his head to Doolan and Brewster to come along.

He led them to a long, folding field table set up away from the rest of the tense activity of the camp.

"Answering your question, Pete, even though you two have been extremely helpful in all this, you're really just informants, and we can't share certain things with you. And, by the way, I hope you'll sit down with our intelligence people because they have a lot of unanswered questions that you can likely help with … in terms of the physical characteristics of the compound and the personalities of the important people there—"

"All I want to know," O'Keefe interrupted, "is that you're not gonna do what it looks like you're gonna do and launch a full military assault on those people as long as there are children still in there—"

"Seriously?" Doolan exploded. "Now that you've collected a truckload of Maxwell's money, you can afford to be the great humanitarian and leave the ugly shit to us. What a phony."

"Kevin!" Redmond said.

"I can't help it, sir. I don't need to be preached at by some greedy hypocrite."

O'Keefe said, "Think what you want about me, Doolan. You may be right. But don't focus on the messenger. Focus on the message." He turned to Redmond. "Before you arrived, Doolan here wanted to storm the place while Sara was still in there."

"You don't know what I would've done in the end," Doolan said. "And it was your stupid escapade that almost got her killed."

With a look that shouted "Boys!" Sara said, "*Please.* None of that's important. It's simple. Don't risk innocent lives. End of discussion."

"I don't know who's innocent in there," Doolan said. "At a minimum they knew all the illegal stuff that was going on and stayed put."

"I can tell, Mr. Doolan," Sara said, "that you've been on the righteous power-exercise end of things all your life. It's a little different at the other end."

"Ms. Sara, what we're on the other end of right now is automatic rifles, machine guns, grenade launchers, and LAW rockets."

"First," Brewster said, taking over from Doolan, "the lawful constitutional government of the United States can't tolerate a bunch of lunatics stockpiling illegal weapons, flouting our laws, and planning to attack its citizens. And not just planning. We think they've progressed with a lot of those actions already, and you know yourself what they intended to do next. And having been exposed, they've now holed up in their protected fortress and are using their wives and children as human shields. Besides, our opinions here at this table don't matter anyway. If we get orders, we have to obey them—"

"Where have I heard that before?" O'Keefe said. "All I can say is that if you attack prematurely, and even one kid gets killed or hurt, I'll go public. And more important, I'll get Maxwell to go public, and he's got pretty big and multiple megaphones."

Doolan stared O'Keefe down. "I guess it's time to remind you and your employer Mr. Maxwell that your actions furthered the conspiracy. You could both be prosecuted."

"That's enough," Redmond said. "I can see now I made a mistake in convening this little session."

"Can I have a couple words with you in private?" O'Keefe asked.

Redmond hesitated briefly, looked at Brewster and Doolan—not, it seemed, for approval, but more to gauge their reaction to this potential act of disloyalty to his subordinates. But he nodded, stood up, walked a few yards away.

O'Keefe followed and said, "Mr. Redmond—"

"It's Charlie."

"I know you're a smart guy," O'Keefe continued. "I've also detected from the very start that you're a decent human being. I understand all the things Doolan and Brewster are saying and agree with most of them. But they're not brave and smart in the way that someone needs to be brave and smart in this situation. It needs to be bravery with decency, and that might actually look to a confused world like cowardice or folly. I'd like to know if you can be counted on to do everything you can as a decent human being in this situation."

"I sure hope so. But understand, I might decide that, considering everything, the only right thing to do is a full-scale assault."

"I know your position is a difficult one," O'Keefe said, "and I sympathize, but I wish you wouldn't use that word 'right.' Abstract stuff like 'right' and 'lawful constitutional government' and 'illegal weapons' and 'flouting our laws' can't justify a pile of dead children."

"Decency will be a big part of the determination," Redmond said.

"And not just decent. Smart. A certain kind of smart. Because the wrong moves here could cause unimaginable damage around the whole world."

"So are you ready to talk to our intelligence people?"

"Sure thing. Tonight or tomorrow morning, whatever. Can we stay here?"

"Of course."

Redmond moved back toward the group still sitting at the table and O'Keefe followed.

"Set them up with our intelligence people. They'll be camping out with us."

Doolan looked surprised but not resistant. He said, "We'll set them up," then smiled, a bit of a smirk but more of a gentle kidding kind of smile. "Two tents or one?"

O'Keefe thought he needed to counter that smirk a bit. "Two. We're sick of chastely sleeping together all these months."

CHAPTER 71

T HEY CALLED BACK three times along their route. She'd watched the television faithfully every minute since they'd left, she told them, switching channels regularly so as not to miss anything. But the news people didn't seem to know anything and had contented themselves with broadcasting interviews with various local townspeople about their interactions with the Ark II people over the years.

The news wasn't all bad for the Ark people as the consensus seemed to be that they were pretty strange in their fanatical devotion to their particular take on Christianity, but at least they were Christians. When asked about their stash of armaments, interviewees often pointed out that the Prophet and his followers believed they needed the weapons for their protection when the world collapsed, which they expected it soon to do. Some even thought it was a shame the Federal government had so little respect for the Constitution's guarantee of the right to bear arms, and the Feds descending on New Ark so fiercely at so apparently little provocation probably proved that they darn well needed to be armed to the teeth.

But the news, either reported by her or on their car radio, had provided nothing in the way of what Sinclair and Darby really needed: the size of the ZOG presence and especially its placement and distribution throughout the area. They did learn that a flotilla of ZOG boats had sealed off the lakeshore, so slipping through from either the west or south was impossible. There were several farms to the east and northeast, all of them served by two dirt-and-gravel "main" roads that intersected not far off the highway.

They left the highway and probed carefully.

"We can't let them catch us," Sinclair said. "For the others, it's jail. For us, it might be the noose."

They rounded a curve and the intersection came into view. Darby slammed on the brakes, and they almost slid into a ditch. The ZOGs were there in force. Nobody was getting down that road.

"We could hike in," Darby said.

"We don't know if they've already lined the entire property with cops."

"They couldn't cover every inch of that."

"But which inches have they covered?" Sinclair said. "We don't know. And I bet they've got dogs."

"Seems like we ought to try though," Darby said. "Get in the fight at least."

"Or," Sinclair said, "maybe it would be better to head back to the city and settle up with Maxwell."

"There's an idea," Darby said. "I'm wishin' now we'd've just stayed up there and did what they sent us up there for, damn the rest of the plan."

"Let's drive over to Beaverton," Sinclair said. "That's far enough away there won't be any ZOGs over there, and nobody knows us. Get some food and study the maps. We might be able to figure some way to get in. If not, head back.

"I bet," Darby said, "Maxwell and his bodyguard have relaxed, thinking the ZOGs got everybody bottled up down here. Be fun to prove 'em wrong, eh?"

CHAPTER 72

OVER THE YEARS they'd built sturdy bunkers at various places around the compound, most of them close to the residences, but none on the Gathering Ground where they now established their main line of defense.

They'd spent the first two days of the siege digging what were initially simple foxholes but were constantly being expanded and fortified into virtual bunkers. Summer had lingered into the early autumn, the sun remaining bright and strong, the humidity high. *At least it's not middle of summer,* Caleb thought. And his special position meant he enjoyed many breaks, often summoned to the air-conditioned front rooms of the Prophet's home where the "strategy sessions" took place—same thing over and over, meandering through the narrowing options again and again.

Despite his prayers and constant self-exhortations to bask in the glory of doing God's work, Caleb felt an increasingly deepening and debilitating sadness. The Gathering Ground had been such a beautiful, peaceful, lovingly tended place. No more. Now it looked like a bunch of giant mole mounds. Over these past days Ark II seemed to be rapidly reverting to a scruffy wilderness. He tried to tell himself that he was exaggerating the extent and speed of this transformation, but it couldn't be denied. All they'd built and cultivated for so many years was vanishing in only a few days, a few blinks of the eye.

Of course it was. It couldn't be otherwise now. The End Times had come. Death or imprisonment was inevitable now. Death would bring salvation. Prison would be horrible even with his Bible always open in his hands. Exchanging this serene beauty for the blank prison walls … unthinkable. But even imprisonment couldn't last long. The Tribulation would be raging outside the walls, the Apocalypse proceeding, the Final Armageddon Battle on the immediate horizon.

And yet it seemed that every cell within him was straining to live to the fullest for the few days, hours, moments of life remaining to him …

And to Marsha and the children.

Why were they a mere afterthought to him?

It came crashing down on him—how he'd always taken them for granted, as just distractions from his contemplation of the Higher Things. Distractions at best. Often irritants. Marsha especially. So loving but so plain, so dumpy. Not that he was exactly an admirable physical specimen himself, but still…

No matter. Now, for the short time remaining, he wanted to be with them all he could. He seized every chance to visit them and take them for walks, silly games, impromptu "picnics" featuring pathetic little treats he'd retrieved from the house or bartered for with his fellow soldiers along the line. Do we always fail to appreciate until it was too late? What was that saying? Something like, *Nothing concentrates the mind like a hanging in the morning.*

And what if they were wrong? Wrong about the approaching End Times?

Banish that thought!

Yet he had to admit that, across the preceding centuries, so many of the greatest of Christians, including even Christ's original apostles and followers, had so many times miscalculated about that very thing, prophesied even down to the specific day and hour the imminence of the Apocalypse, the return of Jesus, and the Last Judgment. Even … yes, so hard to admit … but even Jesus Himself, as reported in Mark's gospel 13:29, had said, "It is nigh, even at the doors. Verily I say unto you that this generation shall not pass till all these things be done."

But that generation *had* passed, and so many more after, and all those things *had not* been done.

If even *Jesus* could be mistaken… At Mark 13:31, Jesus had also said, "But of the day and the hour knoweth no man, no, not the angels which are in Heaven, neither the Son, but the Father. Take ye heed, watch and pray: for ye know not when the time is."

Neither the Son, but the Father. So only the Father knew. Not even Jesus. Certainly, then, "knoweth no man," including Caleb … including the Prophet.

Troubling. But they were still engaged in a great and godly mission. It *could* be now. But they couldn't "knoweth." And he had to admit that the Prophet had prophesied once already that the End Times were coming, even naming a specific day.

And here they still remained.

Now the General was striding toward Caleb with his usual purposeful intensity, though his face was drawn, weary. "David's going stir crazy up there," he said. "I told him he ought to come out and dig with the rest of us. But first he wants you to check the message board … *again.* Then we'll confer … *again.*"

Caleb checked the messages. They revealed nothing but the usual and now tiresome empty hurrahs such as *Like Sampson, You Are Smiting The Philistines. God Be With You. We Shall Prevail.*

What "We" was that? Was a lonely suicide like Sampson's all they could hope for, as the "We" cheered them on while the "We" cowered in safety? And hadn't Sampson taken all the Philistines with him? That's why Yahweh had allowed him to commit the great sin of suicide. Here at the New Ark, they might not take even one of the ZOGs with them.

If they were the spark for the powder keg, where was the fuse? Absent.

Impulsively, he typed out a new bulletin.

WE ARE SURROUNDED AND ALONE,

FORLORN AND ABANDONED,

LIKE JESUS ON MOUNT CALVARY.

WHERE ARE YOU? RISE UP! STRIKE!

GLORY AND SALVATION WILL BE YOUR REWARD!

BUT THE COWARDS WILL BE JUDGED

AS HARSHLY AS THE OPPRESSORS THEMSELVES

ON THAT TERRIBLE FINAL DAY

FLUNG DOWN SCREAMING

INTO HELL—FOREVER.

He should get the Prophet's approval. The Prophet might be very angry with him for sending this.

He pressed the button and sent the message.

"Nothing," Caleb said wearily. "Nothing at all."

A loud snort of disgust from the General. "They're not gonna do anything. This is the Alamo, gentlemen. We're an abandoned remnant, nobody coming to our aid. If we're gonna die anyway, let's take it to them. Bonsai attack. Talk about surprise. They'll shit themselves."

It was Caleb's turn to be disgusted. "Our men out there aren't quite the Japanese army or the U.S. Marine Corps."

"No matter," the General said. "We can make it easy for them. Move up the LAWs and fire them all at once. While the ZOGs are recovering from that, the 50 cals unleash a tornado of bullets. We follow with the grenades. At that point we make a tactical decision: either launch an infantry assault or just dig in and wait for them to carry off their wounded and dead. That will be a glorious moment for us all by itself. But if we can exploit the chaos we'll create with the initial bombardment, we'll follow up with a limited infantry charge. And that will reverberate back to Washington D.C. and all around the world. Who knows what the reaction to that will be? And we'll still be fighting. We'll have fallen back to our primary defensive position and still have tremendous fire power."

He let the Prophet and Caleb chew on that for several moments, then added, "Meanwhile, we organize the women and children and send them out through the Shelton farm on the east."

"They probably have that area fully covered," Caleb said.

"So what? No way they'll fire on a bunch of unarmed women and children. We won't have to worry anymore about them getting hurt."

"But," the Prophet said, shaking his head, "the women and children are no doubt the only thing that's kept them from attacking us already."

He really is using them as shields, Caleb thought, and said, "What if we could negotiate something?"

"Like what?" the Prophet said.

"I don't know. Some kind of plea bargain? I'm no lawyer. Maybe just a weapons charge with some agreed prison term. Maybe they'd allow you to broadcast a statement to the world before we surrender. Any combination of things. We claim we never intended to carry out the attacks. We were just hypothesizing, testing the possibilities. We took not one step forward to execute it. We can claim it was just a wild pipe dream."

"We sent Sinclair and Darby," the Prophet said.

"But maybe they'll never know that. If they do, then we say it was just to take the temperature. Nothing else was authorized."

"And the woman up there?" the Prophet said.

"She seems completely loyal. We flatter her. We crown her queen of the movement. She'll stand with Sinclair no matter what. She drools over him like a desperate dog."

The General intervened. "Even if they allow those lesser charges for some of us, they won't allow it for everyone on everything. Sinclair and Darby have a bigger problem … That woman they found out off Highway 17 … and the trooper."

"How would they even know it was them?"

"There's that Deputy Riggins who came up here poking around about the woman. If they're caught and prosecuted, one or both of them will probably be happy to trade the death penalty for testimony against us."

"Sinclair's a tough customer," Caleb said. "He's the type of sailor who might just go down with the ship."

"But maybe not," the Prophet said, "if his captain *surrendered* the ship."

They sat in silence for almost a full minute. The Prophet broke it, saying, "A lot to pray on for guidance here. Meanwhile, Caleb, all this makes me think you should go and talk to them again. Main thing is to observe as much as you can in as much detail as you can. Also try to gauge how they're feeling about the women and children. If they bring it up, that means it's still heavy on their minds."

"How about the plea bargain idea?"

"Can't show weakness by asking for that. At most say something about how you're between a rock and a hard place. That the Prophet is adamant. Just as you are, Agent Redmond. Tell them they've offered us nothing, even though we know they'll suffer massive casualties if they attack. Tell them, 'We'll make sure the world knows they proceeded recklessly despite the risks to themselves and to our children. They were willing to sacrifice all those lives just to show what big men they are...'And see how they respond."

Caleb rose to leave. Linda was standing a respectful distance away, waiting to speak to her husband.

The second wife.

He'd not seen Naomi in the house since the day of her confrontation with David, though she'd remained a fixture in the Fortress, helping, teaching, leading as always. She hadn't been enough for David, and he'd used his power to reach for more. The Bible recognized polygamy. Why not more than two then?

A disturbing thought surfaced. Samson. What had happened those many times the Prophet and Sara McBride had been alone in the Evangel Room? Had Sara McBride been their Delilah?

CHAPTER 73

WHEN WORD CAME to the headquarters tent that Caleb Nathanson wanted to talk again, Redmond summoned Sara and O'Keefe. "I think it's important that you hear what he has to say. Maybe you'll have some insights of value. But we don't want to risk your presence shutting him down completely, so we'll set up a screen that'll let you hear but not be seen."

Ten minutes later, Redmond stood at the door of the tent as Caleb approached while examining everything around him, taking in everything he could. The reconnoitering effort was obvious. Once inside, he seemed resigned, fatalistic, not trying to persuade like the last time, only going through the motions.

He told Redmond what the Prophet had told him to say with some variations of his own. He claimed he'd volunteered for this to try to negotiate *something* with them, but found himself in an impossible position. The Prophet was adamant that he and his community had done no wrong. They'd tried to live in peace away from the disgusting, vicious Babylonian monstrosity of the world. They'd exercised their constitutional right to bear arms and defend themselves, that's all. The tape had been doctored, he said. And even if it hadn't, that was nothing but a discussion of a possible scenario—nothing but a war game. "Mr. Redmond," he implored, "isn't there something you can offer?"

Redmond shook his head. "Nothing. You're terrorists. We don't negotiate with terrorists."

"Given that you'll suffer massive casualties when you attack us, is there nothing you're willing to give us? For example, I've been thinking … I haven't discussed it with David, but would you allow him to broadcast a statement from the compound for distribution to the media before we come out?"

"No."

"You're a hard man."

"Not as hard as your Prophet."

"How about if you allow him to make such a statement here, at your headquarters, after we've surrendered?"

"No."

"So you have nothing to offer?"

"No more than you do. I saw you gawking around as you were walking up here. You're on a scouting mission, that's all."

"I have nothing more to say."

"How about the women and children?" Redmond asked.

"They stand with their husbands and fathers and their Lord and Savior Jesus Christ and Yahweh, His Father."

"I guess that's it then. And by the way, have you at any point wondered how you were able to send and receive those messages on your message board all this time? You think we were stupid enough to miss shutting off those lines? We wanted to see what you were doing, maybe go visit some of the scum you were communicating with. We know you haven't persuaded anybody to do anything. Your fellow warriors are silent. They've abandoned you. And you know what, my friend? God is also silent. He's abandoned you too."

"I want to go now."

"You'll be able to go, just like before, but please step outside a minute and wait, so I can have a few words with my men here before you leave us."

Something that looked like hope flickered in Caleb's face. "Alright" he said. "But I won't wait long."

With Caleb outside, Redmond brought O'Keefe and Sara out from behind the screen.

"Any insights?" he asked them. "Any suggestions?"

Both shook their heads. O'Keefe said, "Nothing from that conversation, but I wish you'd let me have a few minutes with him."

"Violence won't do any good," Redmond said. "And I can't let that happen anyway."

"I don't intend that. But we spent a lot of time together. I know him well. We were almost friends. What would it hurt? I won't give anything away."

Redmond looked at his lieutenants.

To O'Keefe's surprise, Doolan said, "Why not?"

When O'Keefe emerged from the tent, Caleb looked like he might physically attack, something he'd thought Caleb could never bring himself to do. The moment passed, and instead, when O'Keefe got close, he spat in O'Keefe's face.

O'Keefe didn't wipe it off, letting it slide on down his cheek and go where it pleased.

"We were friends once, Caleb."

"I was friends with a wolf in sheep's clothing."

"Or a sheep in wolf's clothing. But that doesn't matter. I know you, Caleb. I know that, in the end, you won't sacrifice your children for a man like your Prophet."

"He and we are people of God," Caleb declaimed, his voice loud and full of righteous indignation. "The stakes here are the highest stakes in all history. Yahweh will soon be welcoming us into Paradise for ever and ever."

"Blah, Blah, Blah." He slapped Caleb's face hard, a stinging slap that immediately turned the cheek red. "Wake up, Caleb. How can you be so sure? Have you ever been wrong? Has your Prophet ever been wrong? It had better be the End Times because everyone in the world who survives this Apocalypse thing of yours will spit and piss and shit on your names and memories forever. Your children will have died for nothing. And if they're not killed here, their lives will likely be even worse. They'll have to live then as the children of an evil madman ... who was willing to deliver innocent men and women and children including even his own children, to their early deaths to serve his miserable, demented cause.

"And for what? How can you be so confident that God has spoken to your Prophet ... spoken so directly and clearly ... delivered *him,* of all the holy men in this whole big world so unmistakable a message? What if your Prophet's wrong? Has everything he's ever prophesied come to pass? We know the answer to that is a resounding NO. He's named the date of the End Times at least once before, and probably more times I don't know about … *and it didn't happen.* So was he wrong then but right now? What if he's gotten his signals crossed with the Almighty … again?

"That Prophet of yours was trying to fuck Sara every minute they were together. And you know that's true. Two wives weren't enough for him. Would God really have entrusted the most important task in the history of the world to a man like David Dodd?

"King David himself had his flaws, yet God gave him glory."

"What if, instead, God is displeased about what you've done? The great angry God of the Bible that massacred whole peoples including, many times, vast numbers of the Israelites themselves when they took the wrong course. Instead of Heaven, the Prophet, and you, and all who follow you, would be the ones that end up in Hell … with Satan … because that's who you're following now."

Caleb spat again, but his mouth seemed to have dried up. What little phlegm he managed to muster dribbled down his own chin. He turned, staggered slightly, and walked on.

O'Keefe shouted after him, "YOUR CHILDREN DYING IN AGONY, CALEB."

Caleb covered his ears with his hands and marched out of sight.

O'Keefe walked back to tent entrance where Redmond was waiting for him.

"I saw all that. You promised not to beat on him."

"I said that was my intent."

"A wordsmith, eh? You've been hanging around lawyers too long."

"And I didn't beat him."

"Agree. But that was a damned hard slap."

"You ever been slapped like that?" O'Keefe said.

"Not that I recall."

"I have. It provokes a special form of shame and precisely focuses one's attention."

"Anything else worth reporting?"

"I just tried to put some icing on your cake. And maybe a few candles too."

Redmond turned and began issuing orders. "In thirty minutes shut off the rest of the phone lines. Shut down that message board of theirs. Get every helicopter we have into the sky. I want as many of them as possible up there night and day for the next twenty-four hours. Lots of noise. Turn the sirens on. Blast them five minutes at a time every ten minutes until nightfall and start again at dawn. Figure out how to produce every kind of loud noise we can think of.

"Move this tent and all equipment and personnel back so we're out of rocket range. Form a manned perimeter along that 200-meter line. Eyes and ears alert for any movement to the front or the sides. Before the pullback, do two things: Cover the whole parking and entrance area with spotlights and shine them into the compound all night long. Set up our public address system on a pole. Start broadcasting loud and incessant messages of the kind that the people in there aren't gonna want to hear."

As O'Keefe and Sara walked toward their tents, he said, "I don't know how I'll be able to live with myself if any of those kids get hurt. I never signed up for that."

"We never signed up to uncover a planned massacre either," she said. "Whatever happens, it's out of your hands now. You can't blame yourself."

"Oh, yes I can, and I'm sure I will."

"Isn't that a bit self-centered? And don't you guys have a saying about changing the things you can and accepting the things you can't?"

CHAPTER 74

CALEB LET HIMSELF in, kept his head down, and headed for the computer room. The Prophet and the General sat at the table, looking weary and desperate.

"Wait," the Prophet said. "Give us the report."

"I'll be back in a couple minutes. I need to check the computer."

The lights on the machines were still on, the monitor still functioning. He walked over and looked at the screen. Nothing. No response. All those bulletins he'd sent had just been messages in bottles bobbing forlornly on the waves of the vast ocean.

The screen went to black. Redmond had shut it down. A perfect epitaph.

He returned to the front room. The Prophet and the General were both scowling, clearly impatient and irritated with him for not immediately reporting.

"Did you follow the script?" the Prophet said.

"To the letter."

"And?"

"Nothing. One hundred percent rejection."

"You asked him for offers?"

"More than once. Refused."

"Did he ask about the women and children?."

"He did not."

A lie. But hopefully a blessed one.

The General said, "What can you tell us that might be useful for my assault idea?"

"I had to walk a lot farther this time to get to their headquarters tent. They'd moved it. I'm guessing they'll move it again. Redmond accused me of just being there to scout the place. He's a very smart man. Since they've moved way back already, and are probably moving some more right now, doesn't that doom your bombardment and assault plan, General?"

The General's jaw visibly tightened. "Certainly makes it a lot harder to pull off. But I see no other choice here."

"No other choice," the Prophet muttered as if in a trance.

The General alerted on the noise first. He rose, said "I'll be right back," and went outside. They sat waiting for him to return, staring at each other, the walls, the ceiling, the tabletop.

The General's head appeared in the doorway. "Come out here and see this."

The General and all the Ark men on the front line were looking upward toward the sinister roar of many engines in a sky crowded with helicopters.

"What are they doing?" the Prophet said. "Will they bomb us?"

"I doubt that," the General said. "I guess they could unravel ladders and rappel down, but we could easily shoot them before they got to the ground."

"Tear gas? Some other thing? Is there a nerve gas that could incapacitate our people somehow?"

"Can't imagine that, out here in the open."

They flinched when the sirens shattered the air.

"An attack?"

"Could be. I'll send a recon party out to the front. But maybe they're just trying to scare us, drive us crazy."

The General rushed off to organize the recon group.

They waited, again in silence.

When the General returned, Caleb said, "Let's get back inside."

The General shook his head. "I need to be out here."

"Come inside," Caleb said firmly. A command. "I have something to say that you need to hear."

They both shot him a skeptical look, but there was surprise there too. Was this really *Caleb* talking … issuing orders?

When he strode toward the house, they followed.

Caleb rested his forearms on the table and leaned forward. "Please, hear me out. I've had a lot of time to reflect over these past few days. I am, as always, willing to sacrifice my life for our cause, Yahweh's cause. But I've come to believe that the lives of these good men and women and children—and *your* two lives most of all—are better spared, so we and our people with us can continue the struggle."

He noticed their body language change, contort toward a refusal.

Hurry, Caleb. "I know we believe that it's God's will that the End Times begin now and that we're the Chosen Ones to set the spark. But it's possible we may have misunderstood."

The Prophet scowled his disapproval.

"Bear with me, David," Caleb insisted.

He opened his Bible and read the passages from Mark's gospel showing that even Jesus didn't know and even admitted that He didn't know when the great event would arrive ... and that His *own* prediction that the existing generation would not pass before it occurred ... was *wrong*.

"How then can we be confident that we've arrived at the right conclusion? All the signs that God has given us recently suggest that now is *not* the time. He allowed the McBrides, or whoever those traitors really are, in here. He allowed our war plan to be discovered. None of our fellow warriors out there have responded." His voice rose to a breaking, high-pitched near screech. "NONE!"

Startled, the Prophet and the General recoiled.

"I think," Caleb continued, "He is telling us to open more fully to Him and His message. He is telling us we got a bit ahead of things and that we need to play a longer game. And there is most definitely a longer game to play."

He could tell it had moved them, but not enough.

"In 1923 Adolph Hitler led a National Socialist revolution—a 'putsch,' they called it—to overthrow the German government. It failed. Or so it seemed. Several of his party members were shot and killed. Significantly, Hitler, though at the front line, was spared that fate. He was convicted of treason and sent to prison for five years. Devastating, one would think. But it turned out just the opposite. For the first time he became known to the entire nation. He used his trial as a national platform to win more support. In prison he wrote his great work *Mein Kampf.* He obtained early release, after only nine months. It still took him almost ten more years, but he eventually triumphed, came to rule Germany and, ultimately, for a time, until he overreached, *prematurely acted,* he came to rule almost the entire world.

"I think this is the exact plan that God is unfolding for us if we are open enough, anointed and blessed enough, to understand it. What He is telling us, David, is that you, above all of us, but your followers too, *must* be spared. Yes, it would be so beautiful to enter God's kingdom in glory right now, but we must gravely consider that God may be asking us to further endure and persevere … until a time not far away when the fuse we light will not fizzle out … but will stay alight … and the tremendous keg of God's powder that is our movement will explode like a thousand atomic bombs and obliterate any trace on earth of this Babylon in which we're captive."

He stopped. He could go on and on—that was his way—but he recognized a change in the Prophet's demeanor and decided, for once, not to go on, and on.

"What do you think?" the Prophet asked the General.

"I'll be guided by you, David, but I believe it should either be what Caleb's unfolded here or the assault plan I outlined, which I admit that now, since they've moved back, would likely be a kamikaze mission. But the one thing we absolutely should not do is just grovel here in misery until they finally attack … and, to quote the great hero Jim Bowie at the Alamo, 'we die in these ditches.'"

"Alright, General, but which of the two plans would you choose?"

"The assault, of course. But I also acknowledge that there's much wisdom in what Caleb is proposing. I'm not *begging* to die right now, and it would be quite satisfying to someday lead an army a bit more powerful than our good but feeble fellows out there in those ditches."

"The world will call us cowards" the Prophet said.

Caleb replied sternly: "A few. A very few. But surrendering to the fear of *that* will be the real cowardice. Are we so terrified of what the Jewsmedia will say about us that we sacrifice the future of our message and even the lives of our women and children? If we die in these ditches … and worse, sentence all those people out there to die in these ditches … the world will call us demented fools and bury us in scornful oblivion … and our good people out there with us. They deserve better. And, most of all, *you* deserve better. If we allow even one of our women or children to be hurt, the world will call us monsters. Another Jonestown."

The General nodded but seemed unable able to quite let go of his impulse to embrace a glorious martyrdom. "Like I said yesterday, we could send the women and children to safety and still do the assault."

Caleb recognized this as the decisive moment, a moment to flatter the General and use it to make a better point. "The assault plan was brilliant, Leon … *yesterday*. Now that they've moved out of range of the rockets, then we'll have to cover all that ground…"

He left it right there, for the General to ponder.

"Yes," the General finally said. "Pickett's charge."

The Prophet appeared confused.

"Last gasp at Gettysburg," the General said. "Lee sent Pickett's division on a long trek across open ground. They were cut to pieces. No chance after that. A terrible black mark on Lee's reputation."

The Prophet heaved a mighty sigh. "I need to pray on this. Meanwhile, get someone to check it out and make sure they've moved back."

CHAPTER 75

Early morning, shortly after opening time of the saloon-restaurant. The two diners sat at a Formica-topped table at the far end of an otherwise empty dining room but positioned so both could see the television they'd asked the bartender to tune to the regional station most likely to cover the situation at Ark II. Their breakfast plates were scraped nearly clean, only a few traces of egg yolk and a lone toasted bread crust remaining, coffee cooling in half-empty cups, as they studied a map laid out before them.

Sinclair said, "I don't see it any different this morning. It just seems too risky and to not enough good purpose or possible reward."

"So we go back for Maxwell?" Darby said

Sinclair wriggled uncomfortably. "Best option, I guess. Maybe salvage something from this disaster."

A new sound on the TV. Dramatic music. A reporter standing on a dirt road next to a broken fence amid a profusion of scrub grass, weeds, and stunted trees. "We've just received news from an inside source. Ark II has surrendered. Repeat. The Ark II community has surrendered. They are now assembling to march out of the compound in an orderly fashion where they'll be greeted by Agent Charles Redmond of the FBI, the leader of the enforcement action, siege, and standoff that could have resulted in a monumental tragedy. We hope to get an official statement soon."

Sinclair leaned back in his chair and raised his eyes toward the ceiling, letting this news sink in, then said, "Well, I can't say I'm surprised. Almost been expecting it. I always thought the Prophet and Caleb were cowards at bottom, and there was a good chance they'd turn all the way yellow once they had to face the pointed guns themselves instead of sending someone else to do it."

"And the General?"

"You can't lead an army that won't fight."

More nattering commentary on the television.

Sinclair, his simmering rage exploding, banged his fist on the table so hard it knocked over an empty water glass and shook the rest of the dishware, startling the bartender who looked furtively and anxiously toward his guests, then quickly averted his gaze.

"No reason to waste ourselves on this bullshit," Sinclair said. "Let's go back north."

"North?"

"Forget Maxwell. Not worth it now. Idaho."

"Think they'll rat on us?" Darby said.

"It's a possibility, maybe even a probability, but nothing we can do about that. Beyond our control now. If they do, the Zogs'll have to track us down. We'll give 'em some hell if they do. We were willing to give it all up here, why not up there?"

"And the woman?" Darby said.

Sinclair didn't answer right away. Darby, knowing his friend well, waited patiently, until Sinclair's face went hard and he said, "That woman has some good points, but she's a woman. A foolish one too. Can't trust that, especially when it's something we *can* control."

CHAPTER 76

"The Chillren," Caleb said, "will march out first, our warriors after."

It had been agreed that he, accompanied by the General this time, would negotiate the surrender terms.

"There may be a couple of women and teenagers in the warrior group," he continued.

"No weapons of any kind," Redmond said. "And we'll have to frisk them."

"Off camera?"

"What cameras?"

"We think the TV crews should be allowed to film."

"I doubt we'll agree to that."

The General took over. "We insist. Should we go back?"

"We'll take it under advisement."

It seemed worth it, Redmond thought. They had the Ark people where they wanted them. No point in losing it over something silly. This General was a serious man. He might be fanatical enough to let some small, supposed matter of "honor" kill the deal … and a lot of people.

"And stop all the noise, including the helicopters," the General said.

"I think we can do that."

"And the Prophet will make a final statement over our PA system."

Standing next to Redmond, Doolan twitched. "We said no statement."

"That," Caleb said, "was a request for a statement broadcast to the world. All we want now—"

"*Demand* now," the General interrupted.

"All we demand now," Caleb resumed, "is that he be able to deliver a farewell to his friends and neighbors of many years."

The final deal was that television, film, and radio crews would be allowed to record the march out of the compound under certain conditions: One, to ensure that no weapons left the Ark, everyone would be frisked inside the compound. Everyone then would form up under guard.

Two. They would march out in orderly fashion and quietly—no shouting out or singing or demonstrations of any kind. They would halt on the far side of the parking lot. Arrests would occur at that time. For those not arrested, appropriate arrangements would be made for them to travel from the site, all at the discretion of FBI and ATF.

Three. For the remainder of that day and the next, both Caleb Nathanson and Leon Lomax would accompany agents on a thorough search of the entire compound.

Redmond would later be severely criticized from several quarters for agreeing to some of these things, accused of "coddling terrorists." But he believed then and always would thereafter believe that he had done his duty to his country and its people that he had sworn to serve to the best of his ability, and that he had been able to avoid what could have easily ended, instead, in a monumental tragedy and a grievous self-inflicted wound to the Republic for which he stood.

CHAPTER 77

Tʜᴇ ᴍᴇɴ, ᴡᴏᴍᴇɴ, and children of the Ark assembled as best they could among the "mole mounds" of the chewed-up Gathering Ground.

At first, the Prophet had been almost overcome with the dread of this moment. But the more he thought about it, the more he came to understand and then embrace the plan Caleb had laid out and the potentially glorious future it might deliver. This was not a defeat at all. Like Hitler in Landsberg Prison, this was only a beginning. They had shown they were willing to "die in the ditches" as the General had said. This could prove to be a solid foundation on which to erect something so much greater.

So he now addressed his flock. "People, blessed people, of the Ark. In these past few days you have shown, for all the world to witness, that you are most certainly among the tiny sliver of God's Chosen People in this wicked world. Your faith and fortitude in the face of the vicious, bloodthirsty forces of the demon soldiers of Satan sent to destroy us has been a shining beacon that will, I assure you, eventually enflame the whole world.

"After much prayer and contemplation, I decided to stand down, most of all because God has shown me that it is the decision He wants … for now. He does not want a premature shedding of blood where some, many—though even one would be too many—of our cherished women and children, or our stalwart men either, would be slaughtered … The ZOGs were willing to bring that on. I was not."

Tears, weeping, sobs, occasional shouts of pain or rejoicing began to sweep the crowd like a strong breeze bending stalks of wheat on the prairie.

"He does not want us to die now, prematurely. He wants us, for a while, a short while, to continue to live and preach and struggle. The End Times may not arrive tomorrow, but I am certain they will arrive soon. God has revealed to us that we shall certainly be called again, on a day not far away, to offer ourselves once more, hopefully for final victory in the Armageddon battle, to receive a special welcome to, and a special place within, God's beautiful kingdom.

"No matter what they do to me, I shall not allow my voice to be stilled. The word will go out from any and every dungeon they fling me into. And I shall return. Keep the faith. You have done your best to live the lives that God expects of us. Continue that way, and God will bring us back together again in due time.

"The harlots of the Jewsmedia and the rest of the evil ZOG empire of the New Babylon will claim this as a victory. It is no such thing. It is only the beginning of the end ... not of us, but of *them* ... in a conflagration that will torture and consume them all. They crucified Jesus, didn't they? But on the third day He rose from the dead in the greatest of all miracles, and He, today, sits at the right hand of the Father...while his killers, the Roman empire, fell...disappeared forever. And the Jews...look what they brought on themselves and have justly suffered forever afterward and will for all time. And soon, perhaps in only a few months, or even only days, He shall come again in glory on that Last Day to rule the world and gather us into His arms.

"So, my neighbors, my friends, my children ... when we gather up to march out of here, march in straight rows and, most of all, joyfully. Show the world that we are the winners here, for we absolutely are. I love you, every one of you, with all my heart and soul."

Many were on their knees as the weeping and outcries continued. Caleb was sobbing so hard it bent him over. He straightened and reviewed the crowd. The Prophet stood next to him, eyes tearless, brilliant, bright, piercing. Next to him the General was also dry-eyed, but squinting hard, surely fighting back tears.

He looked for Marsha and the children. His wife sat on the ground, inconsolable, her children, his children, beside her, all sobbing, one kneeling next to her, one patting her on the shoulder, one smoothing her hair. He would likely not see them for a long time other than through the iron bars of his cage. But no matter. This, he knew, was a divinely ordained ending to their great undertaking and last courageous stand, an ending that he could say privately to himself and with utmost humility—for it was Yahweh's will, not Caleb Nathanson's, that had been done—but that it was he, more than any other human agent, who had brought this to pass. He had served his God, not perfectly, never perfectly, but well.

Only one incongruence troubled his waters at that poignant moment. He couldn't locate Naomi anywhere in the crowd. She had entirely fallen away from them.

CHAPTER 78

Where was he?

Except for several excursions to probe Maxwell's level of vigilance and protection (which appeared to have waned considerably, and that was *before* the announcement of the surrender), she'd stayed glued to the TV, watching intently for any mention or sign of Matthew in the surrender coverage.

A terrible disappointment that their plan, whatever it was, had failed. But so nice to see them all, some of the children even skipping along as if it were all simply a great and fun adventure. He was not in the march-out crowd. She hadn't expected him to be. *But then, where was he?* Had he been captured somewhere else? Surely, to avoid possible recognition, he'd rushed out of there. And he certainly would come back here? Two of his guns, some of his clothes, even a wristwatch were still here. *She* was still here. Surely she had given him enough pleasure to have pierced or at least threaded her way through a tiny tear or seam in that armored persona. He couldn't get that good of a thing just anywhere, maybe nowhere. And she was perfectly certain that nowhere else in the world did someone exist so devoted to him as she who'd vowed to serve him in all respects.

And what of all the Ark people? Now scattered and leaderless, where would they end up? Some would likely stick together, create a new community. When Matthew returned, maybe they would travel down there if he felt he could risk it, and together they'd help those people pick up the pieces.

Of course there was Darby, stuck to him like a suit of extra clothes.

Be patient. Let that slowly loosen and fall away.

Pondering some more, she decided they must be on their way back to complete the original mission. Surprise, Mr. Maxwell! Surprise, all the rest of you who thought he was safe now!

She believed she could do it herself, and was ready to. No doubt she could get close to him, pistol in her purse. Like that plain, unassuming middle-aged woman who'd almost managed to kill President Ford. They dismissed people like that … well, like me … the invisible people. They might pay more attention in the future.

But could she really bring herself to do something like that? Certainly something like that would never have even entered her mind but for Matthew. And, anyway, it would be foolish to sacrifice herself that way and end up behind bars, especially since they might catch Matthew and send *him* to prison. She needed to be in position to faithfully visit him. Some prisons were even allowing what they called "conjugal visits." He might even marry her for that.

A knock at the door. A surge of joy. She sprang up from the couch and hurried there. She would open the door just a bit at first, smile, then throw it open all the way … and then throw herself into his arms … grab him around the chest (because the top of her head only came up to his chest, he was so tall), and hug him so tight. Then nature would take its ecstatic course.

She inched open the door.

Peeked out.

And found only Preston Darby standing there.

CHAPTER 79

HE HAD NO intention of sticking around for some asinine farewell speech. As soon as he heard that the Prophet intended to surrender, he changed into his swim trunks and thick-soled water shoes, strapped on the belt with a knife scabbard and pistol holster attached, and slipped on the drybag backpack he'd loaded with three grenades, lightweight pants and T-shirt, plus minimal first-aid and survival items. He was sorely tempted to take a couple of his most inventive explosive devices that he'd been working on so assiduously day after day, so happily alone in "his" shed, but they were heavy and would be of no use if he encountered the ZOGs on this critical first leg of his escape. And if he was stopped by the police at some point now or later … forget it, that would cook him for sure. He would even discard the grenades once he got near any form of civilization so there'd be no chance he'd be caught with them.

It would take time to assemble the materials for new bombs in a way that they could almost certainly not be traced. But he had all the time in the world, and this little sojourn at Ark II hadn't cost him much at all. His cash stash was still mostly intact.

He'd never intended to stick around after the ZOGs arrived, no matter how things turned out, though he'd been curious enough to risk remaining until something decisive occurred. When they summoned everyone to the defensive perimeter, he held back, having long ago made sure that the Ark people understood he was never to be issued orders or bothered in any way. He did his valuable work and expected—insisted—that he be otherwise left alone.

He snaked his lithe body through the barbed-wire fence at the southeast corner of the compound. He'd practiced traveling this and other escape routes many times during both daytime and night. He'd checked several times during the siege and found that, except for a desultory halfhearted patrol, the ZOGs were paying no attention this far down the property line.

Once through the barbed wire, only a hundred yards to jog and a dense grove of trees to maneuver through separated him from the lake. The brambly forest extended all the way to the shoreline. There was not even a small beach there like there was on the western side of the compound, not even space to stand. He grabbed a branch and eased himself into the water, swam leisurely, staying parallel with the shore for what he guessed was around 200 yards, a couple of football fields, until he reached a small peninsula. Climbing out on the shoreline, barely breathing hard from the swim, he had enough space to stand up and dress himself. He imitated a wet dog, vigorously shaking the water off himself, then smoothed down his wet hair with both hands.

The stretch of land between him and the road was a ranch property but with no cattle and no ranch house, no danger of encountering a troublesome man or beast. He waited until nightfall, then made his way to the road. Even with the ZOGs infesting the place and the rubberneckers they attracted, the road was seldom traveled at night, and it was easy enough to duck into a ditch or a patch of vegetation if an occasional vehicle passed.

He jogged down one side, then the other, whichever narrow, almost-nonexistent shoulder was more accommodating to a running man on that particular stretch of pavement. Eventually, he came to a small metal building that he'd rented from a farmer who had no other use for it, telling the yokel a story about needing to store his car while he took off into the local wilderness to find out how difficult it would be to survive on his own out there. Without suspicion, but with derision, the man had said, "Whatever floats your boat," and pocketed the large advance rental payment.

The door was padlocked. He entered the combination and it clicked open, smooth as warm butter, just as expected (he'd made several previous trips to check it and to run the engine to keep the car battery charged). The car was there like it ought to be. He turned the key in the ignition with a twinge of anxiety, but the engine caught immediately.

His stay at Ark II had been productive, though only in a negative way. It had confirmed what he already knew—that these organized-group things were a foolish strategy, too vulnerable to spies and traitors like those McBrides and to pusillanimous or megalomaniacal leadership (the Prophet had turned out to be both). The General was alright, but the whole "army" approach was also mistaken. The only way to dismantle ZOG and terrify more or less normal people into doing right themselves would come from individuals like himself, acting as lone wolves, wreaking havoc all on their lonesome, no "comrades" to end up selling them out to the ZOG; people like him, who weren't afraid to bring destruction and death until good moral Christian white people took charge again, and the pinkos and homos and Jews and spearchuckers and mud people were pretty much all banished or exterminated and any few of them remaining rendered forever subservient.

Which prompted the question: Would the Ark II people sell him out? That's why this little spiritual retreat might've been a serious mistake despite having served the excellent purpose of providing him a hideout in case there'd been a witness who could identify him from those baby-killing slaughterhouses back east. Better to give himself time, let those cases settle down, grow cold.

But still, he wouldn't do it again. Any of those Ark people could offer him up. One of those police artist's sketches would likely soon be floating around the country with his face on it. But a beard, a shaved head, and some fake eyeglasses, maybe those wire-rimmed jobs that goofy intellectuals wore, would sufficiently change his appearance, so that sketch of him would soon be useful for nothing except toilet paper.

And he could increase his odds in several other ways. Bury himself in some remote area, rent something in a shabby little trailer park or a mobile home or little house out on its lonesome on some scroungy spot of land far off the road. From there he could foray to carefully chosen targets in places least likely to know or care who he might be. Good planning, placement, body count, and easy escape. Then get in, get out, all fast, very fast. Those were the rules.

But one thing he remembered from some of those crime shows on television. If you hung around the same people long enough, they might see that sketch on TV or in some newspaper or magazine and match it with "this guy I know." Easy enough to have no guy friends. But unfortunately, no girlfriends either, except Mrs. Hand and her Five Daughters.

They'd catch him eventually, but likely not until he'd made them understand that suctioning live babies out of their mothers' wombs or stabbing in there with a knife and scraper and chopping and slashing them into chunks of flesh and tossing them in a trash can would earn severe consequences.

It probably wouldn't be that hard to pick the states that had no death penalty. But he wasn't sure he cared all that much. It wasn't worth anything to live in a world where Herod was allowed, even outrageously cheered on, to daily gather up, on a massive scale, the Holy Innocents and put them to the sword.

CHAPTER 80

Tʜᴇʏ sᴛᴏᴏᴅ ᴄᴏɴᴄᴇᴀʟᴇᴅ behind the first line of trees and watched their former neighbors march out.

The Prophet marched alone in front of them all, the General and Caleb immediately behind him.

Immediately behind them came the children, Caleb's idea of a wonderful "photo op." And Caleb was right. O'Keefe was most pleased to see the little girl bouncing along in her usual way.

The second wave consisted of all the men.

The third wave comprised the women. Sara looked for Naomi, who should have been in the center of the first line. But that position was now filled solely by Linda, who wept and tried to hide her face, her brief ascendancy ending in the worst way, left homeless and penniless.

She finally spotted Naomi in the last line, eyes downcast in shame.

"Naomi is a decent woman," Sara said to O'Keefe. "Not so different from a lot of us … trying to find refuge … and finding it, but, as it turns out, in the wrong place, and, especially, the wrong person."

O'Keefe had no ready wisdom capable of answering that, though he'd noticed that she'd used the word "us."

"I wonder," Sara continued, "how much she hates me now. I'd like to visit her someday."

There was nothing to say to that either.

"What'd you think of that?" she said.

"I didn't like it. Except for the kids, that parade felt all wrong.

"Yeah. Like they were sort of the winners in this thing … or at least not the losers … and certainly not the terrorists they so badly wanted to be.

"The whole story needs to get out."

"It sure hasn't yet," she said.

"And some things are missing."

"Yes. Shame, contrition."

"And something else. Rudy wasn't there."

"Shouldn't we tell them that?" she said.

He sighed and shrugged. "I'm tired. This spy wants to come in from the cold. One of the Ark people will out him."

"He's a bomber. People will die. I'll do it."

He shrugged again, a gesture of shame and surrender. "You're right. I'm just weary. And there's others. Take a guess."

She thought for a moment before it came to her. "How could I forget … Sinclair and Darby."

The processing operation had begun—arrests in several cases, travel and lodging arrangements in many others. Gratefully accepting Redmond's warning that they should avoid any exposure, either to the Ark people or the media, O'Keefe and Sara prevailed on one of the agents to peel Redmond away. Doolan and Brewster joined him.

When they told him about the missing bomber, and Sinclair, and Darby, Redmond turned to Doolan. "Start interrogating all those people before they leave. But wait." He turned to the PIs. "We need the best descriptions you can give us right now, and then to a sketch artist as soon as possible."

Here we go, O'Keefe thought. *Sliding down the slippery slope again.*

After they finished their descriptions, Redmond said, "Let's get out an APB far and wide and in every way possible."

O'Keefe said, "I assume there's no sketch artist on site."

"'Fraid not. But we'll want you in our offices back in the city first thing in the morning. I might even try to roust someone out tonight."

No rest for the wicked … or the virtuous, either. "We'd like to get back tonight, before dark if possible."

Doolan scowled. Redmond looked uncertain and asked, "Why?"

"Because I'm tired of all this. We've got a car phone. You can call us on that if you have questions. And if we think of something else, we promise we'll call you."

"Some of us," Doolan interjected, not hostile this time, just smart-ass, "can't afford to get tired of all this."

Before O'Keefe could come up with something appropriate to counter that, Redmond, with a quick impatient glance at Doolan, intervened. "One condition. Coverage being spotty, you call us every hour on your way back, from a pay phone if necessary, in case we can't reach you."

They shook Redmond's hand. "Good job," O'Keefe said. "Not that I'm any judge, but I don't know how you could've done better."

"I had a little bird on my shoulder who wouldn't shut up about 'decency.'"

They shook Brewster's hand too.

Then Doolan's.

"Even *you* finally did okay, Doolan," O'Keefe said. "But you haven't thanked me for the tape, my boost to your career. To say nothing of the landmines."

Doolan couldn't help himself. He smiled. A rueful smile, but a smile.

"Let's have dinner sometime, Doolan" O'Keefe said. "You never know, this could be the beginning of a beautiful friendship."

Doolan smiled again, less ruefully this time.

"Strange pair, eh?" Redmond said when the two PIs were out of earshot.

"You bet," Doolan said. "Ornery too. Him anyway."

"She's pretty interesting," Redmond said. "What ya know about her?"

"Nothing. And you know what? O'Keefe doesn't either."

"No?"

"Yeah. I asked him. He said she just showed up one day for a job interview as a secretary with an agenda to become a PI and kept moving right along from there. She apparently discloses nothing about herself, and to quote him, 'I decided to honor and respect her privacy.'"

Redmond said, "Weird. And separate tents. You think, like he says, they really spent all that time together as husband and wife and didn't, you know…"

"If you believe that, I've got a famous bridge from London I'll sell you cheap."

CHAPTER 81

THE GOVERNMENT ISSUED a terse statement to the media. The emphasis was only on the illegal weapons mentioned in the warrant. Information about such things as LAW rockets, 50 cals, and a barrel of cyanide were initially withheld. There was mention of a "terrorist conspiracy" but with no details. Thus, the opening "narrative" focused on devout Christians and the right to bear arms.

Interviews with men and women on the street concentrated on locals who seemed to have forgotten the consternation that the New Ark had often aroused. There was no mention of local fears of "another Jonestown." The Sheriff had grudgingly provided a few men to Redmond's task force, but, following the surrender, he'd himself refused, and forbidden his men to make, any comment or provide any information to the media. Which meant there was no interview with, for example, Deputy Riggins, who'd worried out loud and to many people about that Jonestown possibility and his suspicion that some of those "cult people" had been responsible for the vicious bludgeoning and stabbing murder of the still-unidentified "woman in the weeds," and even perhaps the also still-unsolved execution-style killing of a state trooper.

Most of the television preachers explored the theme of "persecution of devout Christians exercising their constitutional right to bear arms," some more gingerly than others, feeling their way toward their own "narrative."

But some were more militant from the start. On his program, broadcast on radio and television stations across the country, the Reverend Billy Bitson, who was often called on to deliver the opening invocations at conferences and other gatherings of Christian Identity, survivalist, militia, and similarly inclined groups, had words such as these to say, incessantly, among many others:

"…A godly group of devout Christians … fleeing persecution and wickedness everywhere … like the blessed founders of our once great country … A city on a hill … A New Ark, as they named their peaceable kingdom … led there by a new Noah and new Moses, David Dodd was both, called by his people 'the Prophet.' Through prayer and hard work and clean living, the ancient American values, everywhere smothering in their death throes now for lack of any political or cultural oxygen … brought forth a new Garden of Eden from the untamed wilderness … and simply exercising their right to bear arms under the Second Amendment of the U.S. Constitution. But the vicious demon forces of our current Tyranny descended on these poor people with a literal ARMY! For what? A few supposedly illegal weapons? A LITERAL ARMY. At least fifty armed men, helicopters, war ships … Issued to God's people an order, one that will live on in infamy, to surrender or they would be attacked … no quarter given even to the little children cowering in their violated homes with their mothers … The New Ark is no more. Let us bow our heads and pray for those holy martyrs … There is no doubt they will be vindicated! But in the meantime, to quote the title of one of the favorite anthems of that true Prophet, David Dodd … KEEP YOUR RIFLE BY YOUR SIDE."

CHAPTER 82

THEY GLIDED THROUGH vistas near and far—down valleys, along riverbanks, up hills that were almost mountains—mile after mile of dying October foliage, the falling leaves bequeathing a last will and testament so much more generous than the alms they had dispensed in their flowering lives of spring and summer. This was a bequest not of bursting life but of expiration and relinquishment, yet so much more glorious than anything they'd revealed in their lush, green prime. Words, concepts—red, scarlet, gold, brown, bronze, yellow, orange—were utterly inadequate to describe these colors. These were colors of some other spectrum, made by Something Like God, an image of the ineffable that would linger in their minds as long as the minds themselves lingered. It seemed like a special providence, a bestowal of fortune far beyond what they may have thought they deserved for that fraught adventure on which they had voluntarily embarked and managed to survive. It seemed like there ought to be some transcendent revelation or at least a bit of wisdom to be gained from all of that, but, as always, it eluded him, seemingly hovering there in front of him, only just out of reach and sight, scattered in the mist. So this, here before him, just this, life itself, would have to be enough.

Finally, they had to stop saying and repeating words like "Wonderful," "Amazing," "Exquisite," "Incredible," "Can you believe that?" and lapsed into respectful silence.

"Well," O'Keefe said, breaking the spell, "it'll probably be the last time for us in the ol' Buick here."

She laughed a little.

Soon she dropped off to sleep.

He knew he should be feeling nothing but grateful that they were speeding far away from their encounter with the New Ark's fateful repetition of humanity's ages-old compulsion to chase the mirage of a lost Arcadia or Eden, the delusion that what never existed can be recaptured, driving men to misery and murder. They had faced great dangers and survived them intact (even Sara's slight limp he had noticed at the hospital had disappeared). They had fulfilled their mission. Only one of the Ark people had been physically harmed in the process, and that harm was only indirectly attributable to their agency. Maxwell was expressing privately and publicly his "eternal gratitude." They had managed to make what was, for them, a large amount of money while serving a higher cause than they normally served. They had been instrumental in saving at least one life, perhaps many.

He looked forward to spending time with Kelly again. He had a lot to make up for there, had missed her entire summer and start of her new school year. She was on the edge of adolescence, and he knew her childhood would soon disappear in what would later seem like an infinitesimal moment of time, and he would always thereafter regret its too sudden disappearance, however inevitable, especially if he failed to fully experience it, carelessly let it vanish without his full focus and appreciation.

Yet he still dreaded the return. Or, not exactly the return itself, but the looming absence of the daily distraction this months-long escapade had provided against the painful reality of his life back home with its constant undertone of irrevocable loss and unassuageable grief.

Annie. A failing. A colossal error. Those words were too tame. It was an unforgivable sin. Long ago he had left her alone with a little girl, and by the time he came to understand what a grievous thing he had done—to her most of all, but also to himself—it was too late. She had hardened against him, and even though he suspected she was melting back toward him despite her best resistance, there was now the even greater obstacle of the life he hadn't really chosen but, like so much of the rest of his life, he'd fallen into out of carelessness and desperation, a life become too crowded with danger and enemies and threat, a life that made it impossible for her and Kelly to live with him.

And even if Annie would, he couldn't conceive how in good conscience he could allow it. Nothing could be more selfish, and possibly fatally so, than that. He could walk away from his new profession. But where could they hide? There was no witness protection program for private investigators who'd had made too many enemies.

The Flying Dutchman, exiled to floating around the world, the only rescue from his aimless loneliness the love of a good woman. But what if he'd already been offered that love but had rejected it?

Or Ulysses, wandering toward home, but no Penelope waiting with infinite patience for him because he'd cast her aside long before.

He was glad when Sara woke up. He needed some conversation.

He thought he'd throw her a softball.

"Well, was it worth it?"

"Oh, yes."

She hesitated, seeming to think about what she might, or might not, say next.

"I've been dodging and ducking those people's bullets all my life."

What was this? A disclosure of some sort?

"You mean, it was personal with you somehow?"

She nodded.

"Can I ask what that is?"

A long pause.

"I'm Jewish."

He looked ahead as that sunk in. Finally, he issued a "Hmph" and shook his head, not sure whether that was a reaction of denial or amazement or both. "Don't be kidding me. I'm the gullible sort."

"No. Really. I'm Jewish … Half …But even observant once upon a time. Like you and your Catholics."

He could only shake his head again and stare ahead.

He thought about all the filthy, antisemitic rants that in these last months she'd been forced to play along with, even on occasion to enthusiastically join in, to solidify her bona fides as a citizen of the New Ark. All those Sabbath services … hard enough for O'Keefe to stomach even though he wasn't personally being constantly reviled as Satan's spawn … and all those bulletin-board modem-conveyed hateful screeds to and from the Prophet, Caleb, the General, and the rest of God's Anointed all over God's Country.

"Esther," he said. "You're Esther."

"Not quite."

"Close enough."

After a few more miles, he added, "I'll bet there's quite a story behind that."

"Esther?"

"No. You."

A smile. The smile of the cat who got the cream. "Yes, Mr. O'Keefe, there is. But that's for another day."

He returned the smile, fully enlisting in the continuing conspiracy. Of course. Why should everything be revealed? About her or anything else. If life wasn't a pilgrim quest, what the hell was it?

So our knight-errant and errant knight—not without qualm, not without pang of reluctance—pressed hard on the accelerator and aimed the mighty Buick toward that darkling kingdom of their captivity, that realm of the sweating strivers, the shills and the suckers, the schemes, scams, and scandals, the soulless spectacles, the sleazy, the seamy, the salacious, and the slanderous, the secret sorrows and stifled screams, and all the suffering sinners and silent saints shrouded in shadow beneath the soaring sullen towers of the New Babylon.

Whoever can make you believe absurdities
can make you commit atrocities.

Voltaire

DEDICATION & THANKSGIVINGS

THIS BOOK IS dedicated to the many Jewish mentors and patrons (Harold Hyman in graduate school, then Frank Morgan in commerce and law) and the far-too-many-to-be-listed (without unforgivably forgetting someone) other Jewish patrons, mentors, teachers, clients, colleagues, and friends who have helped and inspired me throughout my life. Tikkun Olam.

Thanks also to these:

> Editors Linden Gross, Louise Harnby, and Travis Tynan.

> Aimee Ravichandran from Abundantly Social and Deena Rae of eBookBuilders for getting this book from Word document to publication and launch; MilaGraphicArtist for her effort on cover design; Deena Rae for the cover design.

> My friends who put up with reading and commenting on early drafts of this book: Brett Anders, Ann Darke, Gina Harman, Joanna Heimbold, and Chris Parrott.

> Bill Hale, I wish you were still around to again be a member of the above group for yet another book. I won't say that you would have enjoyed it—it's not really a book to enjoy—but you would have appreciated it. But screw the book. I just wish you were still around. All you and Bill Moores ever did

for me was to save my life. And not only mine. You carried the message, buddy. The world could not have asked you for more than you gave it.

Again, my daughter Meghan. Another book. How lucky I am and how grateful I feel that we've been able to move forward in life in closest connection.

And, always, there is you. Sparrow who fell too soon. What more is there to say? Nothing is adequate. I miss you and mourn your absence. But not for one moment do I let any of that diminish what I know was your much greater loss and greater suffering, those months on death row with no possibility of reprieve, endured with quiet tenacity and courage … And yet, when we talk of you, we always seem to be laughing.

Dan Flanigan

Dan Flanigan is a novelist, playwright, poet, and practicing lawyer. He holds a Ph.D. in History from Rice University and J.D. from the University of Houston. He taught Jurisprudence at the University of Houston and American Legal History at the University of Virginia. His first published book was his Ph.D. dissertation, *The Criminal Law of Slavery and Freedom, 1800-1868*.

He moved on from academia to serve the civil rights cause as a school desegregation lawyer, followed by a long career as a finance attorney in private law practice. He became a name partner in the Polsinelli law firm in Kansas City, created its Financial Services practice, chaired its Real Estate & Financial Services Department for two decades, and established the firm's New York City office and served as its managing partner until October 2022. His legal bio may be viewed at https://www.polsinelli.com/professionals/dflanigan.

Taking a break from the law practice for two years in 1983-1985, he and his wife, Candy, founded Sierra Tucson, a prominent alcohol and drug treatment center located in Tucson, Arizona.

Recently, he has been able to turn his attention to his lifelong ambition—creative writing. In 2019 he released a literary trifecta including Mink Eyes, the first in the Peter O'Keefe series, <u>Dewdrops</u>, a collection of shorter fiction, and *Tenebrae: A Memoir of Love and Death*.

Tenebrae is a bracelet of verse and prose poems dedicated to his wife, Candy, to honor her last illness and death and their 40-plus years together, a work that has been described as "celebratory" and "heartbreaking and exquisite." It was a Finalist for both the 2022 IAN Book of the Year in Poetry and in the 2022 American Book Fest "Best Book" Award in the Legacy: Autobiography/ Memoir category.

Dan's novella, *Dewdrops*, was originally written for the stage and enjoyed a successful full-cast staged reading at the Theatre of the Open Eye in New York. Its then well-known and regarded director John Cappellatti described the play as a "powerful" work about "addiction in America—addiction to drugs, alcohol, sex, danger, power, and to finding the Answer," with characters that are "well drawn, real, and actors love to portray them." The short story collection comprised of *Dewdrops*, *On the Last Frontier* and *Some Cold War Blues* was a Finalist in the 2022 Independent Author Network Book of the Year for Short Story Collection and a 2022 American Book Fest "Best Book" Award Finalist in Fiction-Short Story.

In 2025, Dan published a second edition of *Dewdrops* to include a new story (Dude). As an Editor's Pick, Book Life called it "a short story collection that's as heartbreaking, raw, and real as it is beautiful and tender" and said "Flanigan's prose is melodic and hypnotizing, jarring and chaotic, exploring the human condition through a series of tense, often melancholic tales that still capture the imagination with their reality, sweetness, and sadness." *Dewdrops* was a 2025 Global Book Awards Gold Medalist.

The Big Tilt, the second book in the Peter O'Keefe series, was published in 2020 and has been described as "deft, hard-boiled, but literary prose that's reminiscent of Raymond Chandler's best work." *The Big Tilt* won the 2022 National Indie Excellence Award for Crime Fiction and was a Finalist for the 2022 Independent Author Network's Book of the Year in Thriller/Suspense. In 2023, *The Big Tilt* was a Legacy Fiction finalist for the prestigious Eric Hoffer Award as well as making the 2023 Eric Hoffer Book Award Grand Prize Short List.

On Lonesome Roads, published in 2022, is the third book in the series and was a Notable 100 Book in the 2022 Shelf Unbound Best Indie Book Competition and 2023 IPPY Silver Medalist in the Best Mystery/Thriller eBook category. Most notably, *On Lonesome Roads* followed up *The Big Tilt*'s 2022 NIEA Crime Fiction win with a finish as finalist in the same contest and category for 2023. In the 2023 American Fiction Awards, *On Lonesome Roads* finished with its own trifecta: winner for Mystery/Suspense: General; finalist for Mystery/Suspense: Hard-Boiled Crime; and finalist for Thriller: Crime.

The fourth book in the Peter O'Keefe series, *An American Tragedy*, was published in 2024 with the audiobook version following in 2025. This installment has won many awards, including being a 2025 NIEA Finalist (National Indie Excellence Awards), a 2025 American Fiction Awards Finalist, a 2025 BIBA finalist and winning the 2025 Killer Nashville Silver Falchion Best Literary Award.

Soldiers of Babylon, the fifth book in the series, was published in December 2025.

Dan has also written stage plays including *Dewdrops* (already described); *Secrets* (based on the life of Eleanor Marx); and *Tomcat's Progress*, which was awarded, under a different title but the same play, the 2022 Honorable Mention in the 91st Annual Writer's Digest Writing Competition for "Script."

He serves on the Board of Directors of Childhood USA, the U.S. arm of the World Childhood Foundation, established by Queen Silvia of Sweden, working to end child sexual abuse and exploitation everywhere.

He divides his time among Kansas City, New York City, and Los Angeles, and, whenever possible, visits the Catskills in New York and the San Juan Islands (off the coast of Washington state), as well as the Gulf Islands, Vancouver, and the Vancouver Islands in British Columbia.

THE PETER O'KEEFE SERIES

How did we get here?

Dan Flanigan, after a long career as a finance, banking, and bankruptcy lawyer in which he was both a player in and witness to the dramatic transformations of our modern times, intends to provide at least a few of the answers to that question through a series of novels, recounting, from the 1980s to the present day, the life and adventures of his private detective hero Peter O'Keefe and the assorted characters in the O'Keefe orbit.

Welcome, then, to this chronicle of the scams, schemes, and scandals of the last four decades of American life. Flanigan hopes the series will appeal to every generation—from the Boomers, who lived all of it, down to Gen Alpha and future generations who are trying to learn the lessons the immediate past has to teach them and help them to play the hand dealt to them.

In the first four books of the series—*Mink Eyes, The Big Tilt, On Lonesome Roads*, and *An American Tragedy*, which are set during the period 1986 to 1988—Flanigan explores such themes as the disruption and decline of the traditional American Mafia; the Savings & Loan scandal that crippled much of the U.S. banking system in the 1980s and early 1990s; the fallout from the AIDS crisis of that era; the emergence of the surveillance society ("Who is watching? Who is listening?"); the corrosive effect of keeping secrets in both public and private life ("We are only as sick as the secrets we keep."); addiction and recovery; date rape and other sexual violence and the blighted lives that so often result; the Satanic panic that ruined the lives of some innocent people.

In these stories, though teeming with plenty of villains, Peter O'Keefe, a hero for our times, and other everyday people of mostly good will, confronted with extraordinary challenges, struggle to repair and heal themselves and others, and their world, from their wounds, self-inflicted and otherwise.

Mink Eyes
(Peter O'Keefe Book 1)

YOU DON'T SEND AN ANGEL TO DO A DIRTY JOB

It is the tarnished heart of the "Greed is Good" decade. Peter O'Keefe is a physically scarred and emotionally battered Vietnam vet. Struggling with life after war, O'Keefe tries to outrun his vices by immersing himself in his work as a private investigator. Hired by his childhood best friend, ace attorney Mike Harrigan, O'Keefe investigates what appears to be merely a rinky-dink mink farm Ponzi scheme in the Ozarks. Instead, O'Keefe finds himself ensnared in a vicious web of money laundering, cocaine smuggling and murder.

Mink Eyes is available in paperback, hardcover, eBook and audiobook.

"Terrifically entertaining and deftly crafted…"

–Midwest Book Review

THE BIG TILT (PETER O'KEEFE BOOK 2)

NO GOOD DEED GOES UNPUNISHED

The war in Vietnam didn't kill Peter O'Keefe. Neither did his run-in with ruthless crime boss "Mr. Canada" in the Arizona desert. But chasing after justice in his own hometown just might.

A high school crush of O'Keefe's turns up dead, but the details don't add up. His pal, Mike Harrigan, has put his trust in the wrong people and now stands accused of crimes that could put him in the slammer. And O'Keefe? The mafia has put a price on his head.

The Big Tilt is available in paperback, hardcover, eBook and audiobook.

"...Flanigan manages to conjure deft, hard-boiled, but literary prose that's reminiscent of Raymond Chandler's best work. A gritty and eloquent crime novel."

–Kirkus Reviews

ON LONESOME ROADS
(PETER O'KEEFE BOOK 3)

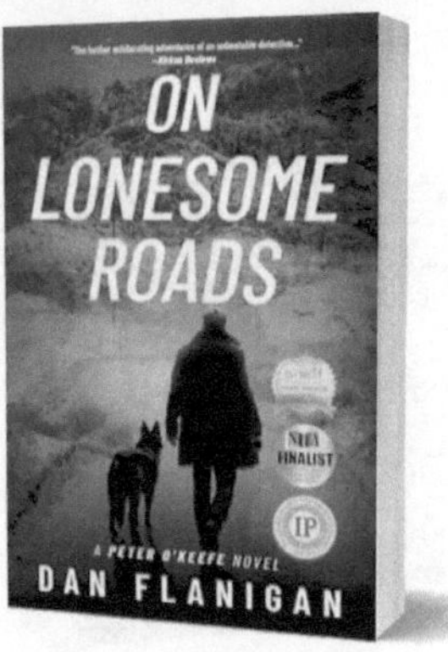

SOME ROADS MUST BE WALKED ALONE

As private detective Peter O'Keefe continues to heal from the burns he suffered from the blast of a car bomb, neither he nor the police can prove who his assailants were. The media speculates that "The Outfit," a mafia group in the city, is to blame. O'Keefe isn't so sure, but he means to find out – and fast. Terrified of another attack, O'Keefe's ex-wife, Annie, won't allow his eleven-year-old daughter near him except under the tightest security, including an armed guard. He can't blame her. It isn't safe for Kelly, or anyone else he cares about, to be near him while his attacker is on the loose.

In a desperate effort to keep his family safe and restore his life to some measure of normality, O'Keefe becomes consumed with solving the mystery of who is hunting him. Along the way, he'll be forced to negotiate with The Outfit – a "devil's bargain" that just might cost him everything.

On Lonesome Roads is available in paperback, hardcover, eBook and audiobook.

"The further exhilarating adventures of an unbeatable detective, packed with tantalizing loose ends."

–Kirkus Reviews

AN AMERICAN TRAGEDY (PETER O'KEEFE BOOK 4)

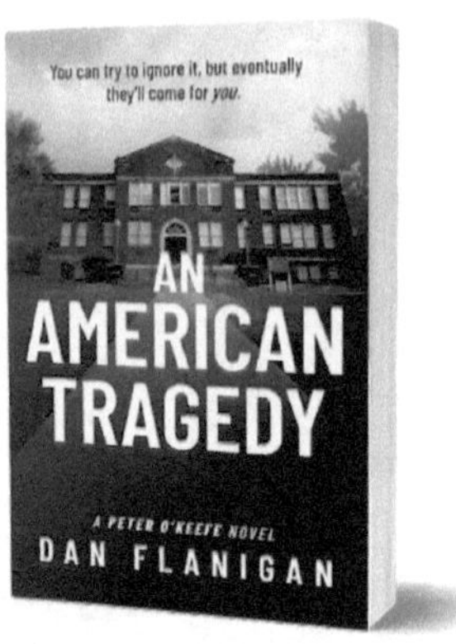

YOU CAN TRY TO IGNORE IT, BUT EVENTUALLY THEY'LL COME FOR *YOU*.

The summer of 1988 is ablaze—not just with heat but with hysteria. As Satanic Panic sweeps the nation, innocent lives hang in the balance.

Private detective Peter O'Keefe never expected to be drawn into the storm, but when his daughter's beloved teacher "Miss Ginny" is accused of unspeakable crimes, he can't turn away.

The case reeks of mass hysteria and hidden agendas but standing against the tide could cost O'Keefe everything. As he fights to unravel the truth, he's forced to go toe-to-toe with shadowy child protection figures more interested in securing convictions than justice.

With lives shattered and the weight of a nation's paranoia pressing down, O'Keefe must risk it all to expose the truth before it's too late. In a world consumed by fear, will justice prevail—or will the innocent be lost forever?

> *"In essence, Dan Flanigan's novel is a masterclass in suspense and social commentary…"*
>
> St. Louis Literary Review

An American Tragedy is available in paperback, hardcover, eBook and audiobook.

DEWDROPS

TALES FROM THE RAZOR'S EDGE

Some Cold War Blues: A neighborhood snowball fight erupts into a thing as close to war as an 11-year-old American boy is likely to face.

Dude: A wanna-be cowboy confronts his last sunset on the ranch.

On The Last Frontier: Old and broke in Juneau with winter coming on.

Dewdrops: The life and death struggles of a charismatic but tormented drug rehab counselor and his patients.

A Book Life Editor's Pick

"Flanigan's Dewdrops is a short story collection that's as heartbreaking, raw, and real as it is beautiful and tender. Spanning decades and following flawed (yet achingly true) protagonists throughout, Dewdrops is an absolute joy to read."

— -BookLife Reviews

Dewdrops is available in paperback, hardcover, eBook and audiobook.

TENEBRAE:
A MEMOIR OF LOVE AND DEATH

"Dan Flanigan is a visionary poet. His series of poems, Tenebrae: A Memoir of Love and Death ... grapples with the death of his wife. In these poems he takes the reader on the journey that his wife endured, and he with her, in her wrenching passage from life to death. ... What he has created is astonishing. There is a humanity at the core of these pieces that shakes the reader to the bone. They are moving. They are elegiac. They are celebratory ... they are the human heart in a singular and authentic voice. Flanigan's poetry is ... playful, intelligent, of the personal and the universal simultaneously ... they are completely of us, for us, the world at large."

"... heartbreaking and exquisite ..."

Tenebrae: A Memoir of Love and Death is available in paperback, eBook and audiobook

Thank you for reading.

If you enjoyed Soldiers of Babylon, a brief review or a rating helps other readers discover the series.

https://www.goodreads.com/author/show/18966479.Dan_Flanigan

You can also stay connected with future Peter O'Keefe novels and other work by Dan Flanigan at:

https://danflaniganbooks.com/

9 798991 232531